WIZARDRY:
PART I

SCOTT CRABTREE

iUniverse LLC
Bloomington

WIZARDRY: PART I

iUniverse books may be ordered through booksellers or by contacting:

iUniverse
1663 Liberty Drive
Bloomington, IN 47403
www.iuniverse.com
1-800-Authors (1-800-288-4677)

ISBN: 978-1-4917-3094-2 (sc)
ISBN: 978-1-4917-3093-5 (e)

Library of Congress Control Number: 2014906013

Printed in the United States of America.

iUniverse rev. date: 04/08/2014

CHAPTER 1

✟ ✟ ✟

"This is a never-ending nightmare," observes a somber younger cleric to a much older one beside him—older as evidenced by the white hair and severe lines on his face and hands that only advanced age can bring along with great wisdom. Although the young cleric's words obviously are a reference to some crisis unfolding, his tone and emotion do not reflect this, as if the nightmare in question has been going on so long now that it has lost its traumatic significance. The two walk down a long corridor of polished marble, though the light emanating from the torches located on the walls throughout is surprisingly weak, which only darkens the gloom in the young cleric's words and his depressing insinuation. But the light is enough to reveal that the two men appear haggard and gaunt with attire that matches their beleaguered appearance as a further indication that something is terribly wrong. The older cleric is carrying a small golden box, its gleaming surface heavily embossed with holy runes. The box would be a great treasure in its own right, but the way the old cleric is reverently holding it indicates that a far greater treasure must lie inside.

"You are only now just realizing that?" responds the older cleric. "But fear not, my young brother, for it will end soon enough. One way or another—it will end."

"No food, no water—," continues the young cleric, "—no healing potions! What good is being a cleric when all our religious knowledge, power, and magic can offer no comfort and only the promise of even greater suffering to come?"

One of the torches along the corridor wall, faint already, now flickers for a moment, and its reassuring glow fades out completely.

"Even the torches are running out of light," laments the young cleric upon witnessing the torch's death throes and ultimate demise.

"I'm afraid fire is a commodity we are in no danger of lacking," comments the stoic older cleric. "One step outside will show you that."

The young cleric now notices the faint wisps of grayish smoke that are seeping into the corridor from an unseen source, which prompted the older cleric's comment in the first place.

"Is there anything you can do?" asks the young cleric. "I'm so weak now that I don't even have enough magic power to heal an injured fly. You are high cleric of the kingdom. At your level of power, you surely must have some magic left."

"I exhausted all my powers after the third day. All of the kingdom's clerics and sorcerers are useless now. But I'll still fight even if I have to put a sword or club in my hand."

"You know clerics are forbidden to carry physical weapons in battle," quickly retorts the young cleric, who is obviously shocked to consider this.

"Does it really matter now?" answers the old cleric, his tone unmistakable in its hopelessness, which the young cleric answers with an impassive shaking of his head with downcast eyes.

"It's unfortunate that our noble paladin has not returned," continues the old cleric. "You would think that after all the blessing spells we put on that man to protect him on his journey he could even walk through the fires of the seven hells unscathed! The queen should not have let him go. A paladin's awesome powers are best used in battle—not in begging."

"Paladins!" scoffs the young cleric. "He will probably cause even greater problems than that first idiot did four moons ago! Where did the queen send him, anyway?"

"The kingdom of the sand elves to try to entreat their aid," answers the older cleric with an apathetic tone.

"Sand elves?" questions the surprised young cleric. "But they're bloodthirsty savages. We've had nothing but trouble from them in the past. Why, they are not even a good race!"

"No, but they're not an evil one either. They are neutral. But they are good fighters, and Cristonn isn't exactly going over there to invite them to a dance. Times of crisis breed strange bedfellows, and we can use them on our side."

The young cleric is not impressed by this at all and responds accordingly.

"Is that the best our mighty queen can do? Ask a treacherous enemy like the sand elves for assistance—a race that wouldn't hesitate to stab us in the back the first chance they get? Doesn't she know her people are suffering? She hasn't lifted a finger to help since this hell began six days ago! She is one of the most powerful sorceresses in the land, and rather than use her awesome magic to fight, she just spends all her time hiding in the temple."

"Queen Valerias is not hiding, my young brother. She has been doing what she can to help—unfortunately."

"Unfortunately is right! How can she possibly be helping by keeping on her knees?"

The scorn on the old cleric's face is readily apparent. Under normal circumstances, the old cleric—especially one at his level of age and advancement—is a kind, gentle, and extremely tolerant soul, but the past days have been agonizing and frustrating for all, and the cleric's patience is at an end. It is against the holy code of the clerical sect to strike a brother cleric—were it not, the older cleric would have done so—but cursing a brother cleric is permissible.

"Now you listen to me, you ignorant ass," the older cleric chastises. "It takes five full days and nights of continuous, devout worship for a high priest or priestess to request a communion with any of the greater gods. Queen Valerias, being the reigning monarch of a kingdom, is therefore high priestess to the god that the temple is dedicated to, which is the goddess Jenyss.

"The first day of worship is one of prayer. The second day is the giving of tribute, and this tribute varies depending on the nature of the god, but for Jenyss tribute consists of food and medicine and effigies of the god from the populace of the kingdom. Day three requires the burnt offerings of one hundred animals. Day four consists of the sacrificing and subsequent destruction of the most powerful and important magical artifacts and jewels that the kingdom has to offer. And that brings us to day five, the day Valerias is at now. And that is why the queen has been in the temple all this time. She is trying to summon Jenyss to help us."

"And what must the queen do on the fifth day?" asks the young cleric. He is hesitant, for although he is unaware of what sacrifice the fifth day entails, he is aware that each succeeding day of worship requires a far greater and more painful level of sacrifice.

The two clerics are now at the end of the corridor and are greeted by a large metallic door heavily embossed with holy symbols. The door opens automatically once the two get near enough, and the dark corridor is instantly flooded with bright, golden light, causing their eyes to squint for a moment, for their sight during their long walk to this point has been limited by the feeble glow of the slowly dying torches.

"*That,*" says the older cleric in answer to the younger one's question, pointing a finger toward a sight that lies beyond the opening.

The sight that reveals itself before the two clerics is the interior of a large and magnificently opulent temple, but they are oblivious to its grandeur, for what instantly catches and holds one's eye is the disturbing sight of two other clerics hurriedly using a white linen shroud to cover some object that lies on a marble altar. The sight is a disturbing one for two reasons: first, there is a woman kneeling before the altar with a blank gaze on her ashen face, a gaze only great shock can account for. She holds a dagger in one hand; the blade drips with blood. And second, the white shroud covering the unseen object is now beginning to become saturated with a dark liquid in one particular area near the center—the color of which eerily matches the blood on the dagger.

"And what is— *that?*" asks the young cleric with even greater trepidation upon seeing the unnerving scene before him. And his apprehension doubles as the other two clerics rapidly leave the altar carrying the shrouded object, darting panicked glances at the woman as if they recently were witness to some horror, and approach the open doorway where the young and old cleric are standing, at which point a human arm drops from under the shroud and hangs there pale and lifeless. Blood trickles slowly down the forearm. As the young and old cleric step aside to allow the other two to pass and quickly disappear down the dark corridor, the young cleric looks questioningly back at the old cleric. He wishes he hadn't when he hears the old cleric's chilling answer.

"That—was a human sacrifice," the older cleric says, greatly subdued and with even a hint of disgust—not disgust at the idea of it but at the fact that this was even necessary.

"What?" comes the aghast outburst from the young cleric, whose shock at hearing this now gives way to disgust. Unlike his older colleague, the young cleric doesn't realize any necessity for such an act of insanity and barbarity. "But why would Jenyss need a human sacrifice? She isn't an evil god!"

"Good or evil has nothing to do with it. Jenyss is a greater god, and therefore any mortal worshipper who dares to seek her favor must pay a heavy and fearful price. That price from the high priestess on the fifth day must be the sacrifice of her firstborn child—her daughter, Princess Arga."

The young cleric is stunned—too stunned even to respond after hearing what price Valerias, who is obviously the woman kneeling before the altar, has paid in order to appeal to her goddess for help.

"Still feel Valerias is not lifting a finger to help us?" the old cleric continues. "I just hope it is worth it. I begged her not to take this drastic path."

The old cleric now makes a move to enter the temple, but the young cleric holds out a hand, stopping him, and gestures to the gold box the old cleric is carrying.

"Why must you give her that? Isn't a human sacrifice and all those made the days prior enough to placate Jenyss now and summon her presence?"

"The human sacrifice was made on behalf of the queen. This sacrifice—" he indicates the box he is holding—"is made on behalf of her people. We the people must now show our devotion at the highest level we can."

He again turns to enter, but the young cleric stops him even more forcibly.

"Don't be a fool. You know she will destroy it. We need it!"

"As a loyal subject to her majesty, I must obey her commands. But I will once again advise her strongly to reconsider this folly she has undertaken before it's too late for all of us. You remain here, my young brother. Only the high priestess and her highest cleric can enter the temple now."

The old cleric turns to leave his young companion, enters the temple, and the door closes behind him. The sound of his footsteps echo throughout the huge interior of the temple as he walks the dozen or so paces toward Valerias—her face still blank and emotionless as she stares at the now empty altar as if her daughter's body were still there. She doesn't even acknowledge the presence of her high priest, a man who has long been her staunch supporter and good friend, who is now standing at her side.

"My queen," he begins somberly, for he too is aware of the painful loss that has just occurred and what the queen must be feeling. "This is the last and most powerful magical artifact in your kingdom. Its sacrifice is the last step you must take in order to complete the summoning ritual. It is my duty to convey to you its immense value by telling you the legend."

He slowly opens the box to reveal a large pearl of unimaginable beauty. Its luster and radiance are so great that it increases the luminosity of the entire temple, and even Valerias cannot help but gaze upon it though she still appears understandably shaken from the act she had to take. But she now is at least moved to speak.

"Very well, my high cleric," she says softly and without emotion. "Proceed. Tell me the legend."

"This is the Pearl of Sinoda," the old cleric begins. "Many moons ago there lived a mortal human youth of unimaginable beauty named Sinoda. His beauty was so great that the goddess Rhasta fell madly in love with him. But Rhasta was married to an evil great god who did not share his wife's love for this mortal, no matter how beautiful, and was insanely jealous of Sinoda because of it—so much so that he punished the angelic youth and his unique beauty by transforming him into one of the most common objects in existence—a grain of sand. Rhasta, heartbroken over the death of one she loved so deeply, could do nothing to restore Sinoda back to his former self, so in order to preserve the memory of his incredible beauty, she put this grain of sand into a giant sea clam—and the Pearl of Sinoda is that which you see before you.

"Its power is great, my queen. It has the power to restore beauty to anything you wish. It can regenerate missing limbs, remove disfiguring scars from battle, curse, or disease. It can restore the gutted landscape of your entire kingdom and give life, vitality, and youth back to your people. It can even restore life to those who have recently died."

He stresses this last sentence strongly as if to tell Valerias that even her daughter's death—which in the cleric's eyes was a horrendous mistake— is something that can be reversed. But Valerias is still unmoved, causing the cleric to continue with a more logical argument, after a frustrated pause.

"If used in battle, it can each day permanently transform ten thousand enemies into harmless grains of sand! I beg of you, Queen Valerias, abandon this temple and this folly of trying to summon Jenyss! Use the awesome power this pearl has to offer as a weapon in defense of your kingdom—and not as a sacrifice to this god. To destroy this mighty symbol of perfection— is a crime against all beauty. Even if you sacrifice the pearl, the chance of summoning a greater god is slim! It's not worth the risk of losing the power of this mightiest of all magical artifacts."

"Your words are sound, high cleric," responds Valerias coldly, not at all moved by her cleric's passionate appeal. "But Jenyss can do all that and more. She can bring life back to my daughter as well as all those who have fallen before, and her divine powers in battle will finally bring us victory. What good is your beloved pearl when we all are dead? I need to save my people—not restore them only to have them be slaughtered later. No, Jenyss will do battle on our behalf. She must! We are her people."

"But even if she does heed your summons, there's no guarantee she will do as you ask! She's a greater god! They think differently than we mortals. Even your paladin, Cristonn, would have told you—"

Valerias raises her head suddenly to look into the old cleric's eyes and grabs him, stopping him in midsentence. Her eyes, which were formerly filled with apathy, now radiate a sense of hope.

"Has Cristonn returned?" she asks hopefully.

"No, Your Majesty."

She releases the cleric and again looks upon the altar with an apathetic gaze. The cleric, almost in a panic over his queen's inability to comprehend the significance of his words, continues:

"My queen, you must listen to me!"

"Enough!" shouts Valerias as she angrily takes the pearl from the box. "Jenyss will come, and she wouldn't dare refuse me. Now go, my high cleric. Only the high priestess can commune with Jenyss in the temple. Go. I command it."

The old cleric feels the urge to continue to protest strongly, but the queen's command to leave overpowers this and he somberly departs through the door from whence he came, leaving Valerias alone in the temple. She stares at the gleaming pearl in her hand. One cannot help but become transfixed by its amazing beauty. But the need of her people and the painful sacrifices all have made that have led up to this moment cannot be in vain. She holds the pearl aloft in her hand—and smashes it hard against the marble altar, shattering the gleaming object of awesome beauty and power into worthless dust. This final act of sacrifice to summon the god of her people now complete, Queen Valerias looks upward at the statue of the goddess Jenyss at the far end of the temple.

The temple is a large room with the impressive statue of the goddess prominently positioned at the far end. This statue, some fifty feet tall, dominates the temple, and one cannot help but be awestruck by its divine presence. The statue is of a human female but with a form that exudes great power. It is made out of a solid piece of gleaming green jade carved with great care and dedication and adorned with the most exotic materials the kingdom has to offer. It sits upon a throne of solid gold, equally adorned, and gives one the impression that although it is merely a lifeless statue it still commands the utmost of respect of those worshippers who kneel before it. At the base of the statue is a large amount of tribute, obviously put there by her throngs of devoted worshippers to entice some aid from the divine being. But the tribute does not consist of the great wealth of jewels and precious metals and silks one would normally sacrifice to a god but something far more significant to the populace at this terrible moment—food and medicine, along with a few trinkets and family effigies lovingly made by the children of the kingdom, for at their innocent age these are all they can offer, though Valerias knows that their time could have been far better spent doing more beneficial things.

The temple floor shines bright with polished marble, as do the ceiling and the pillars supporting it, also heavily encrusted with precious gemstones. The glint of gold and silver everywhere reflects the fires of the dozen bronze braziers providing illumination, which only increases the opulence of the temple. Altogether, it is truly a magnificent sight worthy of its divine purpose. But what stands out most amid this glory, and especially when a muffled explosion from beyond the temple walls causes the room to shudder slightly, is that the ceiling, floor, and walls of the temple appear to shimmer as if covered with a thin layer of pulsating energy put there to prevent any damage from occurring to it.

The temple, in its majestic and pristine condition, is in stark contrast to Queen Valerias who, as she bows her head to further pray for Jenyss' arrival, cannot help but notice her own worn-down condition.

Her robes, which were once flowing veils of heavenly silk with bright, magnificent colors, are now mere remnants of their lavish, regal glory—torn, disheveled, and bloodstained. Those few jewels that remain on her person, which once dazzled in brilliant radiance, are now dull and broken—fitting accessories for her dress, at one time glowing in crisp whiteness but now scorched, gray, and bloody. A melancholy sight, to be sure, but it's the face staring back at her from the mirror finish of the polished marble floor that depresses her most. She has been kneeling in the temple for the past five days, but judging by her appearance it is clear that the first day—the day that caused Valerias to retreat to the temple in the first place—was one of great hardship and combat. Altogether, the six sleepless nights with no food, intense worship, and the constant worry about the suffering of her people and what their ultimate fate will be—not to mention her own—has taken a harsh toll on her appearance.

Valerias now appears much older than the fifty-odd years of her happy and fulfilling life, though there are still traces of the beauty she possessed six days ago. Most women take great care in their appearance, and Valerias is no different, so such a gaunt sight reflecting back at her would normally be cause for tears. But the recent past has drained her of most emotion, and her reaction now is simply one of apathy, though she does make an effort to replace a few strands of hair that cover her face—a futile act considering the severity of her hair's overall condition. It is at that moment that she again lifts her eyes toward the statue of Jenyss, still kneeling in reverent respect before it. The statue remains lifeless.

You must appear, Valerias says silently to herself, though it's clear she is growing impatient, considering the price all have paid to summon the goddess. *What is wrong with you—why don't you come? I must know what will become of my people!*

But again the statue remains lifeless, and Valerias drops her head in despair and falls to the floor and begins to sob

"Oh great Jenyss—can't you please tell me what is going to happen?"

"Death!" The word booms forth like a mighty thunderclap.

This instantly causes Valerias to rise, stunned to hear such a powerful and ominous voice, and she immediately looks toward the statue of Jenyss. The statue's body still remains lifeless jade, but the face shimmers with a glowing aura and is animated to allow it to communicate, and its eyes glow bright blue with incredible power—the great goddess Jenyss has answered the summons, and Valerias quickly moves nearer to the statue to fall upon her knees once again before the mighty deity.

The word "*death*" resonates for some time, fading away slowly, but this isn't due to any acoustical quality that the walls of the temple provide, or purely to the voice of the goddess herself, which would normally send shivers down the spine of any mortal being regardless of royal rank. No, the echoing is purely in Valerias's mind due to the foreboding significance of the word and its chilling finality. But the answer is not as grim as she thought at first, she realizes, for it could easily mean death to the attackers and not necessarily death to the defenders. She was going to ask the goddess, "'Death for whom?'" but now that she has had time to reflect on her own deplorable appearance, it is clear who is going to die. Valerias drops her head as she considers the answer of the goddess and again dreads the chilling and decidedly unwelcome—though perhaps not unexpected—implication, and she raises her head to address the deity once more with her hands clasped together tightly in prayer. Her hands even tremble with gratitude now that the terrible sacrifices of the queen and her people have not been in vain.

"Oh, great Jenyss, mighty and beloved, mother to our pantheon of gods, hear the cries of your people! I have never imposed on you before, but I humbly prostrate myself before you now. I've spent the past five days offering you the painful sacrifices to request this communion. My people have given you food and medicine that were desperately needed. We've destroyed powerful magical artifacts that could have helped in our defense, and your people have suffered greatly because of it—I've sacrificed my firstborn child to you! I have worshipped you devotedly my entire life. My family has worshipped you. My kingdom has worshipped you. I beg of you, mighty goddess of love, compassion, and mercy, use your divine power to help us now. Bring us deliverance, mighty and all-powerful Jenyss! Restore the life to those who have fallen in battle and destroy these infernal invaders in the name of all that is good! I implore you!"

Valerias's plea is sincere, for her situation is indeed dire, and her eyes radiate with the desperate belief that the goddess Jenyss is her last and only hope of salvation. The deity can't possibly refuse to help her people now, not after all the sacrifices that have been made to appeal for the goddess to intercede on behalf of her own people who love and worship her. Jenyss remains ominously silent for several moments, which to

Valerias seems like an eternity. The queen's eyes are wide with hope as she anticipates Jenyss's answer—and then the divine response:

"The gods will not interfere."

Valerias is stunned. Her goddess couldn't possibly give such an incomprehensibly dispassionate and unsympathetic response. If the word "*death*" had an unsettling impact on the loyal human worshipper, the fact that her goddess will not intercede on her behalf is like a sledgehammer to the face. The glowing aura now fades and the face of the statue returns to emotionless, unfeeling, heartless, and ultimately— useless stone.

That's only fitting, thinks the dejected queen. Although she certainly was not expecting this reply, she smiles contemptuously, reflecting on this, for it matches the attitude of her goddess perfectly—lifeless, stone-cold indifference. The communion has ended and not with grateful salvation but with abysmal failure. Valerias closes her eyes, trying desperately to fight back the anger, frustration, and tears, but it quickly becomes a losing battle as the emotions swell within her. It is therefore fortunate that she hears the door of the temple open and the entrance of one of her royal guards.

The guard, in a severely and recently singed uniform still smoldering in one or two areas and with a sloppily bound wound on his arm, pants heavily upon entering. The bandage, once tightly applied with skill, is now a loose rag heavily soaked with blood, which only barely manages to conceal the severe laceration beneath. Obviously, the wound and signed uniform are the results of some unseen traumatic experience taking place beyond the door of the temple in stark contrast to the serene, almost beatific atmosphere of the temple's sanctuary. But despite the guard's exhausted condition, he does manage to prevent a drop of blood from falling to the temple floor as if such an act would have been of the highest blasphemy—a blasphemy not to some divine force— but to his beloved queen.

Queen Valerias, not wanting for any of her subjects to see her in a moment of weakness, immediately regains her composure and regal bearing, though she does not turn to acknowledge the guard so as to have a few more moments to steel her nerves, for only the many years of her steadfast and noble leadership and the unshakeable confidence in her people's faith in her have allowed her the ability to hold on this long in the face of such horrific times.

"Speak," she calmly commands.

"Forgiveness, Queen Valerias," says the guard as he dutifully falls to one knee, "but you wanted me to update you when your prayer had concluded. I regret to inform you, but— it is time."

"They come early this morning," responds Valerias with a slight, sarcastic smile. "How eager they must be to put us out of our misery." But she then lowers her tone so the guard cannot hear as she continues with indifference, "I suppose I should be grateful."

The queen stands, and after taking a moment to draw in a deep though dejected breath to steel herself even further to face the inevitable, she leaves the altar and turns to head toward the temple door. But she stops momentarily and looks perplexed as if to question why she is standing in the first place. She has long been feeling the effects of lack of sleep and utter exhaustion and therefore her ability for rational thought has been slowly draining from her mind. Her moment of confusion is short-lived. A muffled explosion from outside, quickly followed by a faint, shimmering glow that seems to cover the entire room, intensifying as if to counter the explosive destructive force being exerted against it, forces Valerias back into her melancholic coherence, and she once again heads for the temple entrance. The guard also regains his feet and respectfully prepares to open the door for his queen as she approaches, but Valerias raises her hand, stopping him. She then turns to once again face the temple interior and reflect on its awe-inspiring splendor.

"Magnificent, isn't it?" says Valerias with pride. She really isn't addressing anyone in particular, for the guard there is just a convenient excuse, but her voice takes on a more disturbed tone as she continues, "I spent almost my entire life building this temple and lavishly bestowing the wealth of the kingdom upon it to show my loyalty and prove my devoted worship—" she notices the heaps of tribute her people have given, and she knows all too well how painful it was to them to sacrifice such desperately needed items— a sacrifice that obviously was in vain— " —to a god— who won't interfere. So be it." Her lethargic expression now transforms into one of intense hatred as she adds, "I shall not waste any more of my magic protecting you!"

With a wave of her hand, the shimmering glow of energy covering the temple interior dissipates from the walls and ceiling. With her eyes filled with anger, hurt, hatred,— and more importantly, betrayal,— the irate queen quickly raises her other hand and points it toward the statue of Jenyss as all the frustrations that have slowly built up over the past days now burst forth in the form of a powerful bolt of magical energy that instantly discharges from her hand. The bolt hits the face of the goddess's statue, obliterating it completely along with most of the upper half of the body and sending its flaming remnants falling to the floor, leaving only a cracked and smoking stump in its wake. Valerias feels an urge to spit upon the statue at this point but feels a queen is above such a petty and juvenile act—and besides, the distance is too great. But she also knows in the back of her mind that this particular form of insult would be going too far. She knows the disrespectful destruction of the statue will result in some sort of dire repercussions from the goddess, but Valerias didn't care—the queen's bitter disappointment is too deep. Her desire for vengeance abated, she then nods to the guard, indicating that he can open the temple door.

But the guard is stunned. He is awestruck not by the display of magical power but by the fact he has never seen his queen display such anger before—more than anger, hatred. He cannot understand how she has no fear of offending a god, though it is obvious to any mortal being that it is unwise to do so. His hesitation is short-lived, for he certainly doesn't want Valerias' anger directed toward him, and he opens the door far more rapidly than he normally would.

"Remove the food and medicine from the temple," says Valerias to the guard as she passes, "and distribute it back to the people. It serves no purpose here now."

"But my queen," replies the apprehensive guard upon hearing this command, "you can't take back tribute to a god once it's been offered. You might incur Jenyss's wrath if—" He stops when he realizes that withdrawing any tribute is a mild if not wholly irrelevant transgression against the god considering what Valerias just did to her statue. The queen moves on, unmoved by the guard's useless warning. After a stern glare at him, she exits the temple.

The guard, though hesitant, obeys Valerias's command and cautiously approaches the remains of Jenyss's statue, the lower half of which still smolders from Valerias's act of anger. His caution is justified, for even though the statue is only an image of the goddess and not the goddess herself, mere mortals should always show reverent respect. His queen's act hasn't been punished by the goddess, so the guard decides to voice his disappointment as well.

"So you won't help us in our hour of need?" says the guard with a degree of mocking contempt at the smoldering ruin, for he, like Valerias, is angered at the god's lack of pity and refusal to intervene on their behalf.

Had the statue been intact the guard would have been wise to heed his own advice and not desecrate the temple further by showing this lack of disrespect, for a god is a god and therefore commands respect regardless of what condition the god's effigy is in. Even then, the act of removing tribute would most likely be forgiven by a god as merciful as Jenyss. For a queen like Valerias—and therefore high priestess of the temple—a lesser or demigod will allow some latitude toward acts of defiance, and a good deity may also forgive the transgression of destroying a statue of the god. But Jenyss is a greater god and therefore demands the highest level of worship and respect, and a common and lowly guard, ignorant of the laws of divine worship, is another matter entirely. No god—good, evil, or otherwise—would tolerate the sin of disobedience the guard is about to commit.

"Then what good are you?" admonishes the guard again with arrogant defiance.

He arches his neck as a prelude to his unforgivable act of sacrilege, and as his spittle touches the base of the statue of Jenyss—a lightning bolt descending from the ceiling is the last thing the guard sees on earth.

CHAPTER 2

✚ ✚ ✚

Queen Valerias, soon after leaving the temple, begins to walk through the corridors of her castle, and the reason for her anger toward her goddess becomes apparent. In a futile attempt to elicit the intervention of the deity, whose abilities would have been considerable help in her hour of need, Valerias used her magic power to protect the temple long enough for the holy communion to take place— instead of using the power to protect the castle and her people. Now the unfortunate ramifications of that folly begin to reveal themselves.

Large portions of the castle structure are in ruins. Walls have collapsed, and debris of stone and wood litters the ground. Many of the castle's inhabitants, including guards, merchants, and even children are manning defensive positions, repairing and clearing away damage and debris and tending to the many wounded. A considerable number are also carrying white shrouded bundles—obviously dead bodies—and removing them from view.

As Valerias continues down the corridors she notices a group of her guards slumped up against a wall— near exhaustion from the relentless ordeal of the past few days. Most of them show evidence of wounds, some sickeningly severe. The guards notice their queen approaching, and every last one of them makes a valiant effort to stand at a rigid and respectful attention in the presence of the monarch—struggling not to let her see the pain, fatigue, and suffering in their haggard faces. Valerias acknowledges their brave and noble gesture with an understanding nod and a valiant attempt of her own at a smile, though she actually feels like crying upon witnessing this gallant act, for she knows it is not an obligatory show of respect but a demonstration of their love for her. It is at that moment she realizes the alien sensation her lips are making, for she can't remember the last time she smiled. Too much devastation and bloodshed have erased any memory of happiness. Because of this, Valerias would like to cherish this happy moment as long as possible, for she knows it will probably be her last, but she quickly departs. She knows that the attention of her guards must be painful—and she knows she will cry if she stays any longer.

The ever-present smoke becomes thicker as she continues toward an open exit, and now the truth of the older cleric's assurance that they will never be without fire becomes painfully obvious. As Valerias emerges into an open area within the confines of the castle, flames are practically everywhere. Valerias sees a large structure engulfed in a raging inferno with several dozens of her subjects forming a fire-brigade line using buckets of water passed hand-to-hand to combat the blaze, though it is obvious that the fire is far too intense for this pitiful effort to succeed. One of the firefighters notices the presence of the monarch and happily runs to her.

"My queen!" he finally manages to say after a few spasmodic coughs to purge the smoke from his lungs. "Thank the gods you are here! These fires are getting worse, and there's nothing we can do to stop them. It will spread throughout the entire castle. We could use your help."

"And you shall have it," replies Valerias with resolve. "I'm through protecting the temple." And then she shouts to the multitudes before her, "Stand back!"

The people smile broadly once they see who uttered this command and quickly disperse to await the much-needed aid from their much-needed queen. Valerias raises her hands, which begin to glow bright with power, and soon an immense wall of water magically appears in front of her. She sends the liquid wall hurtling toward the burning structure with a thrusting motion of her arms, and upon reaching the flames, it extinguishes them completely, leaving only a few steaming embers which also quickly die. A large tree nearby is also burning fiercely. Valerias quickly vanquishes the blaze with a blast of bluish-white vapor that flows forth from her outstretched hand, instantly covering the tree in ice—a strikingly beautiful sight as the frozen crystals sparkle in the morning sunlight like so many diamonds, much to the delight of the children present, as it provides a greatly needed, if momentary, distraction compared to the death and destruction the youths have been subjected to lately. The queen is pleased that she can offer this brief respite but knows she can do nothing to tend to the multitudes of injured—not to mention the grisly reminder of the white shrouds strewn about. Her faint smile vanishes as quickly as the flames she just fought.

"Do what you can here," the queen says to one of her subjects nearby, "but keep one fire going and put all the debris upon it. We need to clean this area up and get organized."

"Yes, my queen!" responds the subject proudly, confident that his beloved monarch is back to lead them as he turns to obey her command—but Valerias grabs him suddenly, stopping him.

"The bodies of the dead as well," she adds softly. Her desire to remove these constant and tragic reminders to her people of their suffering, and possibly their ultimate fate, is understandably a demoralizing one.

The subject nods, for he understands and heads off to perform the unpleasant but necessary deed.

One of the castle guards soon appears through an entrance and, seeing Valerias, rushes toward her, kneeling at her presence.

"Your Majesty," says the guard, beaming happily, "the paladin Cristonn has returned!"

"Where is he?" demands Valerias eagerly, as she too is greatly relieved and happy to hear this news.

"The courtyard."

In the center of the courtyard, Cristonn is hurriedly trying to cup some water into his hands from a fountain. Like so many of the castle's locations, the courtyard has seen better days. Most of the walls enclosing the section show evidence of recent damage, and the planting areas at the base of each—once vibrant with colorful flowers and shrubs—are now graveyards of lifeless vegetation. The fountain—once the majestic centerpiece of the courtyard—is now cracked and marred, with a grotesque lean to it, giving the impression that it could collapse at any moment. Its life-giving waters, which once flowed in great quantities, have now been reduced to a pathetic dribble. Cristonn has a small pool of the precious liquid in his hands, and he cautiously approaches one of the planting areas. Like all the others, it contains only dead vegetation— except for one tiny sliver of green with a small, fuzzy red top. Cristonn continues his cautious approach, taking great care not to lose one drop of water, but he sees the color of this sole survivor begin to fade and its form shrivel. Alarmed by this, he quickens his pace—but it is too late. The brave little flower dies before he can reach it with his life-saving cargo.

His noble effort now transformed into one of futility, the dejected paladin uncups his hands, which sends the useless water to the ground, where it quickly disappears within the many cracks in the stone floor. Then he sits at a bench nearby to silently lament. After a brief moment to reflect upon his failure to save the flower—and after saying silently, *Life must go on*—he reaches into his clothing and retrieves a small pouch. Untying the opening, he pours a pitiful number of berries into his hand—for even though the pouch is small, it could easily contain more than what has been emptied, indicating that this meager number is the last of its kind and also a further hint that whatever tragedy is unfolding is one that is not limited to Valerias's kingdom. To call them "berries" is debatable, for they have long lost the form of their juicy plumpness and now appear very unappetizing, but his hunger must be satisfied.

He is about to pop them into his mouth when he notices a squirrel warily inching itself close to his leg. Normally the animal–life of the courtyard would be contently plump from the sustenance its gardens supply—but those days are long gone, and the squirrel's body quakes with fear as it cautiously approaches as if this is the first time in many days that the creature has left whatever sanctuary it has retreated to. Cristonn looks at the berries— looks at the emaciated condition of the squirrel— and with a bemused smile tosses the treasured morsels to the pleading creature, which readily takes them, stuffing the booty in its bulging cheeks, and blissfully scurries off. But now Cristonn watches the creature with a slightly disgusted look.

"You could have left me one! You miserable little—" he says, admonishing the squirrel dryly.

He isn't truly angry at the squirrel, for a simple-minded animal like that has nowhere near the intelligence or compassion to consider that Cristonn might be hungry as well, but he knows he did the right thing by giving what was left of his food to a creature that was obviously suffering more than he was at that moment. His smile once again returns, though saddened, as if the thought in his mind is *"some days you just can't win"*.

Cristonn is one of those happy souls that tries to see the good in life despite how bad it sometimes can be, and he has seen his share of this many times during his lifetime. He is human, in his late-forties, though his youthful exuberance tends to make him act more like he is twelve.

Valerias particularly enjoys teasing him over this, though Cristonn defends himself by saying that he can act his age in emergencies, which he has demonstrated many times. Normally his attire would present a far more impressive figure, for the paladin class is indeed a very powerful one and Cristonn's rank among the sect is high, but his clothing is torn, dirty, wrinkled, and bloody; and his cloak has lost its striking blue color, as it is impregnated with dust, indicating a long and arduous journey has only recently ended—a journey rife with savage combat. The sword he has sheathed by his side—and a unique-looking one at that—is the only thing that does not appear blemished, nor does any sign of injury show on his face or body—a surprising fact considering his overall condition.

Valerias now enters the courtyard, followed by around a half-dozen of her royal guards. Cristonn, upon seeing her entrance, smiles broadly, though perhaps with a very slight devious quality, and begins to kneel. But Valerias is slightly annoyed at his respectful gesture, though she does match Cristonn's smile as if she has replayed this act many times —which she has.

"Get on your feet, you fool," Valerias gently scolds. "How many times have I told you that I don't like you kneeling in my presence? You aren't one of my subjects. You would think you would have learned that by now. How many years have you been my paladin? Ten?"

"I would not know, Your Majesty," replies the still-kneeling Cristonn. "I try to forget the bad things that happen to me."

This gets a chuckle from the guards escorting the queen, and she can't help but do the same, shaking her head with a bemused smile, knowing it is hopeless to change him—not that she would even want to try.

Valerias is now standing before Cristonn, who continues:

"But when you stop being a queen—I'll stop kneeling," he says, now looking up at her with deep affection emanating from his eyes.

"I don't think you will," says Valerias, matching the affection in her eyes as she looks down at him. And she is right, for Cristonn would still kneel out of his great respect for her regardless of any royal title.

She holds out her hand, which Cristonn takes into his and tenderly touches to his forehead. As he bows his head to do this, Valerias gently strokes his hair with her other hand as a mother would do to a mischievous child who has committed some mild transgression but in an adorable and easily forgivable manner. The two are not related, and only perhaps five years separate them in age, but their relationship is much like that of a mother and son, with all the mutual respect—and indeed love— that a close, ten-year friendship generates.

"Now, will you please rise," Valerias says softly to her dear friend.

And Cristonn does so. It is then that she notices the ragged condition of his clothing, and she makes an effort to brush off some dirt on his shoulder as she continues:

"You're a mess, my friend. Trouble?"

"A tad."

Valerias knows he is being modest, for the trouble was considerable and she knows it; she is the one who sent him on his mission and knows all too well the dangers it entailed.

"A tad?" she questions with an understanding smile. "But you're no worse than the rest of us. As you can see, this is the fashion in these trying times." She gestures to her own clothing and its similar condition. "You would think," she continues, "that with all the magic out there, some bright wizard would create a spell that can clean clothes! Obviously, we sorcerers aren't that advanced yet."

This gets another chuckle from the guards.

"No matter," she continues. "The main thing is that you have returned safely to us—and just in time too. They're attacking early this morning."

"Yes," responds Cristonn sadly as he gazes off to some unseen point, reflecting on this unwelcome fact. "I saw their formations assembling as I was arriving."

"But now that you are here, we'll give them a taste of their own medicine for a change," says Valerias confidently. "For the first time we have the advantage! Now, tell me where you deployed the army of the sand elves."

But Cristonn doesn't answer and only lowers his head with a disheartened look on his face. Valerias's expression upon seeing this—which only a moment before beamed with hope—now matches Cristonn's dejected face.

"You didn't bring the sand elf army?" inquires an apprehensive Valerias.

Cristonn just shakes his head in silence. Valerias doesn't want to ask her next question, for she greatly fears the answer. But after several moments, she musters the courage.

"Why not?"

"Because there is no sand elf kingdom," responds Cristonn coldly. "They've been annihilated. Not even a sand cat was left alive. I've never seen utter destruction at that level before."

Valerias just closes her eyes, trying not to let her bitter disappointment show.

"My queen, I beg you," continues Cristonn in earnest, "flee before it is too late! You cannot stop them!"

"I will not abandon my people when they need me most. The situation is not hopeless. We've held them off for six days, and we'll hold them off for six more if we have to. And besides, considering the thousands we've killed, I feel they are on the verge of breaking. Come."

Valerias begins to head toward a stairway nearby, but Cristonn does not follow. He stands there motionless, a look of futility on his face. Valerias continues:

"What we'll do is use the archers to—"

She stops when she notices that Cristonn has not moved and turns to face him. Seeing the hurt look on his face, she flashes him a consoling smile, thinking she knows the reason as she continues:

"Yes, yes, I know between the two of us you are the tactical genius. But you have to let me be queen some—"

It is then she realizes that Cristonn's despondent gaze is not due to any usurpation of his military authority but is in fact something far more sinister. Valerias approaches him slowly.

"No," she says, not believing it is possible. "No, there can't be more than yesterday's attack. There can't!"

Cristonn nods in silence, acknowledging this painful reality. Valerias is now standing before him.

"How many?" she asks.

But Cristonn can't bring himself to answer.

"How many?" screams Valerias as she violently grabs him.

But again Cristonn doesn't answer and just shakes his head hopelessly. The horror in Valerias's eyes could not be greater, and as she stares at Cristonn in shock and utter disbelief— the low, rumbling sound of thousands upon thousands of marching footsteps echoes throughout the courtyard. Now in a near panic, Valerias rushes up the stairs, quickly followed by Cristonn and the guards. Upon reaching the top, they enter a large balcony, and from this higher vantage point they can see far into the surrounding countryside and now see the horrific source of the commotion, its thunderous rumbling growing louder and louder with each passing second.

Stretching back far as the eye can see—almost to the horizon—is the demonic horde— numbering into the millions. Although still too far away to ascertain any individual features, the horde appears as an endless sea of blackness slowly creeping forward like some heavily viscous fluid. One might think it were indeed a liquid as it oozes its way across the landscape if not for the glint of the morning sunlight reflecting off the shields, weapons, and armor of the horde, indicating a solid and far more malignant composition.

As Queen Valerias, Cristonn, and the other guards continue to behold in horror the creeping death, the condition of the countryside becomes evident. The castle itself is situated in the center of a wide open plain surrounded by mountains, except for one opening in the distance where the demonic horde is penetrating through. The landscape is now more of a moonscape, pockmarked with large numbers of craters, some still smoldering due to their recent creation. The entire area clearly shows the devastation the past six days of savage battle has brought. Not a blade of grass is seen, not a single tree remains standing intact, and the ground itself takes on a reddish tinge that only blood-soaked soil can account for as corpses—both human and demon and showing the sickening degree of brutality that led to their demise—litter the battlefield. There are thousands of them, and the air is heavy with the nauseating stench of death. Not even the side of the bowl-shaped canyon surrounding the castle's countryside has escaped the disturbing stain of a veritable deluge of blood. The source of this blood, unlike that on the ground, is mysterious and surprising, for the steep and ragged sides of the sharp-rocked canyon preclude any form of combat taking place upon them, and therefore not one single corpse is present.

And yet the battlefield is not silent and still despite the mounds of dead. It is rife with activity due to the constant flying, rapid scurrying, and frenetic gorging of the thousands of vulturats who have been attracted to the carnage. These two-headed creatures are the premiere scavengers of death, with one head that of a vulture and the other of a rat and the body a winged mixture of both disgusting forms. An efficient combination, as the vulture head is quite effective at locating whatever rancid flesh touches its senses while the rat head instantly kills whatever beings or creatures are still alive with one bite from its plague-laden teeth, thereby allowing both heads to feed—for vulturats only feast on the flesh of the dead.

And now, as the demonic army continues its inexorable advance and begins to surround the castle, the thousands of avian-rodent scavengers who were enjoying the grisly feast take to flight, not wishing to be trampled upon by the approaching wave. Most struggle to become airborne with the additional weight their stomachs are now burdened with, but they soon settle upon the rocky sides of the surrounding canyon. It is now gruesomely apparent where the mysterious blood saturating the canyon's sides originated as the dark red droplets drip from beak, teeth, and body in a rain of blood, eventually forming thin, trickling streams and ultimately small bloodfalls that cascade downward from the vast quantities of blood falling from the countless vulturats perched throughout—their black, lifeless eyes watching silently— patiently— indifferently. Silently, for they choose no sides. Patiently, for they know all too well from the days before that the ghastly feast will continue and soon will grow substantially. And indifferently, for to them there is no difference between good and evil—all flesh tastes the same when it is dead. To anyone with a shred of decency, this is truly a hellish scene of nightmarish proportions.

CHAPTER 3

✝ ✝ ✝

A hellish scene of nightmarish proportions—this also must be the thought of those castle inhabitants who witness the scene as they anxiously man their defensive positions along the outer castle wall, awaiting their fate, for what was once a minor concern at the beginning of the battle has grown into a disturbing possibility over the past six days—and that concern is that the castle will fall. In the five days prior, the castle defenders managed to drive off the marauding swarm. Heavy losses occurred on both sides, but there was always a hope that victory could be achieved as long as the castle could hold out long enough. The demonic attacks were intense before and their numbers massive, but not so much so that a valiant and stout defense couldn't withstand it—but this is different, for now, with this vast demonic juggernaut almost upon them, the painful reality that all hope is gone is impossible to ignore.

The paladin Cristonn, still on the balcony with Valerias and the other guards, draws his sword and presents the blade before him. It begins to glow. This sword is different and obviously possesses magical abilities far beyond those of its ordinary metallic cousins. Within the glow of the blade soon a shimmering pool of energy appears that acts like a magnification portal, allowing him to see great distances. With this he can ascertain in more detail the ominous elements that comprise the demonic army.

From afar it appears as a solid mass, but upon closer inspection their numbers are organized into many divisions, the vast majority of which are formed by soldiers. These are man-sized, demonic humanoid creatures clad in spiked black armor, each carrying a sword, axe, spear, or mace. Leading each division is a demon lieutenant, another humanoid creature but of a higher rank than a soldier and wielding a more powerful weapon—an intimidating mace and chain device with a spiked ball at its end that appears to glow with power, indicating an obvious lethal magical property. The lieutenants all ride immature black dragons—horse-sized reptilian horned beasts just as sinister in appearance as their masters and just as evil in nature but lacking the awesome full power and size that a mature black dragon has. Indeed, the mounts must be immature, for a black dragon is the most powerful of the evil dragon classes—and no mortal creature would dare ride a full-grown black dragon. Only several of the most powerful evil gods have the power to keep mature black dragons as their pets. But the real power of this army is not in the masses of soldiers or the magical weapons and powers of the lieutenants and their dragon steeds. The heavy weaponry of the demonic horde comes in the form that follows at the rear of each division—a magmadon, a gruesome, six-legged pachyderm-type leviathan a hundred feet tall and heavily armored and so massive that the ground trembles with every footstep. Not one demonic eye does not glow red with pure evil and hatred. Although the Demonic Abyss is host to a bewildering variety of evil and powerful creatures, these few comprise the elements of the demonic army—for now.

As Cristonn continues to watch the magnified image through his energy portal, he can't help but admire the military precision and discipline of the demons as they march forward with robotic, emotionless steps. But his attention is soon distracted by an object that appears in front of the advancing columns, for emerging from the ground is that same type of little flower that Cristonn heroically tried to save in the courtyard earlier. It struggles to reach the sunlight, as if nature is making a gallant attempt to reclaim the gutted landscape and transform it once again into the pastoral paradise it once was. *A good omen*, thinks the paladin. *Maybe all hope isn't lost after all.* He watches the flower begin to blossom as if in celebration of the miracle of life and the exhilaration it conveys when one is aware of his own existence as Cristonn is now. But the existence of the flower is brief: demonic footsteps crush it into the ground. *A portent of things to come,* thinks the paladin. The sight is understandably a depressing one, and not wanting to see any more, Cristonn dispels the image and the portal vanishes.

"My queen, what are we going to do?" exclaims one of the guards in panic as the demonic forces inch ever closer.

"Give them the paladin!" angrily shouts another guard. "It is his kind that has brought this evil upon us!"

"Silence!" commands an irate Valerias—for the paladinhood is a noble order, and all their kind should be respected. But Cristonn understands the guard's anger and responds accordingly.

"He's right, you know," says Cristonn to Valerias calmly. "A paladin is responsible."

"Stop it. Would any paladin have done any differently? Would you? Would the master?"

"No."

"All right then. The paladinhood could not have foreseen this happening—no sane person could. We need to find a way to end this nightmare, not blame who started it. So I want no more talk about who is to blame."

After several moments of watching the army before her, shaking her head, still in shock at their unbelievable numbers, Valerias again addresses Cristonn.

"If," she struggles to say, her voice trembling as if the thought was once unimaginable, "if we surrender, will they accept it?"

"My queen, they hate us with every fiber of their existence," comes Cristonn's chilling and dejected response. "They don't want our defeat— they want our extermination."

Valerias chuckles softly upon hearing this. But it's not due to any humorous thought, for it is the sound one makes when recalling a foolish act or statement.

"And I said we would resist for six more days if we had to. It will be a miracle if any of us are alive six minutes from now. I just don't understand where they are getting their numbers from. We've killed thousands upon thousands, and they still keep coming—and in far greater numbers each time. It is impossible!"

Although Valerias has been in the temple for the past five days, as the monarch of her kingdom she has been aware of what has transpired. She now slams her hand hard in anger against the railing as she continues:

"And yet here they are—and it is certainly no illusion. They must be regenerating from the Abyss—but how? Not even the demon queen had that power!" She turns to Cristonn. "What does the paladinhood know about any of the other demonic royalty?"

"Not a great deal, unfortunately," says Cristonn solemnly. "In the demonic hierarchy, the queen reigns with total power, and all other demons, no matter what their rank, are subservient. But there has never been a situation like this before where succession to the demonic throne is in question. We know Maggar—the demon king—is ruling, but how and where he is getting this regeneration power of the demonic armies is a complete mystery. There is something terribly wrong going on here, Your Majesty."

"Then how can this be happening?" demands the astonished and still quite angry Valerias. "What about that half-breed abomination of a son of hers? Are you certain Karza is dead?"

"All we know is what the legend tells us," responds Cristonn. "According to legend Karza was destroyed in the Underworld. But with a being at Karza's level of power, the gods only know what really happened to him. But even if he were alive he's a demon prince!—no royal demon ever had this much power."

"Is it possible one of the evil gods could be responsible?" asks Valerias.

"Helping demons? No, demons only worship evil, death, and destruction, my queen. They have no gods. They don't believe in the existence of beings greater than themselves, so I can't see any of the evil gods caring one bit about what happens in the Abyss. Besides, it was the gods themselves that imprisoned the demon queen down there in the first place—even the evil ones—and now they want to help demon-kind by assisting them in their quest for vengeance? That doesn't make any sense."

"Then what is the answer?" questions Valerias openly and to no one in particular. "There must be an answer!"

A panting and terror-stricken guard suddenly enters the balcony. "Your Majesty!" he exclaims, horrified. "We're surrounded!"

An alarmed Valerias quickly creates a ball of energy in her hands, and within it she sees a bird's-eye view of her castle with the massive black ring of the demonic army encircling it. Her expression, though, is not one of terror, for with the encirclement comes the inescapable knowledge that this time the demons will not withdraw like they have each of the five days before. No, her expression now is one of great sorrow and hopelessness as she crushes the ball between her hands and its glittering remnants fall and fade away.

CHAPTER 4

✦ ✦ ✦

On a rocky ledge high above the battlefield on the surrounding mountainside, three demon generals stand overseeing the colossal sea of demonic forces arrayed below with the castle of Valerias and her people in the near distance. These generals are extremely formidable beings. Their black attire is adorned with golden symbols, and indeed their mere presence inspires an intense foreboding worthy of their impressive rank, and like all demon-kind, their eyes glow red with malevolent power. Only the members of the demonic royal family possess a higher level of power than these fearsome creatures. Each general carries an ornate staff topped with a glowing orb that pulsates with energy, indicating some form of a magical power. All three soon raise their hands as they telepathically issue the order to their minions below.

This act causes all the demonic lieutenants to raise their hands, and now every soldier, lieutenant, and magmadon stops simultaneously several hundred yards short of the outer castle wall. The thunderous droning of their movement ceases, replaced by an eerie silence, and only the soft sound of a gentle breeze whistling through their immense formations can be heard. The entire demonic army now turns their heads in unison toward the three generals seen as mere specks and barely discernable in the distance on the mountainside.

The generals turn their heads toward a higher position slightly behind their location as if expecting a signal to soon follow, and from this higher precipice—almost at the highest mountaintop surrounding the area—the heavy footsteps of some large, unseen being echo amid the silence. The sound increases with each step, and an imposing shadow begins to appear on the ground. The shadow is vaguely humanoid in shape, but this being is anything but human, for its demonic origins are readily apparent—and it is huge, as it is easily fifty feet tall. But what stands out most among the features of this shadow is the horny object on its head—the shadow of what appears to be a crown.

It is now clear that all the demons are avidly awaiting a command from this supreme being—the demon king, Maggar. They haven't long to wait, for thrusting into view comes his muscular forearm—slimy skin jet-black in color with a golden bracelet heavily studded with intimidating spikes and laden with jewels. The fingers of its leathery hand end in long, sharp nails resembling talons, with one lone finger pointing menacingly at the castle in the distance. A piercing, bloodcurdling shriek accompanies the gesture, and the command is given. The demon generals instantly drop their raised hands, followed by their lieutenants, and the battle begins—a battle between humans desperate to live and demons eager to die.

The lead elements of the demon soldiers slowly advance, tightening the death grip around the beleaguered citadel. Although this vanguard contains considerable numbers, it is a token display of force; the overwhelming majority of the soldiers of the army remain motionless, and none of the more powerful lieutenants or magmadons move.

Queen Valerias can see these leading forces advance from her high vantage point on the balcony. She makes a gesture with her hand, which sends all her archers—which number in the thousands—to the castle wall. The archers begin to organize along the wall, dozens of lines deep, and they raise their bows and draw them, awaiting Valerias's command to unleash the aerial onslaught.

An impressive display of military might, thinks Cristonn as he watches the maneuver, *and against a typical enemy a highly effective offensive tactic.* But demons are not typical, and Cristonn is troubled to see what Valerias is planning.

"This is unwise, my queen," he cautions. "I've fought demons before. This is merely a ploy designed to count the number of your archers—testing your strength with the lives of a token force of their soldiers."

"Patience, my friend," consoles Valerias. "Have faith in your queen."

She waits for a few moments, letting the enemy get well within range of her legions of bowmen before giving the order.

"Fire!" she loudly shouts.

Thousands of the lethal missiles now catapult into the skies and quickly descend upon the advancing throngs of demons below—their black armor and shields useless against such an overwhelmingly intense barrage. The arrows are so numerous that there is not one square inch that remains without an arrow within it, giving not one soldier in the advancing demonic force any chance to emerge unscathed. Within seconds they all fall as the arrows penetrate deeply into their bodies.

One of the demon generals now raises its staff, confident in the knowledge of Valerias's archer strength, and a force of soldiers far larger than the token one before—too large for Valerias's thousands of archers to combat, let alone defeat—begins to advance.

Cristonn, upon seeing this unstoppable wave approach, again looks at Valerias. He doesn't say a word, but the question is written on his face: *Now what the hell are you going to do?* Valerias only responds to his silent and anxious query with a sly smile.

"Again!" shouts Valerias with a commanding air of confidence.

And again the archers draw back their bows with arrows—but very special arrows this time, ones that glows with power. Valerias looks at

Cristonn with another grin proudly radiating on her confident face. He is surprised upon seeing the glowing arrows but soon appreciates their formidable significance.

"Arrows of demon slaying," he admiringly acknowledges and bows his head to Valerias in respect. "Impressive. You could have told me you had those in your arsenal."

"Secret weapons should remain secret," the still-smiling Valerias replies.

"How many do you have?" asks Cristonn excitedly.

"Only enough for this barrage," she responds.

Cristonn's expression of excitement vanishes upon hearing this and is soon replaced by one of futility, which Valerias fully understands:

"I know, I know—it's nowhere near enough. But do you think I was expecting this?" She gestures to the immensity of the demonic army below.

"Then save them for the magmadons," Cristonn counsels. "They are your greatest threat; for once those damn things start attacking you will have a smoldering crater where this castle used to be."

"No. Those arrows are more than just demon slayers—they are magically charmed. I was hoping that the arrows, in addition to the army of the sand elves, would tip the scales in our favor. But the arrows alone will kill a hundred times their number and will at least put somewhat of a dent in the number of soldiers. Perhaps once they suffer deaths numbering into the hundreds of thousands, they'll think twice about coming any farther. You will see—now, behold a slaughter even the gods have never seen before!" The demon soldiers are now in range, and she eagerly shouts the command to unleash the barrage.

"Fire!"

The glowing projectiles launch, illuminating the sky by their sheer volume and emitting a peculiar crackling sound as they arc through the air and begin to fall like a rain of fire. All the castle inhabitants who witness this fiery display crane their necks as they eagerly await the devastation that the shower of arrows will soon bring upon the dreaded enemy—and maybe, just maybe, give them a remote chance to escape death.

Maggar can see this rain of death descending upon this large portion of his demonic forces from the commanding perch on the mountaintop, and although these demons are certainly not the bulk of the entire army, it still represents a substantial investment in numbers. Not wishing to lose it, the demon king thrusts his forearm forward, and his hand discharges a burst of energy. The demon soldiers immediately stop, and almost as quickly, a wave of magical energy forms high above their heads. It covers the entire mass, a protective roof of shimmering armor. Maggar's maniacal laugh echoes from the mountaintop. Queen Valerias watches her carefully orchestrated attack explode spectacularly—but ultimately harmlessly—on the protective shield covering the demons. Not even her horrified scream can be heard over Maggar's evil laughter.

Now another piercing shriek from the demon king heralds another command. One of the demon generals obediently raises its staff, causing the enormous magmadons to raise their grotesque heads. The behemoths are aptly named, for from their gaping mouths belch forth massive balls of flaming lava, and the fiery orbs streak off toward the castle. The structure is massive, and although it valiantly bore the brunt of attacks in the days prior, its thick walls and elaborate defenses are no match for the ferocity of this latest flaming bombardment. The balls of lava easily smash through whatever they encounter and begin to cause massive destruction and carnage. Those that impact the outer castle wall create huge openings, negating its protective function as throngs of archers fall to their deaths within the flaming ruins. Many of the deadly balls now fall deep within the castle interior, causing equal damage and bloodshed.

The second demon general now raises its staff, commanding the lieutenants to move. The dragon steeds they are riding unfurl bat-like wings and begin to take to the air. As they swarm into the skies, the dragons fire blistering bolts of lightning from their mouths that obliterate any unfortunate human soul they encounter. Their claws and razor-sharp teeth also make formidable weapons as they rend the human victims they catch in flight or those they capture as many now begin to land within the open areas of the castle. The lieutenant riders are also far from feckless beings, for they wield their weapons to devastating effect as the magical power within reveals itself by disintegrating all it touches, be it weapon, shield, or flesh.

The third demon general now raises its staff, and the entire demonic horde is engaged in battle as all the soldiers rush forward in a frenzied rage and begin to flood into the castle through the numerous openings in the smoldering ruins that were once the first line of defense of the castle wall, beginning the final slaughter of Valerias and her people.

A frantic though grimly determined Queen Valerias now reveals the awesome magical power that a royal sorceress of her many years and caliber can unleash. She raises her hands, which glow with power, sending a massive wave of energy toward a large number of demon lieutenants and their black dragon beasts in flight overhead. The wave detonates upon impact as if a massive salvo of fireworks has exploded in the sky with a dazzling display of colors and showers of sparks. Dozens of the winged creatures fall to the ground as masses of burning flesh. She now directs her magical anger at the torrent of demon soldiers infesting her castle like some nightmarish plague of ants.

"Fall back! Fall back!" she cries in desperation to those few guards who have survived the initial onslaught and who are now fighting savagely but are quickly being overcome by the overwhelming might of the demonic invaders.

Valerias's hands again glow with power as bolts of lightning discharge from her fingertips, obliterating large numbers of the demons, whose armor is no match for such mighty magic. But she soon has to stop when she sees the area in her immediate vicinity beginning to glow with red. Looking up, Valerias becomes alarmingly aware of a lava ball from a distant magmadon descending upon her. She urgently fires a burst of energy from her hand at the flaming death, and the ball explodes. Although this act does prevent any harm to Valerias, it unfortunately scatters some flaming remnants into several areas, igniting portions of the castle. One in particular is occupied by a dozen of her people, who are instantly engulfed in the searing flames. Their screams of agony are mercifully short, for Valerias magically summons a wall of water to extinguish the fires—but too late, for the lethal damage has been done. She closes her eyes and lowers her head despondently at the horrible sight, but this sign of anguish lasts but a moment, and she again resumes her battle with fierce resolve.

Cristonn now reveals the fantastic power that a paladin of his high rank commands. The sword in his hand is in fact a mighty soul blade, the weapon all brethren of his noble class wield. He is using it to discharge a blistering array of energy at the masses of soldiers he spies below from his position on the balcony. The armor of the soldiers is useless against his attacks, and considerable numbers of them are destroyed. He stops for a moment to admire the considerable carnage he has inflicted to the invaders, but his smile vanishes when he sees his soul blade flash red. Sensing the danger, he instantly turns to face it and is confronted by a trio of demon lieutenants swooping in for an attack. The dragons they ride each fire a lightning bolt, but Cristonn quickly uses his soul blade to generate a protective shield of energy, which absorbs the otherwise fatal electrical attack. Startled by this unexpected maneuver, the lieutenants strongly urge their dragons to veer off to flee, but they aren't fast enough—a swift counterattack by the paladin sends the three spiraling to the ground in fragments of glowing embers. Cristonn now sees one of the dreaded lava balls descending on him, but unlike Valerias he presents his blade before him as if to brace his body for the impact, and as the blade begins to glow bright with power, his feet skid backward slightly as the momentum of the incoming ball pushes him. But the mighty paladin soon overpowers it and sends the flaming horror hurtling back toward its magmadon creator. It lands on the back of the immense creature, which writhes and bellows loudly in agony as it becomes consumed in flame. Cristonn can see this through the magnification portal he is generating to observe the result, but a quick shift of the image reveals another magmadon preparing to launch a lava ball of its own. The beast's huge mouth begins to open with a fiery orange glow. The alert paladin instantly dispels the image and points his soul blade in the direction of the creature in the distance, and a bolt of energy fires and impacts the lava ball still forming within the magmadon's mouth. The resulting detonation instantly transforms the creature's head into a bloody stump as blood and pieces of gore fly everywhere from the tremendous blast. As the body of the deceased magmadon collapses to the ground, molten lava gushes from the gaping wound, igniting the massed demons nearby, for their numbers are so incredibly huge that many tens of thousands still have not come anywhere near the castle.

It is this realization that has resonated within Queen Valerias's thoughts ever since she first saw the invincible horde earlier that morning. She knows that her and her people's attacks, though individually devastating, are feebly and hopelessly inadequate when pitted against such a virtually unlimited power. Even if there were a thousand times Valerias and Cristonn's numbers, it wouldn't even make a dent in the demons' relentless assaults. Valerias sees the paladin near her and calls to him, "Cristonn!"

Cristonn is standing over a severely wounded black dragon. The body of the demon lieutenant that was formerly its rider is leaning against a wall of the balcony—its glowing red eyes fading into darkness and with a smoking line where the being's neck would be—and as the body slumps to the floor, the neatly severed head becomes detached, obviously due to a slash delivered by the formidable paladin moments before. The head rolls a bit on the floor as Cristonn plunges his soul blade deep into the chest of the dragon, which flails spasmodically in death as electrical energy discharges from the mortal wound. Withdrawing the blade, he then goes to Valerias, who begins to express to him the futility of their plight.

"It is no use, my friend," admits the solemn and defeated queen. "There are simply too many. We can't last much longer."

A demon lieutenant and dragon suddenly come speedily flying by, and the beast discharges a lightning bolt, but Valerias is able to block it with a magic energy shield and retaliates by shooting out a stream of fire from the palm of her outstretched hand, which sends the attackers off in flames.

"Protect me," she commands to Cristonn beside her as she bows her head while clasping her hands together as if to concentrate.

Cristonn stands vigilantly beside her and uses his soul blade when necessary to ward off any attacks. After a few moments, Valerias has generated enough energy in the palm of one hand and raises this over her head. Then, touching Cristonn with the other, she detonates the energy, which creates a blinding flash. Everything for a considerable distance slows to a mere crawl as if time itself is stopping. Only Valerias and Cristonn remain unaffected.

"A 'time-slow' spell," says the amazed Cristonn. "That's powerful magic—my compliments."

"Unfortunately it's not powerful enough," responds Valerias after taking a moment to recover her strength. "I can only maintain it for one minute. Listen to me, Cristonn. I want you to take my son to safety. You are the only paladin under my command, so he'll be safe in your care."

"But Queen Valerias," replies Cristonn, obviously surprised, "I can't leave—"

Valerias interrupts as she reaches out to him, touching his arm tenderly.

"Listen to me, my loyal friend. There is no time for sentiment. Our defense is hopeless against this many, so it is only a matter of time before we all are annihilated."

The mighty queen uses her magic to create a sparkling, blue jewel that pulsates with energy. Holding the gem in her hand, she gives it to Cristonn.

"Take this. It is the only magic jewel I have left that I didn't sacrifice to that useless god! It was a waste of resources to expect any help from her."

"Please tell me you didn't try to summon Jenyss," replies a shocked Cristonn. A despondent nod from Valerias is her only answer. Cristonn continues, "The Pearl of Sinoda—destroyed?"

Another nod.

"Your daughter?"

And another nod, but one with even greater sadness.

"Oh, my queen—what have you done?" laments Cristonn. "The gods rarely help us mortals and especially not a greater god like Jenyss."

"I know that now, my friend, but I had to try. Without Jenyss's intervention, my daughter would have died anyway."

"Yes," says the understanding Cristonn. "It was a desperate gamble, and considering what is at stake, it was worth the risk. I did notice the spell of protection you placed on the temple was gone shortly after I arrived. I hope you didn't do something foolish. The gods can be very vindictive and cruel if you offend them."

"What can Jenyss do?" responds Valerias, shrugging off Cristonn's loosely veiled threat. "Kill me? I'm dead already. But my son is not to blame, so when you reach Rojan, use the jewel. It only has two charges left, and each will teleport two people, but it will transport you both to safety. Then do what you must. Only the paladinhood has any chance of stopping the demons now. In life I cannot help Rojan now—perhaps in death I can."

"If you have a teleportation jewel, then use it! You know I have the ability to escape on my own when necessary, so you and your son should get out of here while you still can."

"No, Cristonn. I couldn't leave even if I wanted to. Jenyss wouldn't let me now."

"Why would your goddess want to keep you here?"

"Let's just say," says Valerias, recalling why her goddess would hold a vindictive grudge against her, "that I did something foolish. But that doesn't matter now. Besides, this jewel's teleport range is only half that of sight, so you can't travel far. My son will need you to take him out of the area—when you have finished what you must do."

These last eight words weigh heavily on Cristonn's mind, for he indeed knows what he must do, but he still is reluctant to leave and is greatly disturbed by what his queen and good friend for so many years is saying. Valerias—seeing the concern and sorrow on his face—smiles comfortingly, for she understands what he feels as she feels the same pain. But it must be done, for these desperate times call for desperate measures, and Valerias is preparing to make the ultimate sacrifice in a last-ditch effort to protect her son.

"Please, Cristonn, obey my last command. Save my son."

"As you wish, my queen," says the reluctant and deeply saddened Cristonn, for he too knows what is soon to come.

The "time-slow" spell's power wanes, and all motion begins to accelerate as the demon attack increases in intensity, prompting Valerias to exclaim to Cristonn in a panicked tone,

"The spell's power is weakening! Go, Cristonn! Hurry!"

Cristonn rushes off toward an exit, fighting his way past several demons that have managed to reach their location now that time has returned to normal, leaving Queen Valerias the sole survivor on the balcony, as the other guards with her have long since been killed.

A large group of demon soldiers scrambles up the walls and rushes toward her position, but the powerful queen unleashes another withering barrage of magical attacks and defeats them all. The impact of another lava ball near her causes a large, marble obelisk some fifty feet high in an area below to crack near its base and begin to fall upon a group of young children who are huddled in a corner for protection amid the demonic attacks. The children scream with terror at the sight of the falling stone, for there is no escaping its crushing impact, but fortunately Valerias hears their screams and quickly uses her magic to stop the obelisk's lethal fall and levitates the massive weight.

She sees a large formation of demons many rows deep and flings the obelisk with great velocity at their ranks. The huge mass of stone easily plows through the demons like so many blades of grass, leaving a swath of bloody emptiness in its wake as hundreds are instantly killed.

The demon king, overseeing every aspect of the battle from the bird's-eye vantage point on the mountaintop nearby, is not pleased to see this gaping emptiness where only an instant before hundreds of his demons were effortlessly advancing, fully aware that this insignificant human female is solely responsible for defeating a large number of his forces. She must be eliminated. And so with another thrust of a demonic appendage (for the creature is still unseen) and with another hideous scream, the king gives yet another command to the three demon generals below. Obeying their master, they teleport from their position and disappear with a flash of energy.

Queen Valerias continues to fight savagely, blasting any demon she sees near her position within her castle walls, but she soon finds herself distracted by a flash of energy as the three very formidable demon generals teleport to her location. They face her, their eyes glowing even more brightly with evil. She backs off in terror at the sight of this evil trio, who easily are twice her size, but her moment of petrified fear is short, and she realizes what she is facing and begins to attack with a frenzy unseen before. But these three demons, being the generals that they are, are very powerful beings in their own right—more powerful than any human queen, in fact—much to Valerias's dismay.

Cristonn, who moments before reached an open area in the castle's upper ramparts, is now on a high walkway and can see Valerias on the balcony below him. He instantly stops, horrified when he realizes her dire predicament, for he can see she is fighting furiously, savagely—terrified, in fact—using every spell and magic power she has to combat the generals who have her surrounded and have erected a ring of energy around Valerias that prevents her attacks from penetrating through to them. The ring of power encircling her begins to constrict slowly as if the generals are toying with some unfortunate trapped animal and are enjoying its struggle and suffering, for the power of the mighty sorceress is simply no match for theirs. They soon grow bored with her pathetic attempts at survival, and the ring collapses upon Valerias, who screams in agony from the painful embrace that now explodes with a flash. Valerias falls to her knees, severely wounded from the blast. The generals, flushed with victory, simultaneously discharge an intense blast of energy from their staffs at Valerias. As she is raked by its relentless power, massive injuries cascade all over her body. Her screams of agony are quickly silenced. Her smoldering body falls to floor. The mighty queen is dead.

Cristonn is extremely distraught upon witnessing the death of Valerias, a dear friend that he loved, respected, and admired deeply, and he drops his head in sorrow. Had her death happened any other way, Cristonn would have spent far more time eulogizing the passing of so great and beloved a person. But the sight of the three twisted fiends that have now become Valerias's soulless assassins quickly replaces any trace of despair with an almost unbridled level of hatred. Valerias's death must be avenged. Cristonn holds his soul blade tightly and, with a flash of energy, it becomes two slightly smaller versions of itself. He puts the two blades together to form an X and fires a powerful bolt of energy at one of the generals below, and the unsuspecting being is instantly blown apart by its impact. The paladin fires another blast, but the other two generals are now aware of the demise of their demonic brother and can see the troublesome cause of it. They create an energy shield to protect themselves from Cristonn's discharge. They then counterattack with their own sordid power. An intense exchange occurs between paladin and demon, but it ultimately is a stalemate, for neither can penetrate the other's powerful shields. But it is the paladin who has the upper hand, for he uses one blade to maintain a protective shield and throws the other violently at one of the generals. The being's energy shield slows the blade's penetration, but it does get through, and as it pierces the general's body, the creature disintegrates with a blinding flash. Cristonn reaches forth with an outstretched hand, and the blade—now lying on the ground and still steaming slightly from the discharge of energy— flies forth and returns to his hand. He prepares to do the same to the last remaining general, but he must act quickly, for separating his soul blade into two has in effect halved his power: the magic attack of the last general is rapidly beginning to overpower the paladin's shield. Cristonn again arches back to throw the blade and sends it hurtling through the air at the demonic target.

The demon king, Maggar, always instantly aware of what happens to any of his demon kind, can sense that the last of his generals is overmatched and will soon die if nothing is done about it and cannot afford to lose this final member of the demonic high command. He quickly raises his hand, and a flash of energy bursts forth.

The general disappears with a flash an instant before Cristonn's blade arrives to kill the being. It harmlessly penetrates a wall and disintegrates a large portion of it before falling to the floor. Cristonn summons the steaming blade to his hand with a look of bitter disappointment on his face at the general's narrow escape. He soon is distracted by a pinpoint of light that he can see out of the corner of his eye on the mountainside far in the distance. Disturbed by this, he puts his twin blades back together to form his soul blade once again, and with it he creates the magnification portal to get a better look. As the image appears within the energy pool, the flash of light reveals the demon general bowing reverently to something out of sight. Intensely curious, the paladin begins to scan the area for whatever the general is addressing, and as he covers several areas of barren rock he begins to see the large form of some jet-black being with glowing red eyes. The image lasts only a fraction of a second, for as soon as he sees the eyes they emit a blinding flash of energy that comes through Cristonn's portal. He suddenly reels in searing pain, screaming in agony, and he drops his soul blade and falls to his knees. His hands instinctively reach for his face as smoke and the dull glow of reddish light begin to seep through his fingers as if his eyes are afire—which they are. The pain is incredible, so much so that any lesser human would be unable to cope with it and ultimately die from the fire that is quickly incinerating his eyes, face, and mind. But this is a high-level paladin, and he therefore possesses a will able to at least withstand the pain enough to frantically grope for his soul blade. The blade is nearby, though out of Cristonn's reach, and since he obviously is blind, his chances of finding it are virtually nonexistent. Fighting the pain with all his might, he manages to call to it.

"Soul blade!"

The blade flies toward his outstretched hand. Cristonn grabs it and puts the blade close to his face.

"Heal."

He can barely say the word as he struggles with the pain, but it soon stops as his eyes begin to glow and heal, and they quickly return to normal. Cristonn shakes his head as if to clear it and blinks heavily several times, trying to regain his lost sight. It returns. He now realizes exactly what he saw fleetingly moments before—for only one kind of demonic being possesses such a formidably evil power.

"Blinding gaze," he begins to say in grudging admiration as he looks toward the being, a mere speck on the mountaintop in the distance. Were Cristonn closer, he would again suffer from the blinding gaze, but at this distance no eyes can be seen without the use of the magnification portal—something that Cristonn is definitely not going to try again. "That's a powerful little trick. So watching the slaughter from the Abyss wasn't entertaining enough for you? You had to come watch it in person, you twisted, demonic—"

He now begins to go but stops when he also realizes something else.

"But," he begins, looking at his soul blade as if considering his options, "it is kind of you to make yourself such a tempting target. All right," he adds sarcastically, "Your Majesty! Let's just see how powerful you really are!"

Cristonn is aware that the guiding force behind this demonic scourge is the demon king, Maggar, easily the most powerful source of living evil that a mortal being can possess—that is, the most powerful source of living evil still living—and with all the incredible powers that his royal title brings, only a handful of the mightiest of evil gods possess more power. But the fact that Maggar is mortal is giving the paladin an idea that he can be defeated—at least he is hoping he can be defeated, but there's only one way to find out. Cristonn raises his soul blade slightly but stops, for he now has another dilemma, and that is to consider Rojan, Valerias's son. What he wants to do is risky—too risky—and perhaps even deadly, but he is a paladin and must do his duty.

Forgive me, my queen, he says to himself, *but I have to try it. If Maggar is out of the Abyss, then we may never have a better chance to kill him and finally put an end to this insanity. It is my duty as a paladin.*

Looking around him, he sees that in addition to the two entrances at either end of the walkway there are two stairways at either end that descend from his location to the balcony where he was earlier. Valerias's tortured body can still be seen as well as a disturbing number of demon soldiers that have overrun the position and are now rushing up one of the stairways to where he is. He immediately fires on them with his soul blade, killing two dozen or so, and then fires on the stairway, destroying it completely. Then he destroys the other stairway, thereby severing any demonic access to his higher level, for what he is planning to do is going to require all his concentration, and in the meantime he will be extremely vulnerable. Although he is safe—for the moment, anyway—from any interference from demon soldiers, a glance skyward reveals several demon lieutenants and their dragons hovering menacingly overhead. There is nothing he can do to prevent this aerial threat from reaching him, though fortunately for the moment they are unaware of Cristonn's presence, for they are engaged in other attacks. Another and perhaps far greater concern is the lava balls falling from the skies that he also can do nothing about.

I'll have to risk it, he thinks to himself, and looking off at the demon king in the distance, he continues. *Now don't move, and I'll give you a pretty present.*

He takes the soul blade and closes his eyes in deep concentration. The blade glows, and its brightness increases in intensity with every passing second. After almost a minute, it has reached a blinding degree of power—more power than he ever has had in the blade before—and his hands tremble, as it is now difficult even to hold the weapon, which vibrates with so much energy contained within. Cristonn opens his eyes, content that he has put all the power he can muster into the weapon. He braces his body with his back against the wall, for he knows what to expect, though he is still very anxious, for again this is a risky maneuver, and with his arms at full extension he points the brightly glowing soul blade in the direction of the hated demon king.

All the stored power within the blade is released at once, forming a huge ball of sparkling energy that shoots off with great velocity toward the demon king in the distance. The tremendous recoil of its launching pushes Cristonn's body hard against the wall. He was expecting this to happen, but what he didn't expect was the intensity of its power. The recoil is so great that its violence creates a spider's web of cracks that spread throughout the surface of the wall directly behind Cristonn's back. The fracturing of stone makes a loud, distinctive sound—but another distinctive sound is heard over this: the sound of fracturing bone. Cristonn's broken body slumps to the floor as his back glides down the wall, small pieces of which begin to pepper his head and shoulders. His face is drained, and not even the pain from his unseen injuries registers on it, for he put all his energy into this attack. Still, he manages to watch the ball of energy continue to streak off into the distance with an apathetic gaze.

Maggar can see this miniature sun approaching. Indeed, the ball of energy is so intense that it is impossible to ignore. Any other creature would flee in terror from the sight, but this is a demon king who fears nothing. Still, this is a potentially existence-ending threat rapidly approaching, even for a being at his degree of almost godlike power, but because Maggar does possess such power, Cristonn's attack is useless. Being the demon king he is, he can easily teleport out of harm's way. Had Cristonn known this, he never would have made the effort to attack. But teleporting would be too simple, for the demon's evil mind operates at a far higher level of diabolically twisted genius and will waste no opportunity to show all the incredible power at his command. He raises his hand, which begins to glow with a purple aura, before the advancing Armageddon. The ball of energy suddenly flashes and takes on the same purple color as the demon king takes control of its power. The ball begins to slow and stops motionless in the sky before Maggar seconds before impact. Now in complete mastery of the ball, Maggar makes a flicking motion with his glowing hand and sends it hurtling back with great speed toward the castle.

A paralyzed Cristonn watches helplessly as the ball—now glowing brilliantly with its disturbingly evil purple color—returns to impact deep within the castle. The resulting detonation is devastating. A large portion of the structure crumbles from the blast. The noble but powerless paladin watches, but what is particularly heartrending is the hundred innocent humans caught within the deadly conflagration that ensues as their mangled bodies are tossed off in every direction. Cristonn shuts his eyes tightly, for although his intentions were sincere, he now is sickeningly aware that he has done far more harm than good.

He laments for several moments what he has unintentionally done, trying to fight back the disgust he feels for himself, before the soul blade lying near him begins to flash red. No sooner does this happen when a shadow is seen creeping across his body and face. His eyes are still closed, and therefore he is unaware of the cause of this imposing shadow as well as his soul blade trying to alert him to its dangerous presence, but the feeling of sunlight on his face vanishes, and finally he opens his eyes. He quickly wishes he hadn't—for the terrible sight that reveals itself is a demon lieutenant and its black dragon mate that have just landed on the walkway. The reptilian creature hisses menacingly as its red eyes of evil meets the paladin's.

Shocked by the sight of the evil pair, Cristonn can see his soul blade near, and although it is easily within reach, he cannot grab it due to his paralyzing injuries. He urgently calls to the blade, which crosses the mere inches between blade and hand. But he is simply unable to grasp the handle in order to use its healing powers, though he is frantically trying to do so, his hand trembling in its struggle.

The black dragon opens its mouth, and the glowing energy of a lightning bolt begins to form. But the demon lieutenant holds out a hand, stopping the beast from discharging the lethal weapon, for the sight of one of the blood enemies of the demonic race—a paladin—slumped helplessly before it is a rare treat indeed. The lieutenant wants the pleasure of sending this wretched human on his journey to the land of the dead itself. It dismounts the dragon, giving a gesture to the beast that sends it flying off to continue its demonic mayhem on its own. The demon, an evil smile on its face, begins a slow advance toward Cristonn as if to savor this victorious moment by not letting it end too quickly. In the background, dozens of its kind fly overhead, the black dragons discharging lightning bolts as several lava balls come smoking by, and the sound of battle is ever present, indicating the intense savagery of the battle has not let up.

The demon lieutenant begins to manipulate its mace and chain weapon so that the glowing, spiked ball spins rapidly, creating an imposing arc of light. Cristonn continues in his panicked attempts to grasp his soul blade with an even greater sense of urgency, but to no avail as his fumbling pushes the blade further away, increasing his panic. The creature is now standing over Cristonn's body and raises its hand, holding the spinning death and preparing to send it crashing down upon the paladin's powerless head. Cristonn is certainly no coward, and his eyes therefore don't display even a hint of horror; but he apathetically closes them, for there is nothing he can do to prevent the deathblow, and he certainly doesn't wish to witness it. But then a glowing arrow streaks in and deeply penetrates the demon's body and knocks the creature to the floor. Its weapon flails about, and with every impact of the glowing ball a small portion of the stone floor disintegrates with a flash and a puff of smoke. The body of the lieutenant also begins to radiate energy, and it too disintegrates into a pile of smoldering ashes.

One of the castle guards now enters the walkway from one of the entrances holding a bow. As he admires the smoldering pile, he catches a flash out of the corner of his eye. Looking around, he can see that another demon lieutenant is beginning to decompose in a similar fashion and falls off the dragon it is riding, quickly becoming a cloud of slowly descending ash—then another and another—one hundred in all, if anyone was counting.

"Wow," he says with a pleasantly astonished look on his face, "those arrows of demon slaying really work! The queen was right when she said they would kill a hundred times their number. Too bad it is the last one."

He sees Cristonn, and though the paladin looks uninjured, his depleted condition makes the guard rush over. He kneels by his side. "How can I help?" he asks.

"My back is broken," Cristonn struggles to say. "My soul blade—I can't hold it. Place it into my hand."

The guard reaches for the blade, but the moment he touches it, the blade gives him a slightly painful shock, causing him to draw his hand away. He gives Cristonn a startled look.

"Sorry," the paladin meekly apologizes, "I forgot," and then, addressing the soul blade, "I permit it." Cristonn nods to the guard, indicating it is now safe to pick up the blade.

He does so after a moment of apprehension and puts the blade into Cristonn's hand.

"Now," the weak Paladin continues, "close my fingers around it."

And again the guard does as he is told.

Cristonn closes his eyes to concentrate and softly says, "Heal."

His entire body glows faintly, and his internal injuries heal, and all his strength returns. "Thank you," he says to the guard gratefully.

"My pleasure, noble one," says the smiling guard. "I guess we all forget that even a mighty paladin is not invinc—"

But his smile and words are instantly cut short by the tip of a bloody sword penetrating through his chest. Cristonn immediately pushes the body aside and sees that the cause of the guard's death is a demon soldier—the first of many who are now beginning to scale the wall to his position despite Cristonn's destruction of the two stairways. He points his soul blade in the demon's direction and instantly blasts the creature away. Several more begin to invade his position by scrambling over the walls. Using his X attack, he manages to blast them away too— as well as a large portion of the castle structure. It is clear that with the exception of the attack he used on the demon king earlier, Cristonn's X attack is his most powerful—that is, when he can use both the blades as weapons.

Although this attack is highly efficient in blasting several demons out of existence, it also unfortunately makes a more efficient entryway for the dozens of demons that follow to get through, for the entrance that is giving them access to the walkway is now ten times larger. Even a lieutenant lands on the walkway now that the paladin's annoying presence is known to all. Seeing this, Cristonn decides that caution is the better part of valor and makes a hasty dash for the only exit available at the other end of the walkway, barely avoiding a lightning blast in the process. Upon entering, he can see the demons rushing toward him, but the entrance has no door—not that it would have made much of an effective barrier against such an oncoming force—but Cristonn does see that the entrance is bracketed by two stone columns. He quickly slashes the top of one with his soul blade. The blade easily slices through as if the stone was made of air, and the cut it leaves glows and smokes due to the blade's energy. He then does the same to the base of the column, thereby severing it from its attachment to floor and ceiling. Holding the blade before him, he levitates the massive weight and guides it in front of the entrance, sealing it completely and preventing any demon from entering.

The paladin eventually makes his way toward another entrance of the castle. Several demons try to stop him, for at this stage in the battle the demons have practically overrun every position and appear almost everywhere in huge numbers, but Cristonn is able to defeat the small group that opposes him. To call it a "battle" anymore is simply being kind, for those people who are still alive are completely overmatched and hopelessly outnumbered by now, and the frantic combat that occurs is more akin to a slaughter than any kind of battle—and it is the humans who are being slaughtered in droves.

A large and strikingly handsome, marble statue of Queen Valerias proudly standing nearby, seemingly in defiance to any threat, catches the loyal paladin's eye. He doesn't feel particularly loyal when the idea racing through his head hits him, for a disturbing number of demons begin to pour into the area.

I'm sorry, my queen, he thinks, *I know you were quite fond of that statue of yourself, but*—

Needing some weapon to deal with this demonic deluge, Cristonn fires a beam of energy at the base of the statue, which severs it from its attachment to the floor. He levitates the weight over the heads of this large group of foes, and another blast detonates the stone mass, which sends a shower of lethal shards hurtling through the air at tremendous velocity and decimates their ranks.

Continuing his way through the interior of the castle, he tries to help those other humans who find themselves on the wrong end of a demonic confrontation, but by and large it is obvious that little can be done to help these people due to the overwhelming number of demons swarming the castle, and many die.

CHAPTER 5

✦ ✦ ✦

Rojan, the young son of Queen Valerias, is in his room sitting on the bed, and like most boys of his tender and innocently angelic age of seven years, he is absolutely fearless when it comes to fighting the forces of darkness. During his countless battles with them, he has always emerged victorious without ever receiving the slightest scratch. Fire hornets or ice spiders, sea warlocks or mountain witches, black dragon queens or green goblin kings—none have been a match for the mighty Rojan. He is particularly fond of recalling how he even defeated a god—a feat up until that time thought to be impossible for a mortal—but Rojan did it, and quite easily too, as he remembers.

It was the evil god of all ogre kind, Vasarak, a very powerful deity indeed, as all gods usually are—but the poor soul just didn't stand a chance against Rojan. And how many times has the heroic boy single-handedly saved all the good races of the land from total extinction? He has lost count. And not one demigod neglects to bow with respect when Rojan walks by. But these legendary adventures were all imaginary, and the epic battles were in reality fought against the dozens of toy monsters seen throughout his room.

Still, he considers himself quite the brave little warrior, and given half the chance, he would gladly prove it without hesitation. Especially now that he is holding the dagger his mother gave him on his seventh birthday three months ago, which inspires him with great courage. It is a far more effective weapon to battle evil than his usual stick. So with blade in hand, he is fully confident in his ability to slay any demon that dares to challenge him. He's never seen a demon, of course, and has no idea what to expect if he ever encounters one, for his school studies have only covered the evil plants and insects of the land and haven't even remotely gotten to the stage of the higher-level creatures yet—especially the horrendous evil that demon-kind is able to inflict—for he is only seven, and such knowledge would undoubtedly be unsettling to any young child, not to mention that his mother would have never allowed him to be in harm's way due to the intensity of the battles during the past six days despite Rojan's pleas to help fight. In fact, the only evil creature that he has killed to date was a small swamp rat that made the fatal mistake of testing Rojan's courage during a recent outing in the forest surrounding the castle—that is, the forest that was there three months ago, for the sylvan glade no longer exists after the recent battles with the demons. The encounter with the swamp rat was a challenge but one that was ultimately overcome due to his nimble use of the dagger. At least, that is the way Rojan likes to tell the heroic tale. In reality, he almost tripped over the creature while it was sleeping—but the point is he did kill it. So dispatching a demon or two can't be much more difficult than that. He honestly felt that way earlier that morning. But now— things are dramatically different.

The booming thuds he is hearing, which were earlier quite distant and only mildly disconcerting, are now almost upon him and have the boy worried. He has no idea what is causing them and has no intention of leaving the sanctuary of his room to find out. It isn't that he is afraid, for although he is, his fear isn't so great that it could overcome his curiosity about the noise, but his mother commanded him to stay in his room, and therefore stay he will. It is a good thing, for if Rojan knew the sounds were coming from the impacts of lava balls from magmadons, he certainly wouldn't leave the room at all, especially now that the proximity of their landings is dangerously close—so close, in fact, that the room shudders with every impact, sometimes quite violently, as various of his possessions tumble from shelves and dust and plaster fall from the ceiling—a very unnerving situation for any small child to deal with. But this is nowhere near as traumatic as the sounds of savage fighting and the bloodcurdling screams of the dying he hears coming from just outside his bedroom door.

The wooden door soon violently explodes inward in a mass of broken splinters caused by the body of some unfortunate human that is being thrown through it with great force. The bloody carcass falls at Rojan's feet with the blade of a sword deeply and grotesquely embedded into the chest. But it is what Rojan doesn't see that is most terrifying, for the body is missing its head. A lesser sight would have caused the young boy to scream in horror and flee the room, but this is so hideously gruesome that it completely stuns the child into a catatonic state of petrified terror, and the sight of a demon soldier entering his room carrying an axe dripping with blood certainly does nothing to alleviate this feeling.

The young boy, who moments before was blissfully ignorant of the horrors of war, is not prepared to handle sights such as these—and the dagger Rojan is clinging to, once a source of his great courage when he fantasized about slaying every demon earlier that morning, slowly slides from his fingers and falls uselessly to the floor.

The demon soldier slowly approaches the boy, drooling in anticipation of an easy kill, and raises the axe over Rojan's head. Rojan, who is still too terrified to move—let alone flee in an effort to save his own life—can do nothing. Then there is a quick flash of a blade falling down the demon's head. The menacing glow of the creature's evil red eyes fades as a large portion of the face neatly slides off, and the dead body collapses to the floor. Cristonn has entered the room. The sight of him snaps Rojan out of his paralyzing fear. He is greatly pleased by Cristonn's presence and attempts to go to him.

"Cristonn!" he happily cries out.

"Stay back, Rojan!" commands the paladin.

A dozen more of the demonic creatures now invade the room. Cristonn separates his soul blade into two and fires off a massive blast of energy with his X attack, instantly blasting away the demonic group—and half the room with it. An impressive display of power and one that would have brought a big smile to Rojan's face along with an exuberant "Wow!" if it weren't for the fact that the missing walls and ceiling reveal another wall—but this wall is far larger, black in color, and appears to be made out of skin. A glance upward reveals that it is the leg of a dreaded magmadon. The stone debris of the walls and ceiling pepper the leviathan's leg after Cristonn's blast, but this is certainly no threat to the massive beast—no more than a flung handful of sand is a threat to a brick wall. Unfortunately, it does get the dreaded demon's attention—much to Cristonn's dismay. Rojan's eyes grow wide as he is awestruck by the sight of the enormous demonic creature, for he has never seen anything so ominous before in his young life, and he stands there shocked as the magmadon lowers its head to focus its red eyes on the insect-sized pair below. The mouth opens, revealing the fiery glow of a lava ball beginning to form.

Cristonn could easily detonate the flaming death with a quick strike as he did to the other magmadon, but because they are so close, it would mean instant death to him and the boy. He quickly puts his two blades back together to form the soul blade, for at this close range he is going to need all of his protective power. He pushes Rojan behind him and generates a shield of energy as the magmadon unleashes the lethal projectile. The impact is tremendous and instantly incinerates everything in the immediate area, leaving only a smoking ring of debris, and as the smoke clears, nothing that was there before remains—except for Cristonn and Rojan. Now that the crisis has subsided, the paladin dissolves the shield and, with the X attack, fires off a blast at the magmadon looming above. The injury it causes is severe and certainly quite painful to the demonic colossus, as it roars in protest, but due to its immense bulk and heavily armored skin it takes several more of the powerful blasts to finally bring the magmadon crashing down in death. The ground trembles as the demon hits the earth.

Unfortunately for Cristonn and Rojan, the protection and secrecy from demonic eyes that the walls of Rojan's room provided no longer exist, for the room and a dozen or so adjacent walls have been completely destroyed by the magmadon's attack, and the two are visible to every demon in the area—thousands of them, far too many for the lone Cristonn to deal with as they all begin to rush toward the two while brandishing their lethal arsenal.

"Stay close, boy," he calmly says to Rojan.

Rojan begins to move closer to his paladin savior but stops momentarily when he sees his dagger lying near his feet. He picks the blade up. Holding the boy close, Cristonn takes out the blue jewel Valerias gave him and throws it on the ground an instant before he and Rojan are overwhelmed by the demons. The jewel creates a blinding flash of light upon impact and the two mercifully disappear by using the jewel's life-saving teleportation power.

CHAPTER 6

✶ ✶ ✶

Reappearing with a flash on a rocky ledge in the surrounding mountains alone and—for the moment, at least—relatively safe, Cristonn picks up the jewel lying beside his feet, which is only glowing with half the intensity it was moments before, indicating that it only has one teleport charge left, and puts it in his clothing for future use. The two walk over and look down to where they can see the demonic army overrunning their former home as the epic struggle for survival continues raging below. Many fires are seen amid the castle ruins as dozens of lava balls streak in, and the flashes of lightning from the hundreds of black dragons are ever present. Even from this distance, Cristonn and Rojan can still hear the faint cries of the dying, as all but a few of the castle defenders still remain alive. The sight is understandably a depressing one, but it is the young Rojan who, even at his tender, innocent age, cannot help but acknowledge the obvious.

"My mother is dead, isn't she?" the boy says emotionlessly as if not wanting to believe it is true.

Although Cristonn would normally try to spare the boy the pain of admitting his mother's death until a more appropriate and less traumatic time, the truth is impossible to ignore.

"Yes, she is dead," Cristonn replies sadly.

Rojan begins to sob. Cristonn also feels painful remorse about the loss of Valerias, and if given the chance might also shed some tears, but he obviously cannot, for that would upset the boy even further. He kneels down beside Rojan and begins to comfort him.

"You must be strong, Rojan. Your mother gave her life so that she could help you later on. In time, you'll understand what her sacrifice means, but for now just remember that her love for you is great, and that love will be with you again."

Cristonn is aware that no human seven-year-old child can possibly understand what someone with a paladin's level of knowledge is trying to explain, at least on a soul level, but Rojan responds with the token answer,

"I'll try and be brave, Cristonn."

Cristonn acknowledges this answer accordingly, and although he knows that Rojan is faithful in his answer, the boy really has no clue what he needs to be brave for. In time he will know the sacrifice his answer entails.

"Good. It looks like we'll be here for some time. Can you make us a fire?"

"Oh yes!" says the boy cheerfully upon hearing this. "My mother taught me how! Watch, you'll see!"

"Make a small one," the paladin cautions. "We don't want to make our presence known."

Rojan cheerfully nods and runs off to gather some sticks nearby. Cristonn smiles, seeing that the boy has something to deal with other than the death of his mother and the horrific crisis at hand—not to mention what the uncertain future will bring. But the smile quickly vanishes as he once again directs his attention to the carnage below, and after a few moments of watching the sickening sight, he turns away in disgust.

Rojan has made a small pile of sticks upon the ground, and with eyes closed, he now holds out his hand above it, taking a moment to concentrate. After a while, he opens his eyes and looks puzzled when nothing has happened. He tries again and concentrates more deeply. Cristonn can see the boy is having trouble, and he knows he could easily make the fire for the boy, but he also knows it would demoralize Rojan if he interfered; but he smiles, for he knows Rojan will soon get the hang of it. The pile of sticks begins to smoke, and soon a very small flame appears which causes Rojan to beam with pride.

"See, Cristonn! I told you I could start a fire!"

Cristonn, however, isn't as enthusiastic as he eyes the rather insignificant flame.

"Rojan, that's a flame—not a fire."

The boy, dismayed by this fact, again closes his eyes in concentration. With Rojan's eyes closed, Cristonn decides that some minor and unseen assistance on his part is now warranted, and with a slight gesture of his hand the pile of sticks ignites, which quickly gets Rojan's surprised and happy attention.

"How about that?" he says proudly, thinking he is the one responsible for this small inferno.

"Very impressive, Rojan—thank you."

And the boy smiles broadly.

Content with the destruction his relentless army has wrought, the demon king, Maggar, decides that his regal presence is no longer necessary. His shadow can be seen transforming into some horrific shape that unfurls large wings and begins to take flight as he leaves the location on the mountaintop.

Cristonn notices his soul blade beginning to glow red, the signal that danger is near, which causes a look of concern to register on his face as he quickly grabs the weapon in hand and scans the horizon. In the distance, the black form of the demon king begins to appear. Though it is still too far away to make out any details, it definitely is getting larger. The sight of this greatly alarms the paladin, for he knows all too well what this approaching threat is capable of doing and how futile his paladin powers would be to do anything about it. Worse, the demon king is flying directly toward Cristonn's location.

"Damn," says the highly anxious Cristonn, but quietly enough not to alarm Rojan. The boy notices the flying black dot getting closer too but has no idea why Cristonn is so apprehensive.

"What's that, Cristonn?" asks the curious child.

But the paladin doesn't answer. Instead, he commands the boy sharply,

"Rojan, get behind that rock—quickly! And for the love of the gods, whatever you do, don't look at it!"

Rojan—not realizing the danger that is causing Cristonn's sense of panic, nevertheless obeys and quickly dashes behind a nearby rock. Cristonn notices the telltale fire that he created, and even though he is far away from it, he still is able to magically extinguish the fire with a wave of his hand so as not to let the flickering light alert the approaching enemy of any human survivors. The paladin moves up against the rock wall for cover as his soul blade begins to glow even more intensely—a glow that also would give away any chance of concealment. He talks to it calmly:

"Yes, I see him, my loves—I see him. Hush now."

He caresses the blade soothingly, and the glow begins to diminish, thereby concealing his presence by the rock wall in relative darkness. But the shadowy image of the demon king begins to appear on the ground and grows larger with each passing second as it comes ever closer to Cristonn, causing his look of concern to grow as well, almost to the point of panic. The paladin takes his soul blade and does something odd—at least odd in Rojan's eyes, for his curiosity has gotten the better of him, and he watches what Cristonn is doing despite the order not to look, for all seven year old boys are intensely curious, and the temptation to watch is simply impossible to ignore. It is fortunate for the boy that the rock he is hiding behind only allows him to see Cristonn. Were Rojan to take even the slightest glance at Maggar almost overhead, he would see his eyes, and the child would instantly suffer the fatal consequences of the burning power of the demon king's blinding gaze, which not even a paladin could prevent, for their healing ability only heals their own injuries—not anyone else's. But the odd thing Cristonn is doing is that he has turned his soul blade around and now has the lethal point of the weapon aimed straight at his abdomen, as if his intention is to impale his body with the blade. Rojan, upon seeing this action, is understandably greatly puzzled by it.

As Cristonn looks down toward Maggar's shadow to judge its proximity to his location—for a gaze skyward would inflict the searing blindness upon him once again—Cristonn is aware that Maggar is now flying directly overhead as the ominous shadow begins to cover Cristonn's anxious but grimly determined face. He takes a deep breath, for the enemy will be upon him in a matter of seconds, and closes his eyes for a moment to steel himself for the act he is about to take. Tightening his grip upon the handle of the blade, he makes a gesture to plunge his soul blade into his body—but he stops when the odious shadow of the powerful Maggar moves on without noticing him. A look of great relief registers on Cristonn's face as he lets out a massive sigh now that the dramatic crisis has passed. Cristonn's hand trembles slightly, for preparing to commit suicide is not one that is usually done without great trepidation, even if the act is a noble one. Seeing Cristonn's relieved countenance, Rojan moves out from behind the rock and approaches him.

"What was that thing, Cristonn?"

"Just a demon," he impassively announces so as not to alarm the child. "He won't bother us."

"Why didn't you kill it?"

Cristonn is slightly amused by Rojan's suggestion, but it is not humor that prompts him to smile but the fact that the boy doesn't know what he is saying. If he did, he would realize the utter foolishness of the idea.

"I'm just a paladin, Rojan," responds Cristonn as he continues to watch the retreating menace warily, "not a god. But at least we don't have to conceal our presence now."

The paladin then points his soul blade in the direction of where the fire once was, and the blade shoots out a bolt of energy that causes a far larger fire than the one before to begin burning brightly. Rojan is impressed.

"Wow!" the boy exclaims.

Cristonn notices a tree nearby.

"Considering the ordeal you must have been through these past several days, I'll bet you are hungry," he says to the boy. He is sincere with his concern over the child's lack of nourishment, but it also doesn't hurt that it gives Cristonn an opportunity to solve his hunger problem as well.

Rojan nods eagerly. "Yes, most of the food in the castle ran out two days ago."

"Let's see what we can do about that. Come."

They both walk over to the tree. Upon closer inspection, Cristonn finds a fruit on one of the branches and reaches to pluck it, but before he can do so, a bird suddenly darts in and snatches it away.

"Hey! Come back here!" demands the annoyed paladin.

The bird returns and lands on Cristonn's outstretched arm, which impresses the young boy.

"We need that fruit, little one," Cristonn continues.

The bird begins to chirp as if talking to the paladin—which it is, but he is not impressed by the bird's excuses and responds accordingly.

"We have all had a busy day. Look, the boy is hungry."

The bird begins chirping again, this time more vociferously.

"Yes, I do have eyes, and I know the countryside has been decimated, but I don't care if this is the only fruit available within fifty miles. He needs it."

But again the bird protests sharply.

"Oh, very well, take it. But you can still help us. Go down to the castle. When the demons have left, fly back here and tell me."

Again the bird chirps its musical response but this time with a more frantic tone, obviously reluctant to follow Cristonn's suggestion. Rojan is greatly enjoying this verbal debate.

"I'm sure the demons have better things to do than barbecue a small, irritating bird. Just stay out of sight and they won't see you. Now go."

The bird gives a final chirp, signaling its obedience, and then flies back up to the tree to put the fruit in a hole there.

"You can talk to animals?" asks the astonished Rojan.

"All paladins can communicate with and command any of the lesser creatures of goodness." The bird emerges from the hole, which Cristonn notices, prompting him to continue sarcastically, "But there are some creatures whose goodness I doubt."

The bird chirps back sharply, prompting Cristonn to exclaim, "Don't use that language with me—there's a child present. Now be gone!"

Cristonn gestures for the bird to depart, and it flies off. He watches the bird departing for a few moments and then reaches into the hole where the bird put the fruit. He says, smiling with triumph, "Birds aren't very bright."

The paladin takes out the fruit and admires his possession, but he is soon distracted by a noise within the hole. As he looks inside, he realizes that there are several chicks that obviously are in more need of that fruit than he and Rojan, so Cristonn meekly puts the fruit back in the hole with a smile and moves away from the tree.

"I'm afraid you'll have to wait a little longer for some food, Rojan."

The boy chuckles at the sight of a mighty paladin being defeated by a humble bird, but even a young child like Rojan knows that it is precisely these unselfish acts that make paladins great. Unfortunately, it does nothing to curb his hunger.

"I'm awfully hungry, Cristonn," says Rojan.

Cristonn looks around the area for anything even remotely edible, but the rocky ledge is quite barren except for an annoying abundance of inedible rocks and that lone—and now fruitless—tree, of course. But he does eye a rather large hole located in the ground nearby and walks over to it. Rojan also sees the hole, and his eyes grow wide with excitement, for it looks exactly like the perfect home for a plump rabbit, and if there is one thing that pleases the boy's tummy most, it is a delicious meal of juicy rabbit. Cristonn takes his soul blade and begins to wave it over the ground near the rabbit hole. After a few moments, the blade gives a faint flash of red, and the paladin tries to zero in on the source, soon finding it as the blade steadily glows red. Cristonn quickly stabs the sword into the ground and withdraws it with a black, furry, rabbit-sized object impaled on the blade. He tosses it to the eagerly drooling Rojan, who can practically taste the rabbit already. But unfortunately what lands at the boy's feet is not a fuzzy and cute rabbit but a fuzzy and repulsive black, rabbit-sized spider, its legs curling in death and a sizzling wound from the soul blade smoking slightly on its body—an extremely unappetizing and actually quite nauseating sight.

"Cook that," says Cristonn to the boy, thereafter taking a moment to energize his soul blade, which begins to glow and burn off the spider's blood, restoring the blade to its bright and shiny luster.

But Rojan doesn't want to touch the thing, let alone put any part of the disgusting creature in his mouth, for it truly is one of the more ugly creatures of the known universe and he eagerly begins to shy away from it.

"Don't worry," says Cristonn. "It tastes a lot better than it looks. I used to hunt night spiders when I was your age, for there wasn't much food near the Blood Sea where I grew up. Just don't eat the head. The poison of a night spider would kill you instantly."

This last sentence doesn't encourage the boy any, but he does reluctantly take the spider and begin to pull the legs off in preparation for roasting it over the fire. Finished with this repellent task, he skewers the body with a stick and begins to roast it over the flames. After a few moments, Rojan notices Cristonn has moved back to the ledge to gaze below.

The boy has known the kind and noble paladin all his life, but he really doesn't know much about the man. Rojan is now at the age when he would like to know more about someone whom he admires greatly.

"Don't you have any children, Cristonn?"

"I have twin daughters," he responds after a poignant moment of reflection.

"Twins?" says Rojan, surprised, for this is the first time he has heard of this. "How old are they?"

"They would be ten about now."

"How come I have never seen them?"

"I see them," Cristonn sullenly responds as he caresses his soul blade tenderly.

Rojan's curious nature prompts him to inquire further, but there is something in Cristonn's tone that makes him think better of it, sensing it is something best not discussed at this moment, so he decides to change the subject.

"Aren't you hungry, Cristonn?" asks the boy.

"A little," says the paladin with an ironic smile in response. Truth be known, he's actually quite famished.

"Why don't you come and eat something?" says the boy, as he has finished with the cooking of the arachnid meal. With an aghast look at the thing, he sheepishly takes a tiny bite, thinking the spider will taste vile, but he is soon pleasantly surprised by how good it tastes.

"I'm a paladin," says Cristonn. "I can't consume the flesh of an evil creature."

Rojan is certainly not a paladin, but upon hearing Cristonn's response he doesn't want Cristonn to think Rojan is less of a man than he is, so he pushes the rest of the spider meat back near the fire. Cristonn notices this and smiles, continuing,

"You can relax—you aren't a paladin yet, so go ahead and eat. Only once you take the oath of the paladinhood do you need to respect the secular laws."

This brings a relieved smile to Rojan's face, for he is very hungry and eagerly continues his meal.

"You must be a great paladin, Cristonn," says the boy with much admiration.

"Great?" the paladin says with a surprised, droll tone. "Why? Because I can kill a spider or talk to a bird? I can't even steal a measly fruit from one of them!"

Rojan laughs, saying, "You know what I mean—you can talk to animals and kill demons! That's what makes you great!"

Cristonn scoffs at this as he replies, "It takes far more than being able to talk to a bird to make a paladin great, my young friend, nor is greatness measured by how skilled he is with a soul blade in battle. The true measure of a paladin's greatness comes from within—from his compassion for others, his bravery, his virtues of goodness, many other things."

"Does it take time to learn all this, Cristonn?"

"Not really, for one is already born with most of these qualities. But it does take time to hone them to such a degree that you can use them in the service of goodness—be it for the paladinhood, as I chose or as a member of the good wizard class like your mother."

"Is that why my mother was teaching me to become a paladin?" asks Rojan. "Because I have these qualities?"

"That's right," Cristonn replies. "When you get a little older, you'll understand more."

"How many paladins are there?"

"Oh, there are about fifty of us. Some are in the service of the good kings and queens of the land, like I was with your mother, but all of us are warriors fighting the forces of evil."

"Are they as powerful as you, Cristonn?"

"All paladins are powerful, Rojan, but some are more advanced than others. Paladins like Zanto, Trajus, Darian—and, of course, the paladin master—but it takes many years to reach their level of advancement and power."

"Like you!" says Rojan with respectful glee, for he is very proud that a boy his age has such a powerful benefactor—and friend. "My mother said you are one of the five arch-paladins—second in power only to the paladin master!"

Cristonn smiles slightly upon hearing this great compliment that Valerias apparently gave him, and although Rojan's statement is accurate, for he is indeed second in power in the entire paladinhood, Cristonn's modesty prevents him from acknowledging this.

"Did she?" is the only response his modesty allows.

"I'll be a great paladin too one day!" the boy proudly announces.

Cristonn laughs at the boy's statement, saying, "Perhaps once you curb that arrogance. But you haven't long to wait. In fact, one of the greatest paladins that ever lived was one not much older than you."

Rojan is pleased to hear this. "Really?" he says with much enthusiasm.

"Yes," Cristonn continues, "his name was Jartan. He was a novice paladin, like you will soon be, but that didn't prevent him from becoming a great one—a paladin we will all remember for his sacrifice."

"People were saying that it was a paladin named Jartan that is responsible for the demons being angry," says Rojan. "Is that true?"

"He did what was necessary," replies the Paladin objectively.

"Cristonn, why are the demons killing us?"

"Because of the demon queen."

"You mean Magdara?" asks Rojan quite innocently.

Cristonn suddenly reacts with great horror upon hearing the utterance of this last word and admonishes the boy sharply, "Rojan!" The paladin quickly grabs his soul blade and looks around the area in a panic as if expecting something terrible to happen, while a stunned

Rojan has a look of frightened bewilderment on his young face, not having a clue about what is happening.

"Cristonn, what's wrong?"

"Never say the name of the demon queen—not while the demons are seeking vengeance. You will summon a shadowlord to slay you."

"Shadowlord?" the boy asks hesitantly, for the very sound of the word conjures up intense foreboding.

Cristonn, still scanning the area apprehensively for he knows what will soon be appearing, coldly responds while shaking his head, for even he doesn't want to think about it. "Bodyguards to the demonic royalty."

Cristonn's soul blade begins to glow intensely, signaling danger, much to his trepidation. Nearby, a surge of energy forms and in the swirling, electrified mist soon appears one of the dreaded shadowlords. This is a tall, cloaked being dressed in black with sharp spikes protruding from its shoulders and two sinister eyes intensely glowing red from the emptiness within the cowl covering the face. It is carrying a large, scythe-like weapon, which seems to glow like the demon's eyes. The combination of the creature's intimidating appearance and its formidable weapon indicates that the shadowlord has a frightening degree of power.

The paladin reacts instantly. He is first to attack with a concentrated beam of energy from the soul blade but the shadowlord is just as quick with a defensive shield, absorbing the blow, prompting a concerned Cristonn to try to defuse the situation without combat.

"Now just relax, shadowlord," he says with resolve but also with a definite hint of nervousness. "The boy meant no harm."

The shadowlord speaks in its demonic tongue, but the paladin understands the language: "He spoke the name of the demon queen," states the creature bluntly and without emotion.

But Cristonn cannot resist the opportunity for a well-timed insult aimed at a mortal enemy like a shadowlord and responds to this statement with a mocking smile:

"So? I say '*bitch*' all the time. How come I never see you?"

This horrifies the shadowlord, prompting the creature to exclaim with anger, "You both shall die for your blasphemy!"

And with a further scream heralding its desire for blood and revenge, it begins to catapult toward Cristonn in a frenzied rage. The shadowlord attacks with a frenzied passion, but the paladin is extremely adroit and uses his soul blade to protect himself and Rojan from the impact of the demonic being's weapon with an energy shield. Cristonn then counterattacks with a slash of his own at the shadowlord, and an intense battle ensues between the two. Rojan reaches some protective cover, as there is simply nothing a boy his age can possible do to help the situation, but he does draw his dagger from his clothing just in case Cristonn calls for his assistance. After several exchanges of combat, Cristonn separates his soul blade into two. With one blade he creates a shield to deflect the shadowlord's attack, and with the other he blasts the shadowlord with energy, causing the creature to reel back.

Putting the blades in the form of an X, he unleashes another blast that causes even more damage, and the creature falls to the ground after being blasted away several yards. Seeing his chance to defeat the stunned shadowlord, the paladin rushes over to it, and putting his blades back together, he beheads the creature with a quick stroke as massive bursts of energy erupt from the wound as the shadowlord collapses to the ground in a lifeless heap of glowing debris until only its black clothing remains. Cristonn stands nearby victorious but quite exhausted from the intense battle.

Rojan approaches him now that the danger has passed, and great remorse shows on his face, for he realizes he was the cause of all this.

"I'm sorry, Cristonn," says the boy sadly as he lowers his head as if to cry. He truly is sorry his act almost led to the death of one he admires greatly.

Cristonn looks down at him and puts his hand on Rojan's shoulder as a comforting gesture, which stops the boy from crying, for the paladin knows the boy was completely unaware of the dire ramifications of saying the demon queen's name. He responds to the boy with a soothing smile: "It's all right, for you didn't know any better. Just never say her name again."

The boy brightens, but the paladin's smile soon vanishes, and suddenly his face shows a slight grimace of pain as he holds his side awkwardly with his hand. Rojan notices this.

"What's wrong, Cristonn?"

"It is nothing. But I want you to do something. Go over to the shadowlord's remains and see if there is a jewel lying within the clothing."

"A jewel? Why?"

"Some of the higher-level creatures and beings have a jewel for a heart, and on rare occasions a shadowlord sometimes has one. These jewels have magical properties."

"What properties?" inquires the boy.

"That depends on the color, but with demons it is usually red. Red means it has magical healing properties. Go and see." Cristonn prompts the boy—rather urgently—to go look, and Rojan begins to search the body, but after a few moments he finds nothing.

"I can't find any jewel here, Cristonn."

"No matter—it was a long shot anyway."

Rojan goes back over to where the paladin is standing. Upon reaching him, he can see that blood is beginning to seep between the fingers that he is tightly holding against his side in an effort to staunch the flow from a rather severe and surprisingly rapidly festering wound he received during his battle with the shadowlord.

"You're injured!" Rojan cries out with much concern.

"I noticed," replies Cristonn mockingly.

"But you're a paladin," a confused Rojan says. "You can heal your own injuries—I've seen you do it before!"

"When you get older, you will find out that there are many creatures that have magical abilities that you cannot counter or can cause wounds that cannot be healed. Unfortunately for me, a wound from a shadowlord's weapon is one of them. I was hoping that the damn thing might have left a jewel I could use—but I'm afraid the irony would have been too great. It tried to kill me and now I need it to save my life? Only fools would see the humor in that."

A frantic Rojan makes an effort to offer assistance, but Cristonn pushes him away, gently adding, "There's nothing you can do. It is not the flesh wound that is the trouble—it is the magical poison that the shadowlord's weapon was laced with."

The paladin begins to chuckle softly, though this quickly turns into a slight cough. He is beginning to cough up some blood as the poison continues its lethal surge through his veins, but he does regain a feeble smile as he recalls the humorous thought.

"At least I won't starve to death." For considering the losing battle with the bird and fruit earlier, and the squirrel with the last of his berries, and the fact that he has given all his miniscule nourishment to whatever poor creature needed it more over the past week—which is exactly what he has done with his food— the possibility of starving has been foremost on his mind for the past few days, and he again laughs; but again it quickly turns to a cough, and he falls to his knees.

"Wait!" cries Rojan excitedly as he remembers something. "My mother taught me a spell that cures poison."

"It won't work, Rojan, but I appreciate the thought."

"Yes, it will!" counters the boy. "I know, because she had me use it on her when she was bitten by a fever fly once—it is really simple," says the boy as he kneels down beside Cristonn to work his spell.

"Of course it worked, you silly boy, for she was your mother. That type of healing spell won't work unless you have that special lo—" But Cristonn stops, for he is astonished to see that Rojan's spell is actually beginning to impart its healing magic to his wound.

And it is an astonishing sight to him, for Cristonn knows that the magical healing power Rojan is using only works when it is used on someone you have a special love for—like family. But as Cristonn thinks about it, it actually makes sense that the boy's spell is working on him. Rojan is not Cristonn's son, for the boy's father died before Rojan was even born, and although the paladin is certainly very fond of the boy, he doesn't possess that special love that one would for one's own child. But due to Cristonn and Valerias's close relationship over the past ten years, the mighty paladin—in the boy's eyes, anyway—is really the only father figure he has ever known, and therefore Rojan does have that special love for him—and it is precisely that special love that the person who is using the healing spell must have for it to work, regardless of what the injured person feels. Cristonn's wound is now completely healed.

"There!" says Rojan, beaming with pride. "See how simple that was?"

"Yes," replies Cristonn, standing and looking down at him with a far greater appreciation of the boy's feelings for him. "Why didn't I think of that?"

"Because you aren't simple-minded like I am," says the boy proudly.

Cristonn laughs upon hearing this, for he is sure the boy didn't mean for his words to come out quite that way, and Rojan certainly is unaware that he has insulted himself. Cristonn replies happily, "You have a point there." And touching the boy's shoulder warmly, he adds: "Thank you for your help."

The paladin notices the boy's dagger.

"Where did you get that?" he asks Rojan, pointing to the blade.

"My mother gave it to me on my seventh birthday."

"Ah yes, I remember. That is going to be a great help to you later on, so you hold on to that—for you will need it soon."

"Will the demons know we are here now?" asks Rojan, looking with a wary eye at the smoldering remains of the shadowlord.

"Not anymore," responds the victorious paladin, also looking at the lifeless pile.

"Would my mother have a jewel for her heart?"

"I'm afraid as advanced beings go, we humans are at the lower end of the spectrum, Rojan. But if anyone deserves to have a jewel for a heart, it would be your mother."

"Cristonn, why is all this happening?"

"I'm afraid that is a very long story and not a very happy one. You may find it frightening, Rojan. But perhaps when you get a little older I might—"

But that simple explanation is nowhere near satisfying for the highly inquisitive child and only increases his curiosity, so Rojan presses further.

"Please tell me, Cristonn. Please!"

The paladin walks over to the fire with Rojan closely following. As the boy sits beside the fire in eager anticipation of hearing the story, Cristonn kneels before the flames and picks up a stick to toss into it. This is a tale that is going to take all night, and seeing how eager the boy is to hear it, Cristonn must relate the story, painful as it is. After all, if the boy is going to die, he has the right to know why.

"As you wish," he begins. "It all began five moons ago—when the demon prince, Karza, was killing the wizards of the Great Council."

And with these distressing words, Cristonn begins to tell the chilling story as he tosses the stick into the fire, creating a fountain of embers as Rojan becomes transfixed by the unfolding tale—so much so that in his mind's eye the boy can actually see, hear, and feel Cristonn's words coming to life before his very eyes within the soft glow of the fire.

CHAPTER 7

✳ ✳ ✳

It is five moons ago.

The almost incessant flashes of light illuminate the rocky gorge even more brightly than the sun shining overhead, and the rolling thunder that quickly follows is deafening. One might think there was a severe thunderstorm occurring in the immediate vicinity from these impressive sights and sounds—if it weren't for the fact of several distressing differences between what is actually happening and its atmospheric counterpart.

First, there is no trace of even a single cloud in the heavens above. Second, the flashes of light are not the monochrome hue of normal flashes of lightning but occur in a variety of striking colors, becoming even more intense as the seconds pass. And third, there is the sight of a large group of dire wolves sprinting through the narrow path of the gorge at their maximum speed—and possibly just a little bit faster than that. Dire wolves are actually quite fearless creatures, and a thunderstorm—no matter how severe—is certainly nothing new to them and would hardly disrupt their usual activities. So that it has sent them fleeing in a terror-stricken panic with their eyes wide with horror is a further hint that this disturbance is not due to some innocent weather phenomenon. As the dire wolves continue to flee, the ground suddenly trembles so violently that it knocks them off their stride and they stumble. They quickly regain their feet, and after darting a frantic look back, they flee with an even greater sense of urgency. Dozens of birds, reptiles, and various other small creatures dwelling within the walls or trees of the gorge also begin to flee with all haste as rocks begin to fall and branches shake from the massive jolts. But it is the sight that soon follows that finally eliminates all doubt whether this disturbance is natural.

A large explosion occurs, creating a huge cloud of dust and flinging debris, and as the smoke clears somewhat, the body of the human wizard Vantor is thrown hard to the ground as he reels in agony and screams in pain from a large, smoldering wound he has just received on his shoulder. He tries to regain his feet—with much difficulty due to the severity of his injury—but before doing so he reacts suddenly and with great alarm to something rapidly approaching that is beginning to inundate the area in an eerie bluish glow. The wizard creates a magical shield of energy with the hand of his uninjured arm just in time to prevent a massive burst of bluish energy from engulfing him, though the burst is so intense that it pushes Vantor back several feet. The weight of his body creates a slight furrow in the soil. When the attack finally subsides after a few moments, the walls of the gorge are covered with a thick sheet of glistening ice.

The wounded wizard retaliates by unleashing a powerful bolt of lightning from his outstretched hand in the direction the icy burst came from; some unseen creature groans in response. This brief respite finally gives Vantor a chance to regain his feet, but as he looks back to see the result of his attack, his face instantly registers great distress, as his lightning was obviously ineffective. He redoubles his frantic effort to escape the area.

Now the heavy thudding sound of massive footfalls can be heard lumbering closer, and soon the blurry image of a huge creature with three serpentine necks, each ending with a different dragon-like head, appears on the mirrored surface of the ice covering the walls of the gorge. The entire area soon glows bright red from a fiery discharge from the creature, which quickly melts the ice covering the walls, transforming it into a steaming cloud that quickly evaporates due to the incredibly high temperature of the flames. When the blast of flame fades away, the area once again glows with a bluish color, and after this frosty discharge the ice returns to once again cover most of the immediate vicinity, and finally it glows with a brilliant whiteness from yet another discharge of some hideous breath weapon from the creature—this time a lightning bolt, but one far greater than any seen before, and the ice shatters like glass due to the vibration it generates. Now only the shadow of the beast is seen on the rock wall, and after a piercing roar of triumph, it rumbles off to continue the pursuit of its human prey.

The frantic Vantor continues to struggle in his efforts to escape, for his body is swiftly beginning to succumb to its many wounds, and he is obviously near total exhaustion. The frenetic ordeal of the chase has been going on for some time—several days, in fact. Three days ago, he appeared as a handsome man full of vitality and in the prime of his late-forties life. But now, the terror of his ordeal has aged him many years, and he is barely clinging to what little life remains in his tortured body. But a glimmer of hope soon reveals itself: Vantor can see his fortress in the near distance as he turns the corner of a rock outcropping of the path. Approaching its thick walls and huge, redoubtable entrance—not to mention the powerful artifacts that he has inside—this offers him the best hope of survival, and the wizard smiles broadly in relief between pants of breath as he finally reaches the entrance, stumbling the last few feet. But his smile is fleeting, and he looks behind him in terror as he hears yet again the shrill, heavy breathing and the sound of the footsteps of his relentless pursuer. Panic flashes on Vantor's face as he raises his hands, frantically trying to catch his breath to speak as he stands before the entrance.

"Open!" commands the harried wizard.

The entrance slowly begins to open, but after another terrified look back and hearing the sounds of his tormentor drawing closer, he redoubles his effort to open the entrance to his fortress. Vantor shouts again much louder and more urgently, "Open! In the name of the gods! Open!"

The massive entrance continues to rise, but the wizard is greatly alarmed at its slowness. "Come on!" he hastily adds.

A loud bellow from the pursuing creature causes the frantic wizard to again look back in its direction. The sound of the footsteps is even louder now, indicating it is very close, and its shadow begins to appear from behind the rock outcropping—the shadow growing larger and larger as it creeps ever closer. Vantor's look of panic only increases as he still waits for the fortress door to open wide enough for him to enter, and after several moments it finally does so, though to Vantor the brief interval seemed like an eternity, and he rushes inside. But now the entrance must be closed for even a remote sense of safety to be achieved. With arms raised again, Vantor shouts the command, "Seal!" and the entrance begins the painfully slow descent, much to the anxiety of the exhausted wizard. He can see from beneath the slowly closing entrance the lower portion of the creature as it begins to emerge from behind the rock outcropping.

Two massive, scaled legs cause the earth to shudder slightly due to the mostly unseen creature's immense bulk—an upsetting sight, to be sure, but one that would be far more unpleasant were Vantor able to see the upper portion of the creature, which is hidden from view by the closing entrance.

The creature—from its point of view—can see the entrance closing, and with a shriek of disgust, seeing that its prey has reached a position of safety, it quickens its pace and rushes forward—not an easy task for a creature this size. Speed is not one of its attributes—but awesome power is. As if to reinforce this fact, the ground begins to glow bright red as the creature breathes a wall of searing fire at the rapidly disappearing Vantor.

The wizard is aware of this oncoming inferno, for he can see it through the half-closed entrance, and it is precisely the half-closed position that makes the wizard hastily create his magic shield of protection moments before the flames snake their deadly way through the opening, but it soon closes enough to prevent any further fire from getting through.

Upon reaching the almost completely closed entrance, the creature violently thrusts two huge, reptilian claws against it. The imposing talons dig deeply into it in an effort to prevent the door from sealing fully. These talons create deep scratch marks on the surface as the door begins to slow—then stop—and the creature begins to raise the barrier.

Vantor is understandably horrified at the sight of his entrance beginning to rise, and he urgently uses his magic to attempt to close it. A contest of will begins between the wizard's mighty magic and the creature's strength—but it is Vantor who ultimately succeeds in closing the entrance.

The creature roars loudly in anger and blasts the entrance with an icy breath of bluish energy, which begins to freeze the inflexible metal surface into something far less formidable.

Vantor looks justifiably concerned; he can see that his virtually impenetrable entrance is quickly being transformed into a frozen sheet of brittle ice, but ice is no match for fire, so he decides to counter this unsettling scene with a magical wall of flame directed against the rapidly chilling surface. After several moments, he is able to overpower the icy effect and restore it once again to the protective barrier. Vantor further adds insult to injury by raising his hands, which begin to glow brightly, and then uses his magic to energize the entrance, thereby sealing it even tighter with a shimmering layer of protective covering.

"You'll never reach me now!" exclaims Vantor, laughing in triumph.

But unknown to the wizard, now safely inside his impenetrable fortress, the dragon-like shadow outside now transforms into something far more muscular—a form with far more strength—and in this form, its huge hands, acting like sledgehammers, begin to pound against the entrance.

From inside the fortress, the entrance begins to buckle from the intense pounding from this new creature outside. Massive dents appear, and Vantor's magical barrier of protection begins to fail. The energy covering the door begins to flicker with every violent impact and ultimately starts to fade. The wizard, whose face moments before radiated triumph, instantly reverts to the horror he has felt since this nightmare began some days ago. He knows the protection of the door won't last for long against such tremendous and relentless punishment. Unfortunately for him, there is no place else to flee, since his fortress is his last refuge, so he decides to make a stand here—for the moment anyway, for he can always retreat deeper into the fortress if what he is planning fails. Taking great pains to calm himself in order to concentrate deeply—which isn't easy, for the pounding on the entrance is deafening—Vantor raises his hands before him, and they again begin to glow with magical energy. The entrance is on the verge of total collapse, dented and covered with a spider's web of cracks. Large chunks of stone begin to tear away from the entryway. The wizard has mere seconds, and with a look of grim fortitude, Vantor awaits the inevitable entrance of his treacherous antagonist. His outstretched hands glow brightly with power.

Unable to withstand any more torture, the door suddenly crashes inward with a mighty explosion of smoke and debris. Vantor falls to the ground after being hit by some of the fragments, for he certainly was not expecting such a forceful entry—and through the smoke the creature enters.

It is a mammoth, heavily muscular, demonic beast approximately forty feet tall. Its skin is almost jet black and smooth in texture and appears to be made out of some substance that is far denser than any flesh could possibly be, giving the impression that this creature is heavily armored with skin that is made out of thick, iron-like metal. Two glowing red eyes radiating malevolence are the only facial features, as if the only law of nature that applies to this creature is that in order to crush something, you must see it. There is no mouth—nose—ears— nothing that would distract it from that purpose is permitted. An almost unbelievable level of physical strength is what this creature's appearance is all about. It is unquestionably one of the strongest creatures in existence—a demonic colossus known as a titan demon.

Seeing Vantor on the ground, vainly trying to recover his senses after its violent entrance, the demon prepares to crush the stubborn wizard with its huge fist, but Vantor miraculously regains his composure and, with the glowing energy still radiating from his hands, discharges an intense wall of flame from his outstretched arms that engulfs the creature. Although the monster has no mouth, it is still able to voice the distress it feels with a loud though muffled grumble.

Vantor, seeing a chance to escape while the creature is reeling from his attack and blinded by the wall of flames, makes his way unseen up the only flight of stairs in the area. When he reaches the small balcony at the top, he uses his magic to create a bewildering number of additional exits and stairways throughout the fortress—a clever ruse to prevent the demonic giant from discovering which route of escape the wizard has taken. With this accomplished Vantor retreats deeper within the fortress.

After a few moments, the titan demon—its skin far too heavily armored and dense for any attack to do much damage— emerges from the flames, which soon disperse, and the creature lumbers farther into the fortress, which shudders slightly with each massive step. Smoke still emanates from the creature's skin from Vantor's fire attack. The creature scans the area, and seeing no one in the immediate vicinity, it transforms into a considerably smaller humanoid form—the normal form of the demon prince, Karza.

He is a chillingly impressive figure with an appearance that radiates intense evil—well over six feet tall, though slender in build and dressed appropriately for his royal rank as the third most powerful demon in existence, with a flowing black robe and attire virtually all black covering most of his body except for a few armor pieces on his chest and forearms. On his head there is an ominous, spiked crown that gives him an air of royal authority—but it is a crown that is not worn or removed, for this is something that all royal demons are naturally born with. His physique is humanoid, but along with the crown there are two other features about him that stand out that are decidedly non-human. First, his face is his most striking feature. It is covered by a smooth, black plate with absolutely no protuberances, which conceals any and all facial features—except two glowing red eyes that seem to penetrate through the metal mask on his face. The second feature is that his right hand is definitely demonic, for it is black and leathery, and each finger ends in a sharp talon. However, considering his overall appearance, his left hand appears surprisingly human. He begins to slowly scan the room he is in for his intended prey. But unlike Vantor, Karza maintains a demeanor of cool and methodical purposefulness—no stress and certainly no fear—as if he knows in advance what the outcome of this hunt will be and it is just a matter of time until his prize is achieved.

"You can't run from me forever, wizard!" he shouts with a mildly irritated tone, for Vantor has proven to have an annoying habit of staying alive.

Karza continues to look around the room, dismayed to see the disturbing number of passageways that the wizard could have taken in his bid to escape. He then raises his human hand, and a rather intimidating-looking sword instantly appears in it. Karza runs the palm of his demon hand across the blade, which creates a cut where steaming blood oozes out, and he then drips it on the floor in front of him. The sword no longer needed, he makes a gesture with his hand that causes the blade to disappear. Stepping back a few paces, he raises his hands, and his eyes glow brightly. Suddenly, a sinister, dog-like creature forms out of the glowing pool of blood on the floor, but this is a somewhat larger, more hideous and decidedly far more menacing creature than any normal canine—for this is a demondog—which bows its grotesque head in the presence of its creator.

"Find him," Karza commands his canine minion.

The demondog sniffs the floor for Vantor's scent and, upon finding it, quickly races up the stairs Vantor took.

The terrified wizard enters a room and falls on the floor, obviously in great pain from the wounds he has received. He fortunately can hear the growling and movements of the swiftly approaching demondog, for its tracking ability is unparalleled in finding whatever it is sent to hunt down. Vantor reacts just in time to blast it with a bolt of energy as it is about to pounce on him and dig its claws and razor-sharp teeth into his body. The dog howls in agony and quickly dies.

Karza, upon hearing the dog scream, looks up toward the direction of the sound. Although his face does not show a mouth to indicate any sign of a smile, for it is covered by the black plate, his eyes are able to convey his emotions, eyes that radiate with a pleased state of evil. This is exactly what he was expecting—his demonic canine to find where Vantor is hiding. Karza's eyes begin to glow brighter, and then his entire body matches the glow and he begins to increase in size as he starts transforming once again into another diabolical creature.

Vantor regains his feet, but this doesn't last for long. The floor beneath him begins to crumble as Karza breaks through in yet another fantastic form of a demonic monstrosity. The wizard frantically fires magical energy at the creature in an effort to protect himself, and as the blasts impact Karza in his demonic form, it distracts the demon enough for Vantor to try to flee the room. The disgusting, snakelike form that Karza has become recovers quickly, though, and it spits forth a concentrated stream of a foul, acidic substance that the escaping wizard barely evades as he dives for cover and ultimately leaves the room.

Making his way into another chamber of the fortress—for his knowledge of the layout of his own residence is the only thing now that is keeping him one step ahead of Karza—he hastily closes the door behind him, and using his adept magic ability to manipulate matter, he cleverly transforms the wooden door so it looks exactly like the stone wall it is attached to, concealing the entrance completely. He then moves over to a mirror located in the room, and as he waves his hand in front of it, a cloud of magical smoke begins to swirl within the polished glass. Within moments the mirror of communication is ready, and Vantor speaks into it with a panicked tone.

"King Morbius! King Morbius! It is Vantor!"

The wall where the door was suddenly explodes, as Vantor's ruse didn't last long against the keen eye of a demon prince, and Vantor flees once again in terror out of the room.

In the mirror appears the kind image of King Morbius. He is a majestic figure seated on a throne with all the royal accoutrements that a human king requires—crown, scepter, jewels, and flowing white robes denoting great wealth and power, but most important for a king of his stature is his white hair, conveying the wisdom of his some sixty years of life—and, consequently, sixty years of magic studies. No one achieves the title of "king" or "queen" solely due to bloodline—it must be earned—and only the great monarchs have the magical experience and power to do that, for in the wizardry world, the older you become the more power you acquire. Morbius is one of the most powerful of the good monarchs of the land. He is the quintessential image of the kind, warm-hearted grandfather any child would love to have.

"Yes, Vantor?" says Morbius, concerned. "What is it? Vantor?"

Suddenly, a giant fist smashes into the mirror shattering it completely and sending its sparkling remnants falling to the floor, abruptly ending the urgent communication Vantor was seeking. Karza, in one of his transformed states, moves past.

Vantor is near total exhaustion, for his effort to escape from Karza has been going on for three unrelenting days, and he stumbles about the fortress in great stress and panic. He enters another chamber and closes the door behind him, not even bothering to try to conceal it, for he knows it won't do any good. Seeing a large chest nearby at the far end of the room, he practically collapses onto it from his utter exhaustion and begins to search among its contents frantically, haphazardly tossing out those useless objects that his groping fingers touch first. He frequently looks back in fear for the pursuing Karza he knows can only be moments behind. He soon finds what he is looking for and pulls out from the chest a scepter with a large jewel on it. His hands grasp the scepter tightly, and he caresses it against his face while making an awkward attempt to smile and laugh between his gasps for breath, thinking that this scepter is what will finally end the horrific nightmare. Hearing Karza approach, Vantor braces himself against a corner in the room, holding the jeweled scepter before him, and with his free hand he begins to charge the jewel with magical energy, which causes the jewel to glow brightly with power, bathing the room with an ever-increasing level of brightness. From the small slit of light coming from under the door, Vantor can see the shadow of Karza approach, and he soon hears him transforming into yet another demonic creature. Vantor's hands tremble as he prepares for Karza's entrance, and the jewel begins to glow even more intensely as Vantor continues to charge it. The door crashes inward, followed by the horrendous sight of a huge demon spider. This is a frightening creature, and though it is nowhere near the most powerful of all the myriad demonic forms available to Karza, this has to be one of the most frightening to humans—and Karza knows it.

Vantor is momentarily distracted by the flying splinters of the door, and seeing the demonic form Karza has assumed doesn't help matters. Soon the instinct for survival takes precedence, and Vantor points the scepter at the terrifying demonic arachnid that is rushing toward him. The scepter fires a blinding bolt of energy, but Karza quickly transforms himself into a ghostly, mist-like form, semi-transparent in appearance, which causes the bolt of energy to harmlessly pass through this phantom fog, although it causes massive destruction to whatever is behind it.

A ghostly face with red eyes begins to form within the undulating vapors of the creature, laughing mockingly at Vantor's attempt, for while Karza is in this particular creature form—the demonic phantasm—very few things, if any, can harm it, for the very nature of the creature is that nothing physical is really there at all.

Vantor is shocked by the failure of his last and most powerful bid to save himself, and he drops the useless scepter apathetically. With one last effort, he musters his last remaining strength and unleashes a crescendo of lightning bolts from his outstretched arms at the demonic cloud that is slowly and inexorably creeping toward him. But as before, the magical bolts pass harmlessly through the monstrous cloud without causing injury and only further destroys whatever is left standing in the room. An instinctive final attempt to flee forces Vantor to his feet, but Karza transforms back into the spider and fires a web from its mouth that ensnares the wizard completely before he can move an inch. The wizard, hopelessly unable to escape the sticky strands, can do nothing as the demonic spider approaches.

"No! No!" screams the terrified Vantor as he struggles in vain to free himself from the sticky embrace of the web.

Karza transforms back into his humanoid demon prince form to stand triumphantly over his helpless foe, the demon's eyes twinkling with evil delight. With a swift gesture, he once again summons his demonic sword into his hand.

"What do you want from me?" Vantor cries in absolute horror.

The helpless wizard screams—as any human would when a horrible death is about to happen—but the bloodcurdling sound is instantly silenced by a slash from Karza's sword. The demon slowly bends over to pick up the severed head that once belonged to the body of the good wizard Vantor. Admiring his grisly new possession, Karza softly chuckles triumphantly—for a demon at his level of cold, calculating evil never displays great emotion—as he answers the brave Vantor's last question.

"I want your head, wizard."

CHAPTER 8

+ + +

Several hours have passed since Vantor's failed warning to Morbius, so the king, concerned after repeated attempts to contact his trusted and loyal friend and fellow Council wizard have failed, dispatches a small force of his warriors to Vantor's fortress a few hours' marching distance away from Morbius Castle. This force, about a dozen in number and led by a young warrior on horseback named Jartan, has arrived.

Jartan is human and fifteen years old, and although quite young, he does not possess the youthful arrogance that those his age tend to project; nor does he feel he is invincible. He is brave, certainly, but not recklessly so—and especially not now, for this is not the first time that his king has sent him to offer assistance to a wizard who is clearly Jartan's superior and easily has ten times the youth's knowledge, fighting power, and abilities. Jartan knows his limitations, and although he would like to ignore them he does have the maturity to at least be aware of them and therefore curbs that youthful and foolhardy overconfidence that his peers tend to have.

But he also knows his skills, and it is not by mere chance that he has been leading these rescue missions, for Jartan is King Morbius's best warrior, despite his age. This is not solely due to his impressive skills with weaponry but, more importantly, to the fact that he has been receiving specialized training since the day he could walk—training in advanced concepts well beyond most humans' ability to comprehend, let alone master—and it is this mastery that is most critical.

Any intelligent being can pick up a toy ball and throw it at a target, but to use only your mind to accomplish the same act is rare indeed. Only those with blood of a higher class of being—such as advanced wizards and sorceresses—have that power and therefore have the ability to master its use. True, anyone can be taught a few simple spells once they attain a certain age of mental maturity—even ogres, the least intelligent of intelligent beings, have a few primitive magic users in their ranks—but Jartan was using his mind when he was not even one year of age and without any previous teaching. And yet he is certainly no wizard—not even close—for his training did not focus on the wizardry arts. That is because of what the infant Jartan did with the toy ball.

The ball in question was the favorite toy of a snow wolf that King Morbius had as a pet. This noble creature was actually Jartan's pet, for the snow wolf was devoted to the boy even at that early age and never left his side. On this particular occasion, the snow wolf was diligently guarding the baby Jartan as he was sleeping peacefully in his crib. This guard duty also happened to be extremely dull, so the creature decided to alleviate the boredom by happily tossing its favorite toy in the air with its mouth and then catching it. Unfortunately for the snow wolf, it misjudged an attempt to catch the ball and sent it flying over the bars of the crib and landing on the head of the sleeping Jartan, who instantly awoke. The boy quickly noticed this shiny new plaything lying beside his head and was thrilled to have it, despite the nasty, wet slobber of the snow wolf drenching the ball.

Now, to the snow wolf this was a major crisis. The creature watched the tragedy unfold as Jartan fondled its property with glee, for the snow wolf was quite fond of that ball and therefore wanted it back, but since the spacing between the bars of the crib was too narrow for the ball to pass through—not to mention the creature's huge head—the snow wolf was unable to retrieve the treasured object. The noble creature would readily have given its life to protect the child, but giving him its favorite toy was definitely crossing the line of unquestioning loyalty, so the snow wolf began to whimper pleadingly for the ball's return.

King Morbius happened to be walking by the nursery at this point and, alerted by the snow wolf's whimpering, looked inside to see this dilemma in progress. If he let Jartan keep the ball, then the snow wolf would suffer from its loss. On the other hand, if he took the ball away from Jartan, Morbius will have an infantile Armageddon on his hands from the vehemently wailing protest of the child. Fortunately for Morbius, the decision was an easy one, and he began to reach into the crib with the determined intention of prying the infant's fingers off the ball. It wasn't that he liked the idea of breaking the poor child's heart; it was just that Morbius had a sleeping spell he could use on the kid if he got out of hand.

But it was Jartan who ultimately solved the problem when, upon hearing the forlorn crying of the snow wolf, he levitated the ball out of the crib and gave it back to its rightful owner. It was then that Morbius knew only one type of person could use the powers with that level of compassion—and Jartan's training followed along those lines instead of magical ones.

Jartan, now near the fortress entrance, is surveying the destruction before him. The shattered entrance and smoldering craters in the ground and on the fortress exterior are clearly evident and are obviously the work of some great malevolence. He then notices something peculiar on the ground and dismounts to get a closer look. Upon further examination, he realizes in amazement what he sees—giant, dragon-like footprints embedded in the soft soil around him, dozens of them, easily large enough to contain Jartan's entire regiment, horses and all. The young warrior shakes his head in disbelief.

The rest of the force emerges from Vantor's fortress somberly carrying a coffin. Reaching Jartan, they lay it before him, and the youth cautiously raises the lid to look inside. The sight is a grisly one—the bloody body of the headless wizard Vantor. Jartan is appalled by the sight and quickly turns away, slamming the lid in the process. This is an act he has replayed several times before, and his bitter disappointment is clearly evident on his face.

"Put the coffin in the wagon," the boy announces to those around him. "We are returning to Morbius Castle." He makes a gesture toward the wagon they have brought, and his retinue begins to put the coffin inside. Jartan remounts his horse, and after one last look at the distressing level of destruction before him, he starts to lead his party out of the area.

"Move out," he solemnly commands.

His tone and demeanor is far more subdued than when he first arrived on the scene. The sense of urgency has long since passed as well as his youthful excitement of facing the unknown. His mission is one of high importance and provides a chance to finally prove himself. But after seeing the brutal condition of Vantor's body and the alarming size of the footprints and considering the fact that his several previous rescue missions ended in exactly the same disturbing manner, he faces the grim reality that there is a great danger present, a danger that the teenage warrior has obviously never encountered before, and for the first time in his life Jartan doubts whether his abilities will be able to cope with it—let alone fight it. And as for defeating whatever this scourge is? The thought doesn't even register.

After an hour of traveling through the lush countryside, Jartan spies Morbius Castle in the distance, with its comforting, majestic spires gleaming in the sunshine, almost tall enough to reach the clouds peacefully gliding overhead; and fluttering defiantly in the slight breeze at the top of the tallest spire is the royal banner of the king, which only further increases Jartan's feeling of peaceful safety.

King Morbius is looking down from a balcony as Jartan and his group approach, and soon he and his party reach the entrance leading to the interior grounds of the castle. Jartan can see his king watching from above, and the boy raises his hand, prompting King Morbius to reach out to touch a large, metallic globe near him. A wave of his hand over the globe causes it to glow brightly, and a shimmer of energy is seen along the castle wall as if a shield of energy has been deactivated. Jartan and his group then proceed through the entrance, and once they are inside, Morbius again touches the globe and the energy shield is back in place.

"Take Vantor's body to the infirmary," says Jartan to the members of his party. His people remove the coffin from the wagon and head toward an exit nearby. Jartan looks up to see King Morbius watching the procession from another vantage point and heads up the nearby stairs to reach him. Morbius, seeing the coffin disappear through the exit, turns to Jartan, who is standing beside him.

"Vantor?" Morbius asks the boy, hoping he doesn't hear the answer he fears.

Jartan nods remorsefully, causing Morbius to angrily slam his fist against the balcony railing in disgust.

"We were too late to help him, Sire."

"I can't believe this is even happening! What form of evil is killing all the wizards of the Great Council? For what purpose?"

Jartan, seeing his king tortured by the unknown, begins to relate what he discovered at Vantor's fortress.

"Whatever it is has fantastic power. There were those same huge footprints of some massive creature near the fortress, just like those found near the bodies of the other Council wizards—footprints unlike anything I have ever seen before."

Morbius, upon hearing this similarity, inquires further.

"And"—he pauses, again not wanting to hear the answer he knows he will receive, "—was Vantor beheaded like all the others?"

"Yes, Sire," replies Jartan as he sadly nods his head. "I don't understand why this thing would want the heads of all the Council wizards."

"It is a mystery to me as well. But whatever the reason, it can only be something dark and twisted. I sense a great evil at work behind all this, Jartan—a great evil."

"It must be another wizard, my king—perhaps several."

"No," replies Morbius after a moment to ponder this. "Vantor was the strongest of my Council wizards. I don't know of any evil sorcerer living that could defeat him. Even an entire coven of night witches wouldn't dare challenge him."

"A demigod then," counters Jartan, "sent as an assassin by a vengeful god?"

"I would tend to believe that if it had been only one of the Council wizards, but not all seven. And besides, that wouldn't account for the footprints you observed."

"True," replies Jartan as he nods his head in approval. "But if whatever is responsible wants the death of all your wizards, then you will be next, my king. You are head of the Council."

"But why?" responds Morbius, the anxious look of concern on his face impossible to ignore. "There has to be a reason! Vantor tried to tell me, but I could not aid him, because here I remain, a prisoner within my own castle walls!"

"You must stay here, Sire. The magic of the castle shield will prevent anyone—or anything—from entering. It is the only way to ensure your safety."

But Morbius is now beginning to doubt this and responds accordingly.

"Safety? For how long and from what—an unseen evil that has the power to kill all seven of my Council wizards? No, if this thing is as powerful as I think it is, then nothing is going to stop it!"

Morbius can see his words have had a somber impact on the young Jartan, so he changes his tone. He puts his hand on Jartan's shoulder in a reassuring gesture and continues. "Except for you, my young friend, for you are my best warrior now, Jartan. I am pleased by the progress you have made in your fighting skills. If this thing does finally reveal itself, then I for one am glad that you will be here to fight by my side. I wouldn't have it any other way."

Jartan is pleased to hear this and smiles.

"Come," Morbius continues, "let us see if Vantor's body can reveal any clues to what we are facing."

And they both leave the area and head down the stairs.

Meanwhile, in another area of the castle, the group carrying Vantor's coffin has reached the castle infirmary. A guard is posted outside and opens the door for them, and upon entering, they place the coffin on a table before the surgeon present. The people then leave, and the surgeon, who is now the room's sole occupant, opens the lid and begins to study the body. In an instant, he grimaces strongly as he sees the unpleasant condition of the headless corpse, for no matter how many times anyone is witness to it, a headless body is a sight one never gets used to. But as repulsive as the act is, the body must be studied, and the surgeon turns away to pick up an instrument on another table nearby. As he does so, Vantor's chest trembles and can be seen shifting as if something is moving under the skin. The surgeon again turns to the body with instrument in hand to begin his examination and notices this movement. With an expression of great puzzlement, he bends over Vantor's body to get a closer look at the throbbing chest, and it suddenly explodes. Emerging from the gaping wound is a large, maggot-like creature with glowing red eyes of evil, which quickly coils itself around the surgeon's body as terror registers on the poor man's helpless face.

Outside the infirmary, the guard posted there can hear the sounds of a scuffle and the breaking of glass as well as objects falling on the floor from behind the closed door, which quickly becomes silent. This naturally alarms the guard, and he draws his sword and slowly opens the door. Peering inside, he can see the room splattered with blood and a multitude of broken objects sent to the floor from the upturned tables located throughout the room, which causes him to rush inside and urgently scan the interior for the cause of the trouble. Seeing none, he calls out to the surgeon, who is nowhere to be seen, but silence is the only response. Confused, the guard cautiously approaches the coffin. The lid is now closed, and with his attention focused on raising the lid to sheepishly look inside, the guard is completely unaware of what is happening on the ceiling above him—for it appears to be moving. After a few moments, a blob of sickly green slime appears, previously and quite cleverly camouflaged to match exactly the ceiling's texture, stonework, and color. This blob also has the sinister red eyes that show a definite pleasure in observing the unsuspecting guard below. The blob soon drops onto the guard, who struggles in vain and whose screams for help are muffled by the green mass covering his face and body. The blob can see that other guards are coming down the steps outside the open infirmary door, and not wishing its presence to be known, it produces an extension of itself that acts as an arm to gently close the door, preventing anyone from seeing what is inside, and the guards pass the door, completely oblivious to the tragic demise of their comrade beyond. The blob transforms into the demon prince, Karza, who grabs the guard's neck firmly in his demonic hands.

"Where is the treasure room, human?" Karza coldly demands of his uselessly struggling captive.

The guard is understandably horrified to be in the clutches of this demonic being, who is clearly something very few humans have had the opportunity to gaze upon—and those few who have did not live long enough to tell about it. Because the very nature and appearance of a demon prince is so foreboding, Karza has an unseen aura of fear radiating from his body that affects any lesser being of goodness that gets near. The guard, too petrified to even speak, prompts Karza to increase the pressure of his grip around the guard's neck in a painful effort to elicit the information he is seeking—for pain overcomes fear.

"I won't tell you!" says the guard, who can barely respond with Karza's powerful hands around his neck.

A displeased Karza transforms his demonic hand into a horrible-looking serpent head. The serpent's fangs drip imposingly with venom, much to the guard's shock, and his eyes widen with horror.

Outside the infirmary, a small boy holding a tray of food happily descends the nearby stairway—the food obviously intended for the surgeon. But upon opening the infirmary door, his blissful happiness instantly transforms into stark horror as he sees the guard slouching to the floor with Karza's serpent-headed hand covering the guard's face. The guard's body writhes spasmodically from the lethal venom being pumped into it by the serpent head, but soon its unsettling wrenching stops, and Karza releases the lifeless body, which falls to the floor. The terrified and stunned boy instantly drops the tray of food at the sight of Karza, too petrified to even flee for his life as Karza extends his snakelike arm and it coils around the horrified child and brings the boy to face him.

"Where is Morbius's treasure room?"

But if an adult guard was too terrified to answer when face-to-face with a demon prince, for a small child to do so would be impossible. In fact, so evil is Karza's influence that if he did not require information from the boy, the demon's very presence would kill any ten-year-old human instantly. Karza transforms his hand and arm back to normal in an effort to be less intimidating. This is only mildly successful, for Karza's mere presence generates intense fear, but he modifies his tone to a more soothing one.

"Don't be frightened, boy," he continues. "Just tell me where the treasure room is and I promise I won't harm you and will let you go."

His words and tone do indeed sooth the boy, and although still frightened, he does respond.

"The—the lower level," says the boy, his voice trembling with fright.

A cold and emotionless Karza—far too cold to respect any assurance not to inflict evil—with a swift twist breaks the unfortunate boy's neck and casually releases his lifeless body, which collapses to the floor. Opening the infirmary door slowly, the demon prince cautiously looks around to see if anyone is nearby to notice his presence. Seeing no one, he transforms into a harmless-looking puppy, thinking that no one will notice—or, at the very least, be alarmed by—such an innocent-looking creature; and it is indeed an adorable puppy, with only the ever-present glowing red eyes betraying the creature's true and far from adorable intentions.

Moving along the castle interior, a puppy-formed Karza descends a stairway and approaches a corridor that leads to the treasure room. As he turns the corner, he stops suddenly as he sees around two dozen guards annoyingly posted there. The guards can see this dog at the head of the corridor, though they are certainly not alarmed by the cuteness of the creature as the lead guard addresses one of his companions.

"Now what in the name of the ancients is a dog doing down here?"

"It must be lost," another guard responds. "What is wrong with its eyes? The poor thing must be sick." The guard then makes a gesture to another guard standing next to him and adds, "You—take that thing back upstairs and get it to the veterinarian."

The guard leaves his post and walks toward the dog, which is sitting patiently and studying the area intently. The dog is particularly careful to notice the number of guards and also the number of torches. Upon reaching the dog, the guard bends over to pick it up.

"Come on, little fellow—I'll help you," he compassionately says.

Obviously unaware of the fluffy bundle of death he is cuddling the guard pets the creature fondly and walks around the corner out of sight of the other guards. But soon the sounds of Karza transforming can be heard, followed by the horrified screams of the guard abruptly cut off. His head emerges from around the corner, rolling on the floor. The other guards are certainly alarmed to see this. They all exchange horrified glances and immediately draw their weapons. A gust of wind comes down the hallway, which extinguishes the torches, making visibility almost nil. The guards begin to panic as they hear yet again the unseen Karza transforming and then the sound of something slithering unseen toward them in the darkness.

"Who is there?" cries the panic-stricken guard. "Who is there? Answer me!"

But only the sound of the ominous slithering can be heard until suddenly from out of the darkness emerges a serpentine face of demonic origin. Its eyes begin to glow brightly, which causes the guards to turn instantly into stone. Karza then transforms back into demon-prince form and waves his hand, making the torches magically ignite as he triumphantly walks farther down the corridor unopposed.

He approaches the treasure room entrance and stops before it. Karza appears concerned as he examines the door and notices a faint shimmer surrounding it. Touching the door gingerly with a demonic finger, he is instantly shocked by a surge of energy, which disintegrates the digit—as well as the hand and most of the forearm. Such a sight would understandably be highly upsetting for a normal being, but Karza is a demon prince, and although he is certainly not pleased to see a major part of his person turning to ashes, he does manage to regenerate the missing limb after a few moments and again looks upon the highly lethal entrance with disgust.

Meanwhile, Morbius and Jartan are descending the stairs leading toward the infirmary, but the youth stops suddenly and puts his arm in front of Morbius, stopping him as well. Jartan realizes the guard usually posted there is nowhere to be seen.

"Wait, Sire! There should be a guard here." Continuing, he calls out, "Guard? Guard?"

The silence is disturbing, so Jartan draws his sword, and the two proceed cautiously into the infirmary. Upon entering, they see the carnage before them and are appalled by this grisly sight.

"In the name of the ancients, what happened here?" asks the startled Jartan.

Jartan rushes over to the small boy's location while Morbius goes over to the guard's body lying on the floor and turns it on its back.

"Let's see if we can find out," says the concerned Morbius.

He reaches to touch the guard's lifeless and ashen face, but he quickly withdraws his hand when he sees two prominent puncture marks on the skin, which begins to sizzle as if the insides are being eaten away by a powerful acid.

"Acid poison," he acknowledges sadly and greatly surprised as he continues, "I'm afraid we won't get any knowledge out of this one. His mind has been eaten away."

"What about the boy?" asks Jartan, kneeling by his lifeless corpse.

Morbius goes over to the body and also kneels beside it. He then places his hand on the boy's forehead, and Morbius closes his eyes in deep concentration.

"Now," Morbius begins, "show me what you know."

The boy's eyes suddenly open wide and begin to glow with energy, though the stare is empty. Jartan is shocked to see this.

"By the gods! Is he alive?"

"No," replies Morbius, shaking his head, "my magic has only temporarily reanimated him so I can probe his mind and know his last thoughts."

"Can you sense anything, Sire?"

Morbius slowly closes his own eyes once again to concentrate.

"An intruder, but not one of this world—evil and very powerful. He is seeking the treasure room."

"Intruder?" comments Jartan, who is surprised to hear this. "But that's impossible! How could he possibly penetrate the castle shield?"

Morbius breaks the spell he is using on the boy, and the dead youth's eyes cease to glow and close in death once again. Morbius rises and, noticing the coffin on the table in the room, opens the lid and examines the condition of Vantor's body, specifically the violently erupted chest.

"Look here. Whoever it is must have been concealed within Vantor's body."

"But what kind of being has the power to do that?" Jartan responds incredulously. "Not even a grand wizard at your level of magical power has that ability!"

Morbius ponders this for a moment and is about to answer when suddenly a deafening pounding is heard echoing throughout the castle. The room shudders slightly, and small pieces of debris fall from the ceiling due to the intensity of the concussions—much to both Morbius and Jartan's dismay.

"That's coming from the lower level," says the disturbed Jartan.

Morbius also has a look of concern on his face, for he realizes what that means as he hastily flees the infirmary.

"It's the treasure room!" he cries with alarm. "Hurry!"

At the entrance to the treasure room, the huge door is being pounded on by the massive fists of Karza in the transformed state of his titan demon creature that he used to break through the entrance to Vantor's fortress—but this door is showing no sign of weakening, as its magical protection is far more powerful. The entrance also has a formidable disintegrating power of protection, and although Karza's fists in this demonic form are far denser and more heavily armored than his normal hands, they still are showing damage with each blow Karza delivers. He soon gives up his futile efforts to break through and transforms back into the demon prince, both hands steaming and bloody and mangled, with pieces of flesh loosely dangling from them because of the door's disintegrating power; but he closes his eyes, and after a few moments his hands have healed. Once again Karza studies the door with dismay, wondering how to enter. He tries another approach with a different demonic form—this time the ethereal phantasm creature. The undulating vapor can easily pass through any barrier, regardless of how thick and regardless of its composition, but magical barriers are another matter, and this particular one is able to discharge a burst of energy and repulses the sinister cloud upon contact with the entrance's surface, sending the creature instantly back several yards. Again Karza transforms into normal form in defeat.

He is completely at a loss as to how to breach this formidable obstacle to his plans, but after a few moments he happens to see crawling on the wall next to the entrance a tiny insect, which soon enters a small crack and disappears. A highly pleased Karza has found his entrance, and he once again transforms into the phantasm creature, whose shapeless form easily is able to seep through the crack like a wisp of smoke, for the entrance's awesome magical power, at least where this crack is concerned, is useless when there was already an entry point available long before the spell of protection was placed upon it.

Inside the treasure room, the phantasm cloud once transforms back into the demon prince. Noticing the darkness, with a wave of his hand Karza ignites the torches located on the walls throughout the room, and a fabulous amount of treasure is revealed in the light—mounds of gold and silver pieces, hundreds of chests overflowing with priceless jewels and artifacts of incredible beauty sparkle intensely in the torchlight. But this appears as so much useless garbage to Karza, for he is interested in another thing entirely. Not content with the sight of anything here, he notices the closed entrance to a small chamber off to the side. Walking over to it, he transforms into a creature that is able to easily rip the door off—for since it is inside the treasure room already, Morbius had no need to magically seal the entrance to this chamber—and transforming yet again to normal, Karza enters the room.

It is a very small chamber, the darkness of which prevents anything from being seen—but another wave of Karza's hand ignites several torches, providing the necessary illumination. After a cursory glance at the chamber's contents of scrolls, potions, and various artifacts consisting of a magical nature, Karza soon finds what he came for. There, resting on a stone table at the end of the room, is the Ring of Angels. This is a large object, far larger than any that could be placed on a human finger, though it can be handled, and it does retain the appearance of a ring of jewelry with a large crystal mounted at the top. This crystal is greenish in color and circular in shape, inscribed with various symbols that seem to pulsate with great energy. Karza lifts it off the table and holds it triumphantly in his hands, and once again his eyes shine brightly with diabolical glee at his new possession.

"Soon, my father," he says with an evil chuckle, "quite soon."

CHAPTER 9

✛ ✛ ✛

Morbius and Jartan rapidly appear at the corridor entrance at the lower level before reaching the treasure room itself. Accompanying them is a large force of Morbius's castle guards, several dozen, whom Morbius ordered to accompany them, considering the gravity of the situation. Turning the corner, they all stop suddenly aghast at the sight of the previous guards turned to stone—the expressions on their stone faces ones of stark terror. Morbius and Jartan cautiously approach as Jartan hesitantly touches one of the victims.

"By the gods! They've all been turned to stone—solid stone! But how?"

"This isn't the work of any wizard," responds a disturbed Morbius, closing his eyes as he also begins to touch one.

"Can't you use your magic to transform them back, my king?"

"No, this stone is natural— not magical. Only a gorgon serpent can do this."

"But gorgon serpents are only found in the Demonic Abyss, Sire," replies a puzzled Jartan. "One couldn't possibly be here."

Morbius instantly opens his eyes, and a look of sheer panic shows on his face as he realizes the evil genius responsible for everything.

"The Abyss. The Abyss! No, he must not get the ring!" shouts an anxious Morbius. He rushes farther down the corridor, leaving a perplexed Jartan.

"Sire? What's wrong? Sire?" Jartan cries as he runs off after him.

Morbius appears at the entrance to the treasure room, with Jartan and the other guards soon joining him, but Jartan, upon seeing that the entrance is still magically sealed, comments:

"The seal is still in place. Whoever this intruder is, he must have given up and fled when he failed to breach it."

"I know he is in there!" Morbius raises his hands, which quickly glow brightly with magical energy, and this soon dispels the seal protecting the entrance and it begins to open. He then rushes inside, followed by Jartan and the other guards, frantically scanning the room for the intruder he knows is here.

"Karza!" shouts an irate and yet highly anxious Morbius.

Jartan and the guards also scan the room, but unlike Morbius, they don't know the reason. Jartan, like the others, has a questioning look on his face as if trying to explain Morbius's bewildering actions to himself. The frantic king sees that the door to the small chamber has been ripped off its hinges, and flickering light emanates from within the chamber.

"Damn it," he grimly exclaims. "Jartan, you and the guards take up positions around the room—quickly!"

Jartan, still showing confusion in his face nevertheless obeys the royal command and gestures to the guards. They all take up various positions throughout the room. All eyes are nervously fixed on the chamber but especially those of Morbius.

"Karza!" shouts Morbius loudly. "I know it is you!"

Meanwhile, in the chamber, Karza slightly turns his head when he hears his name, but he slowly returns his attention to admiring the ring in his possession, apparently unconcerned over being discovered.

"You are too late, Morbius," responds Karza with not a hint of displeasure in his tone. "The Ring of Angels is mine."

Morbius, on the other hand, appears terrifyingly alarmed by this revelation, but he soon answers angrily,

"You'll never live long enough to use it!"

"No?" responds Karza, chuckling softly with contempt upon hearing this. "Foolish human—let's just see you try and stop me!"

And now an alarmed Morbius and baffled Jartan and the others begin to hear the sound of Karza transforming from within the chamber, the light inside of which instantly becomes dark.

The chamber begins to crumble as if something is now far too large to contain it. It suddenly explodes, violently showering the room with stone debris, and from out of the smoke appears Karza in his most powerful demonic form—the awesome tridragon, a fearsome-looking three-headed demonic dragon of massive proportions towering well over fifty feet in height, with each evil head slightly different in appearance and color. The entire body glistens slightly, as its black, armored scales are tinged with gold. Three pairs of menacing eyes glow bright red with immense power and immense evil. Although Karza used this form in his pursuit of Vantor earlier, the wizard only saw its blurry image, its shadow, and some glimpses of body parts. This is the first time any being has seen the hideous creature in its monstrous and highly imposing entirety, which the faces of all the humans present cannot help but show, for they have never faced anything like this before and are stunned by the sight of this three-headed demonic dragon, the form of which radiates an intense level of powerful evil.

The three heads begin to attack, each one discharging a lethal energy weapon. One head shoots a blistering red fire, the middle head a powerful bolt of lightning, and the other a bluish freezing vapor of energy—and many die from these potent blasts.

Morbius, a great wizard and one of—if not the—most powerful, erects an energy shield in front of himself to protect him from the effects of Karza's attack, but the others aren't so fortunate, for they have nowhere near Morbius's incredible magic powers. Some are frozen into human statues of solid ice and shatter like glass; others erupt into flames and burn savagely, quickly becoming incinerated into steaming piles of ash; and still others are blasted into oblivion by the lightning discharges. Screams of terror and death are only barely audible over the demonic discharges, and chaos is everywhere.

Jartan barely manages to dive for cover behind some rock debris that explodes when Karza's lightning bolts of energy hit it. Morbius lets loose a withering barrage of magical energy at the three-headed nightmare, causing the imposing beast to reel in pain from the wounds, but to Morbius's horror, the wounds heal almost instantly. Jartan, with sword in hand, also manages to obtain a shield whose previous owner now lies at his feet, its body a grotesque mass of bloody gore. With the tridragon distracted by Morbius's counterattacks, Jartan manages to make his way toward the tridragon's leg unseen by the demonic beast, but the blade of his simple weapon shatters like glass upon impact with the armored skin. Shocked by this, he quickly turns to flee, but Karza notices this with his center demonic head and fires a lightning bolt at the boy. Jartan raises his shield just in time in defense, and it absorbs the blast, but it sends him hurtling violently backward and his body hits hard against a wall. Taking several moments to recover his senses, Jartan studies his destroyed and smoldering shield with horrified astonishment.

Karza raises his three heads toward the ceiling, and they fire simultaneously at it, causing the ceiling to cave in, with large stones falling to the floor. Morbius is able to magically teleport himself to a safer location in the room, but those others that are still alive are unable to get out of the way of the falling stones and are crushed to death. Jartan, being the nimble warrior he is, barely manages to avoid being crushed by one as well, but due to the number of falling stones, one soon does fall on his leg, causing him great pain and pinning him to the floor of the heavily damaged treasure room, its gleaming wealth covered with a blanket of grayish ash and debris, transforming the once colorful scene into monochrome disaster with only the red of fire and blood present.

The tridragon begins to crawl up through the gaping opening it created in the ceiling until its upper half is on the floor of the upper level. The commotion of the battle can be heard throughout the entire castle, alerting all of its inhabitants to the threat, and large numbers of guards appear with crossbows. They fire wave after wave of lethal bolts into the dragon-formed Karza, but they simply bounce off of him, and the powerful dragon retaliates with a flame attack, incinerating them all.

Morbius, still in the treasure room, fires at the bottom half of Karza which is still hanging from the ceiling, but the demonic dragon soon pulls itself up through the opening. Morbius instantly begins to race out of the treasure room in pursuit but he is stopped by Jartan's cries.

"Sire! Help!"

Seeing the boy, Morbius rushes over. The stone pinning Jartan is far too large and heavy for even a dozen men to lift physically, but a powerful wizard like Morbius has no limitations, and he uses his magic to levitate the stone crushing Jartan's leg. The boy grimaces with the stone's removal, revealing a severe laceration on his leg that begins to gush forth a large quantity of blood. But this too is something magic can remedy, and Morbius heals the severe injury with a glowing touch of his hand upon the wound and then helps the boy to his feet.

"Hurry, Jartan!" he nervously commands. "He must not escape!"

The unstoppable tridragon is slogging its way through the castle, destroying and killing all in its path. The dragon's immense bulk is making progress through the castle's interior difficult but not impossible as the helpless castle inhabitants frantically try to flee from the hideous creature but are obviously no match and are unable to reach any form of safety. Women, children, and castle guards fall before the dreaded tridragon that Karza has become. A lightning discharge from the center head illuminates the area with its bright energy bolts, and the vibration shakes the area enough to cause plaster and loose debris to fall from the ceiling. A crumbling wall reveals an unfortunate woman and her baby that she is holding tightly in her arms in a small alcove. The woman has her hand covering the baby's mouth, preventing the infant's crying from alerting Karza to their presence, which was necessary, for the intense screams of the wounded or dying and thunderous sounds of the battle would make any baby echo such horrors with its own cries; but now that one of the dragon heads has seen this woman and child, her act of concealment is useless, and she removes her hand from the infant's mouth. The child instantly resumes its bawling.

"Please," she pleads before the huge tridragon head looming menacingly above her with its eyes glowing pure evil as the other two heads continue their individual acts of carnage. The woman is obviously terrified, but the safety of her child brings out her motherly instinct of protection, and she braves the wrath of the demonic beast by pleading for mercy as she continues, "Please, I beg of you. Don't hurt my child. Please!"

She holds out her child as if to show this is an innocent soul and therefore deserves compassion—but there is no such word in the demonic vocabulary, and a discharge of freezing vapor instantly freezes them in this pose of death like some sort of grisly memorial to the futility of asking for mercy from a demonic being who possesses such an unbridled level of pure, twisted evil.

In a far more open area within the castle's interior, many castle guards are waiting behind several ballistae that they have wheeled into position now that there is more room to maneuver outside the confining restrictions of the castle's corridors. They work in great haste and panic, struggling to load each weapon with a huge bolt—so huge that it requires a dozen men to manhandle it into the breach. Their fear is justified, for they can hear the rampages and thunderous footsteps of Karza's unseen tridragon coming closer from beyond the blackness of an entrance to a corridor of the castle that leads to this area. Soon, the three pairs of glowing red eyes of the creature loom out of the blackness, and the guards are barely able to launch the three massive missiles the instant the entire body of the dragon emerges through the entrance. Despite the armored scales, the weapons penetrate the dragon's body deeply, and the creature reels against the impacts and collapses to the ground. But although the wounds are particularly severe ones, the injurious effects are only momentary for the tridragon, which pulls the missiles out and, with demonic regenerative powers, is able to heal the wounds.

The creature then unfurls large wings and begins to beat them, which causes a massive explosion of wind to blast forth, hurling people, weapons, and the castle interior away with great force. It turns slightly, and another hurricane blast instantly removes another group of guards trying to organize for an attack. Now seeing the futility of further combat against such a powerful foe, the few survivors attempt to hastily flee, but a final blast of wind from the wings eliminates any and all survivors. The tridragon then begins to fly away through one of the gaping openings that the wind blasts have created amid the castle's interior and heads to the outside.

Morbius appears and launches a ball of intense energy toward the retreating tridragon that, upon impact, covers the creature in a sheet of ice. Its wings now frozen and useless, the ice-covered dragon rapidly plummets to the ground with a violent impact. Although the impact shatters the icy prison of Morbius's magic, for the first time since Karza obtained this dragon form, the Ring of Angels that has always been in its grasp finally falls away.

"The ring!" cries Morbius as he notices the gleaming object falling to the floor. The mighty wizard tries to magically levitate the ring toward him, but Karza transforms himself into a large but very swift cat-like creature called a demonic tigeron and snatches it away in its mouth before it can fall into Morbius's grasp. The demonic cat flees rapidly as Morbius fires magic, frantically trying to stop it, but this creature is an extremely nimble and agile one and manages to evade these attacks without injury. The tigeron turns a corner in its further effort to escape, but it immediate finds itself confronted by Jartan, who instantly thrusts the axe he is carrying deeply into the demon cat's skull, almost cleaving the head in two. The Ring of Angels flies from the creature's mouth and rolls to rest at Jartan's feet.

"Jartan!" Morbius calls out. "Get the ring! Quickly!"

Jartan picks up the ring and smiles broadly, thinking that victory has been achieved, since it appears that the tigeron, with an axe deeply embedded in its skull and thrashing around wildly from the obviously mortal wound, can't possibly pose any further threat. But the taste of victory is short-lived. Jartan is horrified to discover the tigeron beginning to transform into Karza's second-most-powerful form—the huge, muscular titan demon—which tries to crush Jartan with an incredibly huge sledgehammer of a fist. The boy barely manages to avoid the devastating blow, which penetrates the ground deeply, creating a huge crater and churning up masses of earth from the impact as Jartan hastily runs away.

Morbius then attacks by unleashing a blistering wave of magical energy, but this amounts to nothing, as the heavily armored skin of the beast easily absorbs it. Karza retaliates by picking up a huge stone and throwing it at Morbius, but once again the wizard's powerful magic is used to launch a lightning bolt that makes the stone shatter harmlessly—but to Morbius's misfortune, this creates a large number of pieces that begin to cover him. Karza sees the retreating Jartan, and he again transforms, this time into the giant demon spider, and fires off a web at the youth, who instantly becomes ensnared and falls to the ground. The demonic spider soon appears over the helpless boy with fangs bared and dripping with venom, ready to deliver a lethal bite, but before it can do so, Morbius blasts the stones covering him away and launches another blistering magic attack against Karza's spider. The spider, a less armored opponent than Karza's other forms, reels from the impacts and is blasted back savagely, unable to retaliate due to the ferocity of the wizard's attack. Morbius's face strains considerably, for his desperation in trying to kill this thing is summoning all his magic power, and it is indeed a vicious attack by the powerful wizard. He finally uses his magic to once again freeze the demon in a dense block of ice several feet thick, making an impervious prison. The panting Morbius smiles triumphantly at the sight of the immobilized spider but still eyes it warily for a moment, for no one can be too overconfident with beings at Karza's demon-prince level of power. Then Morbius goes over to Jartan and starts to use his magic to free him from the web covering his body.

"Thank you, Sire," says the boy gratefully.

As Morbius continues to offer his assistance, Jartan also apprehensively eyes Karza in the demonic spider form—frozen motionless and apparently helpless and finally defeated.

"By the gods, what is that thing?" says Jartan, astonished and uneasy at the frozen menace that looms before him.

But no sooner do the words leave his mouth when Karza begins to transform into the ethereal phantasm creature, and its ghostly form slowly seeps through the icy prison. Morbius, upon seeing this highly distressing sight, just bows his head in futility at the further prospect of fighting, but he soon manages to regain his fighting spirit and fires several fireballs at the cloud emerging from the ice—but the brightly burning orbs simply pass harmlessly through it. Jartan looks on in horror and turns to Morbius in a panic.

"Is there any way to stop him?"

Once again Karza transforms into the three-headed nightmare of the tridragon.

"Not while he is transformed," replies the exasperated wizard. "Run, Jartan! He must not have the Ring of Angels! I'll keep him busy!"

Jartan runs off as Morbius once again delivers a massive magic attack, causing the dragon to reel from the violent impacts, but as always the wounds heal almost instantly. it counterattacks upon Morbius, who magically transports himself to safety with a well-timed teleport spell, avoiding any injury, and resumes his attack from a different location as the two battle ferociously.

Jartan, who once again has possession of the Ring of Angels, attempts to flee with it, but one of Karza's dreaded and ever-vigilant tridragon heads with its three pairs of eyes sees the boy rapidly departing with the precious object and fires at him. The powerful blast causes a huge explosion near the youth, causing Jartan to stumble and lose grasp of the ring.

Karza, seeing his chance to escape, transforms into a large, demonic dragonfly-like insect—though 'insect' is not quite accurate, for the creature is the size of a large horse—and in this form races off toward the Ring of Angels, grabbing it in its claws an instant before Jartan can regain possession, and then flies away with it at an incredible rate of speed into the distance.

"No!" shouts Morbius, horrified at the sight of Karza escaping with the ring. Rushing after the demon, he frantically fires massive amounts of his magical energy at the retreating form, but it rapidly accelerates into the distance.

"No! No! He must be stopped! He must!" screams the frantic Morbius.

But his attacks are ultimately fruitless, as Karza is almost out of range. In a last-ditch effort to stop him, Morbius, with a look of fierce determination, energizes one hand with his other and begins to form a powerful ball of energy. After several moments, Morbius fires the bolt at the retreating Karza, and the recoil causes Morbius's arm to jolt back sharply.

Karza, still in demonic dragonfly form, can see out of the corner of his evilly glowing compact eyes this oncoming force and instantly transforms into the phantasm creature before the bolt strikes, laughing contemptuously as the energy passes through without injury. The Ring of Angels falls away, as there is nothing in this cloud to retain its grasp, but again Karza transforms back into the demonic insect and quickly regains possession and flies away victorious.

"Karza!" screams the defeated Morbius at the retreating demon, now a mere speck in the distance that quickly disappears. Morbius falls to his knees in despair. Jartan, disheveled, exhausted, but even more confused than ever following the battle with a creature easily the most powerful the young boy has ever encountered, now approaches him.

"How do you fight a thing like that?" asks Jartan, awestruck from his first—and hopefully last (he thinks to himself)— encounter with such a tenacious and formidable adversary.

"If Karza succeeds in what he is planning, we'll be fighting something far worse soon," Morbius responds coldly and almost without emotion, for what he is thinking is so chilling that he doesn't want to even think about it. But the wizard's anger and sense of urgency return, and he jumps to his feet and searches the sky as he continues, "The moon—what moon phase is it?" And now, seeing the moon overhead, he notices that it is a crescent moon. "One week until it becomes full," he continues. "Jartan, how long will it take for the armies to march to Mount Sabo?"

"Mount Sabo?" says the confused boy. "About eight days. Seven if we hurry."

Morbius ponders this for a moment.

"That gives us just enough time. Quickly, assemble the army. We march to Mount Sabo immediately."

"But Sire, what is going on?" asks a bewildered Jartan.

Morbius grabs him violently. "Damn it, boy!" begins Morbius, almost to the point of hysteria. "I don't have time to explain now! But if Karza succeeds, it'll mean the death of us all! Now do as I say, Jartan! Assemble the army!"

"Yes, Sire!" says Jartan as he rushes off to fulfill his king's wishes.

Morbius once again gazes up at the moon as he laments:

"And pray to the gods we aren't too late."

CHAPTER 10

✝ ✝ ✝

High atop Mount Sabo, Karza also gazes at the moon, which is now almost full, and as he directs his attention toward a large assembly of demon soldiers, perhaps a thousand in number, busily clearing away rock from the side of the mountain, the demon prince looks pleased at their progress despite the mask hiding any trace of emotion except for the eyes. A demon lieutenant soon approaches and bows before its master.

"The tomb entrance is almost cleared, my prince," says the demonic minion.

Karza nods in acknowledgement, and the lieutenant stands by his side as the demon prince watches contentedly for a few moments, but his attention is soon distracted toward the ground, for near his feet a fierce-looking snake is slithering. Karza steps on the dangerous creature—not on the head, which is obviously the perilous part, but on the tail. The snake quickly reacts angrily to this and delivers a vicious bite to Karza's leg—but it is the snake that writhes in agony from the bite and not the demon prince. The serpent's body twists and contorts violently in an agonizing death and then shrivels and finally disintegrates into smoke. Karza, his eyes twinkling with sinister delight at the snake's demise, notices a disturbance off in the distance. Curious, he approaches the edge of the ledge he is standing on and looks out to gaze far below, which reveals on the valley floor a large cloud of dust snaking its way through the only path that leads up the mountain. Karza appears concerned at this and transforms into a grotesque and slimy demonic creature with one huge eye. The eye glows brightly, and from it Karza can see a magnified image of the disturbance below. The image that reveals itself is Morbius and Jartan riding in front of a large army about five thousand strong. The demon prince transforms back into his semi-human form, not at all pleased with the sight of Morbius, his army, and his youthful—and, in Karza's mind, pathetic—sidekick, for Jartan has not yet demonstrated any great threat, unlike the powerful Morbius and his annoying wizardry. Karza again quickly glances skyward to check the moon's condition and realizes with distress that the time is almost at hand. Any interference now from Morbius cannot be tolerated.

With a raised hand, Karza turns to face his demon army. They instantly stop working and, facing their princely lord, await his command. Karza gives it by pointing downward to the approaching threat below, and the demons react with frenzied excitement, and suddenly each creates the assortment of weaponry that demon soldiers wield, and upon seeing a clenched fist from Karza, the demonic horde rushes off down the mountainside.

"But they outnumber us, my prince," cautions the demon lieutenant, still by Karza's side.

Karza creates his sword in his human hand and uses it to cut his other demonic hand with the blade, and a small pool of blood forms in his palm. This pool soon forms into a ball of energy, which quickly becomes a large egg of a grotesque nature that vibrates slightly in Karza's hand, apparently due to the movement of some creature within.

"Use this," says Karza, handing the egg to the lieutenant, who smiles eagerly upon seeing the imposing thing, for he knows what lies within the egg's casing. The lieutenant summons its black dragon, which is nearby, and mounts the beast and takes flight to join the demonic soldiers descending like a black wave down the mountainside.

Meanwhile, Morbius and Jartan are on horseback riding in front of the infantry column, and they all proceed down the corridor of the canyon at a slightly greater pace than a normal foot speed, for Mount Sabo can be seen looming in the near distance before them, and they must get there as soon as humanly possible—as per their king's command.

"We should reach Mount Sabo before nightfall, Sire," Jartan observes. "I'm surprised the army did as well as they did, considering the pace of the march."

Morbius glances skyward toward the moon and sees it is almost full.

"Good. We must stop Karza before the moon is full."

"Can you tell me now what is going on? Who is this Karza? Or what is he?"

"Karza is a demon prince from the Demonic Abyss," Morbius dryly responds.

"A demon prince? Here?" gasps the alarmed youth who now wishes he hadn't asked the question in the first place. Fear begins to fill Jartan's eyes—fear that Morbius can't help but notice.

"Does that frighten you, Jartan? Well, it should, because it frightens the seven hells out of me. You are now dealing with beings at one of the highest levels of evil—the demonic royalty. Only a handful of evil gods possess more power."

"So this Karza has been the one killing the Council wizards?"

Morbius silently nods in acknowledgement.

"But why?" continues Jartan.

Morbius is reluctant to relate the painful story but now feels the time is right to explain to Jartan what is going on in full.

"Fifteen years ago there was a wizard of great power named Kordon. Kordon was also one of my Council wizards—my greatest, in fact, for never before has there been any wizard who understood and mastered the magical arts better. His magic became so great that it corrupted his mind, and he turned to evil to satisfy his craving for even higher levels of power. Eventually, he used his diabolical skills and found a way to enter the Demonic Abyss to try to free the demon queen from her imprisonment there."

"Demon queen?" questions Jartan.

"Magdara—she is the most powerful force of non–divine evil in creation. In the time of the beginning, the gods, fearing her power was too great, imprisoned her in the Abyss, for they knew that if she was allowed to roam free, her evil would spread into even their higher level of divine existence. Even the evil gods didn't want that. The seal keeping her in the Abyss is located in the Underworld, which is the plane of existence below ours."

"But why didn't this Kordon just release her from the Underworld then?"

"Because Kordon couldn't reach the seal alone, for the Underworld contains dangers that even magic as powerful as his cannot overcome. He therefore needed a being with demonic powers to help him. So, using his black magic power, he conjured spells to allow him to enter the Demonic Abyss, and once there he sired a son with the demon queen."

"And Karza is this son?" Jartan asks.

"Yes."

"But I thought it was forbidden for any of the demonic royalty to leave the Abyss, Sire."

"True, but since Kordon is Karza's father, this human lineage of his allows him the ability to travel away from the demonic realms into the higher levels. Kordon knew this would happen, for Karza's power, together with his own, would enable Kordon to defeat the many obstacles in the Underworld and reach the seal of Magdara's imprisonment."

"But if all this happened fifteen years ago," comments Jartan, "then Karza would be around my age. How could he possibly be this powerful?"

"Demons age differently than humans, Jartan. For every one year of human life, demons age three. I assure you, Karza is no child."

"So, then why are we going to Mount Sabo, Sire?"

"When I discovered Kordon's insidious plot to free Magdara from the Abyss, I ordered the wizards of the Great Council to destroy him, and when they did so, Kordon's body was buried deep within Sabo in an effort to prevent any of his twisted, maniacal minions from using his tomb as a shrine of evil."

"But if Kordon is dead, why is Karza there?"

"Karza wants to see his mother free from the Abyss just as much as Kordon did, but only Kordon knew the spell to enter the Underworld and reach the seal. Karza is therefore going to resurrect his father."

"Is that possible?" asks an alarmed Jartan.

"It is," Morbius sadly acknowledges, "if he has the heart of a phoenix, which I fear he has, for one was reported killed two moons ago, and only a being with Karza's sordid abilities could kill one of those mighty creatures. And since this is the anniversary of Kordon's death fifteen years ago, and it is a full moon, a resurrection is possible. But in order to fully resurrect an evil human, he would also need the heads of those responsible for his father's death, which were the seven wizards of the Great Council. That is why he has been killing them. If only I had realized all this sooner!"

"What is all this urgency about this ring you were so alarmed over?" inquires Jartan.

"The Ring of Angels. As you know, angels are great guardians, and I knew when Karza was older he would make an attempt to resurrect his father. That is why I used the ring's power of protection and had Kordon's tomb magically sealed with it—only with the ring can anyone dispel the seal and enter the tomb."

"But he's a demon," comments a confused Jartan. "Demons are the arch-enemies of angels, so wouldn't using one of their artifacts kill him?"

"Very good, Jartan, I see your studies of the balance between good and evil has not been in vain. But that is precisely what worries me— why Karza wants it. He knows any attempt to wear the ring on demon skin would slay him instantly—and yet he still took it."

"Then he must be forcing some non-demonic being to wear the ring so he can enter."

"No, Jartan, that's not how the Ring of Angels works. You see, anyone can use the ring's power to protect something, be it an object, person, or in this case a tomb. And that is what I did with the ring; protected Kordon's tomb. But only one who is related to whatever is being protected can dissolve the seal with the ring. Do you understand?"

Jartan certainly is hearing what Morbius is saying and understands to a certain point, but his questioning look prompts him to ask this:

"But what if I was a sword and you used this Ring of Angels to protect this sword. Who is related to a sword?"

"Whoever created it, Jartan—that creator would be the father or mother of the sword, in a sense—and if there were other swords that this father or mother created, these would be the siblings of that sword and therefore related."

Again Jartan's questioning look reveals to Morbius that he doesn't yet quite understand, prompting him to add this:

"Let me put it this way, Jartan. If you died and I used the Ring of Angels to protect your tomb, only someone who is a blood relative of yours could use the ring to negate its protection. And that is why Karza, a blood relative of Kordon, his father—and his only living blood relative, thank the gods—needs the ring. Understand now?"

"But he's still a demon, Sire. How does being a blood relative negate that fact?"

"Exactly," acknowledges Morbius, "and exactly why I am worried. He must have some sort of protection—but what? But it doesn't matter. We must do everything we can to prevent the demon queen from escaping."

"What would happen if the demon queen was free?"

"The end of everything," replies Morbius, shaking his head in despair as he thinks of that dreaded possibility. "At least the end of everything that is good. She would reach the surface and use her power to plunge the land into evil and darkness for eternity—and not even the gods themselves can stop her then."

"But if you knew that Karza would try and do all this when he was older, Sire, why didn't you go into the Abyss and kill him when he was an infant fifteen years ago?"

Morbius, aghast at the boy's statement, just stares at him as if the boy has uttered something so insanely ridiculous that it boggles the mind, but the king does manage to regain his senses enough to chuckle at Jartan's suggestion as he answers,

"I'll give you three reasons, Jartan. One: no good human has ever ventured into the Demonic Abyss and has survived. The only reason Kordon did is because he's just as evil and twisted as the demons. Two: I'm not powerful enough to be the first. I don't even know the spell he used to get down there; nor do I have the magical skills to use or even duplicate his feat. And three: even if by some miracle I managed to kill a member of the demonic royalty, the entire demonic horde would retaliate to seek vengeance. You just can't assassinate a royal demon in its own realm and expect the horde to sit idle. I promise you they would swarm with hatred as if all the seven hells had broken lose."

"Then it's hopeless?" asks Jartan dejectedly. "You saw what Karza did back at the castle, Sire. How can we stop him? He's invincible!"

"True, but only as long as he remains in a transformed state, my young friend. But he cannot maintain such a state for long, especially if he has to use his energy to ward off attacks, and the more energy he uses, the faster he will weaken and be forced to return to his natural, semi-human form. Only when he is in this demon-prince form can he finally be killed—and then we'll crush him like the demonic bug he is."

Jartan is dubious about Morbius's last sentence and voices his concern.

"Isn't that a bit arrogant, Sire? It seemed to me we got our ass kicked back at the castle. He is a demon prince, after all."

"My apologies—we'll crush him like the royal bug he is." But Morbius's hopeful confidence doesn't placate Jartan, and noticing this, the king adds, "Don't worry, Jartan—he can be defeated."

"But if not even the seven wizards of the Great Council could stop him, then what chance have we? He's even more powerful than you are!"

"I am aware of that, Jartan, believe me. But Karza fought them individually, not all at once. That gives us the advantage."

"What advantage? We fought him with everything we had seven days ago and were massacred!"

Morbius smiles as he relates the answer.

"Because we now have a weapon that we and the other Council Wizards didn't have—a force of goodness just as great as Karza's evil. A force that has been fighting all of his evil and demonic kind since time began."

Jartan perks up when he hears this.

"What weapon is that, my king?" he asks with enthusiasm.

"We have you— paladin."

"A paladin? Me?" gasps the incredulous boy.

"Yes. I've been training and teaching you in the ways of the paladinhood since you first were brought to me as an infant fifteen years ago. I knew shortly after I first saw you that you were one of the rare few who possessed the abilities worthy of the paladinhood. It is now time for you to take your place among that noble and powerful sect."

Morbius reaches to the side of his horse and pulls out a unique-looking sword—a soul blade. Jartan is in awe upon seeing this strange weapon.

"What is that?"

"To me," Morbius responds, "it is just a sword. But in the hands of the paladin it was destined for" —he hands the blade to Jartan, and when he holds it, the blade begins to glow and shimmer with energy as Morbius continues—"it is a mighty soul blade. All paladins wield them, though each one physically appears different and has different powers unique to each paladin."

Jartan is amazed at the blade's energetic luster.

"Beautiful!" he exclaims delightedly. "I can feel its power!"

His look of amazement turns to puzzlement as he begins to feel a different sensation.

"It is strange, but—but I can also feel—no, that's ridiculous."

Morbius, though expecting this reaction from Jartan, looks concerned over it.

"Tell me," says the apprehensive Morbius. "Tell me *exactly* what you feel."

Jartan closes his eyes as if in deep concentration.

"I feel a—a sense of devotion—intense loyalty, and deep affection emanating from it—a presence—almost as if it has been reunited with someone it deeply loved—as if it were alive."

Morbius's look of concern grows as he presses Jartan further.

"Who do you feel as you hold the blade, Jartan?"

As Morbius asks this, he raises his hand slightly, and it glows with power as if he is using his magic to elicit the correct response. Jartan tries to answer, his eyes closing even more tightly as his concentration deepens, almost as if his mind is trying to fight whatever influence is forcing him to answer Morbius's question—not that the boy is aware of any of this.

"I feel my—my—s—s—"

Morbius is even more concerned now, and he closes his hand tightly as if to put more power into his mental attempt to elicit the answer he wants to hear as Jartan continues to struggle against it, but he soon smiles broadly.

"My snow wolf! It is my snow wolf, Loba!"

Morbius smiles in relief. Jartan continues,

"I've had Loba as a pet as long as I can remember. But how can that be?"

"Because it is Loba," says the still smiling Morbius.

"I don't understand," the boy replies, confused.

"It is a little complicated, so listen carefully. A soul blade is far more than a weapon—it is a living spirit, a part of the paladin who wields it. When Loba died last month, I used her spirit to power your blade. Loba was your closest companion. She protected you ever since you were an infant. She loved you, and it is that love that gives a soul blade its awesome powers—powers unlike any other class of intelligent beings."

"What can it do?" Jartan asks as he studies his soul blade more closely, thoroughly entranced by the blade and the power it emanates to him.

"Many things, for once in the hands of its paladin master it becomes a formidable weapon. For instance, it has the ability to cut through any non-magical object—and even quite a few magical ones. Try it on that rock face over there."

Jartan, his eyes wide with excitement, rides over to the rock face of the canyon wall nearby. Upon reaching it, he slices the rock with the soul blade, and it cuts through it easily, creating a large gash that steams slightly from the intense energy of the mighty weapon. Jartan is greatly pleased by this.

"Wow!" he exclaims with amazement.

Looking around for even more targets, he sees a tree off in the distance and hastily rides off toward that with a gleeful look. Morbius sees what Jartan is going to do and is greatly alarmed by it. He makes an effort to call out to him but stops himself, though he is very distressed—he is not allowed to interfere. He slumps back in his saddle dejected as he awaits the dire ramifications of the oblivious boy's action.

Jartan has reached the tree and is about to slash the trunk with his soul blade, grinning intensely as he is reveling in the power of his new weapon, a weapon with power he has never experienced before, power so great that anyone could easily be seduced by it. The boy raises the soul blade as a prelude to the strike—but he stops. His smile vanishes as he gazes upward at the immense and quite beautiful tree with its many branches of colorful leaves and blossoms.

Morbius is greatly relieved that Jartan stopped himself from striking the tree and rides over to him.

"Why didn't you strike the tree, Jartan? I know you wanted to."

"I couldn't," he responds. He's not yet aware of the tear that is barely discernable in his eyes. But now that it does become apparent, he shrugs off the emotional implications and responds to the intellectual. "It is a beautiful tree. I just felt that injuring it would be wrong."

"You are wise," says Morbius, smiling. "But it is necessary that you fully understand what harm striking the tree would have done. Look."

Morbius gestures to the tree. Among its leaves and branches are multitudes of birds, insects, and other animals happily going about their blissful business, and large amounts of fruit are among its limbs, which the creatures are eagerly consuming.

Morbius continues as he gestures to what they both can see,

"You see? Killing the tree would have been bad enough, for it is a living entity of goodness and was doing you no harm. But the tree also provides food and shelter to many creatures whose existence depends on the tree's survival. They too would have suffered greatly if the tree had died. Do you understand?"

"Yes, Sire," says the nodding boy, somewhat ashamed that he even considered hurting the tree in the first place. "What would have happened to me if I injured or killed the tree?"

"As a paladin, you are duty-bound to uphold the virtues of goodness. It is a crime against the code of the paladinhood to do any harm to a good creature. Should you do so, your powers would be lost, and the soul in your blade would return to the land of the dead. Remember, Jartan, use the immense powers that being a paladin gives you only in the fight against evil and darkness."

They leave the tree and move back to ride in front of the column as Jartan continues to admire his shiny new possession.

"It truly is a magnificent weapon," he comments.

Morbius, with his greater age and therefore maturity, is fully aware of the blade's non-weapon capabilities, and he makes an effort to introduce these to his teenage companion's consciousness.

"It is much more than a weapon," Morbius responds. "If you ever lose it, and the distance between you is not too great, you can summon the blade into your hand by calling to it."

Jartan finds these particular words hard to believe. He has had many pets that came when they were called. But this is not a living pet but a blade. And even a blade with the spirit of a pet inside should not come when called. So Jartan decides to test this theory out and throws the blade at the rock cliff to the side. The blade penetrates the stone deeply. He then holds out his hand and calls to it,

"Soul blade!"

The blade instantly withdraws itself from the stone and flies off toward a very surprised, though pleasantly so, Jartan, who grabs it.

"Amazing!" he says, thoroughly entranced by this object he is holding in his hand—a weapon that has given him a sense of far more power than any of those swords, axes, and spears that he was previously introduced to, which he now perceives as boring.

"Tell me more, Sire!"

Morbius is certainly aware that giving a youth of Jartan's fifteen years a device of such phenomenal power is quickly overcoming the boy's normal morality to refrain from using such power for one's own selfish purpose.

"That's not a toy, Jartan. You need to get that concept out of your head right now! A soul blade is not designed to serve your selfish whims or abuse its powers. Only when you understand why a paladin is justified to use such a weapon will the powers of a soul blade reveal themselves."

"What do you mean?"

"I mean you cannot use the blade to kill some bee that stung you because you irritated that bee in the first place. Nor can you blast some troll into oblivion because you don't like how it looks. That is why your powers will be severely limited for now."

"What limitations?"

"Because you are a novice paladin, you don't yet have the ability to heal your wounds or create offensive energy yourself—that will come when you are more advanced and understand the paladin laws. The blade's ability to cut through practically anything is more than enough offensive power to let you deal with whatever obstacle or foe you encounter for now. However, you will find that you can summon lightning bolts from a stormy sky, or any other electrical disturbance or discharge, and redirect the energy to a target of your choosing—behold."

Morbius fires a lightning bolt of energy from his hand at Jartan's soul blade, and the blade glows even more brightly as it absorbs the energy.

"Now," Morbius continues, "fire the energy at that rock formation in the distance."

Jartan points the blade at the rock formation nearby, and the weapon releases the powerful bolt of energy at it, causing a spectacular explosion.

"Incredible!" the new paladin says with pride. "When will I be able to create energy myself?"

"Soon," replies Morbius. "Once a paladin has reached a certain level of experience, then they advance to a higher level, and these paladins often have the soul of a loved one—a family member, for example, or someone who was close to them in life and has recently died to power their soul blades. It is these paladins who command awesome power from the love force residing in the blade. But your pet snow wolf, Loba, is strong enough for you to get used to the powers of a paladin. In time, a more powerful soul will wish to serve you."

"What else can a paladin do?" asks Jartan.

"Even though you cannot yet create offensive energy, you do have defensive power. Here, raise the blade in front of you and concentrate on protection."

Jartan does this, though he is apprehensive about what Morbius is going to do.

"Don't worry," says Morbius reassuringly. "Just think of 'protection', and you will survive. Ready?"

The word 'survive' does nothing to bolster his courage, but Jartan nods, though he is still doubtful of the outcome of this—more so than ever when he sees Morbius raising his hand and a rather formidable fireball beginning to form. A blistering stream of flame shoots from Morbius's fingertips directly at Jartan— but true to the king's word, the soul blade immediately creates an energy shield and deflects the lethal blast, much to Jartan's relief.

"Awesome!" says the boy. "What else?"

"All paladins, regardless of their level, have the power to communicate and command any of the lesser creatures of goodness." Morbius looks up to see a silverhawk—a good creature—flying in the sky overhead, and he points to it for Jartan to notice.

"Try it," Morbius continues. "Close your eyes and concentrate on what you want the silverhawk to do."

Jartan closes his eyes and holds out his arm, and the hawk soon descends from above and lands upon it. Jartan is amazed.

"Magnificent!" he says with astonishment as the silverhawk flies off, and Morbius continues.

"Your soul blade will even warn you if evil is present."

"How?" asks Jartan.

"The blade will glow, alerting you of any danger."

But no sooner does Morbius say this than Jartan's blade begins to glow brightly. The two are alarmed by the unanticipated flashing and immediately look around the area for the threat, which doesn't take long to reveal itself, for emerging from behind a ridge on the mountainside directly before them, the demon army of Karza is descending upon them like a plague from above.

CHAPTER 11

✝ ✝ ✝

The battle rages as the two armies fight savagely, and although the demons are outnumbered five to one, the battle is certainly not one-sided, for a demon soldier is slightly larger and stronger than its human counterpart, and this allows it to wield heavier weaponry and carry heavier armor. In addition, it is well known that demons fight in a fearless and ferocious almost berserk state, making them formidable adversaries, which in most cases negates any numerical superiority the enemy may have—and this is the case here. Where the humans have the advantage is in the mighty magic of a formidable wizard like King Morbius, for the demons have no equal here, nor against the recently acquired powers of even a novice paladin like Jartan, for even the limited power of his soul blade at Jartan's low level of experience easily allows the youth the ability to dispatch a dozen times his number as the blade slices through even the heavier weapons and armor the demons possess. Still, the demonic tenacity is such that they are surprisingly resilient and are providing a stubborn resistance.

"Where did all these demons come from?" demands Jartan as he slices a demon or two that come within reach. Morbius blasts a few himself, sending bloody demon pieces flying off in every direction.

"They're Karza's minions, summoned by him to help clear away Kordon's tomb. Jartan, you stay here and take command of the army. I'm going after Karza."

"You can't take him on alone, Sire!"

"Summoning this many demons must have left him severely weakened," says Morbius with confidence. "He won't be able to stay transformed for long; therefore, I will have the advantage."

Morbius rides off up the mountain, but his words of confidence once again do not placate Jartan or override his instinctive desire to protect his monarch. Concerned over his safety, he calls out after him,

"Sire, wait! You'll need help!"

Jartan tries to ride off after Morbius, but a demon soldier jumps on him, and he falls off his horse. The riderless animal rapidly flees from the intensity of combat now that it doesn't have Jartan's commanding influence to overpower its desire to run in terror. The demon soldier is about to put his axe into Jartan's head, but he quickly uses his soul blade to slice it in two and he then gives the weaponless and aghast demon a quick slash with the blade as well—the demon's armor useless against the penetrating power of a soul blade. Another demon suffers the same fate for good measure. Taking advantage of the respite, Jartan now looks around for his horse.

"Damn. Now where did my horse go?"

To Jartan's amazement, his soul blade begins to vibrate, and as if acting on its own volition, it guides the hand that holds it to point off to a rocky crevice where a brief glimpse of the horse can be seen entering and quickly disappearing from view.

"Oh, I'm going to like you, my little friend!" Jartan says to the soul blade with a huge grin, for he is pleasantly surprised at the device's obliging power.

The boy begins rushing over to his horse, slashing a demon or two along the way, and he soon finds himself in the crevice with his horse. He approaches the highly agitated animal, but his soothing words calm the beast enough to allow him to get near and prepare to mount. Suddenly his soul blade once again flashes to signal danger. Jartan turns to face the crevice entrance and sees a large group of demons, about two dozen in number. He looks panicked, for he hasn't fought alone against this many opponents before, and looking around, he cannot see any other way out of the crevice to flee as the demons approach. Jartan talks to his blade:

"I don't know what else you can do, my bright little beauty—but you better do something now!"

The demons charge with berserk hatred, but suddenly the soul blade emits an intense flash of light that blinds the charging onslaught. Jartan, seeing his chance to strike while the demons are in a state of vulnerable blindness, slashes away at them. The demons make a vain attempt to defend themselves by thrashing blindly at their nimble attacker, but in the end it doesn't take long for Jartan to dispatch them all with lethal precision. He then mounts his horse and gives a little kiss to his soul blade in smiling gratitude. But his smile vanishes when Jartan hears the terrified screams of humans from beyond the crevice. A particularly ominous shriek soon follows, which can only be the reason for the bloodcurdling screams in the first place. Jartan hurriedly rides out of the crevice but instantly pauses in shock once this new threat reveals itself to his eyes.

The monstrosity that Jartan can see effortlessly plowing its way through the ranks of Morbius's army of soldiers and just as effortlessly killing them in droves is a giant, demonic scorpion. This is obviously the monster that hatched from the egg that Karza gave his lieutenant, who is on a nearby ledge of the mountainside gleefully watching the scorpion's butchering of any victims that are within reach. The scorpion is highly effective in this massacre, as it uses its four pincers laced with razor-sharp spikes to deliver lethal wounds, and its heavily armored skin prevents any of the nonmagical weapons of the human soldiers from penetrating. But the most deadly attack is in its stinger at the end of its multiple-sectioned tail, for this doesn't deliver poison upon impact; instead, the glowing weapon instantly disintegrates all it touches, and due to this formidable combination of abilities, this demonic giant is quickly decimating Morbius's advantage in numbers over the demon forces.

Jartan rushes over to the creature and dismounts his horse to engage it, for unlike the weapons of the human soldiers that simply bounce off or shatter when they hit the scorpion's armored skin, Jartan's soul blade at least can penetrate and sever parts of the beast. Still, the scorpion's size and weapons make it a difficult opponent, and it is therefore fortunate that the creature cannot focus its attention on any one target for long, as Jartan and the many human soldiers keep distracting it. The battle soon ends thanks to another fortuitous blinding burst from Jartan's soul blade, which causes the scorpion to thrash blindly about, and while it is disoriented, Jartan is able to deliver a lethal thrust of his blade into the creature, killing it.

The demon lieutenant on the mountainside is displeased to see the death of the scorpion and in retaliation commands the black dragon it is riding to discharge a lightning bolt at Jartan below. But Jartan's ever-vigilant soul blade instantly alerts him of the approaching danger, and he quickly turns just in time to block the strike with the potent weapon. Absorbing the energy, he then sends it back toward the source, which kills both the lieutenant and dragon with a mighty explosive blast.

Seeing that Morbius's army has the advantage, for there are very few demon soldiers offering much resistance and the army can therefore handle them without need for his particular talents, Jartan spies Morbius far in the distance and almost to the top of Mount Sabo, so he calls to one of his human comrades nearby.

"You take command," he says to the soldier. "When you defeat these demons, follow me to Sabo. I'm going to help the king." And with that, Jartan remounts his steed and urges the horse to a full gallop to head off after Morbius.

Morbius has gone as far as he can on horse and dismounts, seeing that only a ledge above needs to be reached in order to get to where Karza must be. He begins to climb upward along the jagged surface of the mountainside. But while reaching for a rock protrusion overhead, he notices an alarming sight—the demon prince is standing there looking down at him.

"Karza!" yells a defiant Morbius.

He instantly fires a blast of lightning at the dreaded enemy, but the demon prince transforms into the huge, muscular titan demon, and Morbius's bolts ricochet off its armored skin, sending the bolts skyward without leaving a scratch. Karza then puts his two huge fists together, raises his arms over his head, and slams his fists into the ground in front of him. The phenomenal strength of the titan is so incredible that the shock of this causes a massive portion of the ledge he is standing on to crumble away and begin to fall upon Morbius, who quickly erects an energy shield around himself; but the amount of ruble descending upon him is so great that even his shield is becoming overwhelmed, and he hastily tries to teleport out of harm's way before being completely buried. But this is only partially successful, for although he extricates himself from a rocky tomb, he is unable to prevent himself from being pinned, and rather painfully so, by several large boulders. He screams in agony from the crushing weight. Karza can see Morbius's position of pinning weakness and surprisingly takes no further action against the helpless foe. However, he is satisfied that Morbius is no longer a threat, and with another look upward toward the sky to note the moon's condition, he sees it is now completely full. He lumbers over to the tunnel where his demons were working and, still in this particular demon form, begins to pound away with his fists, breaking away large portions of the rock remaining. After several moments of this effective mining technique, a faint green glow begins to appear. Another round of frenetic pounding from the demon reveals the entrance to the tomb, which is surrounded by this protective green glow. Karza's demonic eyes twinkle with pleasure.

Morbius finally manages to blast free of the rocks covering him and teleports to the top ledge where Karza was. The king can see the titan demon at the huge end of the tunnel silhouetted against the green glow, unaware of Morbius's presence. Taking advantage of this, Morbius hurls a brilliant ball of magical energy into the tunnel, which strikes the back of the demon, causing a huge explosion and collapsing the tunnel, sealing Karza inside. But this doesn't keep Karza trapped for long as he blasts free in his demonic three-headed tridragon form—and once again a bitter battle erupts between Karza's awesome dragon powers and Morbius's mighty magic.

Jartan is climbing the mountain and can see just above him the area where Morbius and Karza are battling. Although he can't see the two yet, the unseen battle is causing explosions to occur, which causes some debris to fall on Jartan, frustrating his efforts to ascend as bolts of energy and flame can be seen shooting about amid the yells and moans of Morbius and Karza in epic battle above.

Morbius is losing this battle, as Karza is simply too powerful to combat when he is in this, his most powerful demonic form. What damage the harried wizard is able to inflict is instantly healed, while Karza's attacks are becoming more and more difficult for Morbius to repel. He falls to the ground unconscious after a particularly devastating attack from Karza and the victorious demon prince lumbers over to the fallen and defenseless wizard, apparently to deliver a death blow. But even though he can obviously easily do so while Morbius is beaten and unconscious, he does not. In all the battles between the two, ever since their first in the castle a week ago, Karza was only trying to escape and keep Morbius at bay and not really try and kill him. Everyone else who got in his way he killed—but not Morbius, as if he was thinking, *You will die Morbius—but not just yet.* Karza turns back toward the tunnel.

But soon Jartan, yelling his defiance, catapults onto the dragon's back from an elevated rock face, driving his soul blade deep into its black, scaled flesh—its protective armor, so effective against nonmagical weapons, appears as scaled butter against the powerful soul blade. The severe wound belches out bursts of energy—as does Karza, who belches out flame, lightning, and freezing vapor from the lethal heads in protest while frantically writhing in agony from this piercing of its skin; but the violent thrashing of the creature's movements throws Jartan to the ground.

The dragon Karza quickly recovers and begins a series of attacks with vast belches of flame, lightning, and freezing vapor—attacks that are quickly waning in their power—but Jartan demonstrates his almost unnatural nimbleness in evading most of these blasts, and his prowess with the soul blade in defense ultimately frustrates Karza's efforts at destroying the annoying youth, so after a few moments he tries a different approach. Seeing a large group of rocks that his demon minions piled there while clearing away the tomb, Karza transforms into a large creature with dozens of tentacles like some demonic, mutated version of a nightmarish octopus. The creature starts grabbing rocks from the pile in its dozens tentacles, throwing them at great velocity at Jartan. The effect is like that of a hailstorm, though of a horizontal and far more deadly nature, and although the severity of the bombardment is quite intense, the youthful paladin uses his soul blade to erect a protective field of energy that causes the rocks to shatter upon impact with it. A frustrated Karza transforms yet again, this time into his massively muscled titan demon form, and slams his huge fist into the earth, which causes the ground to split open, and a crack snakes toward Jartan, the speed of which is too great to evade, and he falls deeply into the abyss.

Stunned from the twenty-foot fall, the boy is unaware of the approaching Karza, who soon appears at the edge of the chasm. Unable to reach his vulnerable prey due to the depth of this crevice, Karza again transforms into the multitentacled creature and in this form is able to grab Jartan. Many tentacles coil around him, and with the helpless boy firmly in his viselike grip, Karza slithers over to the ledge high atop Mount Sabo. The fate that is looming before Jartan's eyes is a horrifying one, for he can see that he is about to be thrown over the ledge—a ten-thousand-foot plummet to his death. He struggles in a panic to break the grip of Karza, but the multitudinous tentacles make this impossible. Karza raises the human projectile over his head and is about to throw Jartan to his death—when suddenly Karza begins to transform back into his demon prince form, causing the boy to fall free. Karza, shaken and alarmed by this sudden and obviously unwanted transformation into this vulnerable form, tries desperately to transform back into some creature, but his weakened condition prevents him from maintaining any shape, and he quickly reforms as the demon prince.

Jartan can see that Karza is struggling to transform and knows that this means he is now too weak to become any of his formidable demonic forms, which would have been a welcoming sight to the youth if it wasn't for the fact that a demon prince, even one in semihuman form, is still a highly imposing sight, with his black robes and armor, crown of regal demonic authority, black mask that hides any face, and evil eyes glowing bright red with power; and only trepidation registers on Jartan's face in the presence of such a powerful enemy as Karza's unseen aura of intense fear generates and begins to affect the youth. Were Karza at his full power, this fear aura would have sent Jartan fleeing in terror, but due to his newly attained paladin rank, he can at least withstand the evil influence. Still, he tries to hide his fear and bolster his own courage by goading the demonic foe now that he is in his weakened and therefore slayable condition.

"What's wrong, Your Highness? Too weak to transform?" says Jartan mockingly while forcing a smile to hide any fear he still harbors. He calls out with an outstretched hand, "Soul blade!"

The blade, still deep in the chasm, begins to fly out to reach its master, and not even the rocky side of the chasm walls is any impediment to the blade's journey; it cuts right through it and emerges from the ground to land in Jartan's hand.

Karza sees this and is concerned, for only a paladin has that ability. A smiling and confident Jartan now approaches the semihuman Karza, but a demon prince, even one that is too weak to transform, is still a formidable adversary. If Jartan had the experience to understand why, he wouldn't feel so arrogant, especially when he sees Karza's eyes appear to smile slyly in return.

"Not too weak to destroy you, paladin!"

Karza summons his own sword to his hand and unleashes a strike, which the paladin quickly blocks with his soul blade. The contact of the two weapons creates a burst of crackling energy, and Jartan is shocked that his blade is not slicing through Karza's sword like it has easily done with all the demon soldiers' weapons and the demonic scorpion, prompting Karza to laugh at the youth's terrified confusion.

"You aren't the only one with magical weapons, boy!"

The two are fairly evenly matched in their combat skills, and they fight for a while until Karza notices the moon and realizes he is running out of time.

"I don't have time to play games with you!" says Karza, clearly annoyed at Jartan's tenacity.

He pushes Jartan away, and with his free human hand he creates a flame and brushes his sword with it. The blade ignites. He then fires off a stream of flame at Jartan, who frantically tries to evade it. The ledge Jartan is on collapses from the fire attack, and Jartan falls with it but manages to cling to an outcropping of rock, which thankfully spares the boy's life, and he quickly climbs back up. Karza is greatly annoyed at Jartan's persistence, and the two resume battle; but after a few moments of intense sword fighting, they part. Both breathing heavily from the ferocity of their battle, each is distracted by a disturbing sight lying on the ground between them. It is a severed human hand, the fingers of which curl due to the freshness of the wound.

Jartan and Karza both look at each other for neither is sure which one of them this hand formerly belonged to. The paladin has a deep cut on his face, and holding his soul blade in one hand he reaches up with the other to wipe the trickle of blood off his face. When he sees that his hand is not the one on the ground, he smiles in triumph. Karza raises his free arm—minus his human hand.

"You'll have to do better than that, prince!" says the laughing Jartan.

But Karza also begins to chuckle slightly, and a glow of energy forms at the site of his wound and a new hand quickly appears, much to Jartan's shock.

"As you wish," responds the confident demon prince with a sinister tone. He raises both his arms, and his eyes glow brightly. From where his severed hand is lying on the ground amid a pool of blood, a burst of energy erupts. The energy soon forms into one of the demon prince's powerful minions—a minotaurus, a fifteen-foot-tall monster with jet-black skin and red eyes of evil with the muscular body of a human but the head of a very unpleasant bull with a decidedly demonic appearance along with an intimidating and surprising number of limbs in the form of four muscular arms. Jartan is understandably greatly alarmed by the sight of this hideous beast as Karza again laughs with sinister delight at the boy's shock.

"You fool! You think transforming is the limit to my power?" says Karza as he walks over to the creature and hands it his sword while adding with a chilling coldness, "Kill him."

He chuckles with evil confidence and walks off toward the tomb entrance, leaving the demonic minotaurus he summoned to deal with the irritating Jartan. The creature creates another sword for each of its hands, wielding four of the intimidating blades. Jartan readies himself for the creature's attack as it rushes toward him with swords flying. The frightened youth tries desperately to repel the minotaurus's relentless blows.

Now that Jartan is preoccupied with the demon he has summoned and Morbius is lying unconscious nearby, unable to offer any resistance, Karza can finally resume his diabolical plan without any further interferences, and he goes back into what is left of the tunnel, for Morbius's attempt to bury Karza and his subsequent eruption to freedom have made a gaping opening, and only a few steps are required now to reach the green glow of the tomb's seal. Standing before the entrance, Karza's hand glows slightly, and a small box soon appears in the hand, which he places on the ground, where it quickly becomes a large chest. Opening the lid reveals eight cloth-covered objects, the cloth hiding from view what is beneath, although one of the objects appears to be moving in a rhythmic fashion. On top of these objects is the Ring of Angels, and he removes this from the chest. The ring is far too large for any normal human being to wear, so Karza magically shrinks it to a size that will fit an ordinary finger. Karza is fully aware that the ring—an artifact of angelic goodness—would be instantly fatal to an evil wearer if it contacted demon skin, so he places the ring on a finger of his human hand. The skin on that hand obviously doesn't radiate the demonic influence of the other, preventing the lethal result.

There is an indentation on the entrance to the tomb that is the perfect size for the gleaming jewel on this ring, and Karza inserts it in the indentation as the green glow of protection dissipates, and a twist of his wrist causes the entrance to open. Removing the ring, Karza transforms the chest at his feet to its original smaller size, and it then disappears in his hand until needed later. He enters the tomb, and once inside, he looks back to see Jartan still in a frantic, losing battle with the more powerful demonic minotaurus—and Morbius lying bloody and unconscious on the ground. The demon prince is pleased and inserts the ring in the indentation on the opposite side of the entrance. The door closes and when he withdraws the ring the green glow of protection returns, sealing the tomb entrance once again. The ring no longer needed, Karza removes it from his finger, and it instantly returns to its larger size. He drops it to the floor and stomps on it. The ring explodes with a flash—thereby making entrance into the tomb virtually impossible. The gleam in his triumphant demonic eye says it all: *Nothing, absolutely nothing, can stop me now.*

CHAPTER 12

✦ ✦ ✦

As Karza walks farther into the tomb along a long, narrow corridor, he waves his hand to ignite the torches lining the way. The corridor ends at a small chamber with very low ceilings and has all the dreary appearance of its purpose. The tomb itself is circular in format and unremarkable in that it is not decorated and has no superficial objects, for it was hewn from the stone in great haste in order to prevent any further evil from developing from Kordon's demise. The only object present is at the far end of the tomb, a stone sarcophagus standing vertically against the back wall—a sarcophagus that both in appearance and presence radiates intense evil and foreboding. But what is remarkable is that the tomb is in pristine condition despite the passing of a decade and a half and lacks the usual additions of cobwebs and throngs of spiders, rats, snakes, and bats—tombs are normally the favorite haunts of such vermin, which revel and thrive within the ghastliness of crypts and graveyards. The Ring of Angels was totally unnecessary to prevent any entrance of such creatures into the tomb, for even after fifteen years of death, Kordon's evil influence still permeates the atmosphere, and no vermin would have dared enter the presence of such intense evilness once the dark wizard's body was laid to rest. Only when the tomb was first being built fifteen years before did one single and clever rat, perceiving that this place would soon contain a convenient source of food—a body—secretly remain to await the feast. Unfortunately for it, Kordon's corpse was deposited and the entrance sealed before the rat could flee. Its skeletal remains can still be seen as far from the sarcophagus as the creature could get. Its teeth and claws have eroded down to smooth, flat stumps from frantic gnashing and clawing against the tomb entrance in a desperate and hopeless attempt to escape the evil in the tomb before the poor thing died of starvation some days later—the marks of its torturous struggle forever embedded in the rock surface. Only Karza, being just as warped and evil as his father, is not fazed in the slightest by the fearful energy Kordon's body still generates, and approaching the sarcophagus, he touches it gently as if the contents are something of great value.

Transforming himself into yet another of his twisted demonic forms—for he has now had time to recover his transformation ability—a grotesque creature with formidable limbs with barbed spikes at each end, he thrusts these spikes deeply into the cover of the sarcophagus, allowing him to easily rip it off and toss it aside; it would have been far too heavy to remove without the abilities of this creature, not to mention that a larger sized form like his titan demon would not have been able to fit within the cramped confines of the tomb. Karza transforms once again into his demon prince form to gaze upon the contents of the sarcophagus, which are revealed in the eerily flickering torchlight. There before him is the dead body of the most feared evil wizard that ever lived—the remains of Kordon.

The body of Kordon is dressed in black robes with a similarly black hood that covers most of the face. The small part of the face that is visible is disturbingly that of a skeleton. The arms are folded across the body, and the hands, like the face, are bony and devoid of flesh—not surprising, since he has been dead for fifteen years. By the light in his eyes, it is clear that Karza is smiling with an evil grin from beneath his otherwise emotionless mask.

Outside the tomb, Jartan continues in his struggle with the demonic minotaurus, and he tries to blind it as he did the demons before, but it is only marginally effective against this creature, for it recovers its sight after only a fleeting moment; but Jartan receives many wounds from the creature's multiple swords, and he is losing ground in the struggle. He manages to sever one of the beast's arms (the magical sword it was holding disappears in a puff of smoke), but due to the fact it has three left to deliver vicious attacks, it is a feeble injury and one that is ultimately too little, too late, for the paladin is quickly becoming overwhelmed and exhausted from the incessant blows of a creature who has no such weakness. The minotaurus soon gains the upper hand as a particularly savage round of strikes sends Jartan reeling to the ground, but before it can deliver a final, fatal thrust, it is fortuitously blasted by a wave of energy and is destroyed (along with the three swords of Karza). Jartan looks behind him to see where the blast came from and is pleased—though "*relieved*" is more accurate—to see the noble Morbius has regained consciousness. The wizard lowers his hand, and its energy subsides after the life-saving blasting away of the daunting demonic foe. A concerned Jartan rushes over to his fallen king to offer assistance.

"Sire! Are you all right?"

"Where is Karza?" demands Morbius, though still somewhat dazed.

"He went into the tomb."

Morbius's face registers with disappointment and anger, and he begins to stand; but Jartan, seeing his king still in a weak and disoriented condition, makes an effort to stop him.

"Sire, you must rest. Your injuries! Sire!"

But Morbius violently pushes Jartan aside and rushes over to the green, glowing entrance of the tomb with Jartan quickly following.

"He must be stopped!" cries the exhausted but highly agitated king.

With glowing hands raised before him, Morbius fires an intense charge of magical energy at the seal and continues to do this for several moments—but soon his face begins to show signs of strain from this effort and his hands start to bleed.

"Sire? Sire, stop!" cries the greatly concerned Jartan upon seeing Morbius beginning to suffer terribly, but Morbius continues to blast the entrance, which only causes his pain to increase, as does Jartan's concern.

"Sire, please!" Jartan pleads in even greater earnest. "You'll kill yourself! Stop it! Sire!"

But the mighty wizard cannot maintain his effort any longer and falls to his knees defeated, panting heavily with hands trembling.

"It is no use," says Morbius, dejected and now totally exhausted. "I can't break through without the Ring of Angels."

Inside the tomb, Karza has set up seven poles arranged in a semicircle in front of Kordon's body, still in the sarcophagus, with one pole in the center. He then produces the small box again and throws it on the ground. The larger chest appears, and when he opens the lid, the cloth-covered contents are once again revealed. The one that is beating is the one Karza removes. When he uncovers the cloth, it is clear why this thing pulsates the way it does, for it is the still-beating heart of the phoenix. Karza carefully puts this on the center pole. From the chest he then pulls out and uncovers the severed head of the wizard Vantor, whom he killed days earlier—the last emotion the human felt before he died, horror, is still visible on the face as if it were chiseled there out of stone—and puts this on one of the seven poles of the semicircle. After several moments, he has all seven of the severed heads of the Council wizards who were responsible for his father's death grotesquely arrayed to form this grisly semicircle of death, obviously in preparation for the evil ritual that will follow.

Karza is aware of the demise of his minotaurus, and he creates his sword again, cuts his hand with it, and drips the steaming blood on each head. As the blood oozes down the face of each, the eyes suddenly open with an eerie, reddish glow from the demonic influence of Karza's powerful blood. He stands back to await the spectacle. Beams of light shoot out from the eyes of the severed heads and focus on the beating phoenix heart in the center. The heart concentrates the beams into a greater bolt of energy that illuminates the body of Kordon, which is bathed in the same reddish glow. The heads erupt into a furiously burning flame and begin to be consumed by it as the resurrection process continues, and after a few moments the skeletal hands of Kordon begin to move.

Outside the tomb, Jartan leaves Morbius's side and rushes toward the tomb entrance. He is leery about his chances of breaching the imposing magical barrier as he stands before the green glow, and looking back to Morbius and his trembling, bloody hands certainly does nothing to bolster his confidence. However, considering the gravity of this situation with Karza safely inside, he must now try his hand at breaking through. Gripping his soul blade tightly with both hands and taking a deep breath, he violently thrusts the blade into the protecting force, which causes bolts of energy to radiate in all directions as Jartan exerts all his strength against the barrier, and the blade slowly begins to penetrate.

Karza, flashes of bright light reflecting off of the black, mirror finish of his face mask, continues to watch the resurrection process unfolding before him, the sounds of which resonate throughout the tomb. But another crackling sound is soon heard over this, coming from behind causing the demon to turn and look back at the source of this disturbance. He can see the tomb entrance down the corridor directly behind him, perhaps fifty feet away. The green glow of protection flickers as bolts of energy cascade along the surface. Although continuing to watch with mild interest, Karza does not appear to be worried by this sight, though he does acknowledge the cause as the tip of Jartan's soul blade slowly pierces the door.

"Paladin," he says with contempt.

Jartan is obviously struggling with the tenacity of the seal's power of resistance, as his hands are trembling violently, and pain shows on his face, increasing in intensity with every passing moment. With every ounce of strength he possesses, the youthful paladin manages only another few inches worth of penetration before he, like Morbius before, is overpowered and can fight the pain no longer. He is thrown violently back with a surge of energy to the ground, defeated and dejected—and again the impenetrable seal remains intact.

A pleased Karza, knowing full well that Jartan's attempt to breach the seal has failed, again turns to watch the resurrection process. The seven heads of the Council wizards have been consumed completely by the flame, leaving small piles of smoking ash on the poles. Only the sound of the still-beating heart of the phoenix is audible. Karza cautiously approaches the body of his father and watches it closely.

Slowly, the black, lifeless eye sockets on the skeletal head of Kordon begin to glow faintly and beat with energy as if they are matching the beat of the phoenix heart, and as the beats of the heart begin to weaken and diminish, Kordon's eyes only increase in power with each passing heartbeat. Soon the phoenix heart is drained completely, having transferred its resurrecting power into Kordon, and stops beating altogether. Although the wizard's body still retains its frightening skeletal appearance, his eyes now glow continuously bright red with immense power—and the greatest evil wizard that ever lived is alive once more. He slowly walks out of the sarcophagus in triumph and begins to laugh—softly at first and then quite loudly with evil delight as he becomes aware that the resurrection procedure was successful. Another maniacal laugh heralds the clenching of his bony fists, and a crescendo of energy erupts from them—energy so powerful that it causes the entire tomb to shudder violently, clearly demonstrating that his virtually unlimited wizardry powers of malevolence have returned. A pleased Karza quickly approaches and reverently kneels before the imposing figure of his father, who affectionately places a bony hand on the loyal son's shoulder.

"You have done well, my son. You have followed the instructions I left you in my testament perfectly. I trust you also did not kill Morbius as I instructed?"

"No, my father," says Karza, rising to his feet. "He is here—alive."

"Excellent. It is imperative that I be the one to kill him in order to make my vengeance complete."

"He has a paladin with him."

"So soon?" responds Kordon, obviously disturbed, after taking a moment to ponder this distressing news. "Are you certain, my son? I killed Morbius's paladin fifteen years ago. How many days have passed since you stole the Ring of Angels from him?"

"Seven days, my father—as you instructed."

"The paladinhood couldn't possibly have sent him a paladin in that time. How advanced is this paladin?"

"Novice—a child, in fact, but a strong one," Karza responds. "And I don't think the paladinhood sent him. I fought this maggot seven days ago, and he had no powers then."

"No monarch is given more than one paladin in a lifetime. Morbius must have been training him and accelerated his advancement once he found out what he was facing. No matter—not even the paladin master can stop me now."

Kordon, with his demonic offspring following, walks back toward the sarcophagus, and with a wave of his bony hand the stone coffin moves aside, which reveals an entrance to another, much larger room. Once inside, they both stand before a large stone circle located on the floor that contains a pool of blackish liquid, and with another wave of his hand, energy can be seen to swirl within the foul substance.

Outside of the tomb, where Morbius, Jartan, and the thousand or so surviving soldiers of Morbius's army still stand, the sky begins to darken with black, unnatural clouds. The low rumble of an ominous thunder sounds from what was, moments before, a cloudless and sunny sky. Morbius and the others can't help but notice this happening, and all are greatly disturbed by it, especially when the ground also begins to shudder slightly.

"No," says Morbius softly, though greatly concerned, as he is the only one who can comprehend the significance of this occurrence.

The dark clouds above begin to swirl, acting like a vortex, and Kordon's evil laugh is soon heard echoing throughout the area. Suddenly, the evil wizard's skeletal face, eyes glowing with power, appears in the vortex—much to the consternation of Morbius and all those present who witness the alarming sight.

"No!" Morbius again shouts upon seeing the malevolent image above. He realizes that this infernal being and onetime implacable enemy has truly arisen from the grave.

"Not pleased to see me, my king?" replies Kordon with an odious chuckle.

Morbius swiftly fires a powerful ball of fire from his outstretched hand at the monstrous image of Kordon overhead. Inside the tomb, the fireball emerges from the energy pool on the floor to impact against Kordon's body. Surprisingly, he makes no effort to evade or deflect it, which he has ample time to do, but instead nonchalantly stands unconcerned to await its impact—but to Morbius's horror, no explosion of flame is seen as the fireball detonates against the wizard's body and fades away.

"Oh dear, we are upset, aren't we?" chortles the evil Kordon with condescension. "By the way, I am immune from all fire spells now. A convenient skill I mastered to keep my soul from being incinerated in the seven hells that you and your wizard assassins sent me to. But it distresses me that you are not happy to see your old friend for I am greatly pleased to see you, especially since you were so kind as to save me the trouble of hunting you down like the treacherous snake you are."

Again, the highly upset Morbius attacks with an incredibly intense discharge of lightning from both outstretched arms, as if the sight of Kordon has replenished his weakened body with untapped power— power of hate. The energy again erupts from the energy pool within the tomb only to be absorbed effortlessly by a single skeletal hand raised by Kordon, which prevents any injury. Morbius, Jartan, and all who witness this are horrified at the evil wizard's power. He laughs mockingly.

"Fireballs?" says Kordon. "And now lightning? That is hardly a fitting gift to give your old friend on his new day of birth. However, it is the perfect gift for you, Morbius—on your day of death—because I am going to kill you now, my friend—and it will be your corpse that rots on this miserable mountain for all eternity!"

Kordon, with an even more chilling and maniacal laugh, raises his hands toward the energy pool. They begin to glow brightly, and suddenly they unleash a torrent of lightning bolts of incredible power into the swirling energy cloud at the evil wizard's feet. Outside the tomb, the clouds in the sky spectacularly electrify with intense energy as massive waves of lightning bolts streak from the sky toward the ground. The bolts of lightning fall like rain, forcing Morbius to quickly erect an energy shield to protect himself from the strikes, and Jartan also uses his soul blade to deflect those that descend onto him—but the soldiers in Morbius's army, having no special powers or weapons, are easy prey to the electrical onslaught, and they all are instantly slaughtered. Jartan is also having difficulty evading such a huge number of strikes, but amid the chaos he manages to see a small opening under a large formation of boulders nearby and rushes toward it, struggling to reach its protection as lightning strike after strike hits the ground, creating large explosions of dust and debris; but soon the agile boy dives for cover beneath the rocks, which afford him much-needed protection from the relentless electrical storm—and also conceal his presence from the evil eyes of Kordon still menacing from above.

Kordon is greatly enjoying the carnage he is causing and continues to fire blistering bolts of lightning from his hands into the energy cloud as Morbius, faced with such a ferocious attack, can only use his formidable magic in a desperate attempt to repel the lethal bolts with his energy shield. Seeing that Morbius is the only one left, Kordon ceases the attack.

"And now, my dear old friend and former monarch," the wizard begins with an evil smile, "you die."

He again laughs maniacally while Karza's eyes smile with delight by his side. Kordon again blasts away with energy at Morbius, but this attack is far greater in intensity, as the good king is the lone survivor below and therefore the sole recipient of Kordon's wrath. Morbius tries valiantly to resist, but soon the effort of his magical defense becomes too much, and he begins to strain terribly under the attack as Kordon's far more powerful magical bolts inch ever closer to Morbius's body.

Jartan can see Morbius's plight from his position, and since Kordon's wrathful magic is being directed only against his king, Jartan is free to leave the protection of the location and rushes over to help him.

"Sire!" he laments loudly with great concern.

But even the noble and mighty magic of Morbius cannot resist the power of a wizard who possesses a far greater level of pure malevolent power, and Morbius screams in agony as Kordon's energy overcomes his defense and hits his body, causing massive damage. Jartan is at his side, though it is too late to offer assistance. Holding the smoldering body of his king, still barely clinging to life, Jartan lays him gently to the ground.

Kordon sees the boy.

"And this is the child paladin you told me about?" he asks his son. Karza nods.

Kordon laughs. "The paladinhood must be desperate. So be it." And Kordon fires once again at the image of Jartan in the cloud of energy beneath him.

Jartan quickly notices the sky beginning to electrify again and raises his soul blade just in time to protect himself from Kordon's attack. He struggles from the impacts against the blade, but it does absorb the energy, preventing the boy any injury. Morbius struggles to speak as this is happening, and reaching up to touch Jartan with a trembling hand, he says weakly,

"Jartan, use his energy against him—like I showed you."

Jartan, after pausing momentarily to reflect on this, retaliates, and an equal number of blistering bolts of energy erupt forth from the soul blade back into the image of Kordon in the clouds overhead.

As Kordon watches from the tomb, Jartan's counterattack comes up through the energy cloud on the floor, and now it is the evil wizard who screams in agony as the bolts hit his body, which sends him hurtling back with great force. Karza, shocked at the sight of his father smoldering on the floor beside him, has now had sufficient enough time to regain his full transformation strength; and since the room he is now in is far larger than the one before, he has the space to immediately transform into his most powerful form—the dreaded tridragon—and launches his own lethal counterattack into the energy cloud at Jartan. However, not wishing to receive an electrical counterattack from the boy, only the fire and freezing heads attack while the center one watches patiently for its chance to strike.

Outside, Jartan does his best to resist. He initially is able to deflect the oncoming salvoes of fire and freezing vapor, but they quickly begin to overpower him. As he tries to evade the blasts, a near miss causes a large explosion that separates Jartan from his soul blade, and seeing a chance to finally obliterate the boy now that he cannot absorb the energy, the center dragon head instantly discharges its lethal ray. Jartan manages to call out to the blade, which reaches his hand just in time to absorb the lightning bolt heading toward him, and again the paladin redirects the energy in the blade back at the sight of the tridragon above. But an adept Karza transforms into the ethereal phantasm, and the bolt harmlessly passes through the form and impacts against the ceiling of the tomb, sending large chunks of stone cascading downward. The impasse between the tenacious paladin and the disgusted demon over (disgusted because this insignificant child still remains annoyingly alive), Karza transforms back to demon prince form to try to aid his smoldering father while Jartan once again goes to tend to the severely wounded Morbius.

"Sire!" he shouts upon seeing the twisted form of Morbius lying half-dead.

He stumbles over to him, as he still is exhausted from the attack. His body shows a few signs of injuries of various degrees of severity but nothing life-threatening, though he does crawl the last few feet to reach Morbius's side. Morbius is lying on his stomach, his bloody body still smoldering slightly, and as Jartan gently turns him over, he sees a sickening number of mortal wounds. Morbius is obviously near death and again struggles to speak.

"Jartan—find my brother—Modex—give him this." Morbius gestures to the necklace he is wearing, and Jartan gently removes it. The once-mighty monarch is in great pain, and talking is obviously requiring a great effort. He manages to continue:

"Go east—to the Undead Forest. You'll find him there. Tell him— tell him—"

"What do I tell him, Sire?" says Jartan, greatly in despair over Morbius's condition and the fact that he can do absolutely nothing to help him or ease his terrible suffering. Morbius almost passes out, but Jartan's urgings force him to remain conscious for a moment. "King Morbius!" Jartan cries. "What do I tell your brother?"

Morbius, the life force ebbing within, says softly, almost in a whisper, "Kordon lives."

Meanwhile, Karza is bending over the wounded Kordon and trying to get him to his feet, but the wizard refuses his help and pushes him aside and then uses his magic to heal the smoldering injury Jartan inflicted.

Kordon is livid and immediately returns to stand before the energy pool, which shows Jartan kneeling by Morbius. Kordon's eyeless sockets burn bright with hatred. Jartan's soul blade flashes violently to alert him of the threat forming above. Gazing skyward, Jartan notices this and can see the huge face of Kordon frowning with a look of determined hatred. Frantically, he tries to move Morbius out of harm's way.

"I must get you out of here!" cries the frantic Jartan as he drags Morbius's body away.

"Join your king in death, boy!" shouts an irate Kordon as his eyes fire into the cloud with a blast of energy.

The paladin's soul blade flashes even more urgently when Kordon's attack emerges from the cloud overhead, forcing Jartan to grasp the blade tightly in defense. He quickly erects an energy shield. This protects Jartan but does nothing to prevent Kordon's merciless wrath directed against Morbius's body. The resulting explosion is tremendous and instantly engulfs all in its wake, and when the smoke clears, there is nothing but a seething crater where Morbius and Jartan once stood.

"So much for Morbius and his pathetic paladin," Kordon announces triumphantly. "And now we finish what I started fifteen years ago. Come, my son."

Kordon waves his hand and magically summons an energy portal, which he and Karza walk into and disappear. Entering anything the Ring of Angels is protecting is impossible without the ring, but leaving its protective seal is easily within the powers of Kordon's magic.

Within the crater, Jartan slowly emerges, covered with earth. His wounds are deep, and it's a miracle the boy is alive at all. If it weren't for the fact that his shield saved his life and that Kordon's wrath was directed at Morbius, he would be dead. As for Morbius, the amount of gore that litters the area reveals the painful truth that the noble monarch is dead, his tortured remains lying nearby.

Jartan, with the once mighty and regal but now twisted and bloody body of his sovereign lord in his arms, sits there impassively, for he has never felt a loss quite like this before—even when his beloved snow wolf, Loba, passed. But soon the thoughts of a man flood his memory—a man who held the infant Jartan in his strong and loving arms some fifteen years ago and has been holding him ever since. A man who was far more than a person he admired and respected, a man who was more than a king, a teacher, a friend. This was a man whom he loved dearly.

Jartan doesn't know how much time has passed as he places the last stone on Morbius's grave, but his face, damp with tears, gives him some indication that it must have been a lot. As he stands silently before the grave, each rock placed with tender care, he notices the magnificent sunset and spectacular view that can be witnessed from high atop Mount Sabo. *A fitting eternal resting place for one as great as Morbius,* he thinks. Looking back down at the grave, he says somberly, "Good-bye, my king—and my friend."

Jartan sees his soul blade lying on the ground half-covered by dirt. He picks it up and dusts it off and sheathes it in its scabbard, and with a face of grim determination, he adds,

"I will avenge you. I swear it!"

CHAPTER 13

✝ ✝ ✝

Swamps, even under the best of circumstances, are still not very far removed from the way they are under the worst of circumstances, and this particular swamp is about as nasty and unpleasant as one can ever be, thinks Jartan as he struggles through it—a thought that has plagued the boy for many hours now. It's not the malodorous stench of the putrid water he finds difficult to endure or the oppressive humidity that hangs in the air like a lead weight. It's not even those pesky swamp pixies that he finally got away from only an hour ago, though Jartan did learn a valuable lesson in that if you want to make friends with swamp pixies, relieving yourself on their royal palace is definitely *not* the way to do it. It was an honest mistake, for swamp pixies are tiny, ant-sized creatures and Jartan just wasn't aware that they were in the immediate vicinity until he noticed the river of yellowish liquid that he was innocently discharging was carrying the imperial structure into the waters of the swamp, where it quickly sank. No, not even this was the worst thing about the swamp.

The worst thing is the incessant buzzing, clicking, whining, and—most irritatingly—biting presence of a bewildering variety of annoying insects, which is getting on his nerves and slowly driving him insane. Often, one will land on him in hopes of making a quick meal, but Jartan ends these attempts with a swift movement of his hand, often adding, "Blood-sucking bastard!" and thereafter flicking the remains off his skin with a finger. Also unsettling are the sounds of the larger and more dangerous denizens of the swamp that get his attention—vicious creatures like swamp dragons and marsh men and an unnerving many others that inhabit the swamplands. These are what Jartan thinks of as the unseen creatures growl and hiss as he wades through the hip-deep muck, constantly turning and anxiously looking around to see if any are stalking him, though mercifully none consider the boy large enough to make a sufficient meal to warrant their interest.

Another nip by an insect prompts Jartan to end its irritating existence, but what was once an annoying nuisance is now becoming a grave concern, for the insect attack increases in its intensity—and quite alarmingly so. The occasional swat here and there will not do against a swarm of this magnitude, for a veritable cloud of these bugs is descending upon him, prompting Jartan to use his soul blade to send out a series of blinding flashes in every direction.

"Let's see you bite what you can't see!" says the paladin to his infuriating miniscule tormenters.

The blinding defense is successful and drives off the marauding swarm.

The injuries he received during his ordeal on Mount Sabo several days ago have mostly healed, thanks to some fortuitous healing fruits encountered during his travels before entering the swamp. As Jartan continues sojourning through the muck, he catches a flash of color out of the corner of his eye, and upon closer examination he sees that it is a very attractive flower. *Finally—a thing of beauty,* he thinks, in the otherwise dismal and depressing mire of this odious swamp. He reaches to touch the delicate petals in admiration of the pretty blossom—but the petals close on his finger with a painful snap, forcing Jartan to withdraw it immediately.

"Damn it!" he exclaims, frustrated. "Even the flowers are vicious!"

He decides to use a blinding flash on the malignant weed, knowing full well the act is useless—there being no eyes on the flower to blind—but the act does make him feel better, and he continues on once again.

Hours of this horrendous traveling have made him exhausted, and he stops momentarily for a rest. As Jartan catches his breath beneath a large tree, a white, gooey substance drops on his head and drips down his face. The boy can feel this and reaches to touch it, but when he sees what is on his hand, he is disgusted. Looking upward to find the source of this gooey unpleasantness, he can see a bird directly overhead chirping gleefully. Jartan looks at his soul blade and addresses it sarcastically.

"I thought you were supposed to warn me of danger."

He washes the avian excrement off of his face and continues on his way, but no sooner does he take a few steps than a similar thing happens to him again. Jartan responds to this with a defeatist tone:

"Not again."

The soul blade he is still holding begins to flash, but Jartan, upon seeing this, doesn't acknowledge the warning, thinking it is just another nonthreatening insult from yet another feathered fiend.

"Oh, now you tell me!" he says mockingly to the soul blade, still oblivious to any danger.

Jartan begins to wash it off, but he soon realizes with shock that this substance is red in color—blood—and he looks up instantly with great concern. In the tree above is a large, catlike beast that is eating some swamp creature it has recently killed, evidenced by the drops of blood that continue to fall. The cat growls menacingly and leaps upon Jartan, but he reacts swiftly and slashes the creature as it passes, slicing it into two halves. With a sigh of relief and a grateful glance at his soul blade, he adds,

"That was close. I won't doubt you again, my friend."

He again heads off through the bleakness of the swamp, unaware that behind him a huge mouth lined with dozens of razor-sharp teeth swallows whole one of the sections of the cat creature that was floating in the blood-stained waters. As Jartan continues blissfully on, he is still oblivious to this new threat—which, judging by the ripples in the water is creeping toward him underneath the surface and rapidly overtaking the boy. The ever-vigilant soul blade flashes a warning, and this causes Jartan to immediately stop to ascertain the source of the danger. Seeing nothing immediately before him, he turns quickly to face what is behind but again sees nothing. A deceptive trick, for slowly and silently emerging from the water behind the confused youth is a hideous and alarmingly huge swamp worm with its razor-sharp teeth dripping drool, but Jartan fortunately notices its reflection in the mirror finish of the soul blade and quickly turns to face it. Upon seeing the monstrous worm, he instantly fires a blinding flash with his soul blade, but this has no effect, for this creature has no eyes and hunts by sound—not sight. The worm strikes and Jartan barely manages to avoid the snapping teeth, although the attack does knock his soul blade from his hand. It disappears into the murky depths of the swamp. Jartan tries frantically to look for it, but the creature, reappearing nearby, makes him quicken his search. Unable to find the weapon, he remembers he can call to it.

"Soul blade!"

The blade erupts from the water, and Jartan grabs it in time to deliver a slash to the swamp worm, creating a large wound. Much to his dismay, the wound heals, forcing the startled youth to rush away from the creature in a panic. The creature discharges a blast of foul, greenish liquid at the retreating paladin, who barely manages to evade its contact, and the noxious liquid hits a tree near him. The tree begins to smoke intensely as the acid eats away at it, giving Jartan an even greater incentive to keep retreating as fast as he can.

He soon finds himself surrounded by dense vegetation, deeper water, and impassible trees with no escape. Hacking through with his soul bade would simply take far too long. The blade flashes, causing the harried teen to look anxiously back to see that looming out of the water nearby is the swamp worm closing in for the kill. But the clever paladin is aware by now that this creature hunts by sound, so he braces himself between two large trees and stays perfectly still and silent, hoping the lethal predator will think its intended human prey has escaped.

The worm enters the enclosed area and Jartan's plan appears to be working, for the worm is unable to locate him who is only a disturbingly few feet away—close enough to touch, in fact. But unfortunately for the anxious youth, the area he has wedged himself into is occupied by a nest of fire ants which do not take kindly to his presence. The nest launches a concerted attack to repel the human and begin to swarm all over his body and bite viciously. The boy's clothing manages to provide some protection from the bites but his unprotected hands and face are another matter, especially once the acidic sting of the ants begin to take their toll for each sting feels like a flaming pin being jabbed into the skin. Jartan's anxiety increases as he struggles not to move or utter a sound amid this painful invasion beginning to cover his body for it would instantly alert the worm to his presence.

Jartan's eyes squint tightly as a layer of fire ants now encroach upon his face but the boy does notice a large, dead tree near him and since he cannot resist the agony of the ant bites and stings any longer he rushes toward it. The sound of his movement instantly causes the swamp worm to blast the area with acid, but Jartan is able to dive beneath the water to avoid it, and surfacing beside the dead tree he uses his weapon to make a deep gash into its trunk which sends the massive weight to fall upon the swamp worm killing it.

After several more hours of thankfully peaceful travel, Jartan finally exits the swamp and walks on dry land. Looking back, he reflects for a moment on the perils of his recent trek and says with a sigh of hope,

"At least nothing could be worse than that nightmare," but he quickly begins to see the error in that logic prompting him to add with a discouraged tone, "Then again, maybe not."

For before him now is a dark, misty area containing bizarre and eerie trees—almost sinister in appearance as their deformed trunks and twisted branches loom menacingly. On the ground are several corpses of animals—and even the remains of an unfortunate human traveler. Jartan, curious at this macabre sight, kneels beside the corpse to study it more closely and is puzzled to see that the skin on the body is pale in color, leathery, and severely wrinkled.

"That's odd," Jartan observes. "It's as if all the blood has been drained out."

As he continues to study the emaciated body, a leaf gently falls upon his neck from the tree directly beside him, but the contact is far from gentle. Sharp pain causes Jartan to jump up suddenly, quickly ripping the leaf off of his neck—which reveals a small, bleeding wound. When he sees that it is just a throbbing leaf in his hand, he realizes with horror what it is.

"Vampire trees!" shouts the horrified Jartan.

More leaves begin to fall and attach themselves to Jartan's body as he tries vainly to bat them away, but the leaves themselves are extremely light, like feathers, and his attempts only succeed in brushing them aside in the air without effect. He then rushes over to the vampire tree closest to him and slashes away at its trunk with his soul blade. Bloody sap oozes out of the gashes the blade makes, but the tree is far too dense and large for it to do much damage. It does, however, unleash an alarming number of leaves in an effort to defend itself, and more and more leaves attach to Jartan's body with painful results. He removes as many as he can, and as he does so, the small wounds caused by the leaves' sucking are revealed. The frantic youth slashes away at those that continue to rain down upon him with his soul blade, but the act is about as effective as using a large stick against a swarm of mosquitoes.

Realizing the futility of his efforts, Jartan runs off in an attempt to get out of their way, but to Jartan's utter horror he can see the leaves are floating after him at a greater speed than he can flee. More leaves attach, and Jartan is quickly becoming overwhelmed by their vast number, and he soon falls to the ground and loses the grip on his soul blade. He desperately tries to call out to it, but dozens of the dreaded leaves smother his face before he can utter a sound, and only the muffled moaning of intense pain can be heard.

A forest elf named Skon fortunately appears from out of the brush, and seeing the writhing pile of blood-sucking leaves obviously gets the good elf's attention. Sensing the trouble, he rushes over to Jartan. Skon uses the flaming torch he is carrying to drive away the leaves floating about, but this provides only a stopgap measure, for the air is practically filled with the dreaded leaves, which begin to attack the elf. Skon takes his bow off his back and pulls back the string, which magically creates a flaming arrow in the bow, and he fires it off toward a vampire tree in the distance. The arrow hits, and the tree instantly erupts in flame. Skon fires off more arrows at more trees, causing them to burst into flame too, and soon the leaves mercifully begin to stop coming. Taking advantage of the respite, he then takes a bottle of liquid from a pouch he is carrying and pours its contents over Jartan's body. As the liquid cascades over the boy, the leaves still attached shrivel up, and Skon easily scrapes them off of the body.

"What kind of idiot travels through the Fens of Despair alone?" says Skon, gently admonishing the severely wounded victim. "Even for a human that's pretty stupid, kid."

Jartan is indeed in a dire state, for his face and arms are ghostly pale and dotted with dozens of red bite marks from the vicious attack of the vampire leaves. If anyone weighed the boy, he would easily be around twenty pounds lighter from the immense blood loss, and his body shows it, for it is almost wraithlike in appearance. Skon struggles to keep Jartan upright in order to get him to drink the liquid he rapidly brings to the boy's lips. Jartan struggles to speak.

"I—I must—"

"Easy, don't talk. You've lost a lot of blood, my friend. Another ten seconds, and you would have been a goner. Here, drink this. It will give you strength."

The elf holds Jartan's head tenderly to give the boy the ability to consume the liquid and then whistles loudly. Soon two of Skon's elf companions—obviously summoned by his whistling signal—come into view.

"Take him. We've got to get out of here before any other foul creatures of the fens appear."

The two elves carry the almost comatose Jartan away. Skon quickly starts to follow but stops when a faint twinkle catches his eye. Bending over toward the source, he brushes away some dead leaves fully revealing Jartan's soul blade lying on the ground.

"Well, what do we have here?" he says cheerfully at this newly found treasure, for a soul blade is indeed an attractive object. "You'll sure fetch a tidy sum when I sell you."

But as he reaches to pick it up, the blade gives him a nasty shock, and he drops it instantly. Skon shakes his hand violently in reaction to the soul blade's painful warning.

"Son of an ogre bitch!" he exclaims angrily, and then, realizing what it is now, he adds respectfully with a smile,

"So you're a soul blade, are you?" Skon then looks back at his two companions carrying the helpless Jartan and addresses the soul blade with a quizzical look, saying,

"That teenaged trash is a paladin? You sure were scraping the bottom of the paladin barrel getting that one. Very well, bright one, I won't sell you, but with your permission I shall return you to your"—again he glances at Jartan while shaking his head in a gesture of disbelief—"paladin master. Agreed?"

The blade flashes in agreement, so Skon again goes to pick up the blade, though he is a bit more hesitant this time; and eyeing the blade warily in his hands, he adds,

"Has anyone ever told you that you have an attitude problem?"

CHAPTER 14

✛ ✛ ✛

Lying on a cot within a primitive but cozy hut and wearing a big smile on his face, Jartan is thoroughly enjoying being tended to by a young elf beauty about seventeen years old. Forest elves are very much like humans except for a slightly green skin tone and pointed ears, but the female elves of this race in particular have a very alluring quality about them that has the human teenage boy barely aware of his surroundings and focused totally on this elf girl. A small dog is also there in the hut with them, happily watching the two as the girl carefully removes some chest bandages from Jartan's bare-chested body, revealing the dozens of small, red wounds inflicted by the dreaded vampire leaves the previous day. She begins to pour a liquid on Jartan's chest, and as she massages the liquid into his skin, the red wounds magically disappear within seconds. Jartan doesn't say a word while she does this, but the gleam in his eye and his mischievous grin indicate he is certainly enjoying her touch. But he actually enjoys the fact that he has this beautiful creature at his disposal in the first place, and at his age, he is going to see just how far he can exploit the situation.

"That feels wonderful," he says with a sly grin—but he only gets a tolerant smile back from the girl in response.

The elf Skon enters the hut carrying a small bundle tucked beneath one arm but stops at the entrance when he sees and hears that Jartan is trying to flirt with the girl. He smiles while shaking his head at the silly boy's youthful and therefore rather clumsily obvious attempt at seduction.

"Lower," Jartan advises the girl as she continues her nursing duties. His grin gets even bigger.

"You aren't injured there," replies the girl with an understanding smile, for she knows all too well what is going on here.

It is becoming embarrassing for Skon to continue to watch this pathetic teenage seduction, and he decides now is the time to make his presence known lest Jartan make a further fool of himself.

"Well, paladin," says Skon as he walks into the hut, "it is obvious that you are feeling much better today."

"I have an excellent nurse—and a very pretty one too," Jartan responds as he again flashes a broad smile at the girl along with a wink. The girl smiles back at him.

"I see," replies Skon. "But take care, my young friend, for a paladin must be pure in both spirit *and body.*"

This news has a markedly disturbing impact on the young Jartan, and his smile quickly vanishes as he gets the demoralizing gist of what Skon is hinting at.

"You mean I can never—?" he inquires, slightly alarmed and looking at the elf girl as if a highly sought-after treasure has suddenly disappeared just when it was within a hair's width of his grasp.

Skon shakes his head with amusement, causing Jartan to add solemnly,

"No wonder there are so few of us."

Skon laughs heartily. "Here." He tosses Jartan the bundle he is carrying, which the boy catches and unfolds to reveal his shirt. "We've removed the blood and repaired it. I'm sure you will be wanting to put your shirt back on." Looking at the two youths, he adds with a smile, "Since any further activities you may have planned with it off are no longer an option."

The two teens look at each other smiling, understanding Skon's implication.

"Come, paladin," Skon continues. "You must be hungry after your ordeal."

Jartan dresses and follows Skon outside with the small dog happily following. It is now clear that Jartan has been taken to Skon's elf village to recover from his injuries. As they walk among the village, they can see all its various residents milling about performing their daily duties—vendors selling fruits (Skon kindly tosses a fruit to Jartan to eat), children running and playing about—all the typical sights, sounds, and smells of a happy, peace-loving, good people. But this serene scene is soon broken when, unobserved by everyone present, a blur of movement swoops in and carries the small dog off silently into a tree, where the unfortunate animal is quickly devoured with one swift gulp by the assassin—a devil hawk. With its formidable talons; feathers gray in color and seemingly made out of metal; black, lifeless eyes; and a face not even its mother could love, the devil hawk is obviously a creature of evil. The speed and stealth of its movements are such that no one is even aware of its presence, especially once it regains its perch high in the branches of the tree, as its feathers change color to match the leafy environment, almost perfectly camouflaged. From its vantage point in the treetop, it continues its stealthy surveillance of the situation below. Skon and Jartan continue talking as they move beneath it—the devil hawk watching them intently.

"How did you know I was a paladin?" asks Jartan.

"Who else would wield a mighty soul blade?" replies Skon, gesturing to the prized blade located on a table nearby. Jartan eagerly picks it up—but as he does so, the blade begins to flash.

"There's an evil presence here!" announces Jartan, alarmed.

"What?" replies Skon, sharing the boy's concern. "But I had my ex-wife banned from the village."

"It's not your ex-wife!" scolds Jartan, not sharing the elf's dry sense of humor.

The two look around cautiously, but no threat is readily apparent, prompting Jartan to ask the blade, "Where is this evil?" As the blade guides Jartan's hand to point upward to the tree, he and Skon scan the tree's branches intently for the evil threat—but the concealing camouflage of the devil hawk is so effective that they cannot see it.

"There's nothing there," says Jartan, confused. "I don't understand it."

"I think I do," responds the elf, his brow slanted with anger.

Skon removes a small vial of purplish liquid from inside his clothing and heaves it skyward at the tree. When the glass breaks upon hitting a branch, a foul cloud of toxic vapor erupts, engulfing a large section of the tree. The cloud of poison is obviously meant to irritate whatever it comes in contact with, which disturbs the hidden devil hawk and forces the creature to fade out of its cloaking camouflage and become its usual gray color. The creature hisses menacingly now that it has been discovered.

"Stand back, paladin!" shouts Skon.

Quickly removing the bow from his back, Skon once again summons a flaming arrow to the string as the devil hawk begins to swoop down with its imposing talons bared to strike. Skon looses the flaming arrow before it can attack, and the evil creature is instantly impaled against the trunk of the tree and begins to burn. It soon disappears in a puff of smoke.

"What was that thing, Skon?" Jartan asks.

"A devil hawk—disgusting creatures. Legend has it they were created by some evil wizard of great power long ago to act as his infernal spies—they've been buzzing around here all day. It's odd, because there hasn't been a devil hawk around for more than ten years. It's as if they've been reawakened somehow."

Jartan, after the past few days' experiences, has a good idea who that evil wizard might be and why these minions of his have been revived, though he keeps this knowledge to himself.

The two continue walking through the village, and after a few moments Jartan says,

"Thanks for my soul blade, Skon. I thought I had lost it and would have to go back into the fens to find it because I was too far away here to summon it into my hands. You've done much to help me. I am grateful. But now I must continue on my quest."

"I gathered as much. No human would travel the vast distance you must have done in order to commit suicide by vampire trees. What is it you seek, paladin?"

"Modex. He's the brother of—"

Skon immediately stops walking and stares at Jartan with a look of great trepidation on his face.

"The wizard Modex?" he asks hesitantly.

"You know of him?" Jartan happily and eagerly responds. "Skon, where is he? It's important I find him as soon as possible."

"Find him? Were you sent to kill him? I hope."

"Kill him?" replies Jartan, utterly confused by Skon's surprising answer. "Of course not! He's a friend."

"If that twisted fiend is a friend of yours, boy, then you are no friend of ours."

"What are you taking about? Skon, where is he?"

"Modex lives in a castle on the edge of the Undead Forest about two days' journey from here. But you're a fool to go there."

"Why?" asks Jartan, again puzzled by the elf's surprising comment.

"Because no one lives for long once they see Modex. He will kill you for sure, paladin—he's evil."

"But that can't be!" remarks an astounded Jartan. "He's the brother of King Morbius! He couldn't possibly be evil. There must be some mistake."

"The mistake is yours, Jartan, and it will be your last."

"But that's crazy. What makes you think Modex is evil, Skon? You must have a reason."

"Oh, I have a very good reason! We forest elves are adept at the creation of potions, but about fifteen years ago the former leader of our village had a curse placed on him by a mountain witch—a curse that no potion could remove. We sent several dozen of our warriors to appeal to this Modex for help, because at that time we were unaware of his true nature and only knew that a powerful wizard was near and thought perhaps his magic could remove the curse. Only one returned and just managed to live long enough to tell what happened. Modex slaughtered the party seeking his friendship—and then put their corpses to rot upon the stake as a grisly warning to those foolish enough to dare to seek his nonexistent compassion and as a reminder of his merciless evil. If you want my advice, you'll go back where you came from and forget all about trying to see that butchering maniac."

"I still can't believe we are talking about the same person. Not a sibling of a good man like King Morbius! No, it has to be some terrible mistake. Look, it is urgent that I talk to him, Skon. I promised my king. Can you take me to him?"

"Take you to that warped wizard?" responds the elf, thoroughly appalled at Jartan's suggestion as his voice quavers with disgust at the thought. "Not I—I've lost enough of my people at the hands of that madman. Besides, the Undead Forest is home to the undead warriors—an evil race and implacable enemies to my people, the forest elves—and we try and avoid the place if at all possible. If I knew this Modex of yours was the evil monster he was, I never would have sent my people through the Undead Forest in the first place. But the river can take you there, and you are welcome to use one of our boats. Just follow the river downstream. But I appeal to you one last time, Jartan—you are committing suicide if you try and see that man."

"It is something I must do, Skon."

They are now at the river's edge, and a boat is visible tied to the dock. Jartan takes Skon's hand in his.

"Thanks, Skon, for everything."

"Wait, paladin—if you truly are hell-bent on going there, then you had better take these with you." Skon hands Jartan two small vials of liquid—one red, the other blue. "The red one is a cure for poison. You may find it useful, for they don't call this the 'River of Pain' for nothing. But the blue one you will definitely need if you manage to reach the 'Falls of Death' other than as a floating corpse."

"What do I do with it when I get there?"

"Don't worry," responds Skon with a chuckle. "You will know what to do. I wish you the luck of the gods, my foolish young friend. Be careful."

"I will be. Thanks again, Skon."

Jartan gets in the boat and paddles off, and after a few moments Skon shouts to him,

"And paladin, beware of vampire trees!" He then adds jokingly, "And especially women!"

Jartan waves back with an understanding smile at the elf's humor and is soon far down the river. Skon continues to watch his youthful friend, but now that Jartan is almost out of sight, the elf shakes his head in disbelief that any sane being would willingly carry on with a journey that is sure to end in total disaster.

"Humans!" he scoffs to himself. "What a silly race—beats me how they ever survived this long. Oh well."

Skon turns to head back to the village—and is instantly greeted by the horrific sight of the wizard Kordon inches away. Skon stumbles as he backs off in a state of absolute terror, but this terror actually increases when he almost backs into Karza. Kordon is just a black-robed, walking skeleton, but even so his presence inspires tremendous fear—but Karza is a demon prince, and his presence is of such a chillingly evil nature that it actually creates a thin layer of frost on Skon's skin. Skon is a forest elf, a race that is naturally sensitive. The terror-stricken elf shudders, and he scrapes the layer off as Karza walks past him toward the river's edge.

"What—what do you want?" Skon says, his voice trembling.

"You killed one of my pet devil hawks, elf," Kordon replies. "That touches me."

Karza slowly walks to the edge of the river where Jartan only moments before departed. Looking out, he can barely make out a person floating on the water in the distance. Karza transforms into the demon creature with the one large eye, and in this form he can once again see great distances. The vision that greets him this time is Jartan rowing down the river.

"Well?" inquires Kordon, prompting Karza to transform back into demon prince form to answer.

"It's that boy paladin again, my father."

"Interesting," replies the evil wizard impassively though with a tinge of concern. "Kill him."

Karza transforms into his muscular titan demon and lumbers over to a very large boulder located nearby—a boulder almost as large as the forty-foot demonic colossus itself—and picks it up with its huge hands almost effortlessly and, with a mighty thrust, hurls it downstream in an impossibly high arc.

As Jartan continues to row downstream blissfully unaware, a rapidly growing shadow covers him and the soul blade begins to flash violently. The youth swiftly drops his paddle to obtain the blade and begins to realize that this shadow must be the cause. With a look behind and skyward, he sees the huge boulder descending upon him from above.

"By the gods!" gasps Jartan, alarmed by this unexpected and certainly unwanted sight. He points the soul blade at the boulder as if expecting to fire off energy at it, but the blade does nothing.

"I can't destroy it! I don't have any offensive energy yet! But maybe I can repel it with my shield." Jartan holds the blade in front of him, and it glows brightly. Although he is trying to repel the boulder, it is far too massive for his novice power to even slow its progress—but the boulder's momentum actually propels the boat. The craft quickly speeds along out of harm's way, and the boulder falls harmlessly into the water with a tremendous splash, drenching the boy in the process and almost capsizing the boat.

Karza is back in the form of his one-eyed demon in order to observe the result of the boulder's impact and is disturbed upon seeing his attack fail. Kordon, aware of this failure as well, orders his son to continue.

"Again," commands Kordon, and once again Karza transforms into the demonic titan and hurls a large boulder at the human speck in the distance.

But this time Kordon quickly raises a bony hand and discharges a powerful lightning bolt that hits the rocky target, which causes it to explode spectacularly into hundreds of fragments. Using his dark magic skills, Kordon with a wave of his skeletal hand transforms the boulder fragments into gleaming daggers, creating a swarm of lethal missiles. A further gesture causes the daggers to glow, indicating they are now magically empowered and far from normal.

Jartan, still alert to any incoming dangers thanks to his soul blade's warning, can see the deadly daggers coming at him, their glowing metallic surfaces reflecting the sunlight. He realizes there is no way he can repel so many, as their numbers have created a blanket of death that blots out a large portion of the sky; nor is their mass enough for him to propel the boat out of range as he did with the first attack. His only defense is his energy shield, which he quickly erects by presenting the soul blade before him. But this shield—much to Jartan's surprise—covers the entire boat like an umbrella all the way down to the waterline. The magic daggers explode upon impact with both shield and water like miniature grenades, and due to their sheer numbers, their explosions are easily sufficient to destroy a boy and his small boat—except that the boy in question is a paladin. Jartan and boat emerge from the attack unscathed, and the youth floats out of sight behind a rocky outcropping along the riverbank to safety, completely unaware of where these attacks were coming from—or why.

Karza, again in the one-eyed demon form to observe the result, transforms into his humanoid form. Kordon patiently looks at him, awaiting the result of these attacks, but Karza's response is just as silent, and he just shakes his head, clearly indicating the attacks have failed.

"I foresee this paladin may become a minor problem," observes the evil wizard with a tone of irritation as he approaches Skon. "Where is the boy going, elf?"

But Skon, with fear still resonating in his voice, is reluctant to respond, for he certainly has no desire to betray Jartan.

"I—I do not know."

"No?" replies Kordon with a menacing grin on his skeletal face. "Then I shall help you increase your knowledge."

With a glowing hand raised toward the elf, the evil wizard blasts Skon with a painful electrical charge, causing the poor victim to scream in agony and fall to his knees. Content that Skon has learned his lesson, Kordon continues, "How about now?"

Skon, his body smoldering slightly and obviously in great pain from Kordon's attack, struggles to speak.

"He's heading for the Undead Forest!"

"Why?" asks Kordon.

Again the brave Skon, not wanting to betray his young paladin friend, is reluctant to answer—so again the impatient Kordon blasts him. Noble bravery makes a poor shield against such incredible pain, so Skon is quickly forced to answer.

"To find the wizard Modex!"

This distressing response causes Kordon to stop blasting Skon, who collapses to the ground from the attack, breathing heavily and moaning.

"Modex," Kordon says as he ponders the elf's answer. "So my old apprentice still lives."

"Why do you think this paladin wants him?" asks Karza.

"Morbius must have told him to find him. As my apprentice, he knows where the spell I use to reach the Underworld is located."

"Will he try and stop us?"

"Modex's commitment to evil was never strong. After fifteen years, he may have changed, so he might help this boy—then again, he may kill him. We cannot take any chances, however."

"Then are we going after the paladin, my father?"

"No," replies Kordon, "we don't have time. My magic can only keep us on the Surface for a short while. We must return to the Underworld soon. Karza, who is the master of the Undead Forest?"

"Zorm—leader of the undead warriors."

"Will he obey us?" asks Kordon.

"If you pay his price."

"Then we pay it. Summon him."

Karza creates his sword and cuts his hand with it. He drips blood on the ground and raises his hands, and his eyes glow brightly. A burst of energy erupts from the pool of blood. Soon, the formidable-looking leader of the undead, Zorm, forms out of it. His features are those of a skeleton though not completely devoid of flesh like Kordon, for there are many patches of rotten skin still clinging to his body, and his appearance suggests he is in some sort of state of eternal decay. The rusted, black armor covered with dull spikes—some broken—that encases most of his body only further enhances his imposing and decayed appearance. The undead leader's presence also exudes a sickening power that affects anyone who gets too close to him, which, unfortunately, affects Skon, who doubles over to vomit. Kordon and Karza, however, being the creatures of high evil they are, are immune to this.

"I obey your summons, princely lord of demons," says Zorm, kneeling in Karza's presence. "I am honored. How may I serve you?"

Kordon approaches as Zorm rises to his feet.

"A paladin will soon be entering your domain," the dark wizard informs him. "See to it that he never leaves."

"Ah, the voice of Kordon—welcome back from the dead, all-mighty wizard. Your level of evil was so great that your soul even bypassed my realm upon your death. As a being of evil, I am obliged to kneel before one who has more power than I, and I do so before you now with pleasure." Again the living entity of undead kneels before Kordon, which the wizard acknowledges with a slight bow of his head. Zorm rises and continues, "So, a paladin is it? It has been a long time since I killed a paladin. They've been avoiding my domain since the failure of the last one the paladinhood sent to kill me. Very well, great wizard, I will slay your paladin, but my services will require payment first."

"Name your price," replies Kordon.

Zorm turns to face Skon, who has just recently regained his feet and has had time to regain his composure enough to resist any further sickness, though he still is disgusted by Zorm's presence. But elves are blood enemies to Zorm and his undead warriors, so with a diabolical grin the undead leader gleefully names his price: "The bodies of one hundred elfin dead."

Skon is understandably horrified to hear this. Kordon turns to face the village and can see many elves in the distance oblivious to the happenings at the river's edge—easily enough to meet Zorm's price—and he turns to face the undead leader.

"You shall have your payment."

"You wouldn't dare!" protests Skon strongly. "My people worship Elestar, goddess of all the forest elves. Her temple is here! If you spill one drop of elfin blood, you will incur her wrath, the depth of which not even your twisted mind can conceive. She will kill you all!"

"He speaks true, wizard," Zorm reluctantly responds. "Forest elves are the mortal enemies of my people—but I want no trouble with

Elestar. Any attack on her people here will summon her. She will want revenge."

But Kordon is unmoved by the justifiable apprehension in Zorm's voice and actually chuckles slightly with contempt.

"Let her try and take it."

Karza, though, does not readily share his father's enthusiasm—and in his mind, overconfidence—for this is a god they are talking about, and he approaches his father to voice his concern.

"Is that wise, my father? You're powerful, but not that powerful. And I can't fight her for long; not a demigod!"

"But not a greater god, my son," responds Kordon as he raises a bony finger to make his point. "She can be defeated. And besides—I *am* that powerful." He points to Skon, adding, "Kill that green-faced fool."

Skon is horrified to hear this and tries to flee, but Karza transforms his arm into a snakelike appendage that coils around the helpless elf, bringing his terrified face up close to Karza's.

"You heard the elf's words, my son," continues Kordon. "His blood must fall upon the ground to summon Elestar—so make sure there is plenty of it. I want Elestar to appear quickly." His evil chuckling only further enhances the sinister implication of his words.

Karza transforms the hand on his other arm into a hideous-looking snake head with demonic features. With fangs dripping venom, it bites the face of the screaming Skon. Karza violently tosses him to the ground as the brave elf begins to writhe spasmodically from the venomous bite. The acidic poison causes Skon great agony as it begins to eat away the interior of his face, which begins to sizzle. The elf's head explodes, splattering bloody gore over the ground. The low, rumbling sound of thunder becomes audible, and the ground soon begins to tremble. A cloud forms near Skon's body. The cloud then begins to glow brightly with energy, causing Zorm to back away from it in fear, for he knows what is coming.

"Elestar comes!" he cries with great trepidation, withdrawing even farther. "Elestar comes!"

"Karza, stand ready," commands the evil wizard to his son as he intently watches the cloud beginning to take shape. Karza moves over to a better fighting position and anxiously watches the cloud, awaiting Elestar's arrival. The cloud of energy reaches its peak intensity, and with a blinding flash the elfin demigoddess Elestar appears.

She appears almost twice the size of an ordinary elf, humanoid in shape, and her garments glow with a divine aura of power. She is carrying a formidable crossbow-like weapon in her hands, and on her strikingly beautiful face is a pair of blue eyes that glow bright with power. Her expression is one of intense anger. Zorm continues to back away in fear, but Kordon smiles at her presence.

"Welcome, Elestar—how kind of you to join us!"

A rapid thrusting forward of the evil wizard's arms unleashes a deluge of powerful magic at the elfin goddess, and Karza transforms into his fearsome tridragon form to join the battle. Zorm watches from a discreet distance, and though he is still near the battle, he does not dare to participate in it lest Elestar's divine and powerful wrath fall upon him as well. The flashes of light from the intense combat reflect from his face and armor amid the sounds of the bitter struggle, but after several moments of watching the slugfest, Zorm's look of dread begins to shape into an evil smile.

CHAPTER 15

✷ ✷ ✷

Fortunately for Jartan and much to his relief, Skon's foreboding revelation that this river is called the 'River of Pain' never really manifested any painful results. Farther up or down stream would have been another story, but this section of the river was not a difficult one. That is not to say that the journey was free of incident, however. There was a cesspool of flaming goo that—once touched—is inescapable which Jartan skillfully navigated around. And his brief encounter with a beguiler snake (the aquatic variety) not long after departing Skon's village wasn't that traumatic either since the snake was just a baby—only twelve feet long with only a tenth of the number of poisonous fangs and no hypnotic gaze that the adults have—so Jartan was able to dispatch it with relative ease. Only the 'Falls of Death' lived up to its name and would surely have led to the youth's demise were it not for Skon's blue potion. He actually found the rapids that preceded the falls to be an exciting and enjoyable challenge—but Jartan's smile vanished once he passed through a deceptively tranquil wall of mist that hid from both sight and sound the liquid horror that followed.

A thousand-foot drop filled Jartan with terror, but what was at the bottom of the falls made the descent far more terrifying. For there, awaiting any unfortunate creature that plunges over the falls, is a water entity—a creature whose size is only limited by the amount of water that the beast resides in. This particular entity— thanks to the amount of water the 'River of Pain' provides it—was so huge that the thousand-foot fall itself is actually the liquid tongue of this water entity and its gaping mouth—which could easily swallow a dozen magmadons—was what Jartan was rapidly falling into. Only the fact that the trip from the top of the falls to the entity's mouth took several seconds gave Jartan the necessary time to recover from his shock and realize that this must indeed be the falls that Skon warned him about earlier. The boy quickly grabbed the blue potion and threw it at the water entity moments before being consumed. The breaking of the glass against the creature created a huge cloud of freezing blue vapor which instantly transformed the entity's mouth into ice, preventing it from closing and delivering a fatal bite with its liquid teeth allowing Jartan and his boat to slide harmlessly through the gaping orifice until the boat once again fell into the peaceful calms of the river's waters and out of harm's way. The water entity could do nothing to prevent this as its mouth was frozen open, but it did manage to eventually break free for the blue potion's freezing power was only temporary, and after casting a stern glare of anger in the direction of its rapidly escaping human prey it resumed its position and its tongue once again became the 'Falls of Death'.

After a day and a night of further paddling without incident, Jartan rows toward a small clearing on the shore nearby, and upon landing he sees a path winding its way through the dark, intimidating landscape of this foreboding forest. The trees—if one can even call them that— look more like huge, petrified beings forever frozen in macabre poses, their branches like deformed arms that stretch ominously overhead completely devoid of leaves and other vegetation—except for some long, weblike growths that hang down, giving the impression of torn and ragged clothing.

Everything here looks like it is in some state of a perpetual advancing death—not quite dead, but very close—as if some unnatural and unseen power here keeps all the forest's sinister and decaying inhabitants alive long after the power of life has left their bodies. Jartan wonders to himself if the sun ever even shines here, but he fears it never does; and he's right, for this is the realm of the unnatural undead, and the only source of light is the frequent flashes of lightning that streak from the creepy, black clouds that completely block out the sky above, and even this appears disturbingly unnatural.

Jartan also begins to wonder if he should even leave the safety of the boat! He is very reluctant to do so, and he has good reason to be so apprehensive, but this isn't solely due to the foreboding scenery; his soul blade has not ceased to flash its warning since the young paladin first eyed what was ahead.

"No need to tell me," says Jartan to the blade, as he understands completely. "I can tell just by looking at the place it is evil."

But he must find Modex if he is going to have any chance of stopping the even greater evil of Kordon and Karza, so with a deep breath (and a silent prayer), he decides he might as well get it over with and exits the boat. He quickly realizes he shouldn't have, for his footsteps make an oddly disturbing squishing sound on the weed-covered sands, and yet there's something strange about the way the ground feels even through the boots Jartan is wearing—almost as if the ground itself is moving. There is no steady source of light here, and the flashes of lightning only provide fleeting glimpses of what is around him, which is hardly a comfort, and it actually increases the eternal eeriness of the place. Jartan makes his soul blade shine brightly, which illuminates a wide area around him and allows him to examine the ground more closely.

The disgusting sight that reveals itself on the ground shocks Jartan, for he sees that he is walking on a carpet of death maggots—slimy, finger-sized grubs of hideous design. Fortunately for the youth, the maggots seem to concentrate at the shoreline, so he swiftly moves farther inland where the disgusting creatures are not so prevalent. The voracious death maggots were beginning to eat through the protective layers of his boots, and Jartan shudders to think what they would have done to his flesh if they had broken through—he would literally have been eaten away from the inside out, a gruesome death indeed.

As Jartan moves further along the path, a small bird perched on a tree branch overhead watches him, but what makes this bird unusual is that it is a bird of the undead. Jartan sees an undead wolf emerging from some undead bushes along the path, and like the bird, this is a walking creature of death with very few patches of fur left clinging to the dry, wrinkled, leatherlike skin still left on its skeletal body. The wolf's face is even more ghastly, for only one eye still remains, and it is a gooey nastiness of rotting tissue. It thankfully doesn't appear to be a threat, so Jartan moves past it cautiously, but upon seeing this oozing creature of death Jartan anxiously remarks to himself,

"Undead Forest is right!"

As the young paladin cautiously continues to move along, he is unaware of a skeletal hand reaching up from beneath the ground and trying to grab the unsuspecting boy's leg. Fortunately for Jartan, this attempt is unsuccessful. His soul blade has never ceased its flashes to alert him of the presence of evil, so Jartan is oblivious to this new danger beneath his feet; therefore he ignores the blade, thinking it is still just trying to tell him of the perils of this unnerving forest in general and nothing specific.

"Yes, yes—I know there is danger," he says to the blade, irritated. "You don't have to keep telling me. Honestly, for a snow wolf you chatter on worse than a human female—now quiet!"

After a few more steps, two more of these undead hands reach up to grab him. Jartan, now thoroughly annoyed at the persistent flashing of the blade, finally gives in to his stubborn companion.

"All right—fine!" chides the peeved paladin. "Where is the danger?"

The blade immediately points downward just as the two hands grab Jartan's leg. Startled by this, he quickly slashes these bony intruders that emerge from the ground, and the blade instantly splinters the hands into many fragments, allowing Jartan to escape. But soon an undead warrior emerges from the ground. It is clad in rusting armor and wields a rusting sword and shield. Soon another appears—and then another and another. Jartan is shocked to see this, and as the ghoulish creatures begin to attack, the youth is once again thrown into the chaos of a bitter battle—this time with Zorm's undead warriors.

The four undead warriors facing Jartan, although fierce and dangerous creatures, are surprisingly no match for the young paladin. His soul blade and Jartan's formidable ability as a fighter quickly overpower his four skeletal opponents. The youth is pleasantly surprised that the combat was woefully one-sided. Thinking the crisis over, Jartan continues along the path as he thinks to himself that this isn't going to be nearly as bad as he thought, for when he first saw this place, he actually began to miss the perils of that miserable swamp. He surely would have liked to be back in that swamp if he only knew what was watching him from above—the flash of lightning reveals the undead leader Zorm, who eagerly watched the minor skirmish below. Zorm is carrying a large, shimmering axe—and although it doesn't have any writing upon it to show this fact, Zorm has lovingly named his favorite weapon 'Paladin Killer'. He certainly isn't finished with the boy yet. One might think Zorm would be upset over the pitiful performance of his warriors against this human, but his devilish smile suggests that he is in fact greatly pleased at their defeat. He raises his hand, and a far greater number of undead warriors emerges, each with an emaciated body and rusted armor in a different state of decay. They quickly begin to surround a very alarmed Jartan. *Four warriors is one thing, but forty is a bit distressing,* thinks the formerly brave youth upon seeing this small army—but the frequent lightning flashes in the sky get his attention.

"Lightning," says the pleased Jartan, for he now realizes the significance of the blasts as he again says with even more enthusiasm, "Lightning—yes!"

The undead warriors launch into a frenzied attack, but Jartan confidently raises his soul blade, and a lightning bolt descends from the sky, striking it. The blade glows brightly with this new power source, and Jartan then redirects the energy toward a group of charging undead warriors, who are instantly blasted away upon contact with the powerful bolt. Their bones scatter. More lightning bolts are summoned from the sky to the blade, and more warriors are annihilated with the redirected energy. With additional blinding bursts and slashing attacks with his soul blade, the highly effective paladin is able to destroy all forty of the undead enemies. Again it is surprisingly easy—almost too easy. Pleased with himself and his apparent invincibility, Jartan turns to continue down the path, a broad grin on his face. The young paladin feels he can handle anything this pushover of a forest can pit against him. Zorm has that same grin on his face.

"This paladin is an idiot," he says softly to himself, and with a soft laugh of confidence—for he knows that Jartan has gone through his complete repertoire of paladin powers—he begins to leave his location.

These words from Zorm illustrate Jartan's greatest liability, for although his abilities are strong, his experience is limited. He has no knowledge of what powers higher level beings of evil like Zorm possess. If he did, he would know that the undead leader is using his warriors to make himself invulnerable against Jartan's powers—for Zorm becomes immune to any sort of attack that slays one of his undead warriors, and now that the young and inexperienced paladin has used all his abilities to destroy the undead decoys, there is nothing that Jartan can use against Zorm that will be of any use whatsoever. A more knowledgeable paladin would have used a mere pittance of his abilities, saving the more lethal ones to use against the leader that would soon appear; but Jartan, completely unaware of this, was seduced by the joy of slaughtering undead and held none of his powers in reserve.

It's not Jartan's fault, for Morbius took the youth's training as far as a nonpaladin teacher could. The additional instruction the boy needs—and the fifteen-year-old needs much more—can only be given by another paladin. Morbius was planning on sending Jartan to the paladinhood shortly, but unfortunately the need to defeat Karza was too urgent and Morbius needed the powers of a paladin immediately. He gave Jartan his soul blade far sooner than anticipated, because he felt the boy had attained enough power and skill in combat to overcome his woeful lack of experience.

Walking along the path and blissfully unaware that he has just signed his own death warrant, Jartan stops suddenly when he sees the imposing figure of Zorm standing in the path before him. The overconfident boy is almost bored by the sight of yet another undead being—albeit one that looks far more formidable, with its huge, gleaming weapon and more powerful and bulky form. The devious smile on its face should be a strong indication to the paladin not to exhibit such temerity, but Jartan arrogantly gestures with his finger for Zorm to advance as if to say, "Come on already, you grinning idiot—you're wasting my time. I have things to do."

Zorm begins to slowly advance with an air of supreme confidence, and Jartan, with his rather cavalier attitude, decides to summon yet another bolt of lightning and fires it off at the approaching Zorm. But this bolt of lightning, so effective in defeating those undead in the recent past, hits the armor of the undead leader and is harmlessly deflected away. An astonished Jartan fires again—and again—and again—but the result is the same. Zorm, laughing at the boy's pathetic attempts, rushes in, and an intense battle begins between the two. The teenaged paladin is a more nimble and agile fighter, but it is soon clear that Zorm is the more powerful, and his shimmering axe is the equal to Jartan's soul blade. The blade would cut through a normal axe with ease, but

Zorm's axe is far from normal, having the same magical properties as Jartan's blade. But even this is not what makes Jartan's face register with utter panic—it's the sickening power of Zorm's mere presence, for the boy is having great difficulty fighting when he is being bombarded with the uncontrollable urge to vomit vehemently and continuously.

The battle continues for some time, for nothing Jartan can do seems to work against this undead foe—lightning is deflected, blinding bursts fail to register, and slashes with the soul blade bounce off Zorm's body no matter where the blade strikes without leaving even a scratch, for Zorm's undead decoys have made him immune. Only Jartan's adept skills of evasion are keeping the boy alive—despite Zorm's nauseating influence, for Jartan has survived long enough to at least become somewhat accustomed to it—but this is quickly becoming an exhausting effort; and Zorm is able to inflict some severe injuries on the paladin now that he is beginning to weaken from the exhausting combat. Zorm finally forces Jartan to the ground after a savage blow with his axe and, straddling the boy's body, tries to implant the edge of the weapon into the youth's skull. Jartan desperately holds his soul blade against the weapon in an effort to prevent this from happening, but since this is purely a contest of physical strength it is the more powerful Zorm that is succeeding in bringing the edge of the axe ever closer to Jartan's head, for the youth just doesn't have the strength to stop him.

"Paladin dies! Paladin dies!" exalts Zorm, laughing in triumph.

Something catches Jartan's eye among the bushes bordering the area, and the snow-white, majestic form of a noble unicorn appears from the brush. Although there is not one blade of vegetation in the Undead Forest, the unicorn makes its own. The magical horn atop its forehead begins to glow, and when it touches a dead bush, plump and juicy leaves begin to form, which the creature readily consumes. It can see and hear the battle between Jartan and Zorm as it lazily looks up between bites, but it apparently couldn't care less about Jartan's life-threatening situation and continues grazing in blissful disinterest.

The struggling Jartan, upon seeing the total apathy of supposedly one of the noblest of good creatures, tries to remember something, and he quickly recalls Morbius telling him about commanding good creatures when they were riding in the canyon on the way to Mount Sabo and how the silverhawk obeyed the boy's command. Jartan closes his eyes in deep concentration—and instantly the unicorn stops grazing and lifts its head. It rushes toward Zorm at full speed with its horn glowing brightly. Zorm is within an inch of ending Jartan's life with his axe when out of the corner of his eye he sees the unicorn almost upon him, but the speed of the creature is too great, and the undead being is unable to evade its attack. The glowing horn of the unicorn deeply penetrates Zorm's armor, creating a surge of energy that violently blasts him off of Jartan, and he flails about on the ground for several yards. The injured and exhausted boy manages to struggle to his feet, and as Zorm is disoriented from the blow of the unicorn, he takes the undead leader's axe—for Jartan has learned by now that his soul blade is useless in delivering any injury to the undead leader—and sinks the weapon deep into Zorm's body, ultimately killing the formidable foe after several spasms of death.

But now the severely wounded Jartan falls to his knees in great pain from the massive injuries he received during the battle, and he urgently holds his soul blade close to his body.

"Can you heal yet?" he asks the blade hopefully—but the blade does nothing. Dejected by this, Jartan adds solemnly, "Oh, that's just great. I'm in a hell of a lot of trouble now."

The paladin grimaces in great pain as large amounts of blood seep from the wounds. He drops his blade and tries to staunch the flow from one of the more severe lacerations with his hands, but the attempt is futile. Dropping to his knees, the boy is beginning to lose consciousness as a prelude to dying.

The unicorn, though, being the compassionate creature of goodness that it is, can sense Jartan's rapidly dying condition. It trots over to him and bows its head so its horn touches his body. The horn starts to glow brightly, and as Jartan's body begins to take on the horn's soothing glow, all of his injuries are completely healed. He is surprised by this and also grateful for this noble, life-saving gesture. As he rises to his feet, he strokes the unicorn affectionately in appreciation.

"Many thanks, my friend. I'm sure glad you were around! You know, I could use a handy creature like you during my travels—for when I recall what I've been through these past days, I can only dread what lies ahead, so I think I'm definitely going to need you! You're coming with me."

Jartan and the unicorn start to head off down the path, but the unicorn is quickly distracted by something emerging from the brush— it is a very small unicorn colt and one of the cutest things living. The absolutely adorable little beast whimpers out a faint cry when it sees its mother walking away without it. Jartan can see the unicorn mother concerned about the welfare of her offspring, and she looks compassionately at Jartan. He understands completely.

"I know. I suppose I could command you to come—but I won't. You've done enough for me as is, and I'm eternally grateful. I won't abuse your powers for my own selfish needs. Go now and rejoin your child."

The unicorn mother happily trots over to her colt, and the two nuzzle each other affectionately. They soon disappear into the brush as Jartan smiles, knowing that he did the right thing. He looks ahead to see what lies before him up the path. Past the eerie-looking and undead vegetation can be seen a black castle looming ominously in the distance—its architecture a decidedly discomfiting sight.

"Modex—I hope," says Jartan to himself. But he adds cautiously as he reflects on the menacing structure, "Then again ..."

CHAPTER 16

✚ ✚ ✚

The intrepid youth is hacking through some dense undergrowth with his soul blade and has been doing so for the past several hours, but to Jartan it seems much longer due to the tremendous effort it requires to make any progress. So much so that he is actually grumbling to himself.

"Potions to cure poison, potions to freeze water entities twice the size of hill giants. Why couldn't that damn elf give me a potion that kills weeds?"

Without the phenomenal cutting power of his weapon, it would be impossible to approach the castle, as the undergrowth makes a highly effective barrier with its interlaced vines studded with sharp thorns forming a dense mass as strong as steel. In fact, the entire area before him is surprising to Jartan, as it doesn't appear at all to be the regal residence of a brother of King Morbius with its sinister and depressing surroundings, which makes the youth begin to wonder as he questions aloud to himself,

"Is this a castle or a prison?"

He soon penetrates the undergrowth after a final slash with the blade, which reveals once again the path that leads toward the castle; but his sigh of relief is short-lived when he sees gruesomely arrayed on either side of the path the long-dead skeletal remains of several dozen forest elves impaled upon stakes—obviously those poor seekers that Skon sent to enlist Modex's aid those fifteen years ago. Jartan is stunned.

"That can't be the result of Modex," he says to himself. "Skon must be mistaken. No, it's just an illusion. That's it! An illusion Modex created as a warning to keep people away from some form of evil that lies beyond. No brother of a good king like Morbius could possibly be twisted enough to kill innocent beings."

Approaching warily despite his own words of confidence, Jartan finds the castle itself, like the area it resides in, is not at all like the gleaming towers one would expect, for it is dark and foreboding— mirroring the overgrown and unkempt landscape. Seeing some stairs leading to the castle entrance, Jartan tentatively climbs them, for he is beginning to doubt it is a good idea to go on. The boy is beginning to feel the power of fear creeping up on him, and he begins to wonder if that grisly warning was just an illusion after all. Still, the thought is a short-lived one, and his confidence once again manifests itself. Besides, he gave his word to Morbius, and proceed he must despite any misgivings.

As Jartan climbs the stairs, he can see two man-sized statues of dragons, one on each side of the entrance to the castle. Although they are motionless and give no evidence of being anything other than harmless statues, they still are quite threatening in appearance, and Jartan cannot help but feel uneasy upon approaching them.

"Is there danger?" he asks his soul blade.

But the blade does not flash or indicate anything of a dangerous or evil nature, so Jartan moves confidently forward and faces the entrance to the castle. Seeing a large, rust-encrusted knocker in the shape of a face of some grotesque creature on the metal door, he reaches out to touch it, and at the sound of the first rap against the metallic surface, the two statues of the stone dragons begin to move. Jartan is understandably startled by this, and with his soul blade still in hand, he immediately slashes one of the creatures. As the blade strikes the creature's skin, the stone dragon shatters like glass as a surge of energy cascades over its body—but it also delivers a blast of painful energy back at Jartan, which throws him violently to the ground. The soul blade's shimmering luster vanishes, and he is greatly alarmed by its condition as he stares at it in shock and utter disbelief. The other stone dragon, obviously not pleased at witnessing the destruction of its mate, begins to attack this human murderer with a hated passion, and Jartan hurriedly regains his feet to protect himself from its charge. But when Jartan strikes it with his previously unbreakable blade, it instantly breaks in two upon impact with the creature's stone skin. The boy is again utterly horrified to see that his formerly mighty and indestructible soul blade is now but a broken piece of junk in his hand.

"What in the seven hells?" gasps the aghast youth.

The creature attacks again, which knocks Jartan to the ground and the broken soul blade is thrown off to the side. Weaponless, the boy uses his agility to flee and barely manages to avoid a lethal bite from the stone dragon's many spiked teeth. He calls out to his soul blade with an outstretched hand,

"Soul blade!"

The object remains motionless on the ground, dull in color and broken. Alarmed by this, Jartan again barely manages to avoid another surging attack and begins to flee in panic from the rapidly pursuing stone dragon as he calls out to the blade with even greater urgency.

"Soul blade! Damn it, what's wrong with you? Soul blade!"

But again it does not move.

From the castle balcony, a figure stands watching the frantic Jartan desperately trying to avoid being killed by the dragon. He is dressed in dark robes and carrying a staff. He is the wizard Modex, an ominous and sinister-looking old man about sixty years of age with flowing white hair, and his eyes seem to glow with a faint orange color as if they radiate some evil power. Jartan notices the imposing figure of Modex standing there dispassionately.

"Modex? Modex, help me!" he cries out to him in desperation.

But the enigmatic wizard doesn't respond and continues to watch, totally unmoved by Jartan's pleas. In fact, a faint smile appears on his wrinkled lips as if he is enjoying the boy's horrifying plight.

Despite Jartan's hysterical efforts at escaping the tenacious beast, the stone dragon captures the frantic youth and has him firmly in its viselike grip, preparing to deliver a lethal bite. The helpless boy again appeals to the apathetic wizard watching from above.

"Modex, please! Your brother sent me! Modex!"

But the wizard is still unmoved. Jartan, terrified by the stone dragon's ever-closer teeth, cries out yet again.

"It's about Kordon!"

"Stop!" thunders out the command of Modex to his stone minion.

The dragon immediately releases Jartan, who falls to the ground. Modex magically materializes close by and hurriedly walks over to the boy.

"What do you know about Kordon?" he angrily demands of the youth.

"What's wrong with you?" says Jartan, panting heavily from his recent ordeal while brushing the dirt off of himself as he rises to his feet. "Why didn't you help me? I was—"

But Modex quickly thrusts out his hand and grabs the boy's shoulder. A painful burst of energy erupts from the wizard's touch and streaks down Jartan's body, forcing him once again to fall upon his knees as he screams loudly from the excruciating pain.

"Answer me, you fool! What do you know about Kordon?"

"He—he's alive!" replies Jartan, struggling to speak from the painful energy.

Modex releases the boy, who collapses to the ground with an even greater level of exhaustion from the experience. Jartan is greatly puzzled by this action from a supposed friend as a disturbed Modex ponders the boy's distressing answer.

"Impossible. His body was buried deep within Mount Sabo and the tomb entrance was magically sealed. How could he possibly be alive?"

"Karza resurrected him by killing all the Council wizards and stealing the Ring of Angels from your brother," answers Jartan, who slowly rises to his feet again after taking a moment to recover his senses from Modex's attack.

"Karza—yes, this would be the time for him to come out of the Abyss to try a resurrection, since this is the anniversary of his father's death." Modex chuckles softly with admiration at the thought as he continues, "So Kordon is resurrected and has a demon prince as a personal lackey. By the gods, that man had such power—such deliciously evil power—power I wish I had."

Jartan is mystified upon hearing these words of admiration coming from the mouth of Morbius's brother.

"But still," Modex continues, "Karza would need the Ring of Angels, and it is useless to him, for it would kill him instantly if it touched his demonic skin. He couldn't possibly use it to enter the tomb."

"That troubled your brother as well," says Jartan. "But I think the answer is that I noticed when I was fighting Karza on Mount Sabo that he has a human hand. He must have put the ring on that."

"Interesting. One of the human features he inherited from his father, no doubt. Kordon was right—his knowledge of evil told him that would happen," adds the smiling wizard with respectful admiration. "And what of my brother?" asks Modex almost as an afterthought.

"Dead," the boy replies, dropping his head sadly.

Modex too displays a faint note of sadness though nowhere near Jartan's level.

"Unfortunate," he coldly responds.

"Morbius never mentioned before that he had a brother. Still, your name sounds—"

"You have delivered your message, boy," Modex hastily interrupts. "Now go!"

He turns to head back toward the castle, leaving Jartan, still perplexed by these surprising acts from the brother of the good Morbius, to follow.

"Go?" he asks, astonished. "Aren't you going to do something? Kordon killed your brother! And now he and Karza are trying to free the demon queen from the Abyss!"

"I know all about Kordon's plans, you fool—and I couldn't care less."

Modex and Jartan reach the castle entrance, but Jartan, thinking that Modex is going to open the door to enter, is stunned when the wizard simply teleports inside—leaving him standing there like a fool.

"Wizards," he says in exasperation, shaking his head.

Seeing his soul blade nearby, he picks it up, and eyeing the blade intensely, he is more puzzled than ever by its broken, dull, and lifeless appearance. He then opens the castle entrance and goes inside where he can see Modex walking away and runs to catch up with him.

"Modex! Wait! Your brother's dying wish was for me to find you. You must do something."

But Modex says nothing and continues walking. Jartan is frustrated more than ever by his total lack of interest considering the dire circumstances and the death of Morbius.

"What kind of good wizard are you?" he angrily shouts at him.

Modex stops walking upon hearing this. Jartan suddenly realizes something.

"Wait a second," he continues. "Modex—Modex—yes, now I remember. You were once a wizard of the Great Council too. But if you were a Council wizard, then why didn't Karza need your head to resurrect Kordon?"

Modex is concerned by the boy's knowledge, as Jartan continues:

"Because you didn't help defeat him—that's it, isn't it? Why didn't you fight him, Modex? Were you afraid?"

The wizard, his eyes glowing with an even greater intensity as his anger increases, turns to face Jartan and grabs him violently.

"I'm warning you for the last time, boy—leave me alone!"

"I think I'm beginning to understand," says Jartan, unfazed by Modex's anger. "That wasn't an illusion of warning outside—Skon wasn't joking when he told me that you slaughtered his envoy sent to seek your aid. You killed them!"

"Of course I killed them."

"For the love of the gods, why?"

"Because I don't like the color green and I don't like the elf race. Put the two together and it is justifiable genocide."

"What?" gasps a horrified Jartan. "But that's crazy!"

"Then I'll give you a better reason. I know they were sent to assassinate me like all the others before. I made many enemies in my past—enemies who would stop at nothing to kill me and send my soul into the seven hells as they did to Kordon's."

"That's not true!" counters a confused Jartan. "They came here to ask your help." But his confusion quickly turns to alarm when he realizes exactly what Modex represents. "Dear gods—now I really understand. You didn't help defeat Kordon because you are two of a kind. Skon was right—you are evil!"

"That's right, you foolish child," replies Modex, flashing a sinister smile at Jartan's realization as the wizard's eyes glow bright with orange hatred, "and you'll die because of it!"

The wizard, obviously reveling in the evil thought of destroying the boy, throws a startled Jartan to the ground and points his staff at him. The tip glows with magical energy as Jartan's expression becomes one of horror, but Modex's expression of evil anger soon fades, and he turns away in disgust.

"You aren't even worth the effort," he says. "Now get out of here before I change my mind!"

"Why didn't you kill me, Modex?" asks Jartan, greatly relieved that Modex did not obliterate him, though he is now beginning to understand why. "You don't want to destroy me, do you? That's why Morbius sent me to you—because he knew your evil would pass in time."

"No, it's too late for me," replies Modex, his head bowed in shame, "for my sins of the past run deep. You were correct. I was one of my brother's Council wizards, but I turned to evil like Kordon. As his apprentice, I was helping him to free the demon queen, but Morbius found out and ordered the Council to destroy him. I was spared because I was the brother of King Morbius, and so I was imprisoned here for life as punishment for my evil ways."

"If you were Kordon's apprentice, then do you know where he is going?"

"He is in the Underworld now. That is where the seal keeping the demon queen, Magdara, imprisoned in the Abyss is. Once the seal is broken, Magdara will be able to reach the Surface—and evil and darkness will reign forever."

Modex smiles slightly as he finishes relating this—not the smile one makes when pleased but the smile one makes when realizing how foolish one has been—but soon he shakes his head in disgust, knowing that he was once a participant in this diabolically twisted scheme, and he continues to walk away.

"Help me to stop them!" Jartan pleads.

"Stop them? And just how do you plan to do that? Kordon isn't some troll you find in the forest, boy. He's the most powerful wizard in creation. It took the combined power of all the Council wizards to defeat him. And that twisted son of his is a demon prince—do you have any idea what that means? He can transform himself into fantastic creatures of tremendous power and destruction, and while transformed, he cannot be killed."

"I fought him before," replies an unimpressed Jartan.

"Then you must have had three hundred luck stones hanging on your body! Or he was in a highly weakened condition. You arrogant fool, a teenage worm like you is no match for a demon prince! Hell, even the paladin master himself would have trouble."

"I'm not afraid," counters the brave Jartan.

"No?" responds the wizard, laughing at the boy's bravado. "Then you go and fight them!"

Modex raises his staff, and it shoots a beam of energy at Jartan, who disappears in a flash of light. In an instant, the boy materializes in a completely different area and is understandably confused by his new and eerily misty surroundings.

"What the hell is this?" he says in bewilderment.

A chilling voice echoes throughout the area—a voice he has heard before, a voice that causes great alarm in Jartan. It is Kordon's voice.

"Greetings, paladin," says the voice of the unseen Kordon. Jartan turns suddenly to face the sound as the evil wizard materializes from a cloud of surging energy. "And welcome," Kordon adds with an evil grin, "to your doom!"

His maniacal laughter precedes a powerful blast of energy from his hands. Jartan vainly tries to use his broken soul blade to protect himself against it, but it is a useless effort, for the blade does nothing to erect any form of magical protection like it has done so many times in the past. The energy bolt throws Jartan violently back a dozen yards in agony, leaving a nasty, searing wound. Suddenly, the ground beneath him erupts, and out comes Karza in the form of some giant, demonic worm-type creature. Jartan is thrown down again from this emergence but quickly recovers and tries to flee. Another blast from Kordon sends him to the ground with yet another massive wound as the evil wizard laughs heartily at the boy's pathetic performance. Karza transforms into the tridragon and goes after Jartan and although the boy manages to hit the demonic creature with the powerless soul blade, it doesn't have any injurious effect whatsoever in its broken condition. Aghast, the youth makes a harried attempt to flee; however, a rapid discharge of lightning from the tridragon instantly obliterates one of Jartan's legs, transforming it into a bloody stump as the boy screams in agony. The explosive force of the blast catapults Jartan's body hard against the misty walls of this twisted arena, and it's clear that he is a mere toy of amusement to the evil pair. There is no chance of escape or respite as Kordon unleashes another round of magical energy; but Jartan, despite his injuries, is able to avoid the oncoming death, and it impacts against the wall, causing a huge explosion. The youth frantically tries to crawl as fast as he can to put some distance between himself and his tormentors, but the evil wizard magically summons a whirlwind that he sends at Jartan. It picks him up and whips him around violently in the swirling vortex, causing the boy great discomfort as his body flails about spasmodically, his blood gushing forth with every rotation from his missing limb as well as the other injuries that the whirlwind is inflicting as Jartan's body begins to tear apart. A laughing Kordon makes a slight gesture with his bony hand that instantly dispels the agonizing whirlwind, causing the boy to fly a considerable distance, and he hits hard against the ground as a fire blast from the tridragon roasts the boy alive.

The once proud, brave, and confident youth—now bloody, broken, twisted, and deformed—lies there, a trembling mass of smoking flesh barely clinging to life. The ground begins to quake slightly as Karza, still in his tridragon form, lumbers over while a gleefully laughing Kordon materializes above the vanquished youth. Karza transforms into the demon prince to stand beside his evil father, and both gaze down triumphantly at the defeated Jartan.

"And now you die," gloats the wizard with a sinister smile.

Laughing contemptuously, Kordon raises his hands, which again glow brightly with energy, and blasts Jartan viciously. The boy screams in agony as his body rips asunder.

A blinding flash of light occurs, and Jartan is instantly back at the castle, lying on the floor in front of Modex apparently uninjured as if nothing has happened.

"Now do you understand what you are up against?"

Jartan, with a look of utter astonishment, regains his feet and catches his breath, taking a moment to recover his senses and then frantically studying his body for any sign of injury only to be amazed that there is now no evidence of any.

"What happened?" he responds confusedly. "I was fighting Kordon and Karza."

"That was merely an illusion I created to show you the power they have. In the illusion they killed you, didn't they?"

"Yes," responds Jartan meekly.

"That's because in your own mind you know you don't have the power to defeat them. I assure you, boy, you would have died just as easily had they been real."

"All right, you made your point. So maybe I can't fight them alone, but you're a powerful wizard like your brother. Together we would have a chance!"

Modex scoffs on hearing this and begins to walk away, but Jartan quickly stops him and adds,

"I can help you. I'm a paladin!"

"You're no paladin, boy," Modex responds with an annoyed chuckle.

"That's not true!"

"Very well, then show me your paladin powers."

Jartan holds the broken blade before him.

"Soul blade—shine!" But nothing happens. With even more conviction, he says, "Shine! I command it!" But the blade does nothing. An anxious Jartan then tosses it on the ground and holds out his hand as he continues, almost in a panic, "Soul blade! Soul blade, come to my hand! Come!"

Again the blade performs as a useless piece of junk. Dejected by the blade's inaction and completely confused as to his failure to make the blade do his bidding, Jartan walks over to it and picks it up.

"I don't understand. Why doesn't it respond?"

"Because you're no longer a paladin," Modex responds matter-of-factly. Jartan looks even more confused, so Modex continues, "Is it so difficult to understand, boy? You broke the code of the paladinhood by using the blade to kill a stone dragon—which is a creature of goodness, not evil."

"But I thought it was going to attack me!" cries Jartan in justifiable defense.

"You thought wrong. The stone dragon was merely greeting a visitor."

"But the other one attacked!"

"Of course it attacked, you idiot!" replies Modex as if stating a fact so obvious it doesn't require mentioning. "You killed its mate. Did you expect it to respond to such an act with kindness?"

"I didn't know," replies Jartan, realizing his error. "I was startled by it. I should have waited. My soul blade would have warned me if I was in danger. I'm sorry. Is there anything I can do?"

"And what is it you want done, boy?"

"To get my paladin powers back, of course," responds the irritated Jartan.

But Modex is not impressed by Jartan's lack of remorse and attitude, so he begins to chastise him.

"But your crime is great. The stone dragon is dead, which is bad enough, but without its mate, the other stone dragon will die from loneliness and their offspring shortly thereafter. Due to your reckless impatience, many will suffer. Now, how do you propose to atone for such an insidious crime?"

"Look, I'm sorry! If I could bring the stone dragon back to life, I would!"

"Then do so."

"How?" asks a bewildered Jartan.

"You took a life," begins Modex, looking the boy coldly in his face, "so replace it with your own. Kill yourself."

"What?" says Jartan, understandably shocked at the thought.

"You heard me. Kill yourself. You just murdered an entire family of stone dragons. Should you not pay for that with your own life?"

Jartan is hurt by these words and backs away from Modex.

"You're insane!" says the boy as he turns away and starts to leave.

Modex can see that Jartan is troubled by all this, but he feels he must go further in his harsh treatment of the boy and follows after him, not really wanting to do what he must. He grabs Jartan and turns him around to face him once more.

"But it doesn't stop there, boy," he continues. "Oh no, for you have done great damage. Not only have you murdered untold generations of stone dragons, but you have also lost the soul in your blade. No longer can it serve you as it was destined to do. And now that you have lost your paladin powers, you have even failed Morbius, one who had such a foolish faith in your pitiful ability to stop the evil of Kordon and Karza. It's because of your ignorance, arrogance, and stupidity that they will ultimately succeed now and we will all suffer because of it. And now you are a coward—too afraid to give your own life to atone for all of your massive crimes. You sicken me. Now crawl out of here and leave me alone—you pathetic little toad!"

Modex angrily strikes Jartan hard in the face which sends the boy to collapse on the floor as the wizard begins to walk off. Jartan, who is deeply hurt— hurt far more by Modex's words rather than the strike—is on the verge of tears. He looks at the remnant of his soul blade, and although it is broken in half, it still has a lethal point. His hand holding it begins to tremble. Modex turns to look back to see what

Jartan is doing, and he can see that the boy is indeed suffering with intense remorse—remorse so great that it makes him consider killing himself. Jartan puts the blade against his stomach and closes his teary eyes. He tenses for a moment, steeling his nerves for the act of thrusting the blade into his body, and as he makes an effort to do this—he is suddenly stopped from acting further by the hand of a smiling and understanding Modex.

"That's quite enough, boy. Forgive me, but I had to make your blood flow with enough remorse that you would offer your own life to replace that of the stone dragon you killed. You can now attain atonement for your crime. Come."

Modex raises his staff, and they disappear in a flash of light. Instantly, they are outside the castle entrance where the surviving stone dragon is standing despondently beside the slightly smoking pile of stone rubble that was once its mate. Modex and Jartan stand in front of the pile, but the stone dragon growls with anger at the sight of the murderous Jartan's presence and instantly lunges forth to attack him with every intention of ripping the boy's body apart; but Modex reaches out and soothingly caresses the creature, stopping it.

"Patience, my pet—patience," says Modex, which pacifies the dragon as the wizard turns and says to Jartan, "Cut your hand."

The boy, understandably dubious over this, casts a wary eye at the wizard, prompting Modex to add,

"Trust me. Cut your hand."

Still confused by this, Jartan nevertheless obeys and uses the blade to cut the palm of his hand.

"Now," Modex continues, "drip your blood onto the remains of the stone dragon."

Jartan does this. Modex then touches the pile of stone with his staff, and both begin to glow. After a few moments, the stone dragon, fully restored and unharmed, suddenly forms from the pile of rubble. Its mate greets it warmly.

"Thank the gods!" exclaims a happy and grateful Jartan.

The beaming boy makes an effort to approach the two creatures as if to share in their happiness with a group hug, for he too is greatly pleased at the creature's return—but they hiss menacingly at him, and he backs off quickly. Modex smiles upon witnessing this, for he understands the reason.

"I don't think they are still too happy with you," says the wizard.

Jartan agrees and rapidly increases the distance.

"Well, thank you for what you've done, Modex. I'm very grateful. But don't you see? This is why Morbius sent me to you. There is still much goodness within you, so use it now to help me stop Kordon!"

"I cannot. You must go now. But if you still desire to find Kordon, then travel south, for there you will find his fortress. Inside you will find the spell to follow him into the Underworld—and I wish you well."

"I'm no wizard!" angrily cries Jartan. "So how can I use a spell like that? And without my paladin powers I wouldn't stand a chance of even getting there, let alone fighting those two even if I did get into this Underworld! Damn it, why won't you come with me?"

"I told you before, boy—I'm a prisoner here, and here I must remain to pay for my past misdeeds."

Modex turns to go, but Jartan remembers the necklace Morbius gave him before he died.

"Wait!" he says. "I remember your brother wanted me to give this to you." Handing it to Modex, he continues, "What is it, anyway?"

Modex smiles slightly as he realizes the significance of this act by his brother.

"The power keeping me imprisoned here."

"If Morbius wanted you to have it, then he's giving you a second chance to use your powers to fight evil as he did. He's telling you that he forgives you for your past. He's telling you that he remembers you as the loving brother you once were—the loving brother that still lies deep down within you. Don't let his sacrifice be in vain, Modex. Please!

I implore you. Help me. And if not me, then help your brother and avenge his death! You owe it to him."

Modex ponders this for a moment and drops the necklace on the ground. The bottom of his staff smashes the jewel within it, which then emits a flash of energy.

"Come," says the smiling and now enthusiastic wizard.

"Where are we going?" asks Jartan, surprised by this change in Modex's demeanor.

"To see if we can find you another soul blade. You don't expect me to fight Kordon and Karza without a paladin by my side, do you?"

CHAPTER 17

✚ ✚ ✚

Inside the walls of Modex's castle once again, the two enter a vast chamber. In this chamber at the far end are two large, marble statues about twice the size of an average human—one of a human male standing proudly with an air of great ability and virtue and the other of a beautiful woman with a similar aura. Modex and Jartan approach them, but it is Modex who is decidedly the more devout of the two.

"Where are we?" Jartan asks.

"The tomb of my parents," Modex reverently responds. "My brother was kind enough to imprison me in the castle where my family lived when we were children. My punishment was to look after and care for the tomb."

They are in front of the statues, and each one has a stone sarcophagus lying before it. Modex looks up to gaze lovingly at the faces of both statues, for prior to Jartan's arrival, love was an emotion long absent from the wizard's heart; but now, thanks to his dead brother's forgiveness, Modex can once again feel the warmth of the emotion—and the orange glow within his eyes that signified his evil has faded away.

"My mother was a sorceress who taught Morbius and me the arts of magic. My father was a great paladin."

"Father?" a surprised Jartan asks when he hears this as he unpleasantly recalls Skon's warning regarding any indiscretions with the opposite sex. "But I thought paladins couldn't—well, that they couldn't be—um— impure with women."

"The act you refer to is permitted after marriage," replies a smiling Modex at Jartan's clumsy attempt to say what he means.

"Thank the gods for that at least!" exalts Jartan with a sigh of relief.

Modex touches the sarcophagus of his father with his staff, and the stone slab lid moves aside, revealing the contents inside. An impressive-looking sword is the only item present.

"Wow!" exclaims an impressed Jartan. "Now that is beautiful!"

"Yes, it served my father well in his battles against evil. This one had the soul of my grandmother within it, but when my mother died it was her wish that she be the one to be with my father, so another sword was used for her soul."

Jartan wonders where the body is, for if this is a tomb like Modex said, then there should also be a body in the sarcophagus—and yet no body is present.

"There's no body. How did your father die?"

"Many moons ago, the king of the frost giants, Utho, was leading his army to crush the kingdom of the ice dwarves, which my father, being a paladin, was protecting. The two races were mortal enemies, and Utho would stop at nothing to annihilate the dwarves. But my father knew that if Utho was killed, then his army would be leaderless and forced to withdraw and thereby spare the dwarves from certain destruction, so my father challenged Utho to single combat."

"I've heard about Utho," responds Jartan, "but I also heard that he had a magical suit of armor that made him impossible to defeat in battle."

"This is true—Utho's armor made him invincible."

"Then why did your father challenge him if he knew the giant couldn't be defeated?"

"Because my father knew that, despite Utho's invincible armor, a paladin has a power that could overcome even this—a power that can overcome anything."

"What power?" asks an eager and curious Jartan.

"The power of self-sacrifice."

"Self-sacrifice? I don't understand, Modex."

"Do you recall what you felt when you killed the stone dragon with your soul blade?"

"I was shocked by a powerful surge of energy," replies the youth after a brief moment of pondering.

"Exactly. That surge of energy was because you caused a paradox."

"A what?"

"A paradox—an imbalance in nature. You used 'good to destroy good' instead of using 'good to destroy evil'. But when a paladin uses his own soul blade to end his own life, then the paradox is on an unbelievably massive scale—and it creates a surge of energy so powerful that no living being can survive the ensuing blast. They say not even a god can survive it, though it has never been tried. My father used this to destroy Utho."

"So that is why there is no body? It was destroyed in the blast?" asks Jartan.

"Yes."

"Incredible," responds Jartan. "There is still so much to being a paladin I don't understand."

"Then you must once again be a servant to the code of the paladinhood. Now that the stone dragon you killed has been restored, you can regain your paladin powers once you have a new soul blade. I just only hope there is another soul that wishes to serve you, but we shall soon see. Take the blade."

"But you said it had the soul of your grandmother within it."

"Not anymore, for once my mother entered my father's new soul blade, my grandmother's soul returned to the land of the dead."

Jartan takes the blade from the sarcophagus, and after a while it begins to glow very, very faintly in his hand.

"I don't feel anything," he says. "Wouldn't I get the same soul that powered my blade before?"

"No. Once a blade is broken, the soul within also returns to the land of the dead and cannot be summoned again. You must request another. Do you know of anyone close to you—a family member for instance—who has died recently?"

"I have no family," Jartan sadly acknowledges.

Modex is surprised to hear this, and he gestures to the blade in Jartan's hand.

"But the blade glows in your hand, so obviously some soul of a family member is close to you and wants to get your attention. Close your eyes and concentrate on the soul energy. Who do you sense?"

Jartan closes his eyes and concentrates for a moment, and soon a broad smile registers on his face.

"Morbius—I sense King Morbius!" he exalts with happy enthusiasm.

But Modex is not so happy to hear this. He is actually astounded by the boy's revelation and responds accordingly.

"Morbius? But that cannot be! My brother had no living family other than me, so how could you two possibly be related? Who were your parents?"

"I don't know who my father was. I know my mother died when I was an infant."

"Ah, a mother's soul energy is the most powerful of all. Paladins who have their mother's love powering their blades are extremely formidable. But if your mother died when you were an infant, then too much time has passed for her soul to power a blade for you. Only the souls of those who have died within a period of one month can enter a blade, so Morbius's soul would qualify, but it doesn't make sense that you are feeling him. Only the soul of a family member through blood or marriage, can serve a paladin. Who was the soul that powered your blade before?"

"It was my pet snow wolf, Loba," replies the boy.

"What?" gasps an incredulous Modex even more dumbfounded than before. "A snow wolf? That's impossible. Animals have spirits—not souls—and therefore are not able to power a soul blade."

"That's what Morbius told me," counters Jartan.

"No, no—that's absurd," Modex responds, bitterly shaking his head. "He knew better than that. No, you must be mistaken if a snow—" But he stops, startled, as he begins to realize something—something that causes the wizard to stare at Jartan with a stunned look. He tentatively moves closer to the boy.

"This snow wolf," he says apprehensively, "was it white with a silver stripe?"

"Yes."

Modex's emotion begins to grow. "Then—then your name is Jartan?"

"Yes, how did you know that?" replies the boy hesitantly, for he is uneasy over Modex's strange demeanor.

Modex closes his eyes, remembering something from his past—fifteen years ago, in fact—and in this memory, he is in a dark room standing before an altar with a burning pit before him while his frantic wife pleads with him by his side.

"Modex, have you gone mad?" she screams hysterically. "You can't do this! Not our child!"

"I must make a sacrifice to the demon queen to prove my loyalty."

"But Jartan is only a baby!" she protests. "Listen to me, my husband. It is Kordon who is doing this to you. You are an unwitting pawn to his will! I know you are a good man! If you just resist him, you can—"

But Modex grabs her violently with a look of pure hatred in his eyes—eyes that radiate with a disturbing orange glow.

"Bring that brat to me, or I'll kill you all."

The wife, horror filling her eyes upon hearing these chilling and malignant words from a man whom until this moment she deeply loved and respected, regains her composure and tries to placate her hopelessly twisted husband.

"All right," she replies calmly, though her voice quavers slightly. "All right, I'll go get him."

Modex releases her, and she starts to back away as he once again tends to the burning altar while chanting ominous words of loyalty to the demon queen as a prelude to the evil ritual he is about to perform.

The wife quickly exits the room and soon enters another chamber where a young girl, about eight years of age, is tickling an infant boy in a bassinet as the happy infant squeals in delight from his loving sister's playful antics. Her face matches her brother's, as she too is reveling in the happiness. But upon seeing her harried mother enter, her happy demeanor changes to concern when she sees the terrified look in her mother's eyes.

"Mother, what's wrong?"

But she doesn't answer and instead frantically searches the room, which contains dozens of vials of potions. She soon finds what she is looking for—a vial of purple liquid. She takes it and, grasping it close to her chest, closes her eyes and takes a deep breath as if contemplating the unfortunate action she is about to take.

"Come here, my daughter."

The girl obeys and stands beside her disheartened mother, who kneels down to look the child in the face.

"Listen to me, my love. Your father has descended too far into evil, and there's no way to reach him. You and your brother must escape from here."

"No, Mother! Not without you!"

"Sweetheart, you must! I have to stay here to give you the time you need." She gives her daughter the vial, and she sobs as she continues,

"May the gods forgive me. I'm so sorry, my love, but this has to be done. You must drink this."

"What is it?" asks the girl as she looks at the vile apprehensively.

"A transformation potion. It's the only way to save you and your brother. Think of a creature and drink the potion, and you will become that creature—permanently."

On hearing this last word, the girl becomes alarmed. Her mother sees her daughter's distress and hugs her tightly, tears forming in her eyes.

"I know—I know. I'm sorry, but it's the only way! You both must escape from here or your father will surely kill us all. Your brother is just a baby—he can't help. So it's up to you. At least you will be alive and safe."

The mother and girl suddenly react with horror as they hear the sound of footsteps coming closer. The mother jumps up and hurriedly locks the door and then returns to her daughter.

"I'll try and hold him off as long as I can. Now, my daughter, think of a creature and drink the vial, but it has to be one that is swift and agile if you are to have any hope of escape—and remember, it is very cold outside, so you will need a form that can adapt to this."

The sound of Modex trying to open the door is heard, which causes the mother to panic.

"Quickly!" she frantically commands her daughter.

The girl closes her eyes for a moment and drinks the liquid in the vial as the door to the room is blasted open with a wave of magic from an irate Modex's hand, prompting his wife to attack with her own magic powers in a desperate bid to protect her children from their maniacal father. Modex counters with his formidable spells, and a bitter battle ensues between the two. The wife puts up a stubborn and brave resistance, considering her children's lives are at stake, but it is ultimately a short-lived effort, for she is no match to the evil power of Modex. It doesn't take long for her body to collapse to the floor in death.

The daughter's body begins to glow bright with purplish energy, which quickly transforms her into a snow wolf—a white creature with a silver stripe. Modex sees this transformation and in a rage begins to raise his hand, preparing to blast the creature—completely uncaring that this was once his loving daughter—but the snow wolf is the first to act. She opens her mouth and discharges an intense blast of cold and snow, which momentarily stuns the wizard; and while Modex is distracted by this, the snow wolf grabs the bassinet with the infant Jartan in its mouth. The cloud of cold and snow quickly dissipates, and Modex recovers his senses just as quickly and attacks with his magic but the snow wolf is a highly nimble creature and is able to evade the explosive onslaught. With bassinet in mouth, she crashes through a window and rapidly runs off into the surrounding snow-covered fields.

Modex is greatly disturbed that his intended sacrifice to evil—in the innocent form of his infant son—is rapidly escaping, and he raises his hands, which causes him to disappear in a flash of light. With another flash he appears on the balcony, and from this vantage point he sees the snow wolf retreating ever farther into the fields.

"Stop!" he angrily commands. "Bring back my son! He must be sacrificed! Stop, I say!"

In a rage he creates flaming balls of magical energy in his hands and begins hurling them at the snow wolf retreating in the distance. The balls of energy impact the ground near the fleeing creature, creating large explosions, but she and Jartan—her infant brother—eventually escape without injury into the dense woods with the evil words of Modex echoing behind them: "He must be killed!"

Modex is still remembering this horrendously twisted past of his, and he understandably has a look of great sadness on his face while doing so. Jartan goes to him, completely oblivious to why he is acting so strangely, and touches Modex gently on the shoulder as if to rouse him from sleep.

"Modex? Modex, what's wrong?" he asks.

Modex slowly opens his eyes and looks at Jartan. He smiles slightly and also touches him gently as he realizes that Jartan is his son, but he certainly doesn't impart this knowledge to him. *Not yet, anyway*, he thinks.

"It's nothing," he responds.

"I don't believe you!" replies Jartan angrily, not satisfied with such a ridiculously simple answer after what he has seen and heard in the past minutes. "I know something is wrong. I feel it! If a snow wolf wasn't in my blade, then what was?"

Modex is obviously reluctant to answer, but Jartan is determined so he presses on.

"Damn it! Answer me!"

"Your sister was the soul," responds Modex, for he knows after what the boy has heard he will not relent in his desire for answers and only the truth can placate him.

"I—I had a sister?" says the dumbfounded Jartan. "But how did she become a snow wolf? Was she cursed? Because only something evil could have caused that."

"That's not important right now."

"What do you mean it's not important? Why didn't Morbius tell me this?"

"And what would you have done if he had?" asks Modex.

"Kill those responsible—that's what!"

"Exactly—for you would want revenge."

"You're damn right I would!"

Jartan is obviously angry and confused, as he is hearing things he isn't meant to know just yet; and the knowledge that the man standing before him is the cause of all his and his family's suffering is not something Modex wants to impart, so he tries to console Jartan.

"Revenge is not the path that one should begin to take toward the paladinhood, Jartan," he begins, "it can only lead you toward great misfortune. Morbius knew this, so he kept your family history secret in order to spare you the pain and therefore keep you on the right path."

Jartan is not comforted by this at all, and he is still very angry.

"I don't give a damn about all that nonsense! I want to know what is happening! Why was my sister transformed into an animal? What killed my mother? Where's my father? Why do I feel the soul of Morbius wants to be in the blade if he's not my family?"

"Look at the soul blade," Modex calmly suggests.

Jartan holds the blade before him. The faint glow of the blade is starting to flicker and weaken.

"See how it weakens?" Modex continues. "Morbius's soul is troubled that you know things you aren't ready for. Let your anger go, Jartan. If not, you will destroy everything Morbius tried to teach you. You must let it go."

"This isn't fair!" replies Jartan, still hurt, angry, and confused.

"You will have your answers in time, Jartan. But for now, let it go. If you truly want to be a paladin—if you want to fight evil—if you loved and respected my brother—then it's imperative that you not seek revenge. You have every right to punish those responsible in time—but not now. You aren't advanced enough yet to handle the negative ramifications that revenge brings. So let it go, for there is far too much at stake here to allow something as selfish as revenge to destroy. Morbius sacrificed much for you, and it's causing him pain that all his dreams, all his hopes, even your own destiny that he labored so hard to give you"—Modex now realizes that his own destiny is also a point of contention—"and the destiny of others all are at risk of being lost. Now it is I who implore you: let it go."

Jartan ponders this for a moment and closes his eyes. He is frustrated that his questions have no answers, but he can feel that even at his young age he shouldn't harbor for long the intense anger that floods his mind. The blade doesn't have Morbius's soul in it just yet, for its glow is only barely discernible—just enough to show that a soul is trying to communicate through it—and Jartan can sense that his anger is indeed painful to Morbius.

"All right," the boy reluctantly says, "I'll let it go—for now." The glow of the blade he is holding begins to increase.

"Well done," comments a pleased Modex. "Everything happens for a reason, though we may not know or even like what that reason is. For the first time in my life, I'm beginning to realize this. There are greater powers than you and I at work here, Jartan, so we both must have faith in Morbius's greater wisdom. Understand?"

Jartan nods in agreement.

"It's funny, but when Morbius first gave me the soul blade, once I held it in my hands I did feel the love of a sister. Morbius must have stopped me from understanding further."

"Oh, I'm sure he did," replies Modex. "The time wasn't right for such traumatic knowledge. So my dear brother wishes to serve you, does he? So be it. He was a powerful man in life and will be powerful again in death through your blade. He obviously wants it that way."

"He was a great man," says Jartan sadly but also with great admiration. "I was alone, and he loved and cared for me when no one else did."

These words have a somber effect on Modex, for as the boy's father, it should have been he who cared for the boy, but he touches Jartan gently as tears fill the youth's eyes as Jartan reflects on Morbius's affection.

"Things will be different now, Jartan," responds Modex tenderly. "You will soon feel his love again. So let's get started, shall we? Where is my brother's body?"

"It's buried on Mount Sabo."

"Then to Mount Sabo we must go."

"Are you crazy?" a stupefied Jartan shouts. "I barely survived the five days' journey from there! We can't—"

Modex taps his staff against the floor, which causes a bright flash of light, and when the light subsides, the two are standing before the grave of Morbius high atop Mount Sabo.

"You were saying something?" says Modex proudly with a sly grin.

Jartan shrugs sheepishly in silence. Modex walks over to Morbius's grave and looks solemnly upon it.

"Forgive me, my brother—I shall not fail you again. This time I shall use my power to do what is right. Jartan, put the blade upon the grave."

The boy does this as Modex raises his staff to begin the summoning of the soul of his loving brother, Morbius. He begins,

"Your life was born in the name of love. Your soul was born in the name of good. Let both be born again—now."

Modex touches the blade with the tip of his staff, and soon a low, rumbling thunder is heard as a brilliant bolt of energy streaks from above and hits the blade on the grave, which begins to glow with intense energy. After a few moments, the energy subsides. Jartan casts a questioning glance at Modex, who nods with a smile, so the boy goes over to pick up the blade. When he does so, it begins to glow brightly now that it has a soul within it—a soul that has been reunited with one that it loved—and a mighty soul blade has been born once again.

"I feel him! I feel Morbius!" the boy exalts happily.

"Then we must waste no more time," says Modex. "Kordon and Karza have a huge head start on us, but I know a few tricks my former teacher taught me—and a few he didn't. We'll give them a little surprise soon. Come," he says, and adds with a smile, "paladin."

A smiling Jartan stands beside Modex, who again taps his staff upon the ground, and the two disappear with a flash.

CHAPTER 18

✠ ✠ ✠

A flash of energy teleports Modex and Jartan into an area of almost total blackness—the lack of light preventing any sight of anything near, which prompts Jartan to raise his soul blade.

"I'll give us some more light," he says.

"No!" quickly responds Modex as he reaches out with his hand, grabbing Jartan's arm to stop him. "Don't do anything here unless I tell you."

"But why?"

"Because you are the intruder here, Jartan—not I. I spent many years as Kordon's apprentice, and I know this place well, so I am not seen as a threat. But as long as you are with me you should be safe."

"Where are we, anyway?"

Modex raises his staff, the tip of which begins to glow, and as he taps the bottom of the staff against the floor, the dozens of torches located throughout ignite brightly to illuminate the area.

The sight that reveals itself is a vast, two-leveled chamber, square in shape. Each of the four walls of both levels is covered with thousands upon thousands of small compartments obviously meant to contain some objects, but they all are empty. A small balcony separates the two levels, and only one large stairway at the end of the room provides access to the upper level, the ceiling of which is covered with smooth, polished black stones; and in the center of the chamber is a large table that has many scrolls strewn haphazardly about. Most of the scrolls on the table are open and show various magical symbols and strange words written on the parchment.

This is obviously a library but a particularly gloomy one, as the illumination of the torches does nothing to brighten the sinister atmosphere, for what overshadows the academic purpose of the library is that placed in each of the four corners of the room is a huge statue of an imposing creature some fifty feet tall. The bodies of the statues appear human, but the heads are those of beasts, each one different from the others, and each carries a different weapon—sword, spear, axe, and mace. They all resonate with an intimidating evil, and it doesn't take Jartan's soul blade long to alert its master.

"There's evil here!" the alarmed boy announces.

"That's hardly surprising," says Modex, unconcerned, "since we are within Kordon's fortress. This is the library of knowledge. Beware, paladin—for there are many of Kordon's minions of evil who inhabit these sinister walls."

Jartan chuckles softly though with a definite resigned tone when he hears this, for he realizes that every place he has been so far has been worse than the one before. First it was that abysmal swamp, then the vampire trees, then the Undead Forest that tried to make him a permanent resident—and the gods only know what this creepy library has in store for him, he thinks uneasily to himself as the two approach the table in the center of the library and Modex begins to search through the dozens of scrolls there.

"What are you looking for?" asks Jartan.

"The scroll that contains the spell that Kordon used to enter the Underworld. I know it is here, because I helped him create it."

"Well, hurry up and find it," replies an anxious Jartan. "I have a bad feeling about this place."

The youth can't help but notice the thousands of empty compartments along the walls and is certainly not impressed by the lack of knowledge in this supposed library.

"Some library," he continues. "It's practically empty except for what is here on this table."

"Oh, there's vast knowledge here, Jartan; make no mistake about that. One just has to know how to find it. And since the scroll I need is not here on this table, that just means it is locked away in the vault at the moment—pray that Kordon has not changed the combination to it."

In the center of the table there is a crystal ball, and Modex touches this with a finger while tracing an intricate series of patterns upon its surface. The ball soon glows brightly with power, and each of the once-empty compartments contains a tightly wound scroll.

"Histories of the Underworld," says Modex with his palm resting upon the ball.

The ball begins to glow yet again, prompting Modex to begin to look around the room in anticipation of the answer to his query, and he soon sees a small section on the upper level glowing, indicating that this is where the histories he is seeking are located.

"You stay here, Jartan, and do me a favor— don't touch anything. Let's see if you can stay out of trouble for once in your life."

"Just find that damn spell and let's get the seven hells out of here. This place gives me the creeps."

Modex teleports to the upper level where the histories are located and begins to search among them as Jartan watches, a bit exasperated at Modex's lack of faith in his abilities to handle himself.

"Crazy old wizard," he whispers softly so Modex can't hear. "Who does he think he is? My father?"

Bored with nothing to do, Jartan begins to scan the scrolls before him. One soon catches his eye. As he cocks his head to get a better look at the title words written on the half-opened scroll, he begins to say them softly to himself.

"Spells to charm human females—now there's some knowledge I can use!"

He glances up at Modex and, seeing that he is preoccupied with a scroll in his hand, Jartan fully opens the scroll of charm spells and begins to mischievously read through it intently.

Unfortunately for Jartan, now that he has broken Modex's commandment not to touch anything, high above his head one of the hand-sized black stones on the ceiling reveals that it is not a stone at all, for two evil red eyes open and eight legs emerge. Soon another stone reacts in the same fashion and then another and another, until the hundreds of creatures that were once cleverly camouflaged as unimposing black stones that comprised the entire ceiling are now alive and aware of the human intruder directly below. These are death spiders—small, jet-black, hand-sized arachnids that look as evil as they are—that slowly descend in unison on strands of web toward the unsuspecting Jartan who, thoroughly engrossed in the reading of the scroll, is oblivious to this descending carpet of eight-legged death inching ever closer. Not even the urgings of his soul blade can get his attention to alert him of this danger, for the scroll he is reading has his teenage mind firmly transfixed.

Modex has his back turned and therefore cannot see the death spiders descending behind him, but he is aware of their deadly descent, for he was the wizard who created this spell of death spiders in the first place long ago when he was Kordon's evil apprentice; and as he closes his eyes with a peevish sigh, thinking of who is responsible for awakening them—despite his explicit warning not to touch anything—he begins to quietly mumble to himself.

"Idiot child—I should have sacrificed him when I had the chance, but that damn mother of his—" Then he adds loudly, "Stop!"

Jartan laughs mischievously when he hears this, for he believes he has been caught in the act of his mild transgression of reading the scroll, so he turns to face Modex to explain.

"Look, I'm sorry, but I had to read this because it—"

But he is instantly stopped mid-sentence when he sees this menacing mass of death spiders with fangs bared only inches from his head, and he instinctively falls to the floor in horror at the sight.

"Sweet mother of the gods!" he screams.

"Is it just me, Jartan," Modex chastises in a light-hearted tone, "or does anyone else think you are a low-grade moron?" He gazes from the balcony at the pathetic sight of Jartan cowering below.

"Don't just stand there like a blithering idiot!" shouts Jartan back. "Do something!"

The wizard snaps his fingers, and the spiders disappear in a flash as their glittering remnants fall to the floor.

"How did you do that?" says an astonished Jartan.

"It was my spell that created the death spiders in the first place to protect the library from intruders. Any wizard has complete dominance over his own spells and can cancel them instantly. Now do you think you can stay out of trouble, or do I have to put a coma spell on you?"

Modex once again turns his attention to searching for the scroll with the spell to enter the underworld as Jartan sheepishly regains his feet, brushing a few spider remnants off his clothing. But Jartan soon notices that one of the statues in a corner of the library is beginning to open its eyes, which glow red. This makes Jartan uneasy, especially when he sees his soul blade confirming his suspicion that this sight is definitely not a welcome one.

"Um, Modex?"

"What is it now?" responds the irritated wizard, still looking through the scrolls and unaware of the statue awakening.

"Please tell me that you had another spell you used to protect the library—like one that animates statues—like those stone dragons at your castle before. That was one of your spells, right?"

"No, the ceiling of death spiders was the only spell I used here—and I thought it quite clever too—but animating statues was actually Kordon's specialty, and he created very powerful spells toward that end. Why do you ask?" Finding the scroll he needs, he adds, "Ah, here it is!"

With the scroll in hand he teleports back down to the lower level and stands beside Jartan.

"Because," says the anxious youth, grabbing the unsuspecting Modex to alert him of what is happening as all four statues open their eyes and fix their nefarious gazes on the pint-sized paladin below, "I see a major problem developing. Modex, get us out of here!"

Modex surveys the dire situation. He too is alarmed to see these statues start to move. Jartan becomes more and more anxious every second—even more so as he watches Modex hesitate to use his teleportation power to transport them both to safety, for the wizard suspects something that Jartan is unaware of. Modex waves his hand, and he now can "see"—due to his understanding of evil magic, which Jartan is unable to comprehend—that a thin cord of energy is emanating from each statue and attached to Jartan's body. Modex is greatly disturbed by this discovery that his suspicion was justified.

"What's wrong with you? What are you waiting for, you fool? Teleport us out of here!" demands a highly agitated Jartan.

Modex stares at Jartan for a moment with a look of futility in his eyes, and he can't help but notice the absolute horror on the youth's face when the wizard is the only one to teleport out of the library to safety—leaving a stunned Jartan to face the stone monstrosities alone.

"Modex!" screams Jartan, aghast at the vanishing form of the wizard that disappears in a glow of energy. Jartan makes a frantic effort to grasp at the fading teleport energy in the feeble hope that it will take him away as well.

Modex reappears outside the walls of Kordon's fortress, and even from this distance and through the muffling nature of the structure, Modex can hear Jartan's scream echoing from the interior. The solemn wizard creates a ball of energy in his hand, and he can see in it the form of Jartan surrounded by the statues.

"Forgive me, my son," he says quietly to himself, "but there's nothing I can do to help you."

The young Jartan is having great difficulty with his giant opponents, as their immense size, armor of dense stone, and great strength and power make them formidable adversaries. Any slashes he is able to inflict on them with his weapon are practically useless, since the statues are far too large for the soul blade to sever any vital areas; but what is particularly troubling for the boy is that the library has no obvious sign of any exit to facilitate any chance of an escape, for teleportation magic is the only way to enter and exit—a power that Jartan simply does not possess. Once again, only his nimbleness keeps him alive. Against one or perhaps two of the larger and slower statues, he would be able to maintain some semblance of parity, but four of the fearsome attackers allow him no chance. It is only a matter of time before they kill him.

Jartan makes an effort to rush up the stairs to the higher level in hopes of gaining some distance, but he only manages to make it up halfway before a slash from a giant axe impacts violently upon the stairs. Jartan jumps off to the side an instant before the staircase collapses completely. The large desk also provides a pitiful degree of protection, which Jartan soon discovers after diving under it when it too splinters completely from the impact of another statue's mace. The four stone statues soon have the overwhelmed and rapidly tiring Jartan on the verge of defeat.

"Modex, please!" he screams again to appeal to the unseen Modex. "For the love of the gods! Help me! Modex!"

Modex, though greatly concerned, continues helplessly to watch the struggling Jartan in his energy ball and can hear Jartan's pleas; but again the wizard does not interfere though Jartan desperately needs his help.

"Think, Jartan—think!" Modex says quietly to himself. "You don't have the soul of an eight-year-old sister in your blade now. Use the power that the soul of Morbius gives you!"

Jartan is knocked to the ground after a near miss, and a statue closes in for the kill. He screams in terror and puts his soul blade in front of him for protection. Suddenly, it sends out a blistering bolt of energy at the huge attacker, completely passing through its body, and the massive creature shatters into a smoking pile of rubble. The boy is obviously surprised by the blade's action (Modex smiles now that Jartan realizes its potential), and he points the blade in the direction of another statue that is almost upon him. It shatters in a similar fashion after a burst of energy from the soul blade, and the third statue falls as well. But as Jartan turns to face the fourth and final statue, he realizes that he doesn't have time to deliver an offensive attack, as this statue is quickly lowering its lethal weapon upon him, so the paladin—now aware of the greater abilities this more powerful soul blade possesses—brings the blade close to his body and creates an energy shield that absorbs the oncoming blow. He then pushes away with the blade and with power he never has felt before, the statue, despite its size compared to the tiny Jartan, is the one who is thrown back with great force. It hits the wall of the library hard and falls to the floor, which gives Jartan the opportunity to fire off another powerful blast of energy that shatters the last statue instantly, much to Jartan's great relief. He falls to his knees to recover his strength now that this near-death ordeal is finally over.

Laughing in celebration, Modex materializes beside him, very pleased with Jartan's performance.

"Well done, paladin!" he says proudly, putting his hand on his shoulder as a congratulatory gesture.

Jartan, though, is not pleased to see him, for—in Jartan's eyes, anyway—his disappearance was a cowardly and treasonous act. As he stands to face him, a look of hate and disgust registers on the boy's face at the sight of the backstabbing wizard, and he violently strikes him hard in the face with the back of his hand, which sends Modex reeling to the floor. Standing over him, Jartan points his soul blade straight at the neck of the wizard, whose skin begins to smoke and sizzle slightly as the point barely penetrates. Now only a very small advance of the blade on Jartan's part is required to end what he believes to be the devious and cowardly wizard's life.

"I should kill you right here and now, you twisted fiend!" shouts the very angry Jartan. "And don't give me any of that troll shit about killing a good creature, because you are definitely not one of them! You sick, evil—"

"Please, Jartan! Let me explain!"

"Talk fast, you bastard, and it had better be good or I'll decapitate that warped head of yours right here! Why didn't you teleport me with you?"

"I couldn't!" pleads Modex in defense, obviously and genuinely distraught that he couldn't offer the boy any assistance even though he was frantic with worry. "Kordon put what is called a 'bloodline spell' on those statues. They were attached to you! Wherever you went, they would have followed—even through a teleport spell."

"You could have at least helped me fight them instead of leaving me alone to be slaughtered!"

"No, no—I couldn't do that either," Modex counters calmly. "You see, a paladin that transfers to a higher-level soul blade must fight his first battle with it alone, or his powers won't come to him."

Jartan, reflecting on the words he hears, decides that they may be logical and withdraws the point of his blade from Modex's neck with disgust, for although he reluctantly understands what Modex is saying he still isn't happy with the way things turned out.

"You know," he begins, "it would have helped if you told me this before!"

"Sorry, I just forgot. I had other things on my mind," says the apologetic Modex, for he is thinking of when he first realized that Jartan was his son. The revelation was obviously so emotional to the wizard that he forgot to address any knowledge Jartan may have needed. He continues, "Please forgive me. But you mean to tell me that you didn't know any of this? Didn't you learn any of these basic teachings from the paladinhood?"

"I didn't go to the paladinhood!"

"Oh, I see. No, I guess you didn't. For there just wasn't enough time for Morbius to send you there, especially when he first realized Karza was out of the Abyss and was planning to resurrect Kordon. My apologies, Jartan. Please believe me that there just was nothing I could do to help—I wish I could have."

The boy just shakes his head, though he's not angry now with Modex as he helps the old wizard to his feet—it's more to do with the fact that all this is confusing and certainly dangerous to his person.

"I don't think I like being a paladin," says Jartan dejectedly. "There's too much I don't understand, and those things that I do I don't even like!"

"Don't you ever say that," Modex responds. "I know it's difficult for you to be thrust into situations you are ill prepared for, for you don't have the training and knowledge of experience that a higher-level paladin could have given you."

"Then why can't one of those paladins be doing this? Why does it have to be me? I didn't ask for any of this!"

"I told you before—there just wasn't time. But I can see why my brother advanced your training, for you have incredible skills, Jartan. Your adroitness with evasion alone is a power not many possess. You were born to be a paladin. It is your destiny. Very few humans have the qualities worthy of the paladinhood, for it's not something one can learn. You either have it or you don't, and you have it, and you command awesome powers because of it—far more than I or Morbius or any wizard could ever hope to attain in the fight against evil. Try and remember that when you feel overburdened by your responsibilities."

"Whatever," says the discouraged Jartan in resigned submission. "I will try, Modex. I just shudder to think what other secrets you are keeping from me!"

He says this half-jokingly, but this statement disturbs Modex, for he would like to tell Jartan that he is his father, but the time doesn't seem right just yet for him to impart such dramatic knowledge; and perhaps the time will never be right, for it will certainly be dramatic and possibly even traumatic for his son when he discovers who is responsible for his mother's death, the curse his sister had to endure, and the boy's own sufferings without a father around to offer the guidance—and indeed, love—that Jartan needed, and still needs today. At least, thinks Modex to himself, looking at the boy tenderly, he can offer his love now—belatedly, to be sure, and certainly a love that must be hidden, but at least it is genuine.

"Well," says Modex with a sly smile, "I think we both have had enough surprises for now. I have the spell to enter the Underworld. Are you ready?"

"Are you giving me a choice?"

"Not really."

"Then I guess I'm ready. Let's get out of here before I change my mind."

"Good," responds Modex, proud at his son's courage and commitment. "There's just one thing I must do before we leave, for there's far too much powerful knowledge of evil here—knowledge that has caused great pain, death, and destruction; knowledge that I am partly responsible for. But no longer!"

Modex takes his staff and begins to create a ball of bright red energy on the floor, which continues to increase in power, and after several moments it has reached a brightly glowing degree of pulsating, fiery red energy. Satisfied with this, he then creates an energy portal.

"Now," Modex says with grim determination, placing his hand on Jartan's shoulder, "you and I shall fight evil together."

Jartan smiles with pride. They both quickly enter the energy portal and disappear from the library room in a flash. A moment later, the energy ball on the floor explodes violently, sending sheets of flame spreading in all directions and instantly igniting the entire infernal library and all its malevolent contents of evil wisdom.

CHAPTER 19

✤　✤　✤

Although there is no hint of sunlight—they are deep below the Surface—the rocky walls of the small cavern that Modex and Jartan have teleported into seem to glow, providing an eerie illumination. Only one opening is visible, which leads off into total blackness. Jartan is surprised, though pleasantly so, as this is nowhere near the foreboding "Underworld" that the word conjures in the mind. In fact, it would seem quite harmless if it weren't for a faint though chilling and unearthly moaning that can be heard echoing throughout. But his feeling of blissful relief that this trek into this unknown realm of darkness will be an easy one lasts only a fraction of a second, for the evil of the Underworld now floods into his body, forcing the boy to tremble and cower in terror. Jartan has never felt such loathsome influences before, and his fifteen years—years that were relatively free from experiences of great evil— leave him totally unprepared for the overpowering malevolence at the level of evil that the Underworld contains, unlike Modex, whose greater level of maturity and evil past have made him immune to such terrors. He can see the

Underworld affecting the boy and tries to snap him out of his petrified state of fear by shaking him back to his senses.

"Jartan! Jartan, can you hear me? You cannot let it affect you! Jartan!"

The Underworld's influence continues to plunge the boy ever deeper into a hysterical state of fear and his body trembles even more violently. Modex doubles his effort to shake the fear out of the boy's body by shouting Jartan's name even louder, and only several strong slaps from the wizard finally bring Jartan out of his terror-stricken condition.

"Jartan? Are you all right now?"

The boy is still slow to recover, so Modex comforts him with some soothing words while gently shaking him and caressing his face.

"Come on, boy—that's it—easy now. Nothing will happen to you; do you understand? Look at me! Just take a deep breath. That's better."

"What—what happened?" the boy asks, still a bit shaken from the experience as his breath labors to take on a more calm rhythm, his body still trembling slightly. "I never felt anything so terrifying before in my life!"

"The Underworld affected you. You aren't old enough yet to have acquired enough experiences to shield you from the powerful influences that this level of evil generates. But you'll be fine now."

"So this is the Underworld?" Jartan comments while looking around cautiously.

"Yes," replies Modex. "This is the level of existence directly beneath our own, which we call the "Surface". Very few creatures of goodness exist here, my young friend, for it is a world of almost total evil as you just found out. We must take great care."

"What other levels of existence are there, Modex?"

"The Demonic Abyss is the lowest level, and that lies below the Underworld. Thank the gods we fortunately have no need to go into those infernal regions. If the evil of the Underworld affected you so violently, you wouldn't last a minute in the Abyss. Even I, at my level of power, couldn't last more than an hour before I would be slaughtered by the evil, demonic hordes that spawn there. But there are also the Heavens, which is pretty much the opposite of the Underworld, and that is the level above the Surface, and above the Heavens is the highest level of existence, the Land of the Gods, where all the divine beings—good, evil, or otherwise—reside. It is also where the Land of the Dead is—the seven hells—many other realms.

"I still don't understand why we needed a spell to get here, Modex. I thought there were many natural entrances to the Underworld from the Surface."

"True, there are. But you have to imagine that the Underworld is a vast maze of caverns and it is not all interconnected, so certain entrances only lead to certain areas. But this is the quickest way to reach Magdara's seal, which is where Kordon is headed. Without the spell and using one of the natural entrances from the Surface could take many weeks to reach the place of the seal. And we don't have that much time—that is, even if we survived the journey, which I seriously doubt. The Underworld is not for the faint or weak of heart—and definitely not for any who are weak in power."

"So we are near the seal now then?"

"Good heavens, no. No, that is much deeper into the Underworld, but this is the closest that Kordon's spell can bring us to it."

"But how can we possibly overtake them? They have almost a week's head start on us. It's impossible!"

"You underestimate the almost limitless perils of the Underworld, Jartan. It is fraught with untold horrors of powerful creatures and devious deceptions, traps, and barriers, and these will take Kordon and Karza much time to overcome. But since we are on the same path that they are using, we won't have to face near as many of these obstacles, because they have already dealt with most of them for us. You see? Worry not, for we will catch up to them."

"If you say so," says Jartan, doubtful of this, for the limited view that this small cavern provides of the Underworld so far is hardly fraught with untold horrors as Modex claims. But as he recalls how even this rather innocuous small area threw him into an uncontrollable fear, he begins to realize that Modex's words may be worth heeding, and Jartan warily walks toward the opening of blackness as he continues, "Well, let's get on with it."

"Not that way, paladin," says Modex stopping him. "This way."

Jartan is surprised by this remark, for there is only one opening visible, and that is the one he was heading for; but his look of astonishment grows when he sees Modex heading for the back wall of this small cavern. *He's lost his mind*, thinks Jartan as he watches this.

"Modex, maybe the fact that you turned to evil in the past has short-circuited your brain in some way—but *this* is the way out of here," says the boy, gesturing to the only obvious exit visible.

"That just leads farther into another area of the Underworld. We want to get to Magdara's seal."

But this statement does nothing to shake Jartan's belief that Modex is clearly befuddled—possibly insane—which prompts him to say, "Modex, I hate to say this, but if you by any chance have a spell that cures senility, I think you should use it on yourself right now."

Modex is at the back wall and sighs heavily with eyes closed as he ponders the ignorant Jartan's sarcastic words. Fifteen years ago, he tried to kill this person when he was an innocent baby. Now that Jartan has the power of speech, that feeling has only intensified—not that he would act on it, of course, but Modex does find the thought comforting.

"Jartan, the gods went to great lengths to make the path to Magdara's seal as inaccessible as possible. Anyone who managed to get this far would assume that this is simply a dead end and turn back. But for those of us who know better"—Modex taps the wall three times with his staff, and the rock facade fades away, revealing an entrance that leads into total darkness—"this is hardly a dead end."

"By the gods!" gasps Jartan upon seeing the entrance. "I had no idea. I'm sure glad you are here to guide us, Modex. I never would have known any of this! I will certainly trust your judgment."

"Really, Jartan?" responds Modex with a decidedly sarcastic tone. "You will really trust my judgment?"

Jartan is somewhat taken aback by this, for it's almost like Modex is being sarcastic—which he is.

"Um, yes," responds the boy warily.

"Well, that's just fine. But if that is indeed the case, then before we go any farther, I would like to make something abundantly clear—may I?"

"Yes," replies Jartan apprehensively due to Modex's sarcastic attitude, unsure what to make of it.

"Don't touch anything!"

"All right, all right! I learned my lesson. You don't have to shout at me."

"I'm not shouting at you—I'm screaming at you! Don't touch anything! Do you understand?"

"Yes!" says the boy defensively.

"Wonderful. I'll sleep better at night now. Let's go."

And the two step through the entrance.

The cavern that greets them is a large, circular one with a path running through it that leads to an exit at the far end. Except for the narrow path, which is clear, the ground, walls and ceiling are covered with stunning jewels of varying sizes and every color imaginable, which sparkle brilliantly in the light, creating a cavern of striking opulence and incredible beauty.

"Wow!" exclaims Jartan excitedly at the dazzling amount of wealth. "This Underworld isn't going to be half as bad as I thought it would be! Modex, we're rich!" But a glare from the wizard causes Jartan to change his joyful tune. "I know, I know—don't touch anything."

"Looks can be deceiving. This is the first of four 'Caverns of Death' we must pass before we can overtake Kordon and Karza, but fortunately for us, this is an easy one to get through. Just stay on the path."

"Caverns of Death?" says Jartan. "That doesn't sound very encouraging. I know I will probably regret asking this, but what are these caverns?"

"This is the Cavern of Jewels, for obvious reasons—but there is also the Cavern of the Vortex, the Cavern of Mirrors, and finally the Cavern of Fire."

Modex and Jartan continue along the path as Jartan fights the temptation to grab an armful of jewels, for the urge to do so is great. Their dazzling beauty has a hypnotic impact on those weakening from being near to so much unimaginable wealth. Modex can see the boy is having trouble.

"Don't give in to the temptation, Jartan."

"I'm trying not to, but it's difficult. It's almost hypnotic—as if they are calling to me to touch them, for they are just so incredibly beautiful! I just want to grab an armful!"

"That is precisely the danger here, for the cavern is trying to seduce you into doing just that. You must fight it."

As they continue to walk, Jartan sees a small pool of blood on the path, and as he looks down, curious at its bewildering presence, he sees another drop of blood fall into it; but looking upward to ascertain the source, he only sees the dazzling array of glittering jewels that cover the entire ceiling. Puzzled by this, he moves on after a few moments to catch up with Modex, and soon they both reach a rocky arch near to the exit of the cavern.

"I'm curious, Modex. What would have happened if I touched a jewel?"

"I'll show you. But you had better stand underneath this arch with me."

Jartan stands close beside Modex beneath the rocky arch. Modex looks to the ground and sees a hand-sized rock near his feet. Picking this up, Modex tosses it into an area of the jewel-covered ground. Faster than the eye can see, the ground and ceiling of the cavern catapult toward each other and would have instantly crushed Modex and Jartan had they not been standing in the safe arch near the cavern's exit, and as the two sections slowly begin to retract toward their original positions, Jartan is astounded to see that they are heavily laden with large spikes. The skeletal remains of several previous adventurers are skewered upon them, and there is one very recent kill, which is where the blood on the path must have come from. After a few moments, the two sections have fully retracted into the ceiling and ground, and the bejeweled illusion again conceals this treacherous death trap.

"Incredible," remarks the astonished Jartan. "It was all an illusion! There are no jewels here at all! It's nothing but an elaborate trap!"

"Exactly," comments Modex, who knew this fact all along. "It took much skill and bravery for those poor souls to get this far only to be killed by their own greed, not knowing that even greater wealth and power awaited them deeper in the Underworld had they freed Magdara from her imprisonment. She would have rewarded them handsomely. We should be grateful they were blinded by their evil lust and greed and too weak to resist it."

"And we have three more of these horrid caverns to get past?" Jartan asks warily.

"I'm afraid so—and each one more diabolically difficult than the previous."

As the intrepid duo sojourn on, they soon are confronted by a curtain of long, tentacle-like growths, hundreds in number, hanging down from the ceiling of this next cavern, almost touching the ground, and they sway menacingly due to a strong wind that is blowing almost as if all the air in this area is being sucked toward some unseen source farther ahead.

"I don't like the looks of those things at all," comments a wary Jartan.

Modex also does not approve of their intimidating presence, and he raises his hand toward them and makes a gesture with it as if trying to use a spell to eliminate this barrier of serpentine vines—but no magic emanates from his hand.

"I was afraid of something like this," says Modex, concerned at the futile act.

"What is wrong, Modex?"

"There are some areas of the Underworld where magic will not function, and this is one of them because of the vortex that lies just beyond those malignant vines. It absorbs everything that comes near, including magical energy."

"If that's the case, then you just stay close to me, old wizard," says Jartan, confidently drawing his soul blade, one with more power than his first, which gives him the idea. "I'll get us through this overgrown patch of weeds—no sweat."

The confident boy nonchalantly fires off a blast of energy from the soul blade. If those stone giants in the library couldn't handle such an attack, then these weakling vines certainly shouldn't pose any problem, and indeed the blade's energy effortless plows through the curtain of vines for quite some distance, instantly severing a large number of them, which shrivel and incinerate—but almost as immediately, they grow back even thicker than before. Modex is not impressed and looks at the boy, irritated. Jartan is also dismayed by the vines' persistence, but not wanting Modex to chastise him, the youth tries to justify his action.

"I was just testing to see how resilient they are," says Jartan.

"Of course you were," replies Modex, knowing full well that was not the case.

"Just stay close, wizard."

Jartan creates a shield of energy with the blade, and he and Modex proceed unopposed beneath the umbrella of power into the curtains of vines. The vines make a concerted effort to attack the intruders but cannot penetrate the paladin's shield. However, halfway through the vines, the shield begins to flicker and fade.

"I'm losing my shield!" cries an anxious Jartan.

"It's the vortex! It's draining your soul blade energy as well! Hurry, Jartan, we must get through before it fails completely!"

They urgently quicken their pace and are almost at the end of this gauntlet of vile vines. Due to Jartan's dexterity, the youth manages to dive for safety out of the vines' reach just as the energy shield fails, but the less agile Modex is instantly ensnared in the vines. They coil around his body tightly and begin to squeeze the very life out of the helpless wizard. Jartan makes a frantic effort to aid him by trying to fire off an energy blast from his weapon, but the blade is barely able to cast a feeble glow at this point, let alone generate any offensive power, and soon all the blade's energy is drained completely. An alarmed Jartan shakes the blade violently as if to force any remaining energy out of it—but the blade does nothing. Although powerless, it is still a sword and has an extremely sharp edge, so Jartan uses this to sever the vines coiled around Modex as well as any that try and do the same to him, and he drags Modex to safety. Once free of any further interference from the vines, Jartan pulls off any vine remnants that cling to the wizard's body and then helps him to his feet.

"Are you all right?" the boy asks.

"Yes, thank you, Jartan. Just give me a moment to catch my breath."

"It is difficult to breathe," says Jartan, as he too is having trouble. "What's happening?"

"It's the vortex. As I told you, it absorbs everything that comes near, including the air. We can't stay here much longer, Jartan. Quickly—we only have a few minutes before we suffocate!"

As they rush forward, they soon reach the imposing Cavern of the Vortex, which lies before them. The cavern is a huge hole that has the glowing, rapidly swirling whirlpool of mist that is the dreaded vortex deeper within it. The exit is at the far end some fifty feet away, but there is no bridge spanning the vortex to reach it; nor is there any way to forge around the gaping pit, as the walls are smooth and nearly vertical, and there is no evidence of anything to grasp in order to pass around it. Not that it would have been much use had there been, for the wind is so strong here that it would have sucked them off with ease and forced them down into the swirling and obviously lethal abyss.

"In the name of the ancients!" says Jartan as he looks over the edge of the pit at the ominously spinning vortex below, taking great care not to let the violent wind pull him into it.

"Damn it!" cries Modex. "There's no bridge here."

"You mean you didn't know?" says a shocked Jartan upon hearing this. "I thought you were supposed to be the expert on the Underworld!"

"Look, I was virtually imprisoned for fifteen years. It's not like I was taking my vacations here! You can't expect me to know everything."

"Great. Well, what are we going to do? Your magic won't work here, and my soul blade has no energy, so we can't go back through those damn vines to try another path."

"My magic and your energy will return once we get past the vortex."

"That's hardly helpful, Modex, when we obviously can't get past and will soon suffocate because of it."

"I admit we are in a little trouble," confesses the wizard meekly.

"A little? If I had more air in my lungs, I'd be cursing you something fierce! How did Kordon and Karza manage to get across?"

"I'm sure Karza transformed himself into one of his twisted creatures and simply flew across while carrying Kordon. See, that is precisely why Kordon needed a being like Karza to help him, for his powerful magic is useless in some places here. But unfortunately for us, we do not possess the power of flight."

"Oh, yes we do!" rejoices Jartan happily, as an idea has entered his head. "Now, you said the soul blade energy will return once past the vortex—correct?"

"Correct," acknowledges Modex.

"Immediately?"

"Yes, once your feet hit the other side, all the power immediately returns."

"I don't care about my feet—what about the blade? Will its power return once it gets past the vortex?"

"It will," says Modex, thoroughly puzzled over what Jartan is asking. "What are you planning to do?"

"We may not be able to fly," says Jartan as he walks the few steps back to where the pile of vines he removed earlier from Modex remains. Tying a long vine to the soul blade's handle, he continues, "but the soul blade can. I'm going to throw it at the ceiling of the cavern near the exit. Once it gets past the vortex, its power will return, and it will penetrate deep into the rock and stick fast. It will then be strong enough to hold our weight, and we can swing across. Here, hold this end of the vine."

Modex takes the end.

Using both hands to grasp the blade and all his strength to overcome the winds within the cavern (lest the blade be sucked into the vortex), Jartan heaves the soul blade across it toward the far side. Once it passes the vortex, the glow of power returns to the blade and it penetrates deep into the rock wall.

"Hold on tight, Modex," he advises, and the two swing across the swirling pit to the far side, escaping from the death trap of the Cavern of the Vortex.

"Soul blade!" commands Jartan, standing safely with Modex on the ledge in front of the exit. The blade emerges from within the rock overhead and shoots into Jartan's outstretched hand.

"Very clever," says Modex, impressed by the boy's method.

"Didn't think I had it in me, did you, Modex?" responds Jartan, beaming with pride.

"No," says the wizard bluntly.

Jartan just glares at him.

"I shouldn't ask this," says Jartan as the two approach the third cavern of death, "but any idea what this Cavern of Mirrors is going to be like?"

"No, but I do know the first two caverns were traps and the last two have guardians that must be defeated in order to pass, and considering how crafty we had to be in order to get through the first two, I dread to think what these last two caverns have in store for us. But stay vigilant, paladin, for it is imperative that at least one of us does not fail."

They reach the dark entrance to the third cavern, and after stopping for a moment to fortify their courage with a deep breath, they enter into it.

The Cavern of Mirrors is exactly what the name implies. It is a long tunnel with a relatively low ceiling of rock, and the walls of this tunnel are smoothly mirrored on either side for the entire length of the tunnel; but what particularly gets both Modex and Jartan's attention, and disturbingly so, is that the mirrored side closest to Jartan reflects his image, but Modex is nowhere to be seen in the glass—and the reverse is true on Modex's side, as his image is visible but not Jartan's. Jartan looks at Modex, concerned by this, and the wizard acknowledges the unsettling sight.

"Yes, I see it. I don't like it either."

But what also gets Modex's attention is that a small section of the mirror wall near the entrance is smashed on either side, further perplexing the wizard. But what is even more unsettling as Modex and Jartan advance are the two figures slowly walking toward them far down the tunnel. The two stop when they notice their unsettling presence, and the two unknown figures also stop instantly. Again Modex and Jartan exchange glances of confusion and cautiously begin to walk forward, and the two unknown figures also advance, though they are still too far away to make out exactly what—or who—they are.

"Oh, now I really don't like this," says Modex nervously as the two figures appear to match their movements perfectly.

The two advancing pairs quickly close the distance between them, and soon the figures reveal themselves, which instantly stops Modex and Jartan in their tracks.

"By the gods, Modex! It's us!"

"Yes," cautiously responds Modex.

He advances slowly, and his mirror twin does the same, and as Modex moves to the side to try to go around the twin, it matches Modex's movements exactly. Modex reaches out to push the palm of his hand against the twin's, who does the same and exerts exactly the same amount of pushing force, causing neither hand to move any farther.

"Hmmm—that's an interesting and quite perplexing little trick," he says, withdrawing his hand and then moving away. The twin continues to match Modex in every detail as Modex continues, "It's obvious we can't go around them, and we certainly can't go through them. I wonder—"

Modex turns to walk farther away, but he suddenly turns to face his twin and discharges a bolt of lightning from his hand at it—obviously trying to catch the twin off guard—but it again mirrors Modex's movements and does the same thing to the real Modex. Both he and the twin reel from the bolt's painful impact and fall to the ground, each one's clothing smoldering slightly.

"Modex!" shouts Jartan.

The boy quickly begins to help the wizard to his feet as Modex grimaces in pain. As he does this, Jartan can't help but notice that Jartan's twin is doing the same thing for Modex's twin, causing Jartan to sneer at this maddening duplication—and of course, his twin sneers right back at him, further compounding the boy's—and his twin's—irritation.

"And *that* is definitely not the answer either," says Modex, taking a moment to recover his senses.

"This is enough to drive you insane!" comments Jartan in frustration. "What kind of sick, twisted mind even comes up with these nightmares?"

"The gods do have a unique sense of humor, this is true. But a better question to ask is how Kordon and Karza got past. They must have encountered their mirror images as well—and yet they got through, so there must be an answer somewhere! But where?"

Jartan tries his luck with his twin and stands before the image, making several quick slashes against it with his soul blade—which the image matches precisely, thereby nullifying the strikes.

"This is crazy! It's like fighting your own shadow!" he says, amazed at his twin's perfect imitation. "Well, at least it can't seem to hurt us."

Jartan turns away and begins to put the blade back into its scabbard. His twin does the same—but then the twin suddenly stops and turns with an evil grin on its face. Modex is alarmed to see this.

"Jartan, look out!"

Jartan turns suddenly, but he is unable to evade a slash that the twin delivers with its soul blade into the unsuspecting youth's side, though fortunately it is a minor wound thanks to Modex's warning. Jartan, shocked by this unanticipated action, is able to react swiftly enough to evade or block any additional slashes from the twin—who is clearly acting on his own volition and totally independent of Jartan's movements. The two exchange intense sword blows, for Jartan is now engaged in the fight of his life with an opponent that is literally his exact equal in agility, strength, and skill. The paladin does manage to deliver a minor slash against his twin's arm—but the wound is instantly duplicated on Jartan's arm at the same location, causing the horrified youth to focus his frantic efforts purely on defense.

Modex is also now engaged in a magical battle with his twin, for it is acting on its own evil volition as well; and like Jartan, he too is purely on the defensive, for he remembers his lightning attack earlier and how it backfired upon him. He therefore has no desire to deliver any lethal blow to his twin—for he himself would be killed by it.

"Jartan, back away! It's no use to fight them!"

The two beat a hasty retreat and once enough distance is achieved, their mirror counterparts once again resume their harmless though highly frustrating mimicry, matching Modex and Jartan exactly.

"That's better," says the wizard. "Apparently when you get close enough to the reflection, it can attack on its own. This is easily one of the most devious barriers I've ever encountered and obviously a highly effective one, and quite frankly I'm at a complete loss as to how to get past them."

"It's not fair!" adds Jartan, more frustrated than ever. "Any wound we make on them instantly registers on our own bodies. How can you possibly defeat your own self? They're our equals in every respect. It's as if the only way to beat them is to commit suicide—and that can't be the answer."

"But it is the answer, my clever young friend!" says Modex, laughing, as he has figured out the key to unlocking this maddening mirror puzzle thanks to Jartan's words. "Jartan, you inspire me. Obviously you inherited your brilliance from m—" He was going to say "me" but that surely would have alerted the boy that Modex is his father, which would have then brought up some unpleasant issues, so the wizard quickly corrects his wording. "Um—Morbius's tutelage."

"What in the name of the ancients are you talking about?" says Jartan, confused.

"We kill ourselves."

"I see," says the youth, understandably wary as he thinks once again that the old wizard has definitely lost his mind—and this time for sure. "Modex, about that senility spell—"

"Would you shut up, Jartan, and listen to me? We don't kill ourselves, you fool—we kill our mirror selves! Watch."

Modex violently strikes his mirror image on the tunnel wall next to him with his staff, and as the glass shatters—his twin shatters too. Seeing the logic in Modex's words, Jartan thrusts his blade into his image on the wall, and his twin shatters along with the glass.

"Finally!" says Modex with a sigh of relief. "I always wondered why we could only see one reflection of ourselves in the mirror wall and not another on the other side. It was this image that was the power creating our twin, so once the image was destroyed, so was our opposing twin. Clever gods to come up with something so devious—very clever indee—" But he stops as a ghastly thought occurs to him and quickly turns to look back toward the cavern entrance.

"Modex?" asks Jartan, obviously disturbed to see Modex's expression rapidly change to one of such alarm. "Modex, what's wrong?"

"Kordon knew this all along. That's why those mirrors were smashed right at the beginning."

"So? He figured it out sooner than we did. What's the big deal?"

"But he shouldn't have—that's the point. Once we entered the cavern, our twins appeared at the far end, but it was only when we went further down the tunnel and our twins did as well that we realized what we were facing. But Kordon smashed his mirror image on the wall long before he could have possibly seen his twin, because he already knew the secret key to defeat the guardian."

"So what are you trying to say, Modex?"

"I'm not sure, Jartan. But it's as if he has access to a higher level of knowledge—a level he should not possess. As if he—but no, that's impossible."

"What's impossible?"

"It doesn't matter," continues Modex, shrugging off the thought. "I'll give it more thought later. Come, paladin. We now only have one more cavern to pass."

Modex and Jartan arrive at the last Cavern of Death, the imposing Cavern of Fire. It is easily the most intimidating of the four caverns encountered thus far, for it is an immense chasm hundreds of feet across where an inferno of molten lava bubbles and gushes turbulently far below, often erupting with fountains of fire of varying height, some almost reaching the ceiling of the cavern. At the edge of this fiery abyss, there are five marble pedestals about four feet high, each topped with a large, hand-sized jewel: blue, red, clear, green, and purple.

"There's no bridge," observes Jartan as he stands at the edge. "This is like that damn vortex, and it's far too big to swing across, so I hope you have a better idea to get us over this, Modex."

"There's a bridge, Jartan," says Modex solemnly, "but I almost wish there wasn't."

"Oh, great," retorts the boy, instantly picking up on the wizard's solemn tone, for it can only bode something dangerous. "I can't wait to hear what kind of depressing gem of information you have this time that is going to make me want to vomit and wish I never started this trek of one tragedy after another. So do tell, Modex—how do we find this bridge?"

"By placing your hand on one of these jewels here—each one creates a bridge to the other side."

"Why are there five of them?" asks Jartan.

"Each bridge, as in the Cavern of Mirrors, has its own unique guardian, and this guardian must be defeated if we are to cross to the other side."

"You are just full of cheerful news, aren't you?" responds Jartan sarcastically. "Why can't you just teleport us over there like you did to Mount Sabo and Kordon's library? They were much farther away than this, and there's no vortex here that absorbs magic."

"Teleporting great distances only works on the Surface, Jartan, but here in the Underworld my teleport spell has very limited range and power. I would have to be a lot closer, and besides, it would only work for me down here."

"Do you know what these guardians will be?" asks Jartan hopefully, but he now thinks that maybe it's best that he doesn't know.

"No, but considering the difficulty we had with the guardians in the Cavern of Mirrors, I can only grimly imagine what foul forms await us here. But there is a glimmer of hope, for if we can choose the same bridge that Kordon took to cross, there is a good chance we won't have to face its guardian because Kordon will already have defeated it for us—so choose a jewel wisely, paladin."

But Jartan just stands there looking at him.

"What's wrong with you?" asks Modex, puzzled by Jartan's stoic stance. "Go ahead and choose one."

"You told me not to touch anything."

"Just get on with it, Jartan!" replies the wizard, not sharing the sarcastic youth's humor.

"All right, here goes," says Jartan, placing his hand on one of the jewels—the blue one.

The jewel glows brightly, and it shoots out a wide beam of light that creates a bridge of glowing energy to the other side of the cavern. It is a pleasant sight to the two, for it doesn't appear threatening at all, and more importantly, no guardian is seen.

"There's no danger," comments Jartan, who has drawn his soul blade in anticipation of facing whatever guardian might appear. The blade gives no warning. "I think we finally got a break for a change! I knew that jewel wouldn't fail me. Blue is my favorite color and always brings me good luck."

But as the two happily step onto the bridge of light, suddenly more beams shoot off in all directions from the center beam that acts as the bridge, and this instantly transforms the upper portion of the cavern above the bridge into an immense spider's web of light strands—and considering the immensity of this web, only an immense spider could have spun it. The sight definitely is not a pleasing one for the two travelers. But what further reinforces this foreboding effect is a sheet of energy appearing directly behind Modex and Jartan, preventing any chance of escape the way they came—and Jartan's soul blade pulsates brightly, signaling danger.

"So," begins Modex dryly, "the color blue always brings you good luck? Was that the appallingly stupid statement you made, Jartan?"

"Well," begins the boy meekly, "maybe if we don't move, this will all go away."

No sooner does the last word leave his mouth than the wall of energy behind them slowly begins to advance, and when it touches Modex's robe, it ignites a small section of the garment. The wizard is now aware of this disturbing occurrence, and glaring at Jartan, he extinguishes the fire with some magical energy and again addresses the sheepish youth.

"For the love of the gods, boy, would you please give your brain a chance?" says the annoyed Modex, who hurriedly steps out of harm's way farther out along the bridge. Jartan follows meekly, for the slowly advancing wall of death gives him no choice.

The two continue to cross the bridge cautiously. It is ominously web-like in appearance, and when they reach the middle they see a huge web tunnel near the ceiling of the cavern almost directly overhead—with the tip of one lone leg of a huge, unseen spider protruding from the opening, touching a strand of light. Modex and Jartan try to tread as lightly as possible for fear of making their presence known; but unbeknownst to them, every step they make causes the bridge to tremble ever so slightly, and this sends pulses of energy up the web strands attached to the bridge toward the web tunnel—and ultimately the web strand that the spider's leg is touching, alerting the creature to the presence of prey. It races out of the web tunnel with surprising speed and scrambles down the web toward the human pair below, who are horrified to see the form of this terrifying phase spider rapidly descending upon them.

The spider's body is a motley mix of black, yellow, and blood red, with piercing white eyes on its grotesque face and spiny black legs, the two foremost ones ending in large, razor-sharp spikes that are obviously used for spearing any prey that comes within reach. Its fangs dripping with deadly venom are an even worse threat and would be instantly fatal to the two humans present, as their size is that of a small insect compared to the spider.

"Modex, look out!" cries Jartan.

The paladin fires at the creature with his weapon, but the spider's entire body suddenly becomes semi-transparent, and the energy bolts pass harmlessly through it. The spider lands on the bridge in front of Modex, and he too is unable to affect the semi-transparent creature with his discharges of offensive magic bolts; but it soon becomes solid once more, and in this state it is able to spit forth a web from its mouth that ensnares Modex in sticky strands as strong as coiled steel, instantly immobilizing the uselessly struggling wizard. The spider prepares to deliver a lethal bite, but Jartan comes rushing in, preparing to slash one of the huge creature's legs; but it can see this attack coming and becomes semi-transparent once again, causing the paladin's slash to pass completely through the spider's leg as if it wasn't even there. Jartan is understandably dismayed by this, as every attempt to combat this monstrosity is ineffective. As the spider becomes solid once more, it fires an energy beam at Jartan from its glowing white eyes; but the boy manages to protect himself from the blast with an energy shield from his soul blade.

Modex, who has had time to magically free himself from the web thanks to Jartan's distractions, launches a magical barrage of fire balls at the eight-legged opponent, but again the phase spider becomes semi-transparent and the flaming orbs pass through without causing injury—but a counterattack at Modex from the eyes of the now solid spider forces the wizard to create an energy shield himself as a protective measure and although it absorbs the attack, the impact is enough to knock him off his feet. He rolls off the bridge, barely managing to grip the side just in time to keep from falling into the raging inferno below.

"Modex, hang on!" yells Jartan, rushing over to help.

"The thought had occurred to me!" shouts Modex back sarcastically.

But the phase spider resumes its attack on Jartan before he can assist Modex, and it fires another blast of energy at the boy, who quickly counters with a shield of protection. Fortunately, as the lethal beams continue to bombard the shield, Jartan is able to deflect them back with the new ability that his more powerful soul blade has, and they return to impact the spider, sending the creature hurtling back across the bridge for some distance. Jartan further increases the somewhat limited level of security the distance provides by launching a few bolts of energy at the spider, causing it to go on the defensive by turning semi-transparent once again, and Jartan has a chance to help Modex back up to the bridge.

"What is that thing, Modex?" he anxiously asks.

"It's a phase spider. It is able to become ethereal at will, making attacks on its body impossible. It only becomes solid to attack."

The spider again spits out a web at the pair, but Modex this time is able to counter with a burst of flame from his hand that incinerates the strands and prevents them from reaching their target. A swift electrical counterattack from the wizard quickly follows, but the spider becomes ethereal and avoids any damage as it begins to rush toward them.

"This is never going to work," says Modex, discouraged at the spider's stubborn persistence and its ability to avoid injury. "The blasted thing is instantly aware of our energy attacks and becomes ethereal before any damage can be inflicted! Our only chance is for you to deliver a physical attack with your soul blade that the spider isn't expecting. I'll try and bait it into attacking me, and when it becomes solid, you rush in and strike. My teleport spell has enough power to at least get behind the thing, and I'll distract it long enough for you to get close to it undetected. Just remember not to use any energy, or it will detect you—understand?"

"Yes, I understand. Good luck, Modex."

"Maybe I should wear something blue," counters the sardonic wizard as he disappears with a flash.

"Very funny," replies Jartan, not sharing the sarcasm.

Modex soon reappears behind the spider and shouts, "Here I am!" He fires a few magic bolts at the creature, which, as always, pass harmlessly through its semi-transparent body. The spider turns away from Jartan toward Modex and begins to rush at him. But Modex holds his ground in hopes the spider will become solid to deliver its attack. It soon does so, and as Modex erects his shield to brave the onslaught of energy and web attacks—the opportunity for Jartan to act presents itself.

"Now, Jartan! Attack its underside!"

Jartan rushes in, and while the spider rears its huge body in preparation to deliver a fatal blow to Modex, he thrusts his soul blade deep into its abdomen. The phase spider shrieks in agony and fires multiple blasts of energy from its eyes as it reels in the spasms of intense pain. They streak off in every direction, and those that hit the ceiling of the cavern sever the web strands that are attached to the bridge, which begins to flicker and fade now that its structure has been damaged and then begins to collapse.

Modex, knowing that the bridge will soon lose its ability to support itself over the flaming lava, immediately turns to look how far the ledge to safety is. He realizes the distance is grim though possible and decides to risk his limited teleportation power in an attempt to reach it, for he really has no choice. He closes his eyes to concentrate on the deed and, with a tap of his staff, disappears with a flash, soon reappearing on the ledge just inches from the edge. A bit shorter would have meant instant death in the lava below.

Jartan, though, has no teleportation powers, and he and the phase spider plummet downward with the remains of the bridge—but miraculously he manages to grab one of the many web strands that are still attached to the ceiling the cavern. Fortuitously, he grabs one that leads near to where Modex is standing on the ledge that leads to safety and the exit to this fiendish cavern. But unfortunately for the boy, this particular strand he is desperately clinging to is too long and is sending him hurtling toward the side of the cavern with an unsettling amount of speed.

The impact of the collision against the rock is a hard one and sufficiently severe to momentarily stun the boy, and he loses his grip on the strand and once again plummets toward certain death. He frantically thrusts his soul blade into the wall in an effort to prevent his descent, but the glowing blade simply cuts through it like it was made of air.

"Stop!" he commands the soul blade, and its glow vanishes. The blade is able to rapidly slow his fall and stop it altogether, allowing him to grab the web strand nearby and start to climb up to safety.

"Jartan—the spider!" shouts a frantic Modex, gazing down from above.

Jartan looks down and can see the phase spider quickly climbing up the same web strand that he is using. The boy begins to scramble up far more rapidly, but the spider, naturally accustomed to using webs, is the much faster of the two and quickly gains on the panic-stricken Jartan.

Modex can see this horrendous spectacle from his position directly above and tries to help Jartan by firing energy bolts at the spider in an effort to stop its advance upon the boy or at least slow its progress, but as always the ethereal defense prevents any harm to the creature and Modex's efforts are ultimately useless. Normally, this act would have been considered a noble and helpful one, but due to Modex's location directly overhead the wizard's magical bolts pass dangerously close to the boy's body—and one of them now alarmingly singes the hair on the top of his head.

"Damn it, Modex!" shouts Jartan—more afraid of being killed by Modex's aid rather than the spider. "What are you trying to do? Kill me? Stop it!"

Modex stops firing but can see the spider is quickly gaining on Jartan.

"Hurry, Jartan! It's almost upon you!"

Jartan is climbing as fast as he can, but the spider is now close enough to begin using its front two legs and their lethal spikes to try to stab the poor youth; but after several more moments of this deadly race, Jartan finally reaches the top of the ledge seconds before the spider, and with a swift slash of his soul blade, he cuts the web strand, sending the dreaded phase spider plunging toward the inferno below. The creature, in a frantic effort to save itself, fires a web strand from its mouth at the ceiling of the cavern an instant before it contacts the lava and begins to scramble up; but Modex has had enough of this infernal creature, and sensing the opportunity to end its existence once and for all, he quickly unleashes a lightning bolt of his own at the ceiling where the strand is attached and blasts away the connection—and finally the spider falls with a fiery splash to be incinerated in the bubbling lava.

"I guess Kordon didn't use that bridge, huh?" Jartan sheepishly says to Modex between gulps of air.

"Apparently not," answers a smiling though greatly relieved Modex, helping the boy to his feet.

CHAPTER 20

✦ ✦ ✦

"Now that we are finally through with those infernal Caverns of Death it should be an easy journey from here on," says Modex happily as the two continue walking along the path. "Now it is Kordon and Karza whose progress will be drastically slowed as they face the further horrors of the Underworld ahead. Just that cave of hell griffins we just passed through must have taken them a good three days to pass—but thanks to their effort, we went through it faster than you can spell *cat.*"

As they turn a corner of the tunnel, they see a large number of harpies—large, birdlike creatures with the heads of evil, hag-like women—frozen in ice.

"Yuck. What are those nasty things?" inquires Jartan with a look of disgust, for harpies are extremely ugly.

"Harpies," replies Modex. "Kordon must have been attacked by a swarm of them as he reached this part of the Underworld, and he froze them with his magic. We are fortunate we don't have to deal with these wicked creatures, for they are absolutely vicious and would make formidable adversaries."

Meanwhile, in another section deeper in the foreboding Underworld, the evil wizard Kordon is engaged in the wholesale slaughter of the last few cave trolls that are offering him resistance. These large, wart-riddled, green-skinned humanoid creatures are strong and fierce warriors and are twice Kordon's size, but unfortunately for them, their dubious intelligence, as evidenced by the crude, simple clubs they wield, does not permit them to grasp the threat they are facing as they vainly try to mount an attack against the far more powerful wizard. The battle has been raging for several hours. Karza is standing off to the side of the tunnel watching and surprisingly not participating in the battle—not that it really is necessary, for the mighty evil magic of Kordon is more than capable of dealing with this pitiful band of trolls, and he soon has killed them all. The heaps of corpses litter the ground, smoldering with savage wounds. The all-powerful wizard is pleased, but he reacts as if something is bothering him. He turns to look back down the tunnel from where they came as Karza stands by his side.

"I sense we have visitors," the wizard says to his demonic son.

Kordon creates an energy ball in his hand that acts like a window into other areas. In the glowing ball, Modex and Jartan appear, walking among the frozen harpies. Kordon is decidedly not pleased by the image before him.

"That wretched paladin again. Obviously our dear Zorm was unable to kill him. You are right, my son, this novice is indeed a strong one—but that may prove useful later. Ah, and he brings my old friend Modex. The fools—they have no concept of the power they are dealing with. So be it. He too will pay dearly for his treachery."

"Then let's get rid of them once and for all," announces Karza, starting to head back into the tunnel—but Kordon quickly stops him.

"No, you must save your strength, my son. That's why I didn't want your assistance in killing these foul cave trolls or any of the other creatures we have had to deal with for the past several days for you have a far more important task ahead of you and one I will be unable to help you with. You alone will have to fight the great diamond dragon we'll encounter soon, and you'll need every ounce of your strength to combat it. However, our visitors do deserve to be welcomed into the Underworld—a nice, warm welcome."

Kordon, with a diabolical laugh, throws the ball of energy on the ground several yards in front of him, which creates an energy portal, and with a further wave of his skeletal hands he magically summons a massive wall of flame that he sends into the portal.

This portal appears approximately a hundred feet in front of a shocked Modex and Jartan, whose horror only increases when the wall of flame emerges from the portal and heads straight for them. There is no room in the tunnel to evade its onslaught, so Modex quickly erects a wall of energy to deflect it, and it moves past them without injury. But unfortunately for them, it was never Kordon's intention simply to sear the intruders, for he has a far more diabolical and far more deadly purpose in mind for the flames. Upon reaching the frozen harpies, the wall of flame begins to melt the icy prisons encasing them.

"Modex, look! The harpies!" an alarmed Jartan shouts. "They're breaking free!"

And indeed the vicious harpies are free from their frozen state and begin to swarm once again with a frenzied passion to slay any living thing they encounter. One soon flies dangerously close to Jartan.

"Jartan, look out!" warns Modex, pushing the boy to the ground an instant before his body is split open savagely by a harpy's menacing, razor-sharp claws, prompting Modex to add, "Be careful of their claws—they are deadly poisonous."

"Now you tell me!" cries the exasperated Jartan.

Modex sends out his own wave of flame, which consumes several harpies flying above him as Jartan slashes a few that make diving attacks on him and also blasts a few flying around with an energy bolt from his soul blade for good measure; but the numerous attackers quickly begin to overwhelm them.

"There are too many of them!" says Modex, greatly alarmed. "Run, Jartan! I'll try and hold them back."

"Don't be a fool, Modex. You can't fight them all!" Seeing the harpy attack intensify, he adds frantically, "We've got to get out of here!"

It is impossible to escape farther forward or back down the tunnel, as this is where the unrelenting swarm of harpies is continuing to flood forth from, increasing their numbers dramatically by the second; but Jartan notices a small crevice off to the side and gestures to Modex.

"Modex, over there!"

The two make a desperate dash for the crevice, but a harpy swoops down on Modex and digs its poisonous claws deep into his back. The wizard screams in pain from the injury. Jartan manages to slash the harpy off of him, practically cutting the thing in two, and it writhes spastically for several moments before dying. Several others that are near enough also fall, and a few blasts from the soul blade create enough of a gap to help Modex to the crevice. It is too small to fit through, so Jartan blasts it with his soul blade, creating a larger opening for them to enter. Once inside, he slashes above the opening, causing a large amount of rock to fall and cover it so that the harpies cannot follow. Modex is in great pain, and he struggles to speak.

"Harpy poison—my magic cannot—heal—" he barely manages to say before collapsing into unconsciousness.

Jartan is greatly disturbed by the wizard's precarious condition and tries in vain to rouse him by shaking him into consciousness.

"Modex? Modex, answer me! You have to tell me what to do! I don't know anything about harpy poison or how to cure it! Modex! Damn you, answer me! Modex!"

But the comatose wizard does not move and only further descends into the grip of the poisonous death as his skin takes on a ghastly pale green color—but then Jartan realizes he has the poison cure that the elf Skon gave him several days earlier.

SCOTT CRABTREE

"Wait a second—Skon's cure for poisons! Thank the gods! I still have it!"

He searches for the vial amid his clothing, greatly relieved that he has an antidote for the deadly poison surging through Modex's blood— but he quickly looks up in horror at the sight of the harpies beginning to claw at the loose rocks covering the opening to the crevice. Jartan hastens his search and finds the vial, but before the frantic boy can open it and deliver the healing liquid to the lips of the unconscious Modex, a harpy is able to slip through the opening into the crevice and attacks Jartan, knocking the vial out of his hands. It rolls into a small crack amid the rocks, disappearing from view.

The youthful paladin battles the harpy and is able to kill it as well as the several others that fly in through the crevice, but he knows that it must be sealed once again and far more effectively. Seeing a large boulder off to the side, he uses his soul blade to levitate it and guide it toward the crevice opening. The large boulder, a long slab of stone that was lying horizontal on the ground, is somewhat too long to stand upright to block the entrance. Jartan's new soul blade with the more powerful soul of Morbius within it gives the youth considerably more levitating power than the old blade, and though it still does require some strenuous effort, he is able to wedge the stone securely between the ceiling and ground, making a very effective barrier and blocking any more harpies from entering. Safe from any further attacks, he frantically looks for the vial he dropped, as Modex cannot live much longer without its curative contents.

"The vial!" he says in panic. "Damn it, where did it go?"

He anxiously searches for it but without result. Jartan then talks to his soul blade.

"Can you show me where the vial went?"

The blade begins to emit a beam of light, which illuminates the crack where the vial rolled. Jartan quickly rushes over to it and kneels down to peer inside the dark opening, but he can't see any sign of the vial, for the crack is many feet deep. He then reaches in with his arm all the way to his shoulder in an attempt to search blindly in the crack, but this also achieves nothing. Almost hysterical now, with Modex on the doorstep of death, Jartan acts as if he is going to use the soul blade to make a larger opening but decides against it.

No, he thinks, *I might break the vial. For the love of the gods, what am I going to do?*

Jartan then notices a ferret moving about the rocks.

"Maybe I can't reach the vial," he says, "but you certainly can, my furry little friend! I just hope for all our sakes that ferrets are good creatures!"

He closes his eyes in concentration. The ferret instantly stops, and after a moment of sensing Jartan's wishes, it heads for the crack. It easily enters the slim opening and shortly reappears with the vial in its mouth, which the boy quickly takes.

"Nice work, little one! I'm definitely keeping you around."

Jartan returns to Modex and, opening the vial, dribbles the precious liquid into his mouth. After several tense moments of awaiting the healing powers, the old wizard recovers, and his skin returns back to its normal healthy color, much to the relief of Jartan, who helps the groggy wizard to his feet.

"Easy, Modex—just take it easy. How do you feel?"

"Ah—much, much better," says the rapidly recovering Modex. "I don't know where in the Underworld you managed to acquire a cure for poisons, but I'm sure glad you had it! Thank you, Jartan."

"Don't thank me—thank our little friend here," responds Jartan, gesturing to the ferret who is sitting there happily as the beaming paladin continues. "Isn't he cute as a button? I think I'll keep him as a—"

Modex, though, doesn't respond to the cute fuzziness with even the faintest degree of grateful enthusiasm, and with a swift flick of the wrist, he blasts the poor thing with a bolt of energy, leaving only a faint squeak and a small puff of smoke where the ferret used to be. Remnants of its fur slowly undulate to the ground like a handful of feathers. Jartan is absolutely dumbfounded by this incredibly ungrateful and certainly unanticipated attack on an innocent creature that just saved the wizard's life; and although Jartan is stunned to silence, his expression says it all; it is one of those what-the-hell-is-wrong-with-you expressions of total bewilderment. He glares at the wizard with mouth still open from his previous sentence about wanting to take the helpful creature along as a pet—a sentence cut short by this insane act by Modex.

"I don't like ferrets," Modex meekly responds in answer to the appalled Jartan with his look of complete shock.

"You still have some evil in you, Modex," responds Jartan, shaking his head in disgust. "You need to work on that."

"But I don't like ferrets!" counters Modex in defense, for in his mind his act was a justifiable one—justifiable to anyone who hates ferrets, that is.

But Jartan shakes his head even more forcefully, not buying his twisted logic for an instant, and moves off toward the crevice entrance, which is still sealed tight by the boulder.

"I hate ferrets," says the wizard quietly, still trying to convince himself that he did the right thing by removing the foul creature from existence as he joins the paladin. Jartan is holding his soul blade close to the entrance and is waving it across the face of the large boulder.

"The blade isn't glowing," says Jartan. "The harpies must have gone."

"I'm sure they have. They have easier prey to find than us."

"Good, then I'll blast us out of here," says the paladin confidently, pointing his soul blade toward the rocks.

"No, paladin!" Modex warns. "You will bring the whole cavern down upon us. This will require a more subtle approach. Behold."

The resourceful wizard raises his staff, which begins to glow, and he then makes a wide arc with it across the face of the boulder, which causes a large section of the rock to glow brightly. The glow soon turns into a shimmering wall of water, which collapses, revealing an effective and far safer passage out of the area, which they take. They are now back on the path and continue to walk through the cavern, but they soon come to a place where there are several routes leading off into blackness.

"Now where?" asks Jartan, discouraged by this troubling sight. "We'll never find Kordon and Karza in this maze of passages!"

"Calm yourself, Jartan. Remember, I helped Kordon map out the route through the Underworld that leads to the seal. I know exactly which passage to take, which is fortunate, for only one passage leads to the seal. All the others are more diabolically lethal traps that await the unknowing. This way."

"And," Jartan adds confidently, "we have the element of surprise on our side, since Kordon and Karza don't know we are coming."

"Oh, they know we're coming, all right," Modex remarks with a pensive tone. "You don't think that wall of fire that greeted us in the harpy tunnel did so because we were cold, do you? I assure you that was Kordon's evil doing. He knows we are here. The question is—what is he going to do about it? He must know by now that his plan to have the harpies rid him of our presence has failed, and he certainly won't stop with that."

"Do you think they have reached the seal yet, Modex?"

"No, for there is one last obstacle they must get through, and—for them, anyway—it will definitely cause much difficulty. They should actually be worried about it—greatly worried."

"That's a comfort, at least. So where do you think they are now?"

"I'm sure they are at the lair of the great diamond dragon."

"Great diamond dragon? I've never heard of such a creature."

"Few mortals have," comments Modex in return. "There are four classes of dragon kind. The lowest and the most numerous is the "nature" class—these are the sea dragons, wind dragons, frost dragons, stone dragons, and many others. Then you have the special class of dragon kind, which includes the dream dragons, magic dragons, teleport dragons, blood dragons, and similar types. The third class of dragons is the colored ones—red, black, blue, and green dragons, for example—with the queen of each color being the most powerful of the race, naturally. But the last class is by far the most powerful, for they are also colored dragons but have reached the "jewel" level. They are so rare and powerful that there are only twelve of them in existence—the great ruby dragon, the great emerald dragon, and so on—and these mighty dragons are used by the gods as guardians to gateways or passages where they don't want us mortals to trespass. The great diamond dragon is the one here."

"Well, it still sounds pretty intimidating to me, Modex," says Jartan, who is now worried. "Shouldn't we be worried about this thing, too?"

"Not at all," responds Modex. "It is, in fact, the guardian to Magdara's seal."

"What?" a stunned Jartan replies. "And that is where they are now—with the seal just beyond? Then we'll never stop them in time!"

"Would you just try and relax for once, Jartan?" the wizard again advises his ignorant companion. "I told you to calm yourself. We have nothing to fear from the dragon. You see, the great diamond dragon is a very powerful creature and one that should be feared, but only to creatures of evil, for it is in fact the last vestige of goodness in this world before you reach those lands that are nothing but total evil like the Demonic Abyss. But since it is the only good creature in the Underworld, it—"

"Along with ferrets!" says Jartan, quickly interrupting, as he is still holding a grudge against Modex for killing one of the innocent animals a few moments before.

But the wizard just looks at him apathetically, still unconvinced as to the benefits that those vile creatures—in his mind, at least—possess, so he continues, unmoved by any hint of remorse:

"As I was saying, it was chosen to be the guardian of the seal specifically to stop any evil beings from reaching it, since no good being would ever dream of trying to free Magdara from her prison—at least willingly and aware of the threat she poses to existence. Because of this, the dragon has great powers to fight the forces of darkness, and one of these powers is that the gods made it impervious to all forms of magic—good or evil—so Kordon can do nothing to affect it, and with that powerful wizard now all but impotent against the dragon, it will be up to Karza to be the one to defeat it—and that will take some time even for his twisted but formidable demonic powers. This is another reason Kordon needed Karza to accompany him through the Underworld."

"If it is as powerful as you say it is, then maybe this dragon can kill Karza," Jartan says hopefully.

"It's certainly possible. As I told you before, Karza's strength lies in his transformation ability, and this diabolical power makes him the virtually unstoppable force that he is, but the more power he exerts in battle the quicker he will weaken; and the great diamond dragon will require every ounce of power that demonic slime has. Eventually, he has to weaken into his prince form, and that is when he can be killed, so let us hope that will indeed be the outcome."

"I sure hope you are right," says Jartan, hopeful but doubtful. "I've seen Karza in that tridragon form of his—that is easily the most formidable creature I've ever seen! It's very powerful. Even your brother, with his awesome magical power, didn't stand a chance against it. That thing tore through the ranks of the castle defenders like they were mere toys."

"Yes, it's powerful—but it takes great power for Karza to maintain it. And besides, the great diamond dragon, being a dragon itself, has certain abilities that Karza's many forms are useless against, so he's in for a shock if he tries to fight a dragon with a dragon. But I can tell you this, Jartan: it will be a battle between two titans unlike any seen before."

CHAPTER 21

✛ ✛ ✛

For a powerful wizard like Kordon, being reduced to a powerless spectator is a bitter pill to swallow. He stands off to the side within the lair of the great diamond dragon—a cavernous chamber with hundreds of stalactites hanging from the ceiling like icicles of stone with an equal number of large stalagmites emerging from the ground like some macabre array of stone teeth. Only about half of these formations remain, as many have fallen to the ground or have been crushed or obliterated by some form of massive violence—violence that has been raging for more than an hour now. For what Kordon is watching quite tensely is an epic struggle as evidenced by the intense sounds of explosions and chilling shrieks and groans that are echoing throughout the vast chamber as flashes of light from unseen powerful energy weapons reflect from his bony and highly concerned face. But this expression quickly turns to anger, and he suddenly erects an energy shield to prevent a large rock, obviously sent hurtling from a powerful nearby explosion, from hitting him.

Hurry, my son, he calmly thinks—for no words from Kordon could be heard over the nonstop chaos of sound echoing within the cavern— *you must defeat her. You must!*

What Kordon is witnessing—as Modex accurately predicted—is one of the mightiest of battles ever waged in one-on-one combat between two beings, though perhaps '*savage*' and '*bitter*' more aptly describe the struggle, for it truly is being waged at a sickening level of barbarity, brutality, and unabated cruelty. Not even the morose and blood-thirsty gladiatorial contests some of the more depraved gods create to entertain their divine lusts could pit such powerful and diametrically opposed beings against each other—a demon prince of merciless evil versus a great diamond dragon, a bastion of good. It is a veritable unstoppable force meeting an immoveable object, a clash of titans in monumental conflict where neither side will show mercy or compassion and neither will surrender, for only one can emerge victorious in battle here—a battle where the life or death of the combatants is of minor concern but where the fate of existence teeters in the balance. The savagely contested prize: whether good or evil will reign supreme.

The great diamond dragon is just that—a huge, reptilian colossus with large scales of white diamond shards of various sizes that cover her entire body and sparkle brilliantly in the light. Four massive legs support her bulk, though she can rear up on the back two when necessity requires, giving her the ability to deliver a vicious, rending attack with her large, dagger-like claws. Her legs provide a surprising degree of agility despite her immense size. The back of the dragon is well protected with an array of diamond shards spiking upward along the spine and descending all the way down the three long, serpentine tails, each of which ends in a club of intimidating diamond shards, a formidable weapon. A similar defensive crown of diamond horns is on her face as well as a formidable set of razor-sharp teeth in her mouth, also of diamond. In fact, the entire dragon appears to be made out of nothing but glittering white diamonds. The only other color present is her two blue eyes, which glow brightly with incredible power from the two diamond jewels located there. Her overall appearance is majestic and strikingly beautiful, as this is easily one of the most magnificent creatures in existence. But her incredible beauty belies a ferocious temperament toward any evil intruders who dare to enter her lair and reveals nothing of the far more awesome powers she commands to prevent those who aspire to pass through to Magdara's seal, the entrance to which lies at the far end of the dragon's lair—powers that Karza is finding increasingly difficult to counter.

What makes the great diamond dragon such a fearsome opponent is not only her total magic resistance as well as the protection her scales of diamond armor provides. Since she is one of the highest class of dragon kind—as all the jewel dragon sisterhood are—she possesses every form of breath weapon a dragon has and can discharge any of these weapons at will. She is also immune to all similar forms of attack, which makes Karza's most powerful demonic form—the dreaded tridragon—virtually useless.

Karza has been using this form virtually nonstop since he entered the lair more than an hour ago, but he is quickly realizing that this, a highly effective force against practically any other opponent, is an ineffective tactic against this jeweled dragon. His normally lethal blasts of fire, lightning, and freezing vapor have absolutely no impact due to the dragon's immunity to all dragon breath weapons. The great diamond dragon's blasts, however, are beginning to register on Karza's body as her lightning, fire, and frost cause damage—as well as further blasts of powerful acid, clouds of poisonous gas, and cyclones of irresistible winds that further frustrate Karza's efforts to defeat the reptilian giant. A particularly devastating blast of wind from the great diamond dragon's mouth sends the tridragon hurtling back violently against a wall of the cavernous lair, the impact of which dislodges several of the large stalactites hanging from the ceiling to crash upon him. A powerful surge of lightning discharges from the great diamond dragon at Karza, but he is able to transform into his ethereal phantasm form before the energy hits, and it explodes against the wall of the lair, sending rocky debris flying. The electrical onslaught now past, Karza transforms into his demonic spider form and attempts to fire a web attack, but a fiery counterattack from the dragon incinerates the ensnaring strands before they can even travel a meager distance; and now, rearing up on her back legs, the great diamond dragon with her front claws is able to launch a salvo of her diamond talons at the spider. The missiles easily penetrate the soft body and fragile legs of the creature, severing most of the limbs and creating large wounds that gush demonic fluids along the body of the spider. It's only the fact that Karza cannot be killed while he is transformed that prevents his instant death.

But two can play at this game, and Karza transforms into a monstrous, demonic, turtle-like creature with dozens of spikes studding its large shell, and in this form he is able to launch a veritable tsunami of spiked death of his own, more devastating than the geat diamond dragon's before—which would have meant instant death for any creature on the receiving end had it not had a skin of armor consisting of layers of diamond scales. The spikes bounce off her body without leaving a single scratch and ricochet throughout the lair in all directions.

The attack is actually more of a threat to the wizard Kordon, who must again quickly erect an energy shield of magic to protect himself from several of the ricocheting projectiles. He can do nothing but watch helplessly, but seeing that Karza is having difficulty battling the powerful dragon, he decides to make an effort to assist: too much is at stake, and his son must not be defeated. The wizard summons a tremendous surge of powerful energy into his hands, and when the ball of energy is intense enough, he hurls the crackling orb of power at the great diamond dragon off in the near distance. The energy would usually go forth with incredible velocity; but since the magic-resistant dragon is the intended target, the ball rapidly slows to a crawl and only manages to travel a few feet before it fades away into nothing. The all-powerful wizard is all but useless here.

Kordon can easily see the exit to the lair that leads to Magdara's seal several hundred yards away, and it wouldn't be any trouble for him to saunter over to it unhindered while the great diamond dragon is busy battling Karza, but even if Kordon were standing inches from the exit, it wouldn't make any difference—only with the great diamond dragon's defeat can anyone pass through. With the way things are now, even a being at Kordon's phenomenal level of power couldn't toss a pebble through to the other side.

The great diamond dragon rushes toward Karza, who counters by transforming into his muscular titan demon form. Picking up one of the large fallen stalactites lying nearby, the demon wields the icicle of stone like a huge club and violently strikes the head of the dragon with it when the beast comes within reach. The strength of the demonic giant is so great that the force of impact sends the dragon reeling back as the stalactite club shatters on contact with the dragon's diamond scales. Although this momentarily stuns the dragon and hurls her body across the floor of the lair—it finally stops only after plowing through several stalagmites and violently hitting the wall of the lair—her armor of diamonds is so hard and resilient that it easily absorbs the strike on her head from the stone club, and the skin shows not even the slightest evidence of damage. Recovering from the blow with a few shakes of her head, she retaliates with a breath of poisonous gas at the advancing Karza lumbering toward her, and he quickly becomes consumed within the sickly green cloud—but his titan demon form has no nose or mouth to inhale the noxious fumes and emerges from the cloud unfazed. Further attacks of fire, lightning, and acid by the dragon only manage to singe the incredibly dense skin of Karza, and surprisingly, only the cyclonic blast of wind the dragon is able to breathe manage to impede his advance at all, stopping the massive demon in his tracks and finally skidding him backward, though the titan demon is far too heavy for the wind to lift him off his feet.

Fortunately for Karza, the dragon's attempt at keeping him at bay is only temporary, for with her lungs now empty, she must inhale another lungful of air to generate another of the impenetrable walls of wind. This gives Karza time to prepare for the next blast, for wind is no impediment to his ethereal phantasm creature—or so he thinks. Transforming into this form he once again advances. But this creature, immune to every other form of attack be it magic or solid, is vulnerable to the wind blast from a jeweled dragon, and the cloud is thrown back and pinned against the cavern wall, unable to move. The wind blast is of such an incredible intensity that it actually rips away large sections of the cloud from the center mass—with the expression on the phantom's face registering complete horror that this is even happening at all! Only another pause from the dragon to inhale gives Karza a respite from the relentless pinning force, but it is not long enough for him to recover into another form to escape, and the dragon once again pins Karza to the wall with another wind blast to continue its torturous punishment.

Kordon, seeing his son's plight, knows his magic can do nothing to affect the dragon itself—but the stalactites hanging overhead are another matter. Firing a lightning bolt at one of them separates the huge stone from the ceiling, and it falls in front of Karza embedding itself deeply into the ground. Although it is a feeble and short-lived barrier against the wind, it is sufficient to allow Karza the time to transform into his fastest creature—the huge dragonfly-insect—and as the stalactite windbreak disintegrates from the wind's ripping power, Karza flies off at the great diamond dragon, avoiding her attempts to force him back with her various breath weapons due to his amazing speed and agility. Once he is too near for the dragon to use the full power of the wind, he again transforms into the ethereal cloud, which covers the dragon. She again tries to breathe wind at the seething swirls of vapor, but due to its close proximity to her body, she only manages to blow a few puffs of the cloud's body away, and blasts of other breath weapons simply pass through the cloud without effect, as do her frantic attempts to slash and bite at the shapeless, phantom form, which begins to coil around the dragon's body. These coils transform into a demonic serpentine creature—a flame snake—and as its oily red skin constricts tightly around the dragon's body, the snake begins to glow bright red with power and the body of the snake erupts into a coil of searing flames. The fire-spitting head of Karza's tridragon is a more powerful weapon, but since it is from her own dragon kind, it has no effect on the great diamond dragon. But a flame snake is not a dragon and therefore inflicts great pain. The great diamond dragon thrashes about violently, but her diamond armor resists the flames and she is able to free herself from the snake's embrace within a few moments after delivering to the snake's body a vicious bite with her diamond teeth and severe slash wounds with her diamond claws, almost severing the snake completely. Tossing the flailing serpent aside contemptuously, she blasts the carcass with a lightning bolt for good measure, sending the gravely wounded snake off into the distance.

The fact that the flame snake is obviously a pathetically useless form of attack quickly forces Karza to another transformation, this time into a nimble, cat-like creature with a massive maw and one glowing, saber-shaped fang so huge and menacing that it gives the impression that it can penetrate practically anything. The saber cat manages to avoid several acid and flame blasts with its agility and eventually leaps onto the dragon to renew an attack by plunging the magically glowing tooth deep into the dragon's body—only to be thwarted yet again by the formidable protection of the diamond scales, which cause the tooth to shatter.

Kordon's anger and frustration only intensify as he continues to watch helplessly while his son rifles through every demonic form in his inventory in an increasingly desperate attempt to find some weakness in the great diamond dragon that can be exploited to defeat it. But as Kordon witnesses failure after failure, one might think that a new emotion is beginning to develop within the evil wizard's mind—panic. He knows Karza will soon weaken and be unable to transform, and once in semi-human form, he will have no chance. Not even the summoning power of the demon prince will be of any use. If even his fantastic demonic forms are hopelessly outmatched, then no creature he can summon could possibly have any impact, even if the great diamond dragon gave him the time to do so—which she won't. And considering the fact that Karza would have to be in his demon prince form to be able to use his summoning power, the dragon would kill him instantly. And yet no panic is evident in the countenance of Kordon, for a being at his level of absolute power is unaccustomed to panic; the possibility of defeat never enters the mind. Even the anger and frustration the wizard feels are not due to the apparent fact that Karza is unable to defeat the dragon, and therefore it will be he who will ultimately be defeated. No, his anger comes from the fact that victory is apparently taking too long to achieve, as if Kordon expected the outcome long before this.

"What is taking you so long?" says the wizard quietly to himself, growing more impatient with every passing second, as Karza cannot maintain transformation much longer. "I know you can defeat her. I've foreseen it!"

He turns to face the lair entrance as once again he is distracted by an annoying disturbance that touches his acute senses of evil, causing the wizard to create the energy ball of vision in his hand to gaze upon the reason. In the ball appear Modex and Jartan, walking amid the twisted corpses of trolls that Kordon killed only moments before, causing the wizard concern, as this means the irritating pair is only in the next chamber of the Underworld before the lair.

"But that," says the displeased Kordon at the sight in his hand, "I did not foresee. I've come too far to have any interference now!"

Dispelling the energy ball, his skeletal face sternly determined, he raises his hands toward the lair entrance, and as the hands begin to glow brightly with power, Kordon creates a magical barrier of pulsing energy within the entrance opening, thereby sealing it completely. But the evil wizard is not content with this and takes several extra moments to put even more of his formidable magic power into the barrier, energizing it even further. With an angry yell of defiance, a final thrust of his hands seals the entrance with a level of energy of tremendous intensity—energy no other single being could possibly generate and that therefore no single being could possibly overcome. Satisfied, he once again turns his attention to the epic battle between demon and dragon.

"You must hurry, Karza!" he says with urgency. "You're running out of time!"

The stalemate continues. Karza is once again in his titan demon form, as this seems to be the only demonic creature that is the dragon's equal and the only one she seems to fear, for it can withstand all of her relentless breath attacks. She is therefore taking great pains to use her breath of wind to keep him as far from her as possible—not that this form is giving him any advantage, for unless Karza can get near his jeweled opponent to use his awesome strength, this form is nothing but a huge target for the dragon. She can afford to waste time in pointless battles, but Karza cannot, as he is beginning to weaken.

The great diamond dragon is an intelligent creature—but not intelligent enough, for if she were she would exploit this Achilles' heel in Karza's demonic nature by keeping him helplessly at bay until his power wanes. But the dragon, frustrated by her inability to deliver a death blow to her tenacious, demonic enemy, makes the fateful decision to summon help to hasten Karza's demise. The three ends of her diamond tails begin to glow, and she pounds the ground twice with them, which creates three portals of energy that soon form into a trio of mature white dragons. These are smaller versions of their great creator, perhaps half her size and white in color, though they lack her dazzling bejeweled appearance and their powers are far less imposing. Still, they are powerful creatures, and the four dragons fighting in unison would quickly spell Karza's doom—were he the sole occupant of the lair.

Kordon, who up until now has been a virtual non-factor in the battle and could only offer minor assistance to his son, poses no threat to the great diamond dragon due to her magic resistance; therefore Kordon has been of no concern or interest to her. But her white dragon minions do not possess any immunity from his magic, and the all-powerful wizard wastes no time in blasting them into oblivion with an onslaught of his mighty evil magic. The great diamond dragon, dismayed at seeing her three minions vaporized before her eyes, directs her attack away from Karza and focuses her wrath upon Kordon, unleashing a torrent of breath weapons of her own. But Kordon's magic can at least be used in his own defense against these attacks, and the shield of energy he instantly creates deflects them.

Karza, who is free from the pinning force of the dragon's wind while she is distracted by Kordon, transforms again into the dragonfly creature to use its incredible speed to fly onto the back of the dragon before she has time to counterattack. Transforming back into the titan demon, Karza has the head of the dragon firmly in the muscular, vise-like grip of his massive arms. The dragon struggles frantically in an effort to escape from the embrace, and although she is larger than the demon, she is only slightly so. Her immense bulk is no advantage against Karza's great strength, and the massive weight he has in this form keeps her movements to a feeble minimum. With her head pinned in Karza's arms, the dragon cannot direct her breath of wind at him to repel his presence, though she does fire several blasts of a variety of breath weapons in a useless effort that destroys large sections of the lair's interior. Only the three clubbed tails of the dragon, heavily embedded with deadly diamond shards, are able to move about freely, and she frantically begins to bash Karza's back, sides, arms, and head with them—anything in an effort to escape. The impacts of the tails are savage, but Karza's armored skin is so dense that only minor dents and scratches appear at first on the smooth, black surface, revealing a surprising gray color and not the red blood one would expect to see from such wounds—for now it is revealed that beneath the thin black skin rests a further layer of solid lead. But even this begins to strain under the ferocious pounding of the dragon's diamond triple clubs, and the damage they inflict becomes more and more extensive with each thrashing blow, almost cleaving off one of the titan's arms. The damage is severe enough that the blows finally reveal a reddish substance that lies beneath the dense lead armor. This is not blood but a further armored layer of iron—for this creature is nothing but a walking mountain of armor upon armor. Coupled with its massive strength, this makes it clear why it is in fact Karza's second-most-powerful form.

As the demon continues to tighten its inescapable death grip with the incredible strength of its vise-like, muscular arms, even the diamond scales covering the dragon's head and neck begin to crack and shatter under the crushing pressure. Victory will be decided in a manner of seconds, for it is now a question of which will weaken first—the diamond armor of the dragon or the ability of the demon to maintain this form—for both are beginning to crumble.

CHAPTER 22

* * *

Modex and Jartan continue to make their way through this chamber of the Underworld where Kordon slaughtered the bands of cave trolls only recently. Their progress is limited as the two wade through the hundreds of bloody and mangled troll corpses that litter the ground, stepping over those that are immediately in their path. Jartan struggles to keep himself from becoming sick at the nauseating level of gore. Most of the twisted corpses are still smoldering from the wounds they received from Kordon's devastating magical attacks, which only increases the boy's urge to vomit as the foul stench of burning troll flesh reaches his nostrils—the effect almost as overpowering as the sickening ability of Zorm, the undead leader.

"We are very close, Jartan," comments Modex upon seeing the smoldering bodies. Indicating their recent demise, he continues, "Kordon and Karza are only one, perhaps two chambers ahead of us now—if the great diamond dragon hasn't killed them already."

"I never thought I would feel sorry for cave trolls," adds Jartan, still disturbed by the level of slaughter. "But after a massacre such as this, they have my sympathy."

"The only good troll is a dead troll, my young friend," replies the uncompassionate Modex. "Kordon did us a favor by slaughtering these evil creatures."

"That's a bit coldhearted, isn't it, Modex?"

"Better them than us."

It is hard for the youth to argue with that kind of logic, which prompts Jartan to respond with a joyful, "True." But his happiness fades when he thinks of another thought, adding, "But I can't help wonder what will stop Kordon from turning both of us into a smoldering mass of bloody jelly too!"

Modex only responds with silence to the boy's remark, for he is beginning to wonder that as well, and turning the corner of the chamber, they come across the magical barrier that Kordon created to seal the entrance to the lair of the great diamond dragon that lies just beyond.

"A magical barrier," a discouraged Modex observes. "This is the work of Kordon's evil magic."

"Can you break through?" asks Jartan hopefully, though he has begun to question this eagerness to proceed farther after witnessing the disastrous fate of the cave trolls.

"We will soon see. Stand back, boy."

And Jartan does so to give the wizard room to use his magical arts. Modex raises his staff and fires at the barrier with an intense magical stream of energy. He continues doing this for several moments, which causes the wizard to strain considerably since this act is using all his power; but the barrier effortlessly resists his attempt to breach the obstruction, and soon Modex is thrown back to the ground with a painful shock from Kordon's evil power. Jartan helps him to his feet.

"Kordon's magic is too powerful," says Modex in defeat.

"Let's see if I have better luck," announces a confident Jartan.

"But you aren't wearing anything blue," says the sarcastic wizard in response.

But Jartan shrugs off the sarcasm with a sneer, and drawing forth his soul blade, he plunges it into the barrier with all his strength. His efforts appear to be affecting the barrier, as it begins to flicker and sparkle in protest as the blade slowly penetrates deeper into it.

"That's it, paladin!" a happily surprised Modex says with enthusiasm. "It is weakening!"

The straining Jartan continues to apply pressure, but he too is soon thwarted in his effort to breach the barrier and is also thrown to the ground with a shock. Now it is Modex's turn to help the boy to his feet.

"Are you all right, Jartan?"

"Yes, but I obviously can't break through it either," he says, discouraged.

"At least you were having some success with your paladin's energy," comments the wizard as he hits upon an idea. "We just need to give your soul blade a little more kick. Let's try it together this time. Point your blade at the barrier."

Jartan does this, and Modex touches his staff to Jartan's soul blade and a far more powerful beam of energy shoots forth from it into the barrier. The barrier quickly begins to flicker once again, but this time with a far greater level of impact.

"It's working! It's working!" shouts Jartan happily upon seeing the effect.

The energy of the barrier continues to wane and fizzle under this combined effort of the two, and after several more moments it finally begins to crack and soon explodes, revealing the black abyss of the entrance and providing clear and unobstructed access into the dragon's lair beyond; for like all entrances to the chambers in the Underworld, only when one passes through the entrance does the sight beyond reveal itself. Jartan makes an effort to move forward—but Modex's hand on his shoulder stops him.

"Wait, Jartan," he says as he turns his head slightly to give an ear a better chance to hear anything from beyond the blackness, "I don't hear anything. I was hoping the battle would still be in progress, but it apparently has ended. Pray, Jartan—pray that we see the destroyed bodies of Kordon and Karza lying crushed into the ground by the power of the great diamond dragon."

As Modex and Jartan penetrate the veil of blackness and enter the lair, they become instantly aware of the massive destruction before them. Huge craters still smolder amid the vast amount of rocky debris caused by falling stalactites and the large chunks blasted from the walls and ceiling of the lair. Blood is everywhere, and it is obvious that a great and horrific battle has taken place recently, for the air still hangs heavy with the hazy mists of combat—never before has such a horrendously savage contest between life and death been waged. Modex and Jartan cautiously proceed through the mist, which obscures anything deeper within the lair, but they soon stop, horrified at the vision that reveals itself.

In the center of the lair lies the great diamond dragon, obviously near death as evidenced by her labored and spasmodic attempts to breathe and her quavering spasms of feeble movement—movement that must be incredibly painful, for it greatly pains both Modex and Jartan to even watch. The creature is a pathetic remnant of the magnificent, proud, noble, and startlingly beautiful dragon it once was. Her body is grotesquely twisted and broken, with deep, massive wounds all over her once pristine diamond skin, which is now stained red with blood. Her injuries are so extensive that one would think that the mere touch of a feather or the faintest breeze against her skin could kill her.

The sight is truly a heart-wrenching one for the pair, and it is difficult for the two to fight back their tears upon seeing the dragon's deplorable condition, particularly for Modex, for unlike Jartan he knows what the dragon looked like in her stunningly beautiful prime—before Karza and his myriad sadistic demonic forms reduced the majestic creature to the mass of trembling, bloody, and shattered jeweled flesh before him. Modex and Jartan approach her cautiously.

"Most unfortunate," says a somber Modex, shedding a tear at the sight, though his demeanor instantly turns to intense hatred as he reflects on the cause as he continues, "May the gods damn Karza and all his infernal forms!"

"Damn it, Modex, do something!" pleads Jartan, also deeply moved by the horrific wounds he sees. "Can't you do anything to help her? Use your magic to heal her injuries!"

"Her wounds are deep, paladin. And besides, all forms of magic are useless on this creature—even healing magic. There's simply nothing I can do."

The great diamond dragon stirs slightly.

"Easy, great one—easy," Modex says soothingly while tenderly caressing her bloody and cracked face with his hand, for it is now obvious that Karza's titan demon was the victor in the struggle and that the diamond armor skin of the dragon was no match to the iron sledgehammer blows that his crushing strength could exert. Modex somberly continues, "Your suffering will soon be over. Sleep now and take comfort in the fact that your brave and valiant efforts will not be in vain."

Her blue jeweled eyes, which once shone with an almost inextinguishable level of brightness and power, are at a barely discernable and rapidly decreasing level that flickers in intensity as the life force of the once mighty dragon continues to seep from her body. The eyes close to await the freedom from pain that only death will bring, leaving the helpless Modex and Jartan to walk away in somber reflection.

The sight of the two continuing to make their way through the dragon's lair within the glowing ball of energy Kordon is creating to view them has also created a stern expression of disgust on the evil wizard's skeletal face, for the breaching of his magical barrier has once again touched his powerful senses, alerting him to the approaching threat the heroic pair present.

"Our friends are persistent," says the evil wizard with grudging admiration. "I should have known my magical barrier would not hold against the combined power of the two. I shall not underestimate them again."

"Then what are we waiting for?" announces Karza, mirroring his father's irritation at the image of the annoying pair. "They will be here within minutes, and my mother's seal lies just beyond the end of this corridor. Their existence cannot be tolerated any longer, my father. My full power has returned now after defeating the dragon, so let's go back and destroy them."

"Patience, my son—patience, for their destruction has always been my intention, but I've been waiting for the right moment, and that moment is now at hand."

"What do you mean?"

"Modex is a powerful wizard, for I taught him well, but my corruptive influence still runs deep within his soul, and I know his weakness. It's this paladin I find disturbing."

"But he is a mere novice," counters Karza. "His power hasn't developed anywhere near the higher levels."

"And that is precisely my concern. He should have died many times long before this, and yet he continues to survive somehow. But the inexperience of this ignorant idiot of a child will be his undoing, for there are ways to turn even the mighty powers of a paladin against himself." An evil grin develops on his face as he contemplates the notion.

"How?" asks Karza, also intrigued by the thought.

"As you know, a paladin cannot use his powers to do harm to another creature of goodness. Therefore, the great diamond dragon will be our key to destroy them both."

"But the dragon only attacks evil," Karza cautions, "and besides, it is near death."

"Which is exactly the way I want it, my son, for she will now be unable to resist my control."

"Control? How? The dragon is immune to magic. Your charm spells won't have any effect on her."

"Your demonic blood has weak charm properties," Kordon explains, "too weak to overpower any creature in possession of full strength, let alone such a powerful one as a great diamond dragon, but in her present comatose condition, a few drops of your blood tainting her body will be sufficient to overpower the meager amount of will the dragon has remaining. I can then control her to do my bidding. Modex can do nothing, because the creature is impervious to magic, and when the boy attacks, his paladin power will be destroyed. This is the moment I've been waiting for, which is why I didn't let you kill the dragon when you had the chance. Now, cut your hand."

Karza creates his sword in his human hand and cuts his demonic hand with it, and soon a pool of the steaming blood begins to form within his palm.

"Now," Kordon eagerly continues, "drip your blood over the dragon."

Karza puts his bloody hand over the energy ball that Kordon is holding with the image of the great diamond dragon focused within it. As Karza's blood drips into the ball, the blood is seen to drip down the face of the great diamond dragon, and after several moments that allow the accursed blood to soak in, her once blue eyes of good now open with a reddish glow of evil.

"Rise!" commands a laughing Kordon to his new minion.

In the dragon's lair, the dragon begins to stir and starts to rise. Modex and Jartan can hear the sound of her movements behind them, and they turn to face it. When Jartan sees it is the great diamond dragon apparently recovering from her injuries, he is greatly pleased by the sight.

"Look, Modex! She's going to be all right! Thank the gods!"

Modex, though, is puzzled by the sight, for the dragon was far too wounded to possibly recover from the massive injuries, and therefore he doesn't share Jartan's enthusiasm.

"But it was near death. How can it?" His expression of puzzlement turns to horror as he realizes the cause of the dragon's surprising recovery when he sees the evil red glow of her eyes. "No—Kordon is controlling her. We must get out of here! Run toward the exit, Jartan! Run!"

Back in the corridor of the adjacent area, Kordon, watching the image in his energy ball, laughs with delight as the great diamond dragon rises.

"Kill!" says the gleeful Kordon, "Your master commands it! Kill them both!"

The great diamond dragon, its eyes glowing with malevolence from the evil control of her puppet master's power, unleashes her lightning breath at Modex and Jartan, who are hurriedly trying to flee for the lair's exit. Her aim is erratic due to her injuries from battle but the huge explosion from the energy blast on the ground near the two causes them to lose their footing and fall tumbling down, throwing Jartan some distance away from Modex. The great diamond dragon lumbers toward Modex, now the nearer of the two, but due to the savage injuries inflicted by Karza during their battle and the fact that her willpower is all but gone from the evil influence of Kordon, her movements are awkward and sluggish as the dragon automaton slowly advances toward the helpless wizard, who is slowly recovering his senses from the dragon's attack. She again prepares to launch another of the lethal blasts.

Jartan, seeing Modex in trouble, quickly regains his feet and rushes toward the dragon with his soul blade in hand in an effort to prevent Modex's impeding death.

Kordon, watching this in his energy ball of vision, laughs with sinister delight as the scene continues to unfold before his approving eyes.

"Good! Good! Strike it, you foolish boy! Begin the path that leads to your own destruction!"

Jartan is near a back leg of the huge dragon, which looms over him, and he rears his arms back as a prelude to delivering a strike with his soul blade. Modex can see this and is greatly disturbed by what the boy is intending to do with the weapon.

"No, Jartan!" he shouts in a panicked voice.

But it is too late. Jartan uses all his might to violently strike the dragon's leg with his soul blade in order to protect Modex. Upon impact, this blow—like his attack on the good stone dragon before—creates a great surge of energy that engulfs both dragon and Jartan. The two reel in agony from the intensely painful energy that the boy's unintentional transgression has brought, and the dragon looses her energy weapon harmlessly at the ceiling, sparing Modex from instant death. Jartan's body trembles from the powerful vibration that his soul blade imparts while still embedded in the dragon's skin, causing ribbons of energy to flow violently over their bodies as the boy cries in agony. A powerful flash is followed by an equally powerful blast that violently throws Jartan's body back a considerable distance—and once again, his soul blade loses its shiny luster of power. The great diamond dragon also suffers greatly as her body begins to spasm and contort grotesquely before ultimately collapsing into death—the ground trembling from the impact of her body due to her immense size. Only a smoking mass of reptilian flesh remains of the once mighty great diamond dragon.

Kordon witnesses this successful outcome to his twisted plan and smiles with victory when he sees the smoking corpse of the dragon—but, more importantly, the now powerless Jartan and his equally powerless blade lying helplessly on the ground.

"And now, my son," says a triumphant Kordon to Karza, who is impressed by his father's evil genius, "we destroy them."

The evil duo head back toward the dragon's lair with an air of invincible confidence.

Jartan struggles to recover most of his senses and clumsily tries to regain his feet after suffering the recently painful ordeal as a stoic Modex approaches his side. The wizard looks over at the dragon's corpse and shakes his head in disappointment before helping Jartan to his feet.

"That wasn't wise, Jartan," comments a grave Modex. "You young fool."

"What—what happened?" asks Jartan, still a little dazed.

"You used your soul blade to kill the dragon. You should not have done that. You did exactly what Kordon wanted you to do, and it was a foolish mistake. You've lost all your paladin powers again."

"But she was attacking!" says the boy defensively. "She would have killed you!"

"She was controlled by an evil influence, Jartan—she wasn't at fault and she had no will of her own to overcome it. It still was a creature of goodness, and therefore killing it was unjustified. I'm afraid we—" Modex stops suddenly and turns to face the lair exit as a look of panic begins to sweep across his face.

"What's wrong, Modex?"

"Kordon and Karza are approaching. I can sense them. We haven't much time." Using his magic to create a magical barrier of his own to seal the opening with a wall of energy, he continues, "That barrier won't hold them back for long. Listen to me, Jartan. Only a paladin would have the power to stop them now. The soul of Morbius has left the blade and returned to the land of the dead, so another soul must be found to replace it—one with a love for you that is even stronger if you are to have any chance against them."

Modex goes over to the body of the great diamond dragon lying nearby, and he raises his staff, pointing it at a small area near the dragon's chest—but nothing happens. He then realizes the cause with disgust.

"Damn! My magic still can't affect the dragon even in death."

He eyes Jartan's former soul blade lying near and levitates it over to him. Although its powers are gone, it still is a blade with a cutting edge, and with the blade in hand he starts cutting into an area of the dragon's chest where enough of the diamond scales are missing from her previous battles to allow this act to succeed, for had the diamond armor remained, the now-powerless blade would not have any hope of penetrating.

"What in the seven hells are you doing?" asks a bewildered Jartan as he watches, somewhat disgusted by Modex's insensitive butchering.

"Many of the high-level creatures have a jewel as a heart. These jewels have powerful magical properties."

"What properties?" inquires Jartan.

"That depends on the color," replies Modex. "Every class of creature has its own unique color, but with good dragons that color is usually green."

Modex reaches inside the gore and soon pulls out a sparkling, hand-sized green jewel. "Thank the gods for that, at least," he softly says, relieved to see the green gem. He then moves to Jartan as he explains further,

"The color green signifies protective powers. This jewel will create an invisibility shield that will conceal your presence, and because it comes from a magic-resistant creature, it will even prevent Kordon's all-seeing magic from detecting you."

"But Modex," says Jartan, thoroughly confused that Modex is even bothering to tell him any of this, "what are you—"

But he is interrupted as the magical barrier Modex created begins to flicker as if some powerful force from the other side is trying to break through.

"There's no time to explain!" shouts the frantic wizard upon seeing the flickering barrier beginning to lose its power of obstruction, his voice trembling with desperation.

Modex thrusts his hand hard against Jartan's chest, which sends a powerful electric shock into the boy's body. After a momentary shriek and grimace of pain, the boy instantly falls into unconsciousness and collapses into Modex's arms. The wizard hurriedly drags the boy off toward a protected corner in the lair.

"Forgive me, my son. But only the love of your father can give you the power to defeat them now."

The wizard takes a brief moment to stroke the blissfully sleeping boy's hair tenderly as he reflects on what he needs to do, for Jartan would not have understood his noble intentions had there been time to even explain—not that his son would have approved of them had Modex done so. He places the green jewel on Jartan's chest, closing the boy's hands around it. He then touches the hand with his staff, causing the gem to glow brightly between Jartan's fingers, and as the green glow slowly covers his entire body, it soon fades away and disappears completely. To Modex's grateful eyes, which show a loving tear, this gives Jartan safety from an otherwise horrific death at the hands of Kordon.

Content that his son is well protected from the unbearable carnage that is soon to follow and that the boy would otherwise have to witness—not that he could possibly survive the ordeal anyway now that his paladin powers are gone—Modex moves over to face the barrier, a look of grim determination on his face as he steels himself to prepare for the dreaded arrival of his former teacher, for the barrier is on the verge of collapse. Its energy continues to flicker violently, and it rapidly loses its power under the onslaught of the unstoppable evil directly behind it.

Modex calmly points the tip of his staff into the palm of his other hand and begins to create a massive amount of energy in it. After several more moments of valiant resistance, the barrier finally gives way with a large explosion, and shortly thereafter, through the cloud of smoke, Kordon and Karza confidently emerge. The energy in Modex's hand is now an intense, concentrated ball of shimmering energy, and when he thrusts the hand forward, the powerful bolt catapults forth with great speed at its intended target—the body of the wizard Kordon. But Kordon reacts swiftly with a flash of energy from his eye sockets, which causes the ball of energy to stop motionless mere inches in front of him. Modex is astonished to see his attack just hanging there, frozen impotently, especially after the considerable effort he took to generate its power of intensity. He is greatly disturbed at Kordon's magical ability to overpower it so effortlessly.

"You disappoint me, old friend," chides an amused Kordon at Modex's feeble attack. "Is that any way to greet your former teacher—with one of my own spells that I taught you?"

Kordon slowly waves his hand, which causes the energy ball to become a delicate globe of transparent glass, and with a slight tap of a bony finger against its surface, the glass globe shatters in a glittering shower of sparkles.

"However," he now continues, though his mocking attitude takes on a far more serious and sinister tone, "I believe *this* was your intention!"

He instantly creates a bigger and more intense ball of energy in his hand with far more speed than Modex could achieve, and it is now he who hurls the ball at Modex. The old wizard quickly raises his staff in defense, using his magic to repel the oncoming magical menace. Straining considerably, he manages to slow the ball's progress, though nowhere near as effectively as Kordon. The momentum of the ball actually pushes Modex back slightly, but he manages to freeze it in the air and then dissolve it harmlessly, but without the dramatic flair of Kordon's magic.

"I'm a quick learner," says the mocking Modex with a sly grin, though his breathing is somewhat labored as the act did take some effort.

"Very good!" comments Kordon with respect, though he is hardly intimidated by Modex's power. "But really, Modex, this exchange of conflict is pointless between such good friends. I didn't come here to fight you. I came to talk."

"I have nothing to say to you, Kordon, other than that death has improved your appearance," comments Modex as a sarcastic reference to the grim, skeletal features of the evil wizard. "I was told you were resurrected, Kordon. It pleases me to see that it failed."

"On the contrary," replies Kordon with a smile—a smile one has when one knows something the other does not, "it succeeded beyond your powers of comprehension," and looking around the lair, he adds, "and where is your pet dog of a paladin hiding?—though perhaps *former paladin* is more precise."

"I sent him back to the Surface. With his powers gone, he is no use to me now."

That alone might have been explanation enough to placate most evil wizards, but Modex knows his former teacher has more knowledge than he does here, so Modex tries to distract his suspicious thoughts by adding,

"By the way, that was very clever of you to use his paladin's power against him like that. I'm impressed." Modex even bows slightly when he ends his sentence—not from respect for Kordon but as a further gesture to thwart any suspicion.

Kordon, taking a moment to reflect on this, soon responds with a suspicious smile. "You don't expect me to believe that nonsense, do you, Modex? I am the only wizard who knows the spell to teleport into—*and out of*—the Underworld."

"See for yourself then," counters Modex. "You have spells that can locate him, if he is nearby."

Kordon creates the energy ball of vision again, but the image that presents itself is cloudy and indistinct—and Jartan is nowhere to be seen.

Modex is pleased to see that Jartan's presence cannot register within the ball of vision thanks to the protective power of the dragon's heart, but his expression quickly turns to one of concern when Modex sees the gaping hole in the chest of the dragon's body where the creature's heart would be. If Kordon notices this, he will instantly be aware of its significance, so while Kordon and Karza are distracted by the ball of vision, Modex discretely levitates a large piece of stone to cover the hole.

"You see?" Modex continues happily. "If he was still in the Underworld, it would reveal that. You forget, Kordon, that I too know a few spells. After all, you were my teacher—and a very great one."

It pains Modex greatly to say this, for he really doesn't want to offer this infernal enemy another compliment, but he feels he should add yet another one to alleviate any other suspicions Kordon may have concerning Jartan's true location, for Kordon was right when he said that only he knew the spell to leave the Underworld, as Modex possesses no such knowledge.

"Perhaps," remarks Kordon suspiciously, taking a moment to ponder this further. This pause causes Modex much anxiety, though he manages to hide it, for he knows Kordon's level of knowledge far surpasses his own; therefore any attempt to deceive him is difficult—if not impossible. But Kordon soon dissolves the energy ball of vision, for he is content with his all-seeing power and falls for the deceptive ploy—much to Modex's relief.

Kordon continues, "But you were wise to send him away, though it is regrettable, for I was so looking forward to ripping the flesh from his body. I'm afraid you, old friend, will have to serve that purpose now, for you're a fool if you think you can stop us. You have always had only a mere fraction of my power."

"Take care, Kordon—much has changed in fifteen years. I have had time to continue with my magical studies while for the past fifteen years all you've done is rot in your tomb."

But Kordon chuckles softly at Modex's ignorance as he responds, "It's a shame you won't live long enough to realize how wrong you are. But fortunately for you, I'm in a friendly mood. Join us, my old friend— with Magdara free, even the gods themselves will cower before us."

"Not this time," responds a defiant Modex. "I'm finished with your school of terror, and I'm happy to say I failed all of your twisted lessons—teacher!" he finishes contemptuously.

"Did you now?" responds Kordon, again chuckling softly at Modex's arrogance. "But I have one more lesson for you, my dear, devoted student—who, as you may recall, once swore unquestioning loyalty to me—and the lesson is 'history'." The red energy that glows within Kordon's lifeless eye sockets increases in its foreboding brightness and now Modex's eyes begin to glow red as well. This has an effect on Modex as if he is being hypnotized, and he drops his staff as the mind-numbing power overcomes him. Kordon continues, "For you and I have had such a satisfying history together. Remember it now, Modex—remember how you felt with the force of evil surging through you, the pleasure it gave you, the exhilaration, the power! Remember?"

Kordon gestures to Karza, who is standing patiently by his father's side. Understanding what the gesture implies, Karza begins to move toward the hypnotized Modex, who is oblivious to anything and all around him due to Kordon's stupefying magic. Modex is obviously straining to resist, but the knowledge of his willing past coupled with the evil wizard's hypnotic power is too strong.

"That was—was—so long ago," Modex responds as if in a trance.

"But not so long ago that you've forgotten," continues Kordon with a sinister grin, knowing Modex cannot resist, since he could not resist fifteen years before. "Feel it now again, Modex—as you did once before. Remember the satisfaction you felt as you killed thousands by my side, the destruction you caused, the evil. Oh, how you enjoyed it—and you did enjoy it, Modex—as they begged you for mercy while you stood there laughing and spat in their faces. Remember?"

"Yes!" cries Modex ashamedly as he recalls the feeling, straining painfully to resist Kordon's seductive influences. But his shame turns to pleasure as the evil memories once again begin to seduce Modex's mind.

"Good," continues Kordon with delight, seeing that Modex is weakening, "Feel it once more. Remember the anger and hatred you felt at your brother? You were the older—you were the one who should have been king—but they told you that you weren't strong enough. Remember?"

"Yes, I remember—I hated him. I hated them all!"

"I know you did, my friend," chuckles Kordon at Modex's weakness. "Only with my evil teachings did you become more powerful than your brother. Feel the incredible power and become my servant of evil again. You could not resist me before, Modex—and you cannot resist me now."

Karza is now behind the unsuspecting Modex, and he transforms himself into a demonic creature with large, dagger-like blades at the tip of each of its dozen slimy appendages and places one of the gleaming edges in front of the helpless Modex's neck as a prelude to slitting his throat—but a raised hand from Kordon bids him to stop, for the wizard waits to hear Modex's answer to his next question—a question that will decide whether Modex dies.

"Will you join us, Modex? Join us to free Magdara, and we will rule in darkness for all eternity!"

Modex is straining considerably in his mental battle to honor his pledge to resisting turning to evil yet again, a pledge he so wants to keep—or to succumb to the malignant urges Kordon is giving him by recalling his malevolent past. This past makes resisting the truth of Kordon's words impossible, and Kordon's offer to join once again into the insidious plot for Magdara's freedom is a highly seductive and tempting one, for the power the demon queen would bestow to her loyal followers would be considerable. But as Modex ponders the evil advantages, a distinct disadvantage now enters his mind—the thought of his son, a son he has grown to love deeply, as a mindless slave of evil in the dark, bleak horror of existence under Magdara's monstrous reign. This thought is intolerable as Kordon's words echo in the now loving and protective father's mind.

"This is your last chance, old friend—will you join us?"

The red glow of evil in Modex's eyes suddenly disappears, and he is able to overpower Kordon's influence—thanks to the loving thoughts of his son.

"Never!" he angrily shouts in defiance.

The evil wizard grimaces now that his hypnotic mental bond is broken, and it registers quite painfully, causing Kordon to grab his face with both hands, moaning. Modex instantly summons his staff, which was lying by his feet on the ground, and when it reaches his hand, the tip begins to glow brightly with energy. He rapidly spins around to strike Karza with it. The demon prince was unprepared for the breaking of Kordon's mind control as well as for the ferocity of Modex's demeanor—and the impact of the staff against his transformed skin creates a blast of energy that sends the creature hurtling backward with a mighty explosive force.

"This time," says Modex proudly and with a steadfast level of defiance as he addresses Kordon once more and for the final time, "I will do everything in my power to stop you—old friend!"

Kordon can see Modex is steadfast in his newfound nobility and goodness. He is definitely not pleased to see this in his former student of evil.

"You may find that difficult," responds Kordon angrily, "when I blast you into oblivion!"

The irate wizard unleashes a formidable energy attack at Modex, who quickly counters with his magic to create a shield blocking it, and the two mighty sorcerers exchange several barrages of magic as Karza quickly recovers and transforms into his potent tridragon form to join in the fray. If the lair was a mess after Karza and the great diamond dragon's monumental fight, it is quickly becoming a complete shambles now, for the blistering exchanges of magic and the awesome powers of Karza in his insidious forms are causing total destruction.

It is easy to see why Kordon is the most powerful wizard that has ever lived, as his magic ability is truly frightening. Modex, though, is no weakling, and he is managing to hold his own. Against either one of them in single combat, Modex might—might—stand a chance, albeit a slim one; but against two evil beings that possess such tremendous power, he is beginning to lose ground. When Modex does manage—after a Herculean effort—to temporarily incapacitate one, the other attacks, allowing his evil partner time to recover. But there is no respite for the brave Modex. A glimmer of hope arrives when Karza, who has by now transformed into his titan demon form, picks up the carcass of the great diamond dragon and hurls its massive body at Modex. The wizard tries in vain to use his magic in an effort to deflect it, but the creature's magic resistance prevents this, and he is barely able to teleport out of the way just in time before being crushed by the reptilian mass. As Modex instantly reappears in another location nearby, the hope comes in the form of one of the dragon's diamond scales, which dislodges from the impact. The ground of the lair is strewn with glittering diamond scales, but they all are broken and shattered and therefore useless, but this diamond scale that has just landed at Modex's feet is one of the few that are still intact. Because of this, Modex eagerly picks it up, and with the magic resistance of the scale, he is able to finally put Kordon on the defensive, as Kordon's magic cannot affect Modex with the scale acting like a shield that imparts magic resistance to the wielder. The scale is even effective against all of the fire, freezing vapor, and lightning discharges from Karza's tridragon (to which the great diamond dragon was immune), which the demon prince once again has transformed into now that Modex has teleported too far away for his titan to attack.

"Clever," remarks an irritated Kordon with grudging admiration, "using the magic resistance of the dragon for protection. You may be safe from my magic, Modex—but not from its effects!"

Kordon levitates a huge boulder among the many strewn about in the lair and hurls it with great velocity at the ceiling over Modex's head. The ceiling is still covered with dozens of large, hanging stalactites, and the boulder breaks many of them loose, and they fall as a veritable avalanche of stone. But Modex raises his staff, which shoots out a dazzling array of lightning bolts, disintegrating any of the rocky objects that fall upon them, which spares the wizard from being crushed to death.

Although the dragon scale is a clever and useful tactic to keep the evil wizard's otherwise devastating magic at bay, it is useless against the various demonic weapons of Karza and the malignant forms he can assume other than the tridragon—or so Karza thinks. Seeing a chance to attack while Modex is dealing with the falling stalactites, he begins to transform into the gorgon serpent whose eyes have the power to turn any creature into stone. But fortunately for Modex, he is aware of this creature beginning to form, and he uses the diamond scale to shield his face. As the gorgon serpent appears, the mirror finish of the scale reflects its gaze back—and it is the serpent that turns to stone, the face of the creature petrified into one of horrified astonishment. But a stony prison is no match for the phantasm cloud creature that now begins to seep through, and once it fully emerges, it transforms into the titan demon, which smashes its huge fists into the ground, causing the whole area to shudder from the major earthquake and creating a large fissure that begins to expand toward Modex. The wizard barely manages to jump aside before falling within—but in doing so, he loses grip of the dragon scale.

The battle rages and only increases in its savagery as Modex continues to fight bravely, but now that he has lost any hope of advantage he is simply overmatched; and the battle soon turns hopelessly against him. His wounds increase as Kordon's mighty magic and Karza's various demonic forms begin to overcome Modex's efforts at attack and defense. A particularly devastating attack by the evil pair comes as Karza, as the fearsome tridragon, once again attacks Modex from one side. The wizard uses his free hand to erect an energy shield to deflect his lethal breath weapons, but Kordon attacks him from the other side and Modex uses his staff to create a shield against that. But this overwhelming onslaught ultimately overpowers the valiant wizard's shields, and as the beams of energy inch ever closer to his body, Modex's failing struggle to repel them only increases the agony on his face. The deadly force coming at him from both sides contacts his body with a mighty explosion and sends the noble wizard to the floor in a bloody, smoldering heap. Modex is in great pain from his injuries. Half a leg is gone, an arm is missing, and other deep wounds cover his broken body as he crawls in agony to reach his staff, which is lying nearby—for although he is half dead, his determination to fight with his last breath overpowers the incredible pain he must be feeling.

"You have fought well, my old friend," says the victorious Kordon as he watches, amused by this heroic but hopeless act, "much better than that weakling brother of yours. Do you know he was on his knees sobbing and begging for mercy long before this?" This isn't true, but Modex doesn't know it; it's just another stab Kordon wants to evilly inflict. "But now, I'm happy to say—it's time for you to die."

Karza transforms into his demon prince shape to stand beside his father to enjoy the sight of a helpless, broken, and thoroughly beaten Modex crawling before them. The demon prince's eyes twinkle with delight at the pathetic image.

"The old fool deserves a decent burial, at least," continues Kordon with an ominous smile. "Give him one, my son."

Karza matches his father's sinister grin of triumph with his eyes and transforms yet again into the massive titan demon and lumbers over to the bloody and gravely injured Modex, the earth shaking with each massive footstep of the demonic colossus. Although still alive, Modex cannot possibly defend himself further, as his wounds have brought him near death.

The demonic titan stands over him and raises its giant fist. With a tremendous impact, the titan smashes Modex's body deep into the ground, creating a large, deep crater. Kordon laughs triumphantly and raises his arms to fire a lightning bolt at the rock ceiling, which causes a massive amount of rocky debris to fall onto Modex's grave below, thereby completing the unceremonious and sordid burial.

"And now," says Kordon, grinning with evil satisfaction over his decisive victory, "we complete our task without any further interference. Come, Karza."

The two walk out of the lair to disappear within the blackness of the exit, leaving the faint traces of smoke seeping upward from the pile of rocks covering Modex's grave as the only sign of movement within the once-majestic lair of the great diamond dragon, now transformed into a virtual crypt of death. The smoke emanating from the tortured corpse of the wizard Modex buried deep below, which still smolders from the searing attack that led to his demise, is the only evidence of the brave father's unselfish act of sacrifice—a decidedly tragic and ill-fitting memorial.

CHAPTER 23

✦ ✦ ✦

Jartan begins to materialize where Modex left him now that the protective energy of the green jewel that was the dragon's heart is losing its power. A steady green glow appears first, but then it flickers and finally gives out completely as Jartan begins to stir and slowly regain consciousness. He takes a few moments to recover his senses while trying to stand upon his feet, but his attempt to do so is awkward, and he stumbles a bit, for he is still stunned by Modex's act—stunned mentally and physically. Stunned physically for obvious reasons—but stunned mentally because the image of Modex thrusting his hand into Jartan's chest and the subsequent electrical discharge that sent the youth into his unwilling unconsciousness in the first place still registers bewilderingly in the boy's mind. Now that his senses are beginning to return he considers this act very, very disturbing, and he is becoming quite angry because of it.

"What did that white-haired cobra do now?" wonders the boy, miffed by Modex's unwarranted attack as he stumbles about the lair, still a bit unsteady after the forced slumber. He trips over a rock, for his eyes haven't had time to focus yet on his surroundings—not that his mind would be able to grasp the significance anyway.

"Modex? Modex, where are you? Where are you, you—" Jartan is not accustomed to swearing, and he's not even sure if it is a crime against the code of the paladinhood to do so, but since he has been continuously rubbing his chest in the area of Modex's electrical contact since he awakened, he decides that perhaps swearing is warranted here, because it hurts like hell. He continues, "Where are you, you son of a bitch! And I don't give a damn what your excuse is this time—because I am going to beat the seven hells out of you! Modex?"

Several pieces of stone have been falling at random intervals due to the total devastation, and one finally gets Jartan's attention as it falls near him. With his mind rapidly clearing, he suddenly stops in his tracks. The massive destruction before him now reveals itself to his eyes, and it's clear to him that a savage battle must have ended only recently. Jartan's anger at the unseen Modex disappears, and he calls out to the wizard, confused and gravely concerned over the fact that he is nowhere to be seen.

"Modex? Damn it, answer me! Mo—"

He instantly stops, feeling great alarm as he notices a trail of blood. His eye follows the trail up and stops when it reaches a disturbing pile of stones—a pile very similar to one the youth made himself only days ago atop Mount Sabo. Fearing the worst, he rushes over and frantically begins to remove the rocks from the pile—the wisps of smoke emanating forth becoming thicker and thicker with each stone that is uncovered, which only causes Jartan's expression of panic to increase in intensity. His frenzied removal ceases when one stone's removal reveals the smoldering, smashed hand of Modex protruding upward from the pile of rocks that conceals the remainder of his corpse—the hand's few bloody fingers that remain curled grotesquely in death.

Jartan closes his eyes tightly in despair now that his fears have been justified, for even though the two had their minor moments of conflict, the boy has genuinely grown quite fond of the old wizard—not that he would have ever admitted this to him—and seeing that Modex is dead is very painful to him—a pain that should not feel so acute as it does.

"Oh, Modex," he says solemnly, "you old fool—why did you do it? You knew you couldn't fight them alone! Why? Why? Now what am I going to do? Without my powers I am helpless, and without your guidance I couldn't get out of this bloody nightmare of an Underworld in a thousand years!"

Jartan's despair continues for a few moments, though he actually is becoming angry that Modex has left him and that he is now totally alone. But out of the corner of his eye he notices a faint glow and, rising to investigate further, sees his soul blade off in the distance—pulsating ever so slightly with a barely detectable glimmer of energy. Jartan picks it up to examine it more closely.

"The blade shouldn't have any power," he says as he eyes the blade suspiciously, "so why is it pulsating?"

It dawns on him that the blade is performing exactly like it did when he first held it back at the tomb of Modex's parents.

"I think I understand now," he says. "You sacrificed yourself so I'd have a soul to power the blade again—that is what I'm sensing from it. But how do I summon your soul into it? I don't have the magical knowledge for that or even the ability—or do I? I wonder …"

He goes back over to Modex's grave and puts the blade on it—but nothing happens.

"But you did something else," says Jartan. "You said some words, almost like a prayer, to summon the soul of Morbius when we were at his grave on Mount Sabo—but what was it?" Closing his eyes and trying to remember, he continues, "Your life was born in the name of love—your soul was born in the name of good. Let both be born again now."

But nothing happens.

"It's not working," says a confused Jartan. "Why is it not working? Those were the exact words! It should have worked. You said the words and—" He stops as he recalls what is lacking in the summoning. "Your staff! That's what is missing! You touched the blade with your staff!"

Quickly scanning the lair for the staff, Jartan finally locates it after a search among the debris and again stands before Modex's grave with staff in hand. He touches the blade with the tip of it.

A bolt of energy streaks from above onto the blade on the grave as Modex's soul descends from the land of the dead and the weapon is again reborn into a mighty soul blade, glowing with an even greater degree of energy now that Jartan has the love of his father's soul powering it from within—not that he is aware of this yet. Jartan picks it up reverently, smiling with pride that he has once again rejoined the ranks of the noble paladinhood—and this time, nothing is going to stop him.

"Your sacrifice will not be in vain—" Jartan says with grim determination. He was going to add: "—my friend", but as he holds the blade more closely, he gets another feeling that puzzles him at first, a feeling of intense love he has never felt before—love far greater even than that which emanated from the souls of his sister and uncle within the blades previous—souls that didn't want Jartan to know that they were members of his family. But this soul has a love for the boy that is now impossible to conceal, a soul that wants Jartan to know who he is, and as this love continues to emanate from the blade, it causes the boy to beam with an understanding smile. With a tear forming in his eye as the emotion begins to sweep through his own soul, Jartan adds with pride: "—my father."

CHAPTER 24

* * *

As Kordon and Karza emerge from a tunnel, they are confronted by a huge, jet-black pyramid, the gleaming material of which appears to radiate with power and crackle with foreboding energy, looming several hundred feet before them. It is situated on a column of stone—a virtual towering island—for it is surrounded by a vast, seething sea of molten lava extending as far as the eye can see, casting an eerie, reddish glow throughout the entire area. A long, narrow bridge spans the fiery abyss leading to the pyramid. Soaring high above the pyramid is the rocky roof of the Underworld, which also extends as far as the eye can see, with only the ground of the Surface—the next level of existence above this one—beyond.

"There it is, my son!" exalts Kordon. "There it is! The black pyramid where Magdara's seal of imprisonment is located! After all the years of planning—after fifteen years of death waiting for this moment—soon the demon queen's power will be released and our reign of evil darkness will begin! Nothing can stop us now!" His maniacal laughter of triumph—laughter which almost borders on the insane—now echoes throughout the area.

After crossing the bridge, a closer inspection of the entrance of the pyramid reveals that there are actually three entrances equally spaced apart.

"Three entrances," comments Karza, concerned. "Which one do we take?"

"All three, of course. But the trick is knowing how to open them. The first entrance is simple enough. It only requires someone to open it."

After hearing these rather innocuous words from his father, Karza moves to touch the first entrance but Kordon holds out a skeletal hand, stopping him.

"I suggest, my son," says Kordon with a sly grin, "that you have one of your minions do it for you."

"Why?"

"Upon trying to open each entrance, a death ray descends from above to slay the opener—a further protection from the gods, and their last attempt to prevent access."

Karza summons his sword, and with his blood he creates another of the four-armed minotaurus creatures. With a commanding gesture from Karza, the demonic minion moves to open the first entrance and is instantly slain by a powerful bolt of energy that disintegrates the minotaurus completely—but the entrance does open, revealing a portal of total darkness.

"As I said, Karza—simple. But you must open the next entrance yourself, for only a blood-relative of Magdara is allowed to do so. But more than that, it requires a special kind of blood-relative— one with a special power."

"What power is that, my father?"

"Your tridragon form has the ability to discharge a prismatic beam. The entrance won't be able to withstand it—nothing can."

"I have prismatic weaponry?" responds a stunned Karza. "Why didn't you tell me this before?"

"Because had you known you would have used its power long before this in your many battles and I could not let you do that. This entrance must be your first target."

"No being is given a special power as great as that without also given a special weakness to balance it", says Karza. "What will happen to me after I fire this prismatic beam?"

"It takes all your power, you will be forced to transform back into your demon prince form and it will take some time before you are able to recover."

"How am I going to survive the death ray?"

"I will protect you from it, my son. Have no fear. But before you transform, summon a flame demon. We will need its illuminating power once we are inside."

"A flame demon? Why?"

"As you know, no natural form of light can exist in the presence of Magdara or any of her images—light is too benevolent for that—and since her statue is inside, we will need another source of light, one that is unnatural and pure evil. Summon the demon."

"As you wish, my father."

And Karza soon summons the flame demon. It is a surprisingly small creature around a foot tall that in appearance is like an animated flame, but it does have a demonic face and evil eyes that appear within the glowing fire that makes up its body.

"Good. And now, my son, become your tridragon."

The demon prince transforms into the tridragon. Kordon addresses it.

"You fire the prismatic beam by touching your three heads together."

The mouth of each of the three dragon heads opens and glows bright with its blue, red, or white breath energy. The three heads touch each other, and as their breath combines, it creates the awesome energy of the prismatic beam weapon, which discharges at the entrance. The dazzling array of ever-changing colors that compose the beam form a strikingly beautiful rainbow of power— a hypnotically awesome sight to see a creature of such evil generating a force of such beauty—and a frighteningly destructive one.

The second entrance quickly begins to crumble, but Karza is just as quickly drained of all his transformation power. The death ray that the gods have placed there to destroy any being that tries to enter the pyramid instantly discharges once Karza's prismatic beam hits the entrance; but true to his word, Kordon uses his magic to create a protective field of energy over the tridragon's body, sparing Karza from instant death. The prismatic discharge lasts only a brief period, but it is more than enough to open the second entrance—and not just open it. The beam is so powerful that it destroys a large section of the pyramid, creating a huge opening that also leads to a portal of total darkness, and the death ray ceases. Now drained of all his power, the highly exhausted demon prince returns to his humanoid form and falls to his knees. Kordon helps him to his feet.

"Well done, my son," says Kordon. "And now I will take care of the last entrance personally. This one requires magic to open—very powerful magic of evil."

"But you can't use your magic on the entrance and protect yourself from the death ray at the same time, and with all my power drained, I can't do a thing to stop it. I don't have a form that can block a death ray of the gods even when I regain my strength."

"No ray will descend upon me, my son."

Kordon blasts the third entrance to the pyramid with a surprising degree of violence, for the wizard is impatient now that his goal is within reach, and the last entrance to darkness reveals itself—and no death ray tries to stop him. Now that all three are open, they dissolve into a single but far larger entrance of darkness as Kordon laughs with triumph. Not even the light of the Underworld is evil enough to penetrate the blackness more than a mere few inches—it takes evil at the Demonic

Abyss level to exist inside the pyramid in the presence of Magdara's statue—evil that only one of her demonic kind possesses. Karza gestures for his flame demon minion to advance, and once inside it divides with surprising speed like wildfire into several hundred flame demons. Each one flies toward the hundreds of torch posts that line each side of a long passageway. The ghoulishly evil light they generate is sufficient to reveal the entire interior.

The walls and ceiling are jet black in color, but they glisten from the light as if made out of some strange form of obsidian. In the center is the long passageway made from blood-red marble that leads toward a large chamber of pyramidal shape. At the end of the chamber is an immense statue about a hundred feet tall of the demon queen, Magdara.

The statue is the image of a humanoid female, and although it appears to be made out of the same materials as the pyramid, one can see that the body is dressed in a flowing robe of darkness. Surprisingly, the figure is also unremarkable, and her body is very slender in build. Were it not the image of the demon queen, one might call its appearance frail, for it appears nothing like the heinous demonic figure one would expect. Only her face—which is completely devoid of eyes, nose, or mouth—and the imposing crown upon her head give a hint to the horror and total power that the stone image signifies. On her forehead, though, is a small depression for something to be inserted. Kordon and Karza stand in front of a small marble altar before the statue.

"Very soon now, my beloved," Kordon says reverently to the image as he gazes upward, "we will once again be together."

Meanwhile, Jartan is at the pyramid entrance, which has fortunately been blasted open. He gazes in disbelief at it, for even though he has no idea of the power it required for Kordon and Karza to gain access, he senses it must have been incredible.

"By the gods," he says dejectedly, "is there any limit to the power of those two? I don't stand a chance." He actually begins to back away, and his soul blade instantly flashes danger. "I know there's danger, you idiot!" Remembering whose soul is now in the blade, he corrects his attitude to one with a slight degree of respect. "I mean, *father*. But I feel what you are trying to tell me—the greater danger lies in not facing them. All right, at least when my soul is being tossed into the fires of the seven hells it won't be due to cowardice—beating you to a bloody pulp, maybe—but not cowardice. Let's go."

The boy certainly doesn't mean this; it is just his way of telling his father that he isn't happy with the way things have turned out, but the blade stops flashing. Modex's soul is proud of his son's determination. The youth, with soul blade in hand, walks into the pyramid. The sound of Kordon's voice chanting strange words echoes from deeper within, and although Jartan can barely see Kordon (who is a mere black speck at the far end of the pyramid before the towering statue of Magdara), the boy's presence has not been noticed by the unsuspecting enemies ahead. Realizing the advantage, he quickly hides behind a column. For Jartan to launch an attack from this distance would be pure insanity, and there's no way for him to stealthily approach due to the vast length and lack of cover in the passageway, but he does see off to the side of the marble interior a small crevice in the wall and decides to enter it. Moving along the wall's interior is difficult, as the space is narrow and very cramped, but Jartan can see it is an inner passage that must surround the entire pyramid. It actually is an area that minutes before contained a vast reservoir of holy water that was used as a sealant of protection to keep Magdara from breaking through—holy water that Kordon eliminated.

As Jartan continues to struggle deeper down the cramped inner passageway, he eventually comes to a small crack in its surface, for the wall's stone construction is so ancient that it is only loosely held together, forcing the boy's movement to be extremely cautious lest he bring the whole wall crumbling down upon him. Peering through this crack, the view is narrow and a highly restricted one, but he can see he is now parallel to Kordon and Karza's position, the wizard kneeling before the altar with Karza nearby. Kordon is still chanting his strange dialect, the words obviously part of the evil ritual he is performing, while using his hands to begin to materialize something on the altar. The shapeless energy begins to settle into a spherical form. Karza, standing by his side, has his back turned to Jartan, which gives the boy an idea.

If I could only get a shot off at Karza while he's in that semi-human form of his, thinks Jartan, *I could kill him instantly.*

He tries to reach for the soul blade sheathed by his side, but the area he is in is very cramped, making even the slightest movement almost impossible. After almost dislodging a loose stone on the wall with his clumsy attempts to retrieve his blade, he decides to wait, for a stone falling would alert his foes to his presence, something Jartan would like to avoid until he can make his presence known in a more lethal way—lethal to Kordon and Karza, that is.

He continues to watch intently, for the sight is a curious one, and there is nothing he can do anyway as long as he is squeezed between the walls.

A large and quite hideous-looking hand-sized spider creeps along the wall directly behind the boy. When it crawls on his shoulder, a startled Jartan twitches, and the loose stone in the wall falls. As it hits the marble floor on the other side of the room, it makes a muffled thump—a quiet noise, much to Jartan's relief, for the sound could have alerted them to his presence. But Jartan is still nervous, and he once again looks through the crack to see if Kordon or Karza has noticed the falling stone. Kordon, thankfully, is still chanting and oblivious, for he is engrossed in the ritual he is performing. Jartan breathes a silent sigh of relief at the sight. As he turns an eye to Karza, the demon prince is staring right at him—his evilly glowing red eyes are not pleased.

The boy, his eyes wide with fright, is horrified to discover that Karza is staring right at his location as if his gaze can penetrate the concealing obstruction. Though this is not the case, the stone's disturbance is enough to cause the demon prince to leave Kordon's side and begin to approach the wall where Jartan is looking through. Jartan again tries frantically to reach his soul blade but is still unable due to the cramped area. But Karza has no such encumbrance and creates his sword. Using his free hand, he creates a flame that he touches to the blade. The sword ignites, and he points it at the wall, preparing to discharge its fiery, lethal blast.

A terrified Jartan, seeing all this through the crack, is powerless to defend himself, but seeing the spider now crawling on the wall before his eyes, he manages to calm himself and picks up the creature—though he is disgusted to do so, as it is a small horror in its own right—and pushes it through the opening of the crack. As it scrambles along the other side, it dislodges another loose stone, which crashes to the floor.

Karza can see the spider and stops walking, confident that it was the spider's movement that must have caused the first stone to fall. He blasts the scurrying creature with his flaming sword, which obliterates a large section of the wall, creating a gaping hole, and returns to Kordon's side.

Jartan breathes another silent sigh of relief that his rather simple trick actually worked, but he is doubly relieved when he sees that the hole Karza created in the wall miraculously ended inches away from where it would have revealed Jartan. And since the hole is behind him, he can move farther along the wall without being noticed. He continues to watch the two evil beings through the crack.

Kordon continues to chant his spells, but he soon finishes. A gleaming, black orb now sits on the altar before him and appears to glow with power.

"It is done," he says, satisfied. "Karza, take the orb of summoning and place it within the depression upon Magdara's forehead. You have regained your transformation ability by now. But take great care not to damage the orb, for it would have dire repercussions, and Magdara's summoning would fail."

Jartan, intrigued upon hearing this, decides now is the time to make his move. He knows Magdara's statue is perhaps only a dozen yards ahead, and he cautiously and stealthily moves farther along the wall toward the statue.

Karza takes the orb and transforms himself into a winged creature similar to a praying mantis, but like all his forms, it is not just a larger version of a common insect but one far more menacing and demonic in appearance. He flies off toward the statue of Magdara clutching the orb in two spiny forelimbs, and upon reaching her head he clings to it with his other legs and begins to insert the black orb into the depression there. Soon two large, glowing red eyes radiating intense evil and malignancy begin to form on the otherwise blank face of the statue.

Jartan has reached the back wall and finally has room to maneuver and can take out his soul blade.

"Now, where is the statue of Magdara?" he asks the blade.

Moving the blade along the back wall to ascertain the statue's exact location, Jartan sees it begin to shine when it moves over a certain point. He then slashes the wall with the soul blade, and part of Magdara's statue can be seen once the stones are removed. Jartan fires a beam of energy from the blade at the statue, which begins to crack.

Kordon, although he cannot see Jartan due to the immense size of the statue blocking his view, can see something is terribly wrong as the base of the statue begins to crack and move.

"No," he exclaims with alarm at the shocking sight.

The statue of Magdara begins to crack further as Jartan continues pushing it off of the base using the power of his soul blade, and after a few more moments the stone goliath begins to fall directly in Kordon's direction like an immense tree being felled. Helpless, Karza is still clinging to the statue's head. The expression on the mantis monster's face registers with utter horror as the floor of the chamber rapidly approaches.

"No!" shouts Kordon with an even greater sense of dread.

Raising his hands before him, he quickly tries to use his magic to prevent the statue from crashing to the floor, but Jartan redoubles his effort to send the demonic object crashing downward. The soul blade glows even brighter to compensate for Kordon's magical resistance, and a battle of strength begins between paladin and wizard. But for once the evil wizard is the one overpowered, and his eyes glow with anger as he is unable to stop the statue from falling. He teleports out of its way as it crashes to the ground and shatters while Karza, still transformed, is buried under the rubble of Magdara's immense statue. Huge quantities of demonic mantis blood splatter under the crushing weight. Smoke from the fracturing stone of the statue fills the chamber, obscuring everything within, and when it slowly dissipates, all can see the shattered destruction that once contained Magdara's mighty image in beautiful, polished marble and obsidian.

"The orb!" Kordon cries out in horror as he reappears safely in another location.

The orb of summoning is bouncing on the floor, cracking with each bounce, and bluish vapor begins to seep out of the fractures on its once-pristine surface. It rolls along the floor and finally comes to a stop. Jartan comes out of the hole in the wall where the statue of Magdara once proudly stood, eyeing the destruction he has caused in triumph.

"Let's see you try and summon that demonic bitch now, wizard!" says the boy proudly.

"You!" Kordon hisses with even greater horror now that the cause of his troubles reveals himself. "You have plagued me with your infernal interference for the last time, boy!"

The wizard angrily fires a blast of energy from his skeletal hand at the persistently annoying youthful target, but Jartan is able to use his soul blade—which now has the very powerful soul of his father, Modex—to easily deflect the energy. Without the added power his father's soul gives the blade, Jartan would surely have been incinerated by Kordon's evil magic.

"Impossible!" remarks Kordon with shock, for the boy should have been instantly vaporized by the magical discharge. "Your paladin powers were lost! I know I destroyed them!"

"Now it's your turn to feel Modex's wrath, wizard!" Jartan responds proudly in defiance, for he has supreme confidence now with the greater power he has at his command.

Jartan, seething with vengeance, unleashes his own paladin-powered devastation upon the hated Kordon, who instantly uses his powerful magic to generate a cone-shaped shield of protection that encircles him. The blasts Jartan fires at it are more intense than any he has seen before due to the love of his father's soul in the blade, and as they explode spectacularly against Kordon's shield, the clouds of smoke they leave begin to obscure the sight of the wizard. Jartan continues his blistering assault for several more moments, which only increases the thickness of the cloud. Convinced that Kordon couldn't possibly survive such a relentless beating, he ceases his attacks and waits for the dissipating clouds to reveal the dead wizard's twisted and mangled corpse—only to gaze in shock as the smoke clears to expose Kordon standing unscathed, a contemptuous grin on his skeletal face the only sign of Jartan's attack.

The sight of Kordon mocking him only redoubles Jartan's hatred and intense desire to slay the evil wizard once and for all, and summoning every ounce of strength he possesses, the boy fires a continuous stream of energy—the most powerful he and his soul blade can generate. Kordon counters with an energy discharge of his own, and as the two concentrated beams meet, it becomes a contest of which one can overpower the other.

What makes this renewed battle of strength between paladin and wizard particularly disturbing for Jartan is that he is using all his power to maintain his attack and is straining painfully to do it, whereas Kordon is maintaining his almost effortlessly despite the energy it requires on his part to generate his attack, and no sign of strenuous effort shows upon him. But what fortifies Jartan's courage to continue is that his attack is beginning to overcome Kordon's. It starts to creep closer to the wizard's body, and yet Kordon astoundingly is apparently not intimidated by the sight of this approaching beam of death and comments accordingly.

"How droll," he says, unconcerned and even amused.

But it is Kordon who ultimately has the advantage here, for although the two opponents are using both their hands in an effort to overpower each other, the wizard has other weapons at his disposal. As his anger at Jartan's existence returns, Kordon begins to combine the energy he can fire from his glowing eye sockets with that of his hands, and this rapidly repels Jartan's attack back at him. His scream of protest is a futile gesture, and seeing that he cannot repel Kordon's advancing energy, he quickly ends the hopeless struggle by trying to create a shield of protection. But the advancing beam's progress at this point has come so close to Jartan's body that this is only partially effective.

The shield does manage to absorb most of the energy and thereby save Jartan's life—but just barely, for the resulting detonation rips through the boy's body causing severe injuries and he collapses to his knees in defeat, his skin and clothing smoldering. All his strength is gone as his feeble attempt to raise his soul blade demonstrates and it's a small miracle that he remains upright at all, though his body wavers from the total exhaustion and severe injuries.

"Frustrating, isn't it, boy," remarks a chuckling Kordon, "to come so far only to realize at the end that you are hopelessly outmatched. You fool! Can't you see your childish powers are no match for mine? But don't feel so bad, for you did surprisingly well considering your infantile level. So Modex's soul is in your blade now, is it? That must mean he is your father. His love for you gives you a fair amount of power. Now, if you were an arch-paladin, I might even fear you, with the soul of a loving parent in your blade. Unfortunately for you, your father's love manifested itself far too late." He chuckles derisively at the knowledge. "You know that he tried to kill you as an evil sacrifice of loyalty to Magdara when you were a mere, sniveling infant?"

Jartan is far too exhausted, injured, and near death to speak, but the hurt look in his eyes upon hearing this betrays his thoughts as Kordon continues his verbal abuse.

"Oh yes—it's true, boy. You weren't conceived out of any love on his part—only evil."

Jartan's mind floods with hate for Kordon, but his broken body struggles to summon enough strength to lift his soul blade to act upon the hatred. His arms tremble violently in the attempt, but the blade fails to leave the ground, and Kordon's evil laughter is the only other result of the brave act.

"Oh dear, I sense you want to kill me, boy. That is unfortunate, for I am very fond of you. So fond, in fact, that I am going to help you with some further knowledge you are unaware of. Now that you have the soul of such a close and loving family member serving you, your blade has the power to heal your injuries. So, go ahead, boy—heal yourself."

Again the look in Jartan's eyes betray his feelings of doubt, for a being at Kordon's level of diabolical evil does not show mercy.

"Think I am being merciful, do you?" says Kordon. "I'm not. For I am going to take great pleasure in torturing you mercilessly before I finally kill you—and I want your body healthy to take the excruciating torment I will unleash for ruining Magdara's summoning—if you have the courage. But I don't think you have the courage not to maintain your family's tradition of dying on your knees like your uncle and father!"

These words combined with the sound of Kordon's maniacal laughter are too much for the boy to bear, and with a Herculean effort, Jartan closes his fingers around the handle of the soul blade tightly. With his remaining breath, he manages to utter loudly in defiance, "Heal!"

A wave of energy engulfs the boy's body, which causes it to glow brightly, and all his injuries disappear as the healing glow fades. Recovering all his strength, the agile Jartan, seething with hatred, jumps to his feet once again to battle the evil wizard—a battle to the death.

CHAPTER 25

✝ ✝ ✝

In a world of mighty magic, mighty weapons, mighty abilities, mighty intelligences, and the even mightier beings that possess them, the eternal struggle between the forces of good and evil tend to be decided by which force has the most power—unless the other is very, very lucky. Luck is a matter of random circumstances, but power can be achieved. Power comes from knowledge. Knowledge comes from wisdom. Wisdom comes from experience—and experience comes from age. It is not some lucky coincidence that the most powerful of beings are the most ancient—the gods—and when one reflects upon all the many pantheons in existence and the even greater number of gods each contains, not a single one of the divine beings is a child. Age equals power here. No student can defeat the master, just like no acorn can defeat the oak—and no teenage paladin can defeat the most powerful wizard in creation unless he is very, very lucky. Jartan's luck is running out very, very quickly.

But *luck* is not the word for it is time he is really running out of— time that is solely at the discretion of Kordon's whim, for the more powerful wizard could use his dark magic arts to crush Jartan like a proverbial bug if he wished. The boy, even with his more powerful soul blade—possibly the most powerful he is capable of wielding at this stage in his life—is of little use, for he would need far more experience to use it more effectively to have any chance, especially against an all-powerful being like Kordon. Not even Jartan's youthful and adroit nimbleness, which saved his life many times in the past, and the more advanced defensive powers the blade imparts are the reasons he has survived this long in the battle. Only Kordon's desire to see the boy suffer greatly is the reason Jartan remains alive—a groveling toy of amusement for the twisted wizard's sadistic brutality and vindictive evil.

The explosive force from the blast of a mighty magical discharge against the soul blade Jartan holds before him sends the boy's body hurtling back violently. He flails along the floor and collides against a huge block of debris, which stops him instantly. Quickly recovering his senses, Jartan sees a particularly large mass of marble debris from Magdara's statue nearby and uses his blade to levitate it. He hurls the immense stone in Kordon's direction with great velocity—but the evil wizard immobilizes it in midair with a mere raising of his hand and instantly sends it back at Jartan with even greater force. The boy, understandably horrified to see his attack backfire against him, raises his soul blade for protection. The blade generates a protective shield, and the stone shatters upon impact with a mighty explosion, leaving Jartan unharmed.

"Arrogant little swine," says Kordon, unimpressed. "Do you really think a pitiful child like yourself can possibly defeat me? I've destroyed demigods infinitely more powerful than you!"

And again his maniacal laughter, which almost borders on the hysterical, precedes another onslaught of his incredible magical wrath upon the hopelessly overmatched youth. Jartan miraculously survives, though barely, for his efforts at defending against the relentless torrents of magic from Kordon continue to wreak havoc on Jartan as his body displays more and more sickening wounds. The increasingly desperate paladin does manage to counterattack with a discharge of energy at Kordon from his weapon, but the wizard simply teleports out of its way only to instantly reappear some distance behind the unsuspecting boy, leaving Jartan to watch helplessly as his powerful bolts explode against the wall of the chamber, sending debris flying. Kordon summons a magical whirlwind, which he unleashes toward Jartan, and although the flash of his soul blade alerts him to this new danger, his effort to combat the wind with several blasts comes to no avail, as the swirling wind has nothing solid to impact against. Unable to evade its power of attraction, Jartan is snatched up within the churning vortex, spinning around violently. The boy groans loudly due to the highly unpleasant forces trying to rip his limbs from his body. His yells increase to a frightening level of intensity as Kordon shoots a stream of flame into the whirlwind, causing the cyclone of death to ignite. Jartan, who is slowly being incinerated within, screams in piercing agony.

The evil wizard, obviously enjoying the suffering of his searing opponent, isn't ready to kill him just yet, even though he could do so on a whim, as Jartan obviously has nowhere near the power to combat him. Kordon waves his hand, which dispels the flaming whirlwind; and the severely burned Jartan, his body smoking from the flame attack, is catapulted some distance away to land violently against the floor. His soul blade, also smoking from the incinerating heat, is tossed off as well and lands far from Jartan's reach leaving a highly pleased Kordon to laugh with victorious delight at the sight of the severely burned, mortally wounded, and trembling Jartan. The dying youth makes a feeble effort to reach forth for his soul blade, which he blurrily sees off in the distance with the one good eye he still has, his outstretched arm and hand trembling.

"Soul blade!" commands the boy, struggling greatly to even generate enough breath in his failing lungs to call to it for its healing energies.

The blade flies off toward Jartan's hand—but Kordon, seeing this from his location, fires a bolt of lightning at the groping hand of the boy before the blade can reach it. The bolt instantly transforms his arm into a sickening, bloody stump—and the soul blade continues to fly past Jartan who has no means now to grab it. The soul blade does manage to land mercifully near, so Jartan crawls in its direction to obtain it with his remaining hand. The ten feet to the blade's location is an agonizingly slow journey for the boy, and it takes him some moments to crawl the torturous distance as Kordon watches with his ever-present, odious smile. He could easily kill the boy with a mere snap of his fingers at this point, but indulging his delight at seeing Jartan suffering greatly with each inch of progress, he allows him to reach the blade—only to once again blast the boy savagely once the fingers of his remaining hand touch it. The impact of energy against Jartan's body sends the blade flying before Jartan can utter the command to heal, and he falls to the ground as a mass of scorched flesh with only a few seconds of life remaining in his grotesquely broken body. Laughing with contempt, Kordon now materializes over the defeated youth, who is obviously at the powerful wizard's nonexistent mercy.

"Infantile idiot," he gloats over the boy. "I see stupidity flows in the blood of your entire family. You dare to challenge one with the power of a god? There will be no healing for you this time, boy, although I did enjoy your agony. Many thanks for being such an amusing kill."

Kordon kneels down beside Jartan and painfully clutches the helpless boy's neck with his bony fingers, bringing Jartan's bloody and burned face close to his as if to examine it more closely.

"I expected the paladinhood would send one of its kind to stop me—and I need a paladin to fulfill my purpose—but you?" He laughs with contempt yet again. "No, boy, I cannot use you."

He releases his skeletal grip on Jartan's neck, causing the boy to once again collapse upon the ground. Jartan can't help but notice that Kordon is leisurely walking away from him with his back turned—a further act of contempt, for the evil wizard is not concerned that he has placed himself in such a vulnerable position. Kordon knows that Jartan, with his massive injuries, can do nothing to exploit it. And now that Kordon has achieved the few yards of distance necessary to unleash his last and fatal insult, he turns to face Jartan with his hands glowing bright with lethal energy.

"You are going to die now, paladin, so it's time for you to join your family's legacy—on your knees, boy!" commands the wizard with a thrusting forward of his hand as he uses his magic to force the unwilling Jartan, unable to resist, to the humiliating, subservient position on his knees, causing him great pain as his broken body contorts to Kordon's forceful will. "And pray to me—pray to your new god—that you die quickly. I want to hear two words from your lips before you die: 'kill me.'" Kordon, laughing maniacally, continues to inflict his painful magical energy on Jartan, obviously enjoying his tremendous suffering. "Say it, boy. Say the two words that will end your suffering and send you to your doom!"

Jartan, the boy on the verge of death, can see his soul blade sticking out of the floor where it landed—directly behind Kordon.

"Here are your two words," Jartan shouts defiantly with practically his last breath. "Soul blade!"

The blade flies too fast for Kordon to react to this unexpected act of defiance, and he does not see the blade before it hits Kordon in the back and passes completely through his body to land in Jartan's remaining hand.

The wizard screams in agony, but it's not blood that flows from the two gaping wounds on Kordon's body made by the blade's entry and exit—for that dried up and disintegrated over a decade ago along with the wizard's flesh—but waves of powerful energy that gush forth as if released from under great pressure. Kordon continues to reel in pain, and it is now he who is on his knees, giving Jartan time to heal his massive injuries now that he has the soul blade in hand. He holds the

blade close to his body and, closing his eyes in deep concentration—
which is not easy, given the incredible pain he is experiencing—says in
a mere whisper,

"Heal."

The soul blade glows brightly and again covers Jartan's bloodstained
and still smoldering body with its soothing radiance. All the horrendous
damage of scorched skin, severe lacerations, and missing limbs disappears
or regenerates within the healing energy. Now fully healed and all limbs
restored, he regains his feet, vigor, and visceral hatred and rushes over
to Kordon, who is still writhing in agony on his knees—and it is now
Jartan who stands over his helpless, defeated opponent. Kordon can
do nothing to stop the flow of energy leaving his body, for the wound
on his back is unreachable; and his bony fingers, devoid of flesh, make
a feeble barrier over the wound on his chest as Jartan puts the blade
of his weapon in front of Kordon's face, for the boy wants Kordon's
eyes—which for the first time since the wizard's unholy resurrection fail
to glow bright with power and begin to flicker and fade as his energy
continues to seep from his body—to see who the real victor of the battle
is: Modex. Triumphantly, Jartan raises the blade over Kordon's head,
stopping only for a moment to spit upon Kordon's body. Only a swift
though incredibly satisfying thrust downward is required to decapitate
the greatly loathed and once greatly feared pitiful form of the most
powerful evil sorcerer, who kneels inches below the gleaming blade—a
blade which seems to glow with an almost imperceptibly higher intensity
as if the soul of Modex is smiling with pride for its wielder.

Suddenly, the interior of the chamber is showered with stone debris
as Karza, in his tridragon form, erupts from the pile of rubble he was
buried under, and several of the violently flying stones hit Jartan, which
knocks him to the floor before he can kill the dreaded wizard. The sight
of the demonic enemy that was supposedly destroyed forces the alarmed
youth to urgently recover to try once again to deliver a decapitating
blow to Kordon—who even in his defeated state still appears the more

dangerous of the two—but a discharge of lightning from one of Karza's dragon heads distracts the boy into trying to block the energy with his weapon for defense, the impact of its arrival sending Jartan hurtling back a dozen or so yards from the defenseless Kordon, who is still painfully clutching his wound, for its severity is so incapacitating that he is unable to act otherwise.

The youthful paladin angrily counterattacks with a blistering attack of energy from his weapon at the rapidly approaching demonic tridragon, but Karza transforms into his giant titan demon form in anticipation of the onslaught. The beams of energy hit the black, armored skin and surprisingly blast away a few sections of it from the creature's body thanks to the added power of Jartan's new soul blade, but the attack does nothing to faze the far denser skin of iron that armors the beast beneath this outer layer and does not inhibit its lumbering progress at all. Jartan hurriedly avoids the ensuing onslaught of deadly, crushing blows.

The massive weight of the beast cracks the marble floor of the chamber with every footstep, but the impacts of its fists upon the surface cause huge chunks of stone to erupt, further increasing Jartan's difficulty, though his nimbleness does allow him a few opportunities to strike—but the incredibly dense skin easily absorbs the slashing effects of Jartan's blade. The boy manages to scramble up a large pile of debris from Magdara's statue and from this higher vantage point is able to leap onto the shoulders of Karza's titan demon. He tries to plunge his soul blade into the huge, demonic skull, but again the density of the creature's construction impedes the blade's progress. Karza transforms into his ethereal phantasm form, causing Jartan to fall the thirty or so feet to the floor with a painful impact.

The phantom cloud engulfs the boy, its eyes showing the gleeful radiance of victory, and then Karza transforms into sickly green blob creature that smothers the boy like a heavy carpet of thick, oozing jelly—its form bulging slightly from Jartan's frantic but useless attempts to escape. Even the large holes he makes when blasts from his blade penetrate the slime almost instantly coalesce back into shape due to the creature's almost liquid composition. But soon its entire body begins to glow, which causes the creature's evil red eyes to glow with concern; and after a few moments during which the glow grows more intense, the entire slimy mass of the thing is blown off into dozens of pieces, leaving Jartan standing and catching his breath with his glowing soul blade shining brightly. The dozens of slime pieces, though, quickly merge back into one, and Karza once again transforms into the titan demon to renew the attack. Jartan retaliates with another barrage of energy blasts, but again this form of Karza absorbs them without any major damage, forcing the youthful warrior to try another approach. He levitates a large slab of stone, almost the same size as the demonic juggernaut, and hurls it at the onrushing creature—but the stone ultimately becomes nothing more than a virtual piece of glass as it contacts the far denser metallic body, shattering completely without leaving even a dent of injury.

While paladin and demon are busy fighting ferociously, Kordon manages to use what's left of his magic energy to heal himself of his massive, encumbering injuries, and once again his eyes beam with almost godlike infernal power and evil now that he has fully recovered. His anger at Jartan is unparalleled, and as the boy is engaged in battle with Karza, the wizard prepares to blast the unsuspecting Jartan with a raised hand that glows bright with lethal power—but he is quickly distracted by a flash of light he sees in his peripheral vision. As he turns his head to focus on the cause, he is alarmed to see the damaged black orb of summoning continuing to belch out blue vapor as it begins to crack further and flash spasmodically. Its glowing energy begins to flicker, further increasing Kordon's horror.

"The orb!" he cries, "I must repair it before—"

But the orb's energy now fades completely.

"No," whispers an extremely worried Kordon, and then he says quite loudly, "No!"

From the area where Magdara's statue once stood, a beam of brilliant energy erupts from the floor.

Karza, still in titan demon form, at this point has a helpless Jartan firmly in the clutches of his vise-like grip. He chuckles softly (for the creature has no mouth to sound anything louder) and slowly crushes the boy between its fingers—his fragile, human bones making a disturbing cracking sound under the pressure. Thin trickles of blood come from his ears, nose, mouth, and eyes, and only the fact that Jartan is instinctively closing his eyelids so tightly due to the tremendous pain he is experiencing keeps his eyeballs in their sockets. But the beam of light erupting from farther in the chamber is so intense that Karza can't help but notice, and sensing the far more important cause, he tosses his boring plaything away, totally engrossed by the beam's presence as he transforms into the demon prince to gaze upon it.

The broken body of Jartan rolls a bit, but remarkably he still has a grasp on his soul blade as if the intense pressure of Karza's iron grip has fused the handle of the blade into his smashed hand, and he soon heals himself from the crushing injuries to regain his feet once again. Like Kordon and Karza, he is virtually paralyzed by the hypnotic, pulsing beam with its powerful radiance. The beam slowly condenses and, with a blinding flash, forms into the awe-inspiring presence of Magdara, the dreaded demon queen.

The awe she inspires does not come from her appearance, for she is much like the image of her statue in that her humanoid build is relatively unremarkable and even fragile in its slimness. She appears much like Karza, but her face does not contain a black plate that obscures any facial features, for there is no face beneath the cowl of black that covers her head—just an emptiness of infinite blackness. She does not even have the towering height her statue had, though she still is a respectable and imposing ten feet tall. But what does exude an almost unlimited level of awesome power and evil—making this infernal being one that should never be underestimated or trifled with, let alone summoned in person to be gazed upon by mere mortals like the three present, no matter how powerful they are—is the glowing red aura that surrounds her entire body and the even brighter glowing eyes. Her eyes closely match Karza's—but these eyes are flame and radiate a far greater level of power. The crown on her head is also more imposing than Karza's and conveys a higher level of regal authority and power worthy of the supreme monarch of all unholy evil. Kordon and Karza both drop to their knees to kneel before her, for even their level of evil pales in comparison to that of Magdara. Jartan is paralyzed at the sight of her, and if it wasn't for the fact that he is holding his soul blade, he would surely die from her mere presence, for no human possesses enough goodness to overpower Magdara's evil—only Modex's soul that exists beyond the grave and therefore is not affected by evil gives the paladin the protection to survive a demon queen's presence—and Jartan's Soul Blade glows bright with danger as it never has done before.

"Magdara," begins Kordon with great trepidation, for even though he has wished for this moment to arrive for a long time, and has gone to unimaginable lengths to achieve it, the damaged orb weighs heavily in his mind, for this is not how her summoning was supposed to happen. He tentatively continues,

"Magdara, almighty power of darkness—my beloved! It is I, Kordon. After an eternity of imprisonment in the Abyss, you are finally free—free to rule over all the realms of existence in total evil!"

But this gets no emotion from the demon queen, though she is aware of Kordon's presence as she lowers her head to watch him slowly move toward her.

As Kordon cautiously approaches with outstretched hands, a gesture signifying complete harmlessness and kinship, the two glowing eyes of flame within Magdara's otherwise infinite face of darkness appear to grow even brighter—a show of great anger and perhaps even unbridled hatred that causes Kordon to stop and then rapidly back off in fear—and fear is definitely an emotion that the all-powerful evil wizard with all his diabolical genius is completely unused to.

"Magdara—don't you know who I am? I have freed you! Don't you understand? You are finally free of imprisonment. No—don't!"

But it's too late. Bolts of intense energy shoot from Magdara's eyes as Kordon frantically erects an energy shield to protect himself, but a demon queen's power is of a kind that one cannot hope to protect against, and the bolts pass through the shield and hit him, causing a massive explosion that sends the wizard hurtling backward.

Karza, aghast at this unwarranted wrath from his mother toward his father, rushes toward her, feeling that a familiar face—that of her own son—will be sufficient to calm her.

"Mother, what are you doing?" he shouts, completely bewildered by her angry and destructive act toward one she hoped would eventually release her and who was father of her offspring.

But there is no sign of motherly affection from the demon queen as she raises her demonic hand and points a terrifyingly glowing fingertip at her son, discharging a number of potent energy bolts from it.

An astonished Karza instantly transforms into his ethereal phantasm creature, the eyes of which radiate horror and astonishment. The energy passes through him without damage. He then transforms into his massive titan demon form. Then, three times Magdara's size and a thousand times her physical strength, he charges at his mother in an effort to stop her from any further acts of mystifying violence. He has her in his grasp—but only for a meager second, for Magdara transforms her body into a far more massive, far more imposing, and far more hideous creature than Karza could ever hope to become. It is a creature so hideous, in fact, that any being with a lesser constitution that gazes upon this creature either dies instantly of fright or flees in eternal terror, the image burned forever on the eyes of the poor soul—and the tables have turned, for the titan demon is now in Magdara's inescapable grasp.

Karza, who is obviously helpless in the grip of the far more powerful creature that his mother has become, is understandably concerned by this. This demonic form of his—one that was up until now so incredibly dense that its weight was of such magnitude that nothing could lift it off its feet—is now but a mere toy for Magdara.

She quickly rends Karza's titan demon nearly in two—making that particular sound that metal makes when it is being ripped apart accompanied by a shower of sparks. Magdara has split the creature from the shoulder to the groin—another act Karza thought impossible for any but the mightiest of supreme gods. Karza's two sections writhe frantically, gushing with blood and gore, and he lets out a piercing shriek. The body section minus the head falls on the floor and instantly transforms into a large portion of Karza's semi-human body, which spasms sickeningly and soon erupts into flames and disappears in a puff of smoke. Magdara then violently throws the remaining section of the spastically flailing titan demon—its body still gushing enormous quantities of blood—against the wall of the pyramid like so much useless trash, and it smashes completely through to exit the other side and falls into the fiery inferno below, creating a massive fountain of flame upon impact with the seething lava. The black hand of the once mighty and unstoppable demon thrusts upward out of the lava as if to save itself from the burning lava, but even the metal skin begins to melt from the hellish heat, and the smoking hand slowly disappears into the bubbling inferno.

Jartan, awestruck upon seeing the attack on Kordon—and particularly the horridly unpleasant fate of Karza—wants no part of any of this family squabble and starts to discreetly back away and leave the area with as much haste as possible without getting Magdara's attention.

Meanwhile, Kordon slowly recovers, his black robes still burning slightly from the impact of Magdara's attack, trying to placate her yet again with a display of arms raised as a nonthreatening gesture along with what he hopes will be his soothing words.

"Magdara, you must listen to me! Your mind has been affected by the damaged orb! Do you understand? The damaged orb has damaged your mind as well. Stop what you are doing. Do you hear me?! Stop what you are doing! I can repair the orb! I came here to help you! Magdara!"

But the impassive demon queen ignores Kordon's pleas and once again begins to attack him, and the wizard has no choice but to retaliate. The two powerful beings become locked in ferocious battle.

While Kordon and Magdara are distracted battling each other, Jartan is able to make his exit with greater speed, but he stops when he notices the orb—still seeping vapor slightly—lying on the ground nearby. It occasionally flickers with power, so he decides it might come in handy. He picks the orb up and exits the pyramid—which is not easy, due to the amount of debris lying about, as he has to scramble over several large pieces. Outside, Jartan rushes across the bridge as the sounds of Kordon and Magdara's intense battle can be heard echoing out of the pyramid interior and several explosions send pieces of the structure's exterior flying off.

Back inside the pyramid, the struggle between the two titans of evil continues, but even Kordon's formidable magic is unable to offset the awesome powers of the dreaded demon queen. The evil wizard is beginning to panic—another alien emotion for him.

"Stop! I command you!" he cries.

Kordon continues to blast away frantically, unleashing every ounce of power—power of such magnitude that the entire area begins to tremble from its ferocity—in a hopeless effort to save himself.

"Stop! Stop! Stop!" he shouts but to no avail.

Even a frantic attempt to teleport out of the Underworld to safety is quickly nullified by Magdara's powerful influence, and Kordon manages only to fade feebly before reappearing. The immense and monstrous form of Magdara is now upon the wizard. She prepares to crush him between her huge demonic hands, and Kordon makes a last-ditch effort with his awesome magic in a futile attempt to repel them—but Magdara is simply too strong and overpowers Kordon's effort within mere moments.

"No!" he screams—the final word of the most powerful evil wizard that ever lived.

The blinding explosion of energy that erupts from Kordon's crushed body is commensurate with his incredible power, and its explosive force completely shatters the pyramid structure. The blast is so powerful that it also sends Jartan to the ground, and he has to defend himself from the barrage of large pieces of the shattered pyramid that begin to fall upon him, using the soul blade to make a shield.

The victorious Magdara transforms yet again, becoming even larger, and towers over what's left of the pyramid. Jartan can see that Magdara is now of an alarming and perhaps unstoppable size—unstoppable for his powers, certainly—and seeing that he has reached a secluded area where he may be able to avoid detection, he thinks that now is the time to put an end to the demon queen's existence or at least send her back to imprisonment in the Abyss. He places the orb on the ground before his feet.

"Back into your eternal prison, demoness!"

With a quick blow, he strikes the orb with his soul blade causing the sinister object to shatter with an accompanying discharge of energy that cascades along its already cracked surface and turns to see what effect this has on Magdara in the distance. This same discharge of energy radiates from the demon queen's head which causes her intense pain, momentarily stunning her. But the effect is ultimately useless for it does nothing even remotely lethal; nor does it send her unwillingly back into the Demonic Abyss. In fact, it only succeeds brilliantly in focusing her attention on Jartan, who up until now has avoided her notice. Judging by the look in Magdara's eyes—she is furious.

Jartan, realizing that destroying the orb has only alerted her to his presence and increased her anger, makes a concerted effort to run for his life.

"That wasn't smart!" he says as he hastily flees.

Magdara fires a blast of flame at the retreating Jartan, whose soul blade alerts him to the incoming danger, and he turns just in time to protect himself with an energy shield. The blast of flame is of considerable magnitude due to Magdara's size, and it covers a large area. When it finally subsides after several moments that, to Jartan, seem like an eternity, he is the only thing undamaged by it. Everything around him for a considerable distance has been incinerated by the incredible intensity, leaving only blackened and charred earth smoking profusely. He is amazed at the destruction.

"By the gods!" he exclaims with awe.

Jartan counterattacks with energy bolts at Magdara's immense body, but she is far too large now for the pitiful damage he inflicts to matter, and he only succeeds in once again incurring Magdara's wrath. Not wishing to tempt fate by testing whether his power can repel another searing attack, he decides that discretion is the better part of valor. Seeing that the only chance of safety for the youthful paladin is to retreat farther into the Underworld from whence he came, the entrance to which lies some dozen yards away, he rushes toward it, soon reaching the protective cover of the tunnel. But his sigh of relief is short-lived, for the flashing of his soul blade warns of danger, and the earth shakes violently, sending the boy diving for cover to a small ledge several feet below him as the entire tunnel area is virtually swiped away by a sweeping blow from a huge demonic appendage. Nothing remains over Jartan's head other than the ceiling of the Underworld high above. Further retreat into the Underworld is now impossible, since for a considerable distance the concealing protection that the tunnel provided no longer exists and only open skies remain. Jartan can only shake his head in shocked amazement at the degree of destruction. No words could possibly describe his awestruck emotions.

Incredibly, Magdara increases in size once more, and now she is able to reach the very ceiling of the Underworld. Her appendages claw and tear into it, dislodging massive amounts of earth as she attempts to make her way upward to the Surface—where her infernal power will be absolute.

"She's heading for the Surface!" Jartan screams in horror. "I must stop her!"

Jartan scrambles out of his position, shaking off the debris that covers him, and begins to head back toward the ruins of the pyramid where Magdara is still located. But as she continues to break through to the Surface, large sections of earth rain down on practically the entire area below. Jartan evades as many as he can with his youthful agility, and those he can't dodge he uses his soul blade to deflect or blast away. He crosses the bridge amid the bombardment and jumps across the last few feet just before a large piece of earth crashes into it, causing the structure to collapse completely and its remnants to fall into the lava below.

If exiting the pyramid was difficult before, entering it—now that it is in ruins with debris that continues to rain down as a veritable avalanche of earth—is a far greater challenge, and only the fact that Magdara is so huge now makes getting close to her possible. Her demonic skin is like an oozing wall of slime. It is impossible to find a handhold or foothold, so Jartan plunges his soul blade into the flesh all the way to the hilt— not that this trivial injury is even noticed by Magdara. Holding on to the handle tightly, Jartan is pulled upward as the demon queen breaks through to the Surface.

Those creatures that were peacefully grazing and foraging on the Surface here raise their heads in unison as the ground trembles violently beneath their feet, and they make a panicked attempt to flee. But as the ground erupts beneath them, they quickly become buried alive by the millions of tons of earth that billow upward. Magdara is now of such mountainous size that her dimensions can only be described in acres and not feet, and not one creature in the immediate vicinity has any hope of survival.

Although the sun is shining brightly, once Magdara's rising presence appears on the Surface, the sun's warming glow begins to fade and the sky darkens. This is not due to her tremendous bulk that blots out the sun but to the power of her evil influence, which drains all benevolent light only to replace it with eternal darkness.

Jartan, after hitching a ride, falls from his parasitic position on Magdara's body along with a large amount of earth and debris, and he strikes the ground violently but soon recovers and is greatly alarmed to see she has reached the Surface. Again he uses his soul blade to attack the unbelievably immense creature that Magdara has become. Although his attacks are again some of the most powerful he is able to inflict, her incredible size makes the damage insignificant—though it does get her attention.

This is unfortunate for Jartan, for had he not attacked it would have been impossible for Magdara even to notice him, for her head brushes the clouds slowly meandering by, and from this height her eyes could never have distinguished the less-than-ant-sized Jartan from the surroundings below, especially as the light from the sun continues to drain in the presence of her evil powers of darkness. However, the thin slivers of energy he is firing are visible, easily pinpointing his highly vulnerable location.

Magdara's eyes glow even more brightly with hatred, and this illuminates the entire area with an evil red light, outshining what little light the sun is able to generate by a considerable margin. Jartan puts all his strength into his soul blade to generate a protective shield, for he fears what is soon to follow. The eyes of the demon queen fire a powerful bolt of energy that rapidly descends toward the pinpoint of light below that signifies Jartan and his shield, and as the bolt impacts against the human flea, a mighty explosion erupts. The blast obliterates everything within its radius, and as the smoke subsides, only Jartan remains, standing on a tall, narrow column of earth—the only ground protected from Magdara's attack by his shield. But this soon crumbles under his weight, as there is no earth around the dirt column to support it. He falls into the immense, smoldering crater the bolt from the demon queen's eyes created.

Although Jartan managed to survive the demon queen's attack with his shield, he is nevertheless severely injured from the phenomenal destructive power unleashed by her wrath, and only his healing ability prevents his death. Now fully healed and recovering from the fall, Jartan makes a hasty dash to the wall of the crater in an effort to escape from it, but upon reaching it he finds that its steepness and height make an escape impossible. He claws at it only to slide back as his flashing soul bade and the darkening sky only compound his level of terror. Turning to face the approaching danger, he gazes skyward to see a gigantic appendage of the demon queen rapidly descending upon. The sound it makes as it plunges through the air is thunderous. The paladin frantically fires up at it, tearing off pieces of its flesh, but the appendage is far too large for the feeble damage to make any difference. A shield of defense would be an even more futile gesture against such a massive force.

His look of sheer terror only increases to the highest level possible in a human being as Jartan, in a virtual hysteria, frantically digs his soul blade into the earth of the crater to try to find some leverage to lift his body, but this also fails after a few attempts. The loose soil of the crater wall gives way, sending the horrified and frustrated youth sliding once again down to the bottom of the crater in defeat—he is trapped, unable to flee or protect himself from the approaching doom.

But now, as he realizes the hopelessness of his situation, a profound sense of tranquility floods through his body, transforming his terror into a surprising epiphany as thoughts of his father; his uncle; his sister; and even his mother, whom the boy never knew, begin to resonate within his mind. It is as if all their souls and love are emanating from the soul blade he carries, and he feels all the selfless sacrifices they all made for him. *Why should I be any different?* he thinks. He turns the point of his soul blade toward his body, pressing its glowing tip against his abdomen.

"If I'm going to die, then I'm taking you with me!" says Jartan with proud defiance—and as the shadow of Magdara's demonic appendage begins to cover him, Jartan plunges the blade deep into his body.

The sun has lost all its warmth and burning brightness, and the land plunges into total darkness. Only the glowing, evil red eyes of Magdara provide illumination throughout the entire realm of the Surface. Suddenly, a blinding burst of light—light more brilliant than the brightest sun could possibly radiate—bursts forth with incredible intensity, flooding the landscape with pure whiteness. The energy unleashed from the paradox of Jartan's act of self-sacrifice is unbelievably powerful as the souls of his loving family are used to end the life of their loving son, nephew, and brother. The shockwave from the blast travels an incredible distance, instantly destroying everything in its path.

Unfortunately for the demon queen, her death isn't as merciful or as quick as Jartan's, for despite all her malevolence, hate, and pure evil, not even the mighty Magdara can withstand the self-sacrificing power of a paladin's paradox. She is engulfed in the blast and writhes in agony from the incredible conflagration, and not even the loudest thunder could equal the sound of her shrieking cries of pain. Her skin rips from her body in massive pieces, leaving only the bones, but these too also quickly become consumed, and she finally collapses to the ground as a mass of burning and charred and twisted flesh.

The demon queen is dead—and the sun shines once more.

CHAPTER 26

✝ ✝ ✝

Cristonn and Rojan are still sitting by what is left of the fire. It has long since consumed all the wood. The paladin uses a stick to push around the few glowing embers that remain. It is early morning of the next day as Cristonn finishes relating the story to a thoroughly entranced Rojan. The boy's eyes are wide with excitement as Cristonn continues:

"And so Jartan used the paradox power of sacrificing himself to destroy the demon queen. But unfortunately when she died, her blood was spilled onto the Surface—a place where the gods ordained she was never supposed to set foot—and because of this, a portal straight into the heart of the Demonic Abyss was created, which summoned every demon in creation to seek vengeance. And we—meaning all of the non-evil forces in the many lands—have been fighting the demonic hordes ever since, for the demons won't stop until we all have been annihilated."

The story now ended, Cristonn leaves the remnants of the fire and walks toward the ledge to ascertain the situation below that the morning sunlight reveals, leaving Rojan to ponder his chilling last words in silence. As the solemn paladin gazes at the smoldering ruins of the castle off in the distance, he turns slightly to see that the black swarm of the demon army is advancing. The faint sound of marching footsteps fades as the army continues on its relentless path of evil and destruction toward the next inhabited settlement. The battle has ended, and it has ended in crushing defeat for the forces of goodness—not that Cristonn expected it to end otherwise. He slowly shakes his head despondently, knowing that this will soon be the fate of all that the demonic horde encounters with its unstoppable wrath of extermination.

Soon the bird Cristonn sent forth to spy on the demons the previous morning flies toward him and lands on the paladin's shoulder. It chirps a brief message, which Cristonn acknowledges by nodding, for the message is that the demon horde has moved on. This is good news, of course, but Cristonn cannot bring himself to celebrate with even so much as a slight smile when the only reason the enemy has left is that that there is nothing left alive within the ruins of the castle below to slaughter—and he also knows that the future holds far more carnage in store. The bird's scouting mission now completed, Cristonn gestures with his head for the bird to depart, and the creature flies off back to the tree and disappears within the hole there.

"Wow," says Rojan, finally breaking the silence, "that's an amazing story. But it's a story without an ending."

"That will reveal itself soon enough, my young friend," responds a crestfallen Cristonn as the depressing image before him of the ruined castle and its slaughtered inhabitants continues to impact his teary eyes, which prompts him to add quietly so the boy cannot hear, "Not that it hasn't already."

"Cristonn? Will we be able to stop the demons?" asks Rojan hopefully.

Cristonn, his back still turned to the boy, closes his eyes as he ponders this for a moment, his face betraying his thoughts of futility and hopelessness. However, not wishing to disillusion the boy with what he feels is the painful reality of the truth, he turns to face Rojan with the forced bravado of an enthusiastic grin and an exuberant demeanor.

"Of course we will! Once we have enough warriors to fight them with. And a warrior who defeated the mighty god of the ogres, Vasarak—a feat I've heard tell of so many times now that even the gods must have lost count—is certainly one I want fighting beside me."

"That was just a fantasy," says Rojan with a sheepish chuckle.

"Oh, so now you finally admit that?" replies a smiling Cristonn, who of course knew that the boy's fantasy was just that all along. But his smile becomes a stoic blankness as he ponders his next thought. "Well, even fantasies can lead to reality on some level. I had fantasies myself at your age, some of which I never dreamed would happen—but they have become real now—which reminds me, your mother has a gift for you. Come."

An eager Rojan—and what seven-year-old child would not be eager to receive a gift—moves to embrace Cristonn, who once again retrieves the teleport jewel from his clothing. He tosses the jewel on the ground. It creates a flash of light, and the two disappear within its blinding glow and instantly reappear amid the devastated ruins of the castle. It is a particularly distressing sight for Rojan, for his young eyes have never before witnessed the results of such horrific violence. Massive amounts of rubble and debris along with untold numbers of human and demon corpses are strewn about with vast amounts of sickening gore from the brutal carnage. And once again the thousands of vulturats have returned to gorge on the dead. They become aware of the two humans and raise their heads for a moment to watch them, seemingly concerned but not threatened enough to leave their meals. Only when a particular sound reaches their bloody ears do they feverishly take to the air and leave the vicinity for the safety of the nearby hills—the sound of Cristonn removing his soul blade from its scabbard, a sound that usually does not bode well for any evil creature.

"Rojan," begins Cristonn as he warily eyes the retreating clouds of vulturats, "let me have that dagger of yours."

The boy, confused by this request, nevertheless hands the paladin his dagger.

"You remain here. You understand?" Cristonn sternly orders the boy, for he does not want him to see even more horrific scenes deeper within the castle ruins, and he begins to leave.

"But what if I am attacked?" asks Rojan. "I have no weapon."

Cristonn knows an attack is unlikely, but he also understands the boy's desire for protection now that his comforting dagger is not in his possession. He looks around the immediate area for a suitable substitute form of courage. Seeing a large, spiked mace lying on the ground near the corpse of its human owner, he effortlessly picks it up and hands the imposing weapon to the boy.

"Sweet!" says the smiling Rojan, as he is greatly pleased that he is being presented with such a formidable device. But as Cristonn relinquishes the mace into Rojan's hands, the young boy has nowhere near the strength to hold the heavy weapon—let alone wield it in any kind of battle—and its lethal end falls to the ground with Rojan barely able to hold his end up. Cristonn now heads off, completely unconcerned over Rojan's plight. It's not that he isn't concerned about the boy's safety; it's just that he knows no demon here is left alive to threaten the boy. But Rojan doesn't know this, and he watches Cristonn depart with an exasperated look on the young boy's face.

After several minutes, Cristonn walks deeper into the castle ruins, which are extensive, and the castle's once-familiar layout is now a virtual maze of towering debris and clouds of smoldering ruin that hide from view much of the surroundings. Body parts and gore from the countless dead, both human and demon, are everywhere. He is obviously searching for something, for he has his mighty soul blade in hand and is waving it about, letting the blade alert him which direction to take when it flashes. It does so, and Cristonn moves off in the direction indicated.

A blast from the blade obliterates a huge obstructing pile of debris caused by a collapsed castle wall, but the disturbing sight that confronts him is the corpse of Queen Valerias—her body mutilated and bloody. This is precisely what he was searching for, but the sight is still a highly depressing one, and he stops for a moment to close his eyes to fight back the tears before moving on to kneel beside her body.

Taking Rojan's dagger from within his clothing, he looks around to find a demon corpse, which isn't difficult, for they are virtually everywhere—a tribute to the heroic resistance to the human defenders— and stepping the few paces to the nearest one, Cristonn stabs the corpse with the dagger so the blade drips with demonic blood. He places the blade reverently on Valerias's body.

"The blood of a blood enemy—just to give the boy a little edge," says Cristonn quietly to himself. "He's sure going to need it." But as he holds the dagger in his hand, he begins to doubt whether this weapon is adequate. In a more peaceful time, a dagger would be a perfect weapon for a small boy like Rojan to practice the paladin arts with, but now that the demons are on the warpath seeking death to all, a dagger is hopelessly inadequate—as Cristonn laments:

"But unfortunately a dagger just isn't much of an intimidating weapon for a soul blade, and certainly not one with the love of a mother's soul within. What we need is something that can utilize that power far more effectively but still be small and compact enough that Rojan can wield it until he reaches a high enough level that his mother's soul power can be fully brought to bear."

Cristonn starts to search around the immediate area and picks up two additional undamaged daggers from the hundreds of weapons lying about.

"These two in addition to the dagger you gave him should help the boy."

Cristonn places all three daggers upon Valerias's body, and with the tip of his soul blade, he touches the daggers, which instantly begin to glow. A peal of thunder precedes the blinding lightning bolt of powerful energy that descends from the skies above and strikes the daggers, which glow even more brightly as they absorb this new energy source. The bright glow quickly subsides, and the daggers are transformed into a single, three-bladed weapon, which has now become a mighty soul blade. Cristonn picks it up and caresses it gently, for he knows that the soul of his beloved friend, Queen Valerias, now rests within the blade.

"Yes, I am happy to see you too," says the smiling paladin now that he senses Valerias's presence. "It will be some years before Rojan can take advantage of the power that a mother's love will give him. Do you mind if I test you out to see what powers you possess?"

The soul blade flashes in approval. Cristonn points one of the three blades at a pile of debris, and the blade discharges a potent energy bolt at it, causing a respectable explosion. Turning the weapon slightly, from the second blade he discharges a stream of fire; the third discharges a freezing ray.

"Not bad," says Cristonn, impressed.

Seeing a half-standing marble column that once was part of the castle's structure, Cristonn heaves the weapon toward it. The soul blade effortlessly cuts through the column, felling it to the ground, and the weapon quickly returns to Cristonn's hand. The felling of the column disturbs a vulturat that was behind it feasting on the remains of some unfortunate soul, and the creature hurriedly takes flight as it sees a paladin near. Cristonn points the weapon at the creature.

"Do you see it?" he asks the soul blade, and the weapon flashes in acknowledgment, prompting Cristonn to add, "Seek."

Surprisingly, he now tosses the weapon not at the rapidly escaping vulturat but off to the side, testing its seeking ability. The weapon quickly corrects its heading and flies off at great velocity toward the vulturat, killing the creature instantly as it rips through its body, creating a slowly descending cloud of blood and then returning to Cristonn's hand.

"Very good," he says with pride as he admires the weapon. "Your son is going to need powers like those soon. I just hope he lives long enough to achieve enough experience to use it. Until then, I may just use you myself."

Although Cristonn is joking about this, it does not sit well with the souls within his own soul blade, and his own weapon gives him a slight shock out of jealousy, forcing the paladin to drop it.

"Oh, now don't you two start!" says a slightly peeved Cristonn at the weapon as he picks it up. "I was only kidding. You know I wouldn't replace you two for anything. By the gods, you females can be sensitive." He now addresses the other soul blade with Valerias's soul and is obviously overcome with emotion now that he is, at least to a certain extent, reunited with Valerias once again and must relate to her the ordeals that the future will bring.

"It won't be easy, my queen," he continues. "They are so many, and we are so few. I'm taking Rojan with me to the Circle of Paladins. It's up to the paladin master to decide his fate now—the fate of us all."

Cristonn is pondering whether to give the boy the blade yet, but he soon comes to the conclusion that he is still too young to appreciate and understand all the powers and sacrifices that the blade implies. After all, it is his mother in the blade. Such knowledge would be difficult for a small child to comprehend. Rojan is no paladin yet and won't be for some years to come.

"When the time is right," he says to himself, concealing the blade within his clothing, and he begins to head back to the boy.

Rojan is patiently waiting for Cristonn's return when he notices the corpse of a demon soldier disturbingly near to him. Wanting to demonstrate his bravery and superiority—which isn't too difficult, considering it's against a foe that's probably been dead for two days, though this doesn't hurt Rojan's pride one bit—he decides a further blow from his mace weapon is warranted here. However, the mace's weight prevents this, for it is simply too heavy despite Rojan's concerted effort to lift it. An angry kick from his foot to the demon's head satisfies the boy.

But a more disturbing sight reveals itself: a vulturat has alighted upon the ground some ten feet from his person—and then another and another. Soon there are several dozen of the disgusting half bird, half rat creatures surrounding him. An arch-paladin like Cristonn is a being to be greatly feared, but a small boy is merely a fresh meal. Since the vulturats are nearly Rojan's size, they are not intimidated by him one bit. Rojan becomes aware of this as he sees that the feathered fiends are making an effort to advance closer, so the boy quickly starts to throw at them whatever he can pick up—hand-sized rocks, bricks, and debris—to ward them off. He knows his heavy mace is useless, but he sees a sword sticking out of the chest of a nearby corpse and wisely decides that this will be more practical. He drops the mace to wield this instead—only to be defeated once again by its ungainly weight, though he can at least make some clumsy attempts to slash at the nimble vulturats, which easily avoid the strikes. Seeing that the boy is far from a worthy opponent, even more vulturats alight in the area to join in the fray, and several hundred of them soon have Rojan surrounded. The boy's frantic attempts to keep them at bay with his sword slashes becomes more and more pathetic, and as his strength wanes with each strike, the look of panic on his ashen face increases. The plague-ridden teeth of a vulturat need only to break the skin in order to kill a small child like Rojan within seconds.

Suddenly a sword lands at Rojan's feet. The blade buries itself halfway into the ground, and within a fraction of a second it creates a shield that surrounds Rojan before the hundreds of vulturats overwhelm him—the creatures bouncing off of it as they try to reach the boy. It is now the faces of the vulturats that display fear and alarm as they see another sword come spinning in. The creatures take to the air with great haste and rapidly flee in a state of panic, for when this sword strikes the ground it creates a powerful wave of heat that begins to incinerate anything nearby. Rojan, however, is safely protected from the inferno by the shield still generated by the other sword.

Large numbers of the vulturats burst into flames as they all try to escape from the burning area. The vast majority soon becomes engulfed in the searing inferno and fall to the ground as ashes, leaving only a few survivors trailing smoke and shrieking from the searing pain. A stunned though happy Rojan sees Cristonn walking toward him. The paladin summons his twin soul blades back into his hands, and they instantly become one again, which further broadens the smile on the boy's face. He knows that Cristonn has once again saved his life. Cristonn also is aware that saving Rojan's life seems to be becoming a habit.

"You, my young friend," he says to Rojan with bemused annoyance, "have a natural talent for getting into trouble." But he smiles at Rojan in return, and upon reaching the boy, he puts his arm around him and begins to lead him away from the castle ruins.

"Come, Rojan. We've done all we can do here."

"Where is my dagger?" asks the boy. "And this gift from my mother you said I was getting?"

"You will receive both soon, Rojan—you'll just have to trust me. In the meantime, you can practice two of the paladin virtues—patience and silence."

The first is indeed a paladin virtue, but the second is just Cristonn's way of keeping the boy quiet.

"So what do we do now?" asks Rojan.

Cristonn can't help but smile, knowing that for the boy being silent is not possible—not at his age of seven years.

"We travel south," replies Cristonn, "across the Emerald Sea."

"Why are we going there?"

"That's where the Circle of Paladins is. But to get there, we are going to need transportation."

"But the teleportation jewel is out of power."

"I know a friend that can help," says the paladin with a sly smile.

He runs the palm of his hand along his soul blade, making a small cut. Blood begins to flow from the minor wound, and he drips it on the ground. Stepping back a pace or two, he raises his hand, and his eyes glow. From the small pool of blood, an energy surge begins to develop that soon forms into a magnificent blue dragon. The handsome creature, with its light blue scales tinted with gold sparkling in the sunlight, colorful wings, and pleasing face, is one of the most beautiful and powerful of the entire good dragon race. But her gentle disposition and stunningly majestic appearance—like those of all of the good dragon class—hides a ferocious tenacity should her anger ever be aroused toward evil. She bows her head as Cristonn approaches. He smiles in return, for he is always pleased to see those noble creatures he summons to aid him, and he caresses her face affectionately.

"Awesome!" shouts an amazed and highly impressed Rojan at the sight of the magnificent creature. "That's a blue dragon! Paladins can summon?"

"Not exactly," responds a humble Cristonn somewhat unemotionally, for although he certainly does not take his ability lightly, it's just that he has summoned so many creatures by now that he isn't as impressed by the gift, though he can understand why a young boy like Rojan would be awestruck by such a tremendous power; but Cristonn is fully aware of his responsibilities toward those he summons. He continues, "You see, when you reach the level of arch-paladin, you get a special power—a power that is unique to each arch-paladin. Mine is summoning."

"That's incredible! What special power will I have when I become an arch-paladin?"

"No one knows, Rojan. The special power chooses you—you don't choose it."

"What special power does the paladin master have?"

"Well," Cristonn begins, chuckling slightly with a smile of admiration as he reflects on this, "let's just say he's master for a reason.

That is one powerful old man. I sure wouldn't want to mess with him in battle."

"Could you beat him if you did fight him, Cristonn?"

"What kind of question is that? He's a dear friend. I owe him my life a dozen times over, so why would I want to fight him? Besides, doing harm to a good creature is a violation of the Code of the Paladinhood."

"But I heard paladins can challenge each other for the mastership through combat."

"How did you hear about that?"

"Some of the other students at school told me. Is it true?"

"Yes, it's true. But it's also rare, Rojan, for the circumstances of the challenge must be extreme and are not to be taken lightly—for the price the loser must pay is severe. I know because there was a time not so long ago when I was the paladin who was third in power. But the paladin who was second made a challenge for the mastership; and now I am second in power. So don't you get any bright ideas of challenging the master just yet. I'm afraid you'll find him a far more formidable opponent than that swamp rat you killed."

Rojan smiles, for he knows Cristonn is making fun of him once again about his playful antics as they both move toward the blue dragon. Once Rojan gets close enough to the creature, she licks his face affectionately, causing the boy to laugh happily.

"Look, Cristonn! She likes me!"

"Either that or she's seeing how good you'll taste when she gets hungry."

This causes Rojan's smile to vanish instantly, and he eyes the creature with extreme wariness and backs away. Cristonn smiles at this, for he was only joking about the dragon eating him, but the boy doesn't know this. When Rojan sees the paladin smiling slyly, he picks up on the jest, albeit with a slight degree of caution toward the dragon, for she exudes an imposing air of power—no matter how good a creature she may be.

Cristonn lifts Rojan up and puts him on the blue dragon's back and then mounts the creature behind the child.

"Cristonn?"

"Yes?"

"Can you summon my mom?" asks Rojan, a look of sadness on his youthful face.

Cristonn, fully aware of the touching significance of the boy's question, looks down at him with an understanding eye, and where the blade with Valerias's soul is concealed beneath his clothing, he presses a hand against it tenderly. Rojan cannot see this, of course, and after several moments of silence, the boy turns to face him to elicit an answer from him. The paladin's eyes greet the boy's, and a smile begins to form on Cristonn's face—a smile one has when one knows a secret another does not.

"I'll see what I can do, Rojan."

Rojan smiles back. The boy obviously doesn't have a clue what Cristonn means, but his words are soothing. In time, that same smile will return on Rojan's face—but in a far more profound and deeply loving manner. A command from Cristonn to his dragon steed prompts the blue dragon to unfurl her wings, and Cristonn and Rojan fly off toward the adventure ahead.

End of Part I